W9-BSL-215

Praise for *Dark Reservations*

"*Dark Reservations* is a novel of power, written with confidence by a veteran in the investigative field. He is also, by the way, an artist, using words as if they cost ten dollars apiece, achieving his effect in short order, with resonance after the fact. There is humanity here, along with a world-weary tolerance of weakness and temptation, and something of the clean, pure wind-driven strength of the best frontier fiction, which is to say the best in the English language."

—Loren D. Estleman, author of *The Sundown Speech*

"Provocative and convincing . . . the best mystery writing about Native American culture since Tony Hillerman. John Fortunato delivers compelling insight into the human condition and a rare peek into the evil that men do as only an experienced FBI agent can."

—Patrick W. Picciarelli, coauthor of *Undercover Cop*

"John Fortunato takes us on a fifty-two-day ride with lawman Joe Evers you won't soon forget. Joe owns the ground he walks on here, but there's nothing overly familiar with this lawman's manner and means. For those of us who long for a story with that real feel, John Fortunato's G-man background gives *Dark Reservations* just the right punch."

—Robert Knott, author of *Robert B. Parker's The Bridge*

"Ancient Navajo artifacts have gone missing, and when these thefts are tied to the disappearance of a U.S. senator, BIA agent Joe Evers knows he has an explosive case on his hands. *Dark Reservations* gives a full, rich picture of the beauty and complexity of the Navajo Nation in northern New Mexico. A rewarding read."

—Mary Logue, author of the Claire Watkins mystery series

"Fortunato spins an intricate tale, overlaying multiple story lines with a galaxy of characters, some of whom have much to hide. Readers who relish mysteries against the backdrop of the Southwest and who are fans of Tony and Anne Hillerman will savor this page-turner."

—Library Journal (starred review)

JOHN FORTUNATO

DARK
RESERVATIONS

SOUTH C
22 STATION ROAD
BELLPORT, NY 11713

MINOTAUR BOOKS

A THOMAS DUNNE BOOK

NEW YORK

OCT 2 3 2015

This is a work of fiction. All of the characters, organizations, and events portrayed in this novel are either products of the author's imagination or are used fictitiously.

A THOMAS DUNNE BOOK FOR MINOTAUR BOOKS.
An imprint of St. Martin's Publishing Group.

DARK RESERVATIONS. Copyright © 2015 by John Fortunato. All rights reserved. Printed in the United States of America. For information, address St. Martin's Press, 175 Fifth Avenue, New York, N.Y. 10010.

www.thomasdunnebooks.com
www.minotaurbooks.com

Designed by Kathryn Parise

The Library of Congress Cataloging-in-Publication Data
is available upon request.

ISBN 978-1-250-07419-5 (hardcover)
ISBN 978-1-4668-8583-7 (e-book)

Our books may be purchased in bulk for promotional, educational, or business use. Please contact your local bookseller or the Macmillan Corporate and Premium Sales Department at (800) 221-7945, extension 5442, or by e-mail at MacmillanSpecialMarkets@macmillan.com.

First Edition: October 2015

10 9 8 7 6 5 4 3 2 1

To my wife, Kim,
and my children, Samantha, Sabrina, and Sydney
(who just wanted to see their names in print)

I love you.

In memory of
Frank Friel
a fine cop, a fine mentor, a fine friend

DARK
RESERVATIONS

When Joe Evers arrived, his squad was already donning their vests and checking their weapons. He was late and had missed the briefing.

"You're with us," Stretch said. "Sadi and I have the rear. You have outbuildings and vehicles." He handed Joe a picture of the subject, Roy Manygoats.

Cordelli was the case agent and had designated the casino's rear parking lot as the staging area. From here, they would go to Manygoats's residence to make the arrest. If he wasn't there, they would go mobile, trying to track him down as quickly as possible.

Standing beside his vehicle, Cordelli spotted Joe. He shook his head and said something to Dale, who glanced at Joe and laughed.

"Let's hurry up," Dale said. He wore his vest high over his rather generous gut, the large, yellow BIA letters sitting just below his chin.

"What are you doing here?" Joe asked.

Dale walked away, ignoring his question. He rarely went on

operations, not since becoming squad supervisor six years earlier, which coincided with his outgrowing his tactical vest. Too much desk time, he'd said. Too many tacos, the squad had said.

Stretch charged his M4 carbine. "He thought you would be a no-show." The assault rifle appeared petite in front of his six-foot-seven frame.

Perhaps it was guilt, but Joe thought his friend and former partner was going to add *again*. He put on his vest and started for the passenger door of Stretch's unmarked Suburban.

"Don't even think about it," Sadi said, and reached past him for the handle. She jogged a thumb toward the backseat.

They traveled in convoy, three vehicles, into the heart of Acoma, which was located off I-40, west of Albuquerque. This was Indian Country. Reservation land. Rural, desolate, and hard.

Four dirt roads later, they arrived at a trailer a little more than a mile from an adobe village that sat atop a plateau and was known as Sky City. As they pulled up, a couple of scrawny rez dogs came from behind the building, both mutts, both starving. Stretch drove to the rear, stopping ten feet from the back door. They climbed out, guns drawn.

The other half of the team was at the front door, making entry.

A few hundred feet behind the trailer were the remnants of a corral, two abandoned vehicles, and an outhouse.

Cordelli's voice came through the radio. "His mother's saying he's not here."

Joe checked the vehicles. Empty. He made his way to the dilapidated corral and searched behind a pile of car tires. The land here was devoid of trees, only scrub grass and a few scraggly bushes, no place for a person to hide.

He moved on to the outhouse, a plywood special in need of paint. From twenty or so feet away, the air was already redolent with the smell of human waste. Tasking him with the outhouse was punishment. He was the senior agent, but he'd been put on the perimeter. He'd been put on shit duty.

A dog barked.

Sadi and Stretch were by the back door of the trailer, which was now open. Cordelli stood in the entryway. One of the mutts challenged them from the building's corner.

A sound emanated from the outhouse, a soft creaking. Joe raised his Glock.

"Police! Come out!" he said, not sure if there was someone inside, but not wanting that person to hear his uncertainty.

The door burst open and a skinny kid in a blue T-shirt came running out, away from Joe, into the open field beyond.

Joe cursed and holstered his weapon, then took off after him. It wasn't a kid, but a teenager. He called for the teen to stop.

The runner ignored him, heading toward an arroyo some two hundred yards beyond. The ground was rocky and dotted with flat cacti and mesquite brush, but the teen proved agile. Joe knew he was too old and too out of shape to chase this guy far. All he could do was try for an all-out sprint and get him quickly, or else let him go. He took longer strides and focused on his breathing. The gap between them closed. The teen turned.

It was Manygoats. All nineteen years of him. He had the look of a rabbit chased by a dog—an old dog.

Joe reached out and grabbed for his shirt. Fabric ripped. The effort threw Joe off balance and he stumbled forward, taking long, erratic bounds to stay upright. But he was going too fast. He fell to the ground, dragging the teen with him. They rolled. Joe lost hold of the shirt. They both came up on a knee. Manygoats's eyes revealed the terror of a man facing a lifetime in prison.

"Don't make it worse," Joe said between breaths.

Manygoats tried to get to his feet.

Joe lunged and slammed him to the ground. They wrestled. Joe felt movement by his right hip, his holster. Manygoats had the Glock halfway out. Joe clamped his right elbow down over his weapon and the young hand, then raked it backward with all his strength, knocking the weapon away. He seized the teen's arm and wrenched it behind his back. Manygoats shifted and tried for the gun with his free hand, but he didn't have the reach, and before Joe could retrieve it, a boot came down on the grip.

Cordelli stood above him.

Joe cuffed Manygoats, then dusted himself off.

Stretch grinned as he handed the weapon back to Joe. "Maybe I should hold on to that for you, seeing how much trouble you're having with it?"

The rest of the squad gathered around them.

Dale wanted to know what had happened. Joe told him, leaving out the part about losing his weapon.

"Good work," Dale said.

"Tell him about your gun, cowboy," Cordelli said. Half Italian and half Ute, Cordelli had the face and body of Michelangelo's *David*, with a mouth that spat arrowheads. Joe carried a few scars.

Stretch came to stand next to Joe. "Why don't you shut up, Cordelli."

"What about it?" Dale asked.

"Nothing. The punk tried to grab for it when I put him on the ground. I had it under control."

"You're just lucky I came along." Cordelli pointed a finger gun at Joe. "You might've been retiring in a box."

Stretch pulled Joe toward his vehicle.

"Write it up, Joe," Dale said. "Get it to Cordelli before the detention hearing."

A report would be embarrassing, but Joe didn't argue. He had only three months left. At least things couldn't get any worse.

❖

Joe and Stretch stood in the middle of the squad room, looking up at the television suspended from the ceiling. The news ticker scrolling across the bottom of the screen announced breaking news. Authorities had found Congressman Arlen Edgerton's vehicle on the Navajo reservation.

What the ticker did not tell viewers was that the congressman, two of his staff, and the vehicle they'd been traveling in had gone missing more than twenty years earlier. But soon the news anchor, a young, attractive brunette who looked strikingly similar to every other brunette news anchor, reported the full story, punctuating the facts with provocative questions that rivaled the skills of the most accomplished true-crime writer: Did the corruption probe prove Edgerton was taking money? Why, after a two-year-long investigation, did the independent counsel find only one suspicious transaction involving Edgerton?

"They'll be spinning it by noon," Stretch said.

"Who?"

"His wife. Her campaign. She's dirty, just like he was."

Joe nodded, not really caring. He knew his friend, knew he enjoyed passing judgment, everything black and white, never a shade of gray, never a faded edge.

On the screen, superimposed over the background to the assembly-line brunette, was a picture of Congressman Edgerton and his secretary, Faye Hannaway, he in a conservative dark gray suit, she in a red look-at-me dress. The photo appeared to have been taken at a campaign party. A banner in the background read ARLEN EDGERTON FOR CHANGE. It seemed only the candidates got swapped out, never the slogans.

"Joe!" Dale called from the doorway to his office. "Get in here."

When Joe entered, Dale waved him to a seat in front of his desk. He ripped a sheet of paper from his notepad and handed it to Joe.

"That's the number for the officer who found Edgerton's vehicle."

Joe stared at the paper, confused. On it was written "Randall Bluehorse," below that a phone number.

"What's this for?"

"You're catching it. The FBI's letting us run with it. We handled the disappearance back in '88."

"And I'm handling it? Bullshit. I'm out of here in three months."

"Clear it and you go out big."

"Is this because of this morning?"

"No. It's because you're still my senior agent."

Dale didn't say *best agent*. He wouldn't say that. Not anymore. Joe tossed the paper to Dale. It landed atop a red '76 Datsun 510, part of Dale's model-car collection, a replica of the car Paul Newman had driven to win several of his first professional races.

"Get Stretch. Or your wonder boy Cordelli."

"You refusing the assignment?" Dale leaned back in his chair. "If so, I can put you out right now. You're the one with a kid in college, not me."

Joe lowered his gaze, not because he was hurt or beaten, but because he knew if he stared at that puffed-up face any longer, he might launch himself across the desk.

"You're an asshole." He snatched up the paper and stormed out.

He marched past Stretch to his own cubicle, where he flung down the officer's number.

What the hell was Dale's game? He'd already won, had already gotten the board to force through Joe's retirement, had already ruined his life. In the end, they had agreed that if Joe didn't fight the review board's decision, he could use his remaining time to wrap up cases and find a job. Now it seemed that deal was off.

He opened his center desk drawer and grabbed for his bottle of aspirin, what he thought of as his morning-after pill. He fumbled with the lid, his fingers jittery. It had nothing to do with his need for a drink. He wanted to punch Dale in his smug, fat face, not fiddle with the childproof dot and arrow.

He threw the bottle at his computer. The lid popped. White tablets sprayed over the papers and folders and a crumpled burrito wrapper on his desk.

He picked up two pills. Chewed them. Their chalky texture coated his mouth, not quite overpowering the bitter taste Dale's words had left.

"What'd he want?" Stretch asked.

"He wants me to work the Edgerton case."

"The vehicle? It's FBI. What's he want you to do with it?"

Joe picked up the paper with Bluehorse's phone number.

"I guess he wants me to find Edgerton."

Arthur Othmann unfolded the clear plastic painter's tarp and spread it over the bone white carpet in his study. He stepped back to appraise his handiwork and then repositioned it so the sides were parallel to the display cabinets that ran the length of the room.

"Perfect," he said to no one.

Muted voices carried from another part of the house.

He checked his watch, then smiled up at the oil portrait of his father, Alexander Othmann, founder of the once Great Pacific Mining Company, now both defunct. "They're right on time, Pops."

The portrait's massive gold-leaf wood frame, ornately carved, clashed with the Native American artifacts displayed in the cabinets along the walls. Its shimmering trim and grotesque size gave it an otherworldly quality, a doorway to the spirit world, what the Navajo might call *Xajiinai*. According to their creation story, the Navajo emerged through *Xajiinai*, a hole in the La Plata Mountains of southwestern Colorado that allowed them to ascend from the underworld. Othmann knew all about Navajo history. It was, after all, their past that fed his passion for the arts. His father had never shared that passion. In fact, he hated that his only son, the last male carrier of the Othmann bloodline, was interested in the arts and was "a little light in his goddamn pants!" Toward the end of his life, his father would growl those words through wrinkled brown lips wrapped around a Padrón cigar, which looked like a shovel handle sticking out of the old man's face.

The son didn't care about understanding his father, only outliving him. Not hard, considering the old bastard had been in his seventies when Arthur finished college. And during those seven years after his return from Stanford, where he'd studied art history, they had lived together in the house, with only a maid and a nurse (his mother had died his first year away—not a great loss), and it was during those seven years that the son had often fantasized about that shovel handle.

Once, after acquiring a rather spectacular ninth-century Anasazi watering bowl, he had shared his thoughts of the portrait with his bodyguard, David "Books" Drud, over a glass of celebratory scotch. "I like to think it's a portal to the afterlife, and my father visits from time to time to see how I'm spending his money. And I get to kill the old bastard all over again." Books gave a respectful chuckle and sipped the five-thousand-dollar-a-bottle whisky. But Othmann had not been joking.

The voices were in the hallway now.

He strode over to the stone mantel behind his desk. Atop it sat a wood carving of a rug-weaving loom. The tiny weaver's seat had been hollowed out and a miniature camera installed. In a darkened room ten feet below the study, a twenty-five-terabyte digital recorder captured every moment on Othmann's estate. He never skimped on security.

The door opened.

A middle-aged Navajo man stumbled in. Strands of long, black hair stuck to his face. His dirty clothes and the black patch over his left eye gave him the appearance of a down-on-his-luck desert pirate. At one time, this had been Othmann's prized silversmith, whose work had been shown at the Smithsonian and sold in the Faubourg Saint-Honoré district in Paris. But when the Navajo silversmith had lost his eye in a drunken brawl four years earlier, he also lost his talent. Now he was just Eddie Begay, the snitch.

Books stepped behind Eddie, his imposing figure clogging the doorway. He shoved the skinny man forward. Eddie's feet failed to keep up, and he fell to his knees onto the plastic tarp.

Eddie had grown comfortable groveling these past few years; alcohol seemed to lubricate his humility. Kneeling on the floor, he actually looked somewhat at ease.

"You doing some remodeling, Mr. O?" Eddie said.

Books moved to stand behind their guest.

"I thought we were friends, Eddie," Othmann said, his voice soft, with just a touch of hurt.

"We are. You're my *bil naa'aash*."

"Cousin-brother. I like that. Yes, I suppose we are brothers of a sort. Brothers in art."

Eddie must have put up a fight because Books's right trouser leg was muddied and torn. Othmann was curious.

"His dog didn't like it when I put Eddie in the car," Books said, his voice slow, tired, as though his words had traveled a long way before passing his lips.

"He killed my dog, Mr. O. He slammed her head in the car door."

"It was practically dead anyway," Books said. "Nothing but skin and bones. You people don't take care of your dogs."

"Fuck you, man."

Books was fast. Othmann almost missed it. He heard a slap, and then Eddie's head snapped forward.

"Eddie," Othmann said. "Look at me, Eddie. A little birdie told me you got caught diddling a kid."

"I never done nothing like that. I got a woman. I don't touch kids. If anyone told you that, they're just trying to mess up our business arrangement."

"That's exactly what I wanted to talk to you about, our business arrangement."

Eddie squinted. "I thought you were happy with the carving."

"Oh, I'm very happy with it. And I have it on good authority it's authentic."

The carving was a chunk of stone with a thousand-year-old petroglyph of a spiral-beaked bird that Eddie had chiseled from a cliff at Chaco Canyon. It now sat below them as part of Othmann's very private and very illegal collection in an environmentally controlled vault. And in that same vault was the recorder that was, at that very moment, capturing Eddie Begay's every word.

Othmann continued. "Why don't you tell us what the police are accusing you of, Eddie?"

"This is bullshit. I'm not telling you any—"

Books drove a knee to the back of his head. Eddie did a face plant on the tarp. He didn't move.

They waited.

"I hope you didn't kill him."

Books shrugged.

Eddie let out a sound somewhere between a whimper and a groan and struggled back to his knees. His eye patch had shifted, granting Othmann an unwanted view of a black sunken hole. Was that what *Xajiinai* was? Black and bottomless? Not like his father's portrait at all. Maybe Eddie was the portal to communicate with the dead, to communicate with good ol' Pops.

"What did they say you did?" Othmann asked.

Eddie took several deep breaths. His good eye seemed unable to focus. "They said . . . they said I touched my sister's boy. But I didn't."

Othmann walked around to the front of his desk, careful not to block the camera's view. "And what did you tell the FBI about me?"

"How did you know it was the FBI?"

"Eddie, it's time to be honest. I need to know I can trust you. Now, what did you tell them about me?"

"Nothing. Why would I talk about you? They were asking about my nephew."

"Did you tell them about the carving?"

"No." Eddie's voice was high.

"What do you think, David? Did he talk?"

"He talked. A man that can't take care of his dog isn't loyal to anyone."

"Are you loyal, Eddie?"

"Yes—"

Another knee to the back of his head.

They waited.

Books wrinkled his nose. "I think he shit himself."

A minute passed.

Eddie regained consciousness. He groaned. Blood dripped from his nose onto the plastic.

"Oh man." Eddie pulled at the seat of his pants.

"Stay on the tarp," Othmann said.

The broken man sat back on his knees, swaying. A silver and turquoise squash-blossom necklace, which Eddie usually wore beneath his shirt, now hung exposed on his chest. It had been handed down through his family, originally belonging to his great-grandfather, who had been the chief of his clan before the Long Walk. Its craftsmanship was some of the best work Othmann had ever seen. But no matter how tough things had gotten for Eddie, he had never parted with his great-grandfather's legacy.

"Eddie, Eddie. Why are you doing this to yourself? It's a simple question. I already know the answer, but I want to hear you say it."

"Okay . . . but don't let him knee me anymore. I'm seeing double."

"David, don't knee him anymore."

"Okay, boss."

Eddie stared as Books unbuckled his belt. Books pulled it from his waistband and grasped both ends in his right hand, letting the loop dangle by his side.

Eddie whimpered.

"What did you tell the FBI about me?"

Eddie licked his lips, smearing the trickle of blood from his nose, spreading it wide, giving himself a clown's red mouth.

"You're right. I'm sorry. I got scared. Real scared. I was never in trouble like that before."

"What did you tell them?"

"That I used to make jewelry for you, and when I couldn't do that anymore, I started getting you things."

"What things?"

"I told them about the prayer sticks . . . and the artifacts."

"Did you tell them about the Chaco carving?"

Eddie hung his head.

"And they want you to talk to the grand jury, right?"

"I'll disappear. I have a cousin in California. I can hide out there. Really. I won't talk to them again. I promise."

"I know you won't."

Books dropped the belt loop over Eddie's head.

The silversmith clawed at the thin strip of leather.

Othmann stared into the dying man's empty eye socket.

Later that night, in the environmentally controlled vault below, while replaying the hidden-camera footage, feeling the effects of Cuervo Black and a line of Christmas powder, Othmann would think about this moment and tell himself he saw his father staring out of that depthless black hole, the tip of his cigar glowing with the brilliance of hellfire, and his wrinkled lips mouthing the words *You're a little light in your goddamn pants!*

Supervisory Special Agent in Charge Dale Warren thumbed through a copy of that month's issue of *Model Cars Magazine,* pausing on an article about applying alclad chrome to bumpers and grilles. His cell phone rang. He recognized the number and answered.

"It's assigned," he said. "I gave it to one of my . . . older agents." Dale disconnected the call without waiting for a response.

Then he picked up the 1952 Moebius Hudson Hornet convertible parked at the edge of his desk and eyed its bumpers. The metallic paint was dull and pitted from a poor application he'd attempted the previous summer. He laid the car back down and returned to the article.

Joe pulled his Tahoe behind the marked Navajo Police vehicle and stepped out. They were parked on the side of Jones Ranch Road in Chi Chil Tah, a small Navajo community twenty miles southwest of Gallup, consisting of a school, a small housing development, some scattered trailers and ranch homes, and a chapter house, the

Navajo equivalent of a town hall. The blacktop had ended about four miles back, and now he stood on hard-packed clay surrounded by piñon trees.

The officer, who had been leaning against his ride's front fender, approached. He wore the tan uniform of the Navajo Police Department, and wore it well, crisp and clean. A rookie.

"Agent Evers?"

"Call me Joe." He flashed his credentials, then slipped them back into his sport coat. He didn't ask the officer's name. His name tag read R. BLUEHORSE.

A big grin spread across the officer's face. He reached out and pumped Joe's extended hand with all the enthusiasm of a teenager being given the keys to the car for the first time. "Glad to meet you. I'm pretty new to the force. My first week out on my own and I caught this case. Lucky, I guess."

Lucky? A cold case? Lots of work and little chance to clear it. The kid had no idea.

Joe pulled his hand to safety. "Sorry, I'm a little late." Mornings had become more and more difficult for him over the past year.

Bluehorse looked at Joe's shoes. "Did I tell you it was in the woods?"

The cuffs of Joe's wrinkled khakis sat atop a pair of tasseled loafers. No doubt boots would have been a better choice. "They're old." They weren't.

The officer seemed to be waiting for something.

"You want to show me what you found?"

"Isn't there anyone else coming? You know, to process it."

"I need to check it out first."

Officer Bluehorse looked down the road one last time, as though willing there to be more attention to his find. Then he walked to the north side of the road and set off through the woods. Joe followed.

This was the high desert, six thousand feet above sea level, just enough rainfall to support life. The trees were spread far apart, with a sprinkling of sage, rabbitbrush, and brown grass between them. The scent of sage was strong, almost overpowering. Joe studied the distance between trees. He guessed a car could zigzag a path through these woods if the driver didn't care about beating the vehicle to hell.

"I plan on putting an application in with BIA or FBI when I finish my bachelor's," Bluehorse said.

"Go with the FBI. They offer dental."

"Really?"

Joe smiled, something he'd not done in some time.

"Which would you recommend?"

"Either," Joe said. "FBI if you don't care where they send you. BIA if you want to work reservations the rest of your life." And don't mind being screwed over once in a while by your supervisor.

"I think I want to work reservations."

Enjoy the screwing.

"So how did you find the vehicle?"

"We were searching for a missing hunter, and I just came across it."

They arrived at a shallow arroyo. Joe slid down and could feel loose soil spill into his shoes. When they climbed out on the other side, he was breathing hard. It had to be the elevation and not the four or more beers a night—usually more—he told himself.

"Hold on." Joe leaned against a tree and took off his shoes, one at a time, shaking them out as he filled his lungs. "What made you run the vehicle?"

"The bullet holes."

"Bullet holes? Why didn't you tell me about them when I called?"

Bluehorse shifted his weight to his other foot. "The car's been here a long time. They could be from hunters having target practice. I didn't want to sound the alarm. And you didn't ask any questions."

"I shouldn't have to ask."

The officer lowered his gaze. "Yes, sir. Sorry."

Joe hadn't meant to come off so harsh. "The news didn't mention bullet holes."

"I haven't turned in my report yet. I wanted to keep that and the location quiet until you arrived."

"That's great, but how did the story even get out?"

"This is Navajo land," Bluehorse said. "There are no secrets. I guess someone in the department talked."

Joe slipped his foot back into his second shoe. He patted the trunk of a tree. "Is this oak?" he asked, trying to stretch out the break a little longer.

Bluehorse perked up. He peered toward the tree's canopy. "A real fine one, too." He touched the bark with his hand. "There's a lot of oak here, mostly down by the canyons. The name Chi Chil Tah means 'where the oaks grow.' My grandpa was Hopi, a kachina carver. Do you know what they are?"

Joe did. Small colorful carvings of Indian dancers representing various spirits.

Bluehorse continued in a soft, almost sad voice. "He used to take me out this way when I was a kid to gather wood. Most kachinas are made from cottonwood root. It's soft and easy to carve. But my grandpa made a special oak kachina for men with what he called 'the wandering spirit.' Oak is heavy, he'd say; it plants the man firmly with his family. He also made it for people who suffered great losses because oak was strong and could bear great burdens."

"He sounds like a wise man."

"He was. He died a few years back."

Joe's chest tightened. He felt for Bluehorse. For this young man's loss. He thought of Christine, his own loss. Memories flashed through his head like a silent montage. Images of her. Images of them. He pushed them out of his head. Those memories were for the nights when he lay awake in bed, not having had quite enough alcohol to dull the pain, to bring on the blackness and the comfort of oblivion. On those nights, his memories would infiltrate his mind like termites, trying to destroy his will to go on without her. He stood in the woods now, struggling to catch his breath, but he couldn't. He faced away and inhaled deeply. After a bit, he turned back. Bluehorse had his eyes closed and his left ear pressed against the tree.

"We'd sometimes wander these woods for hours till we found the right tree. He'd say he could hear the tree's energy, its life. He'd take wood only from a healthy tree, never a sickly or dying one." Bluehorse pushed himself off the trunk, turned, and started again through the woods.

Joe followed. He knew he had just witnessed something profound, something that should have given him a flash of insight into the human condition, or some glimpse of a universal truth. Instead, he just felt dull. His head hurt, memories of Christine still fighting to get back in. He trudged on, following the young officer, weaving between trees both living and dead.

They hiked the next ten minutes in silence, Bluehorse in front, maintaining an easy pace; Joe, some distance behind, breathing hard, trying to keep up. Finally they arrived, quietly, solemnly, forgoing any discussion that might herald the journey's end.

Between two dead piñon trees, surrounded by sage and rabbitbrush, painted in shadows, out of place in this seemingly untouched wilderness, sat the remains of a bone white Lincoln Town Car.

Bluehorse had not downplayed its condition. There was little left. The doors were angled open, seats missing. The dash had been ripped apart, its wire innards dangling. Only brittle shards remained of the rear window. All the tires were gone, the axles resting on an assortment of logs and stones.

Joe made a slow circle around the remains. He detected the faintest scent of engine oil, surprising considering all the years the vehicle had rested there. Yet, at the same time, he knew the longevity of odor. He had been to many body recoveries over the years. And he knew how strong the smell of decay could be even after a decade under the earth, as if the dead refused to break their connection with the living.

The vehicle's vinyl roof was shredded and its four headlights broken. Its front bumper lay lopsided, like a stroke patient's smile. Three evenly spaced bullet holes cut across the windshield. Possibly some idiot's idea of target practice, but it challenged the idea that Edgerton had simply skipped out with the money, which had always seemed a little too storybook for Joe.

He bent down by the rear bumper. On the left, faded, peeling, barely legible, was a sticker that read EDGERTON FOR CONGRESS. To the right of that was DUKAKIS FOR PRESIDENT IN '88.

"Nice work." Joe was being honest, but he wished the officer had waited three months to call it in. That way, Joe could have read about it at his new job. If he could find a new job.

"Thanks, sir."

"Call me Joe."

"So what's all the fuss over Edgerton? I mean, I know he ran off with some money, but it's not like he killed anyone."

"At the time, it was pretty big. Right after the Iran-Contra scandal. People were upset about political corruption. I think Edgerton became everyone's target. Also, it was sort of a mystery. What happened with all the money? Sort of like D. B. Cooper."

"Who's D. B. Cooper?"

Joe grinned. "When were you born?"

"1990."

"Forget it." Joe turned his attention back to the Lincoln. "Why don't you give me your take on this?"

Officer Bluehorse straightened. "Yes, sir—I mean, Joe." He walked to the engine compartment.

"The whole car's been stripped, even the engine."

Joe looked under the hood. In place of the motor was a pile of sticks and shredded bark. A pack rat's nest.

"At first I thought the vehicle may have been put here after being stripped somewhere else. But I found an old trail right over there." Bluehorse pointed north. "It's overgrown now, but that must be how they got the engine out. Also, I found some of the engine parts under the car, so that told me they dismantled it here. Same with lug nuts and some dashboard pieces.

"I can't be sure, but it looks like those three shots through the windshield were fired from a downward angle. My guess is the shooter was standing on the hood and fired down into the dash."

Joe poked his head inside. A gouge ran down the front edge of the dashboard, over the missing radio console, showing the trajectory of a round. It seemed unlikely the shooter had been aiming for the occupants.

"And there's something else," Bluehorse said. He closed the driver-side door and then walked around to the passenger side. Joe followed. They squeezed between the piñon tree and the front passenger door. They crouched down. Joe looked to where Bluehorse pointed, at the now-closed driver-side door. The door's plastic panel had long since been removed, and Joe could see the fabricated metal frame and mechanical components inside. A single bullet hole, round, jagged, had ripped into the frame at the base of the window, just below the pop-up lock lever. He hadn't noticed them on his walk around the vehicle, but he had noticed that the paint had peeled at the top of the door and that rust had begun working its way down from that same corner.

"I don't know the caliber," Bluehorse said. "But it's big."

Joe walked around and examined the hole. After a moment he said, "Forty-five." This bullet hole was interesting—and troubling. It was larger than the rounds in the windshield. He looked down. At first he thought he was looking at a brown carpet, but then he realized the entire floorboard was covered in rodent droppings. The rug had been removed.

"You want to stay involved with the investigation?"

"Yes, sir."

"You're going to have to keep quiet about what we do, even to your supervisors. Is that going to be a problem?"

Bluehorse hesitated. "The chief asked me to keep him updated."

"You can keep him updated, but we'll have to agree on what those updates will be. If that makes you feel uncomfortable, tell me now. I can't have any more leaks to the press."

"I don't think the chief would leak to the press."

"That's the deal, Bluehorse. I like how you've handled it so far. I think you should be part of the investigation, since you're the one who found the car, but it's your call."

"Are you going to bring out a crime-scene team?"

Joe shrugged.

"Okay. I'm in," Bluehorse said, smiling. "But please give my chief decent updates, so I don't lose my job."

"Welcome to the team."

"What's next?"

"Well, we have no idea if the bullet holes are related to Edgerton's disappearance. It could've been some hunters having fun."

"What if it wasn't?"

"That's why we cover our asses and bring in an FBI evidence team."

Officer Bluehorse watched Joe's Tahoe disappear down the road. He couldn't help but grin. He was on the case. Only a rookie and he was going to be working one of the biggest cases to hit the reservation since . . . since he didn't know when.

He wanted to tell someone, but he didn't know who. He'd have to wait until he got home tonight. He saw himself sitting around the dinner table with his folks, forking a few peas, offhandedly mentioning the investigation. Oh, by the way. That Edgerton case. The BIA wants me to work it.

He couldn't wait.

But for now, he'd have to satisfy himself by telling someone else. He took out his cell phone.

"Chief, this is Officer Bluehorse. We just finished." He told the chief about Joe's inspection of the Lincoln, grinning the entire time. "He said I could assist with the investigation, if that's okay with you, sir."

His good mood soured slightly. "I'm not sure what his plans are, sir. He's going to call me tomorrow."

After he disconnected, he stood there for a bit, not moving, still flying high, but beginning to see the ground. Joe had given him a chance; he wouldn't let him down.

He punched in his grandmother's number.

"*Shi másání*," he said. "I'm in Chi Chil Tah and was thinking of *Shi chei*."

They talked a little about family and about why he hadn't been out to see her the past couple weeks. He didn't mention the case to her, though. She didn't follow the news, and it would have taken too long to explain its importance. But he did have a reason for calling.

"*Shí másání,* do you still have any of *Shi chei's* oak kachinas?"

❖

For the past month, the two dozen volunteers who staffed Grace Edgerton's campaign headquarters buzzed with the excitement of an impending win. The polls predicted it. Her staff echoed it. In four weeks' time, Grace Edgerton would be elected governor of the great state of New Mexico. And she was ready. Ready to lead New Mexico to a prosperous future that would embrace the multiethnic population and leverage the state's technological centers, the backbone of its economy. She would also protect the border, not to keep Mexicans from following their dream and coming to the United States, but to stop the flow of drugs and violence. Those were her campaign pledges. And any one of her volunteers there in the office would swear she planned to do just that. She loved New Mexico. To her, it *was* the Land of Enchantment.

But yesterday, things had changed. Brooding silence descended upon her headquarters. Volunteers spoke in hushed whispers as they stole furtive glances toward Grace Edgerton's office and the battalion of senior staff dashing in and out. The change began right after Channel 13 reported her husband's vehicle had been found.

In less than a month, voters would go to the polls and decide which lever to pull—or rather, which button to push. Her volunteers started talking about defeat. That morning, two had called in and said they could no longer volunteer because they had found jobs.

Now, Congresswoman Grace Edgerton rocked back and forth in her tufted high-backed burgundy office chair. That morning's edition of the *Albuquerque Journal* lay on her desk. The photograph above the fold showed a smiling Arlen and Grace Edgerton, their hands joined and raised in a victory pose. Arlen's first election, in 1986.

Gabriella Soyria Cullodena Sedillo-Edgerton began to cry.

Cullodena was her grandmother's first name on her mother's side, the Gilchrist side. A proud Scottish family. Her father, Gustavo Alejandro Sedillo, came from a wealthy Mexican family. Both sides opposed her parents' union. But when Grace was born, their families put aside their ethnic differences and doted on their *pequeño joya*, their little jewel.

Grace's parents lived in Matamoros, a city on the U.S.-Mexico border, across from Brownsville, Texas. But a few months before Grace was due, her mother moved to Brownsville and delivered her first baby at Mercy Hospital, or La Merced, as the locals called it, ensuring Grace's birthright citizenship. Grace grew up attending the best private schools in America. Later she attended the University of New Mexico, which wasn't the best, but it did have the largest Hispanic population in the country and was close enough for Gustavo Sedillo to check up on his only daughter. At age twenty-two, she met an older man, Arlen Edgerton, a transplanted blue blood from Massachusetts, who became a campus activist and her college lover. At age twenty-six, she was the wife of Congressman Arlen Edgerton, the beloved New Mexican, the celebrated liberal, and her political role model. At age thirty, she was Congresswoman Grace Edgerton. And now, at an age that she tried her best never to divulge, she would be Governor Grace Edgerton.

Her office door flung open. She wiped away a tear.

"We've got trouble." Christopher Staples, her campaign manager, strode into the office, an invisible cloud of cheap aftershave in tow. He plopped his two-doughnut-a-day bottom onto the burgundy leather couch she kept in there for those long nights during the campaign. "Big trouble. *Godzilla* sequel–size trouble. King fucking Kong–size trouble. This is the shit you can't foresee. The shit that can torpedo a run at the last minute."

Her chest fluttered. "What is it?"

"This could sink us. Sink you."

"Chris, calm down and tell me."

"So close. So freakin' close."

"Chris!"

"Arlen's vehicle was riddled with bullets."

"Oh God."

"See what I mean. A shitstorm is about to hit and stink up your campaign."

"Oh God."

"You can say that again."

She whispered, "Arlen."

Chris stared at her.

"I'm sorry," he said, but his tone didn't agree. "I shouldn't have dropped it on you like that. But we need to move."

Grace took a deep breath and wiped away another tear.

"Why?"

"Kendall called. There's a *Washington Post* reporter already sniffing around, working the angle that you knew about the affair and maybe you put a hit out on your husband and that tramp."

"Her name was Faye and she wasn't a tramp and they weren't lovers. I shouldn't have to be telling you this. You're supposed to be on my side." She looked down at the paper on her desk. At the picture of her and Arlen holding hands. "Those rumors are old. No one cares about them now."

"This is the *Washington* fucking *Post*. You know, the Watergate folks. They put the FBI to shame." He shook his head in disbelief. "Damn it, Grace. Take your blinders off. Arlen's disappearance never amounted to much back then because no one had any answers. No one knew what happened. Anything goes now. They could find the gun in your desk drawer, for all I know."

She sprang to her feet. "What the hell do you mean by that?"

"Kendall's concerned, and I don't blame him. If he endorses you now, there can be blowback later. He wants you in office so you can return the favor when he announces his run for the White House. But you go up in flames with this, he gets burned." He leaned his head back, pressing the palms of his hands against his eyes. "Shit. You may have been considered for the VP ticket. I so wanted out of this state. You know, I was even checking out condos in D.C."

"Knock it off. I'll talk to him."

He dropped his hands and met her gaze. His expression suggested he was witnessing humanity's fall from grace. "Look, I'm neither your priest nor your lawyer. I was hired to get you elected. If you had anything to do with it, I don't care. But if you, by some wild chance now, do get elected and the feds come knocking at the governor's mansion someday, perhaps it would be in your best interest to start planting a few seeds of marital discord. It might help you later. I get paid either way; just give me the word."

"Let me make one thing perfectly clear. I love—loved—Arlen, and I want to know what happened to him, just like everyone else. And if you don't believe me, then maybe you need to consider joining Percy's camp."

"Don't think I haven't." Chris struggled to his feet. "And remember what I said. Marital problems make you sympathetic."

Joe parked in a no parking zone. He tossed his placard on the dash. The laminated card read FOR OFFICIAL USE ONLY—FEDERAL LAW ENFORCEMENT VEHICLE. He hurried into the building.

Inside, he scanned the tenant directory posted on the wall.

THE HAMILTON GROUP . . . 17th Floor.

He checked the time. He was late.

On the drive over, Joe had received a call from Bluehorse. The Gallup newspaper had printed a story about Edgerton's vehicle being found bullet-riddled.

With his finger, Joe wrote the words *shit happens* in the condensation on his mug of beer. He appraised his work. Andy Warhol had nothing on him. Pop art at its finest.

"Wanna talk about it?" Mickey Sheehan said as he sorted through the quarters in the bar's register, forever on the lookout for rare coins.

"Not right now. I'm finding my muse."

"Ask her if she's got a sister."

"You need a bingo partner?"

"One of my waitresses quit."

Mickey started on the nickels. Joe watched. Back in August, Joe had been sitting on the same stool when Mickey yelled, "I'll be damned. No *P*." He repeated that a few times, slapping the mahogany bar top and laughing. He later told Joe that all the dimes minted in Philadelphia after 1980 had a *P*, designating the city. In 1982, the mint accidentally omitted the *P* from a small batch. Mickey's dime would fetch a couple thousand dollars, though he'd never sell it. "I got a spot for it right next to my 1955 doubled-die penny." Joe had no idea what a 1955 doubled-die penny was, but he appreciated Mickey's enthusiasm, especially when he gave the bar a round of drinks on the house.

Mickey finished his coin hunt and limped to the other end of the counter to check on the only other customers at the bar, two men in suits and ties who huddled together and talked in whispers, as though they were discussing trade secrets. Maybe they were.

Mickey's Bar & Grill had the feel of an old-time saloon. The walls were of wood panel and exposed brick, and the thick oak tables and chairs were covered with liberally applied coats of varnish. The place smelled of smoked ribs and frothy ale. War photographs decorated the walls. Mickey had served in Vietnam with the Screaming Eagles. He once told Joe how he'd earned his Purple Heart. "During the war—and don't believe that conflict bullshit; it was a goddamn war—I was at Firebase Ripcord when the shit hit the fan. We was getting pounded by mortars. I jump in a foxhole and feel a sting on my right calf. I reach down to rub it, thinking I got nicked by a flying stone or something, and the son of a bitch is gone." He looked Joe in the eye. "Now my foot powder lasts twice as long." He'd winked then, but Joe had been too involved in the story to laugh or smile, or whatever the old war vet had expected.

Joe liked Mickey and he liked the bar. It relaxed him. He sipped his beer and enjoyed the relative quiet of pre–happy hour. Mickey would turn the music on around 4:30, sometimes Tony Bennett, sometimes something more current. And then the after-work regulars would start to trickle in, most sitting at the bar, a few grabbing tables for dinner. Joe knew the routine of the regulars. He'd become a member two years ago, ever since Christine's . . .

He downed the mug and set it at the end of the counter, indicating to Mickey he wanted—no, needed—another. Mickey hobbled over, took out a fresh mug from under the counter, and filled it.

"Ready to talk?"

"Yeah. Just needed to get one down."

"I'm listening."

"Had a job interview today. I was late and it didn't go too well. The guy was younger than my daughter."

"Don't worry about it. You got a good reputation and you know your shit. It'll work out. But next time, don't forget to shave."

Joe stroked his face. Shit. Actually, he'd hadn't forgotten. He just hadn't bothered. Shaving was one of those things that didn't seem so important anymore.

Mickey went on: "How's Melissa?"

"Top of her class, as always. Just like her mom." He took a swallow of beer, a long swallow. "Nothing like her dad. At least I can be thankful for that."

"Snap out of it, Joe." Mickey's voice was serious. "I don't mind your business. Hell, I appreciate it. But you got more going for you than coming in here and drinking by yourself every night. You're still young—younger than me, anyway. Get out and meet people. Meet some women."

"You're a broken record, Mick."

"See what I mean. You're outta touch. They ain't got records no more. You gotta say, 'Mick, you sound like a skipping CD.'"

Joe smiled. "I don't think anyone says that."

"They should. 'Broken record' sounds old-fashioned."

Joe wrote *skipping CD* in the condensation on his mug, wrapping the letters all the way around so they started and stopped at the handle. No, it didn't have the same ring as "broken record."

"We may have a prospect," Mickey said.

Three women walked toward the bar. They didn't look over. Joe knew two of them, Linda and Sue. Two very nice, and very loud, married women who came to Mickey's a couple times a week to grab a drink and do battle with the bar's sound system. They worked for a large development company down the street. Joe liked them because they were fun to listen to. He didn't know the third woman, a blonde. She walked between the other two, laughing a nice laugh, a friendly laugh. Joe immediately liked her. She filled out her beige pants like roses fill out a bouquet—and she wore sensible heels. If she had been wearing high heels, he'd have pegged her as high-maintenance. Christine, his wife, had never worn stilettos, but she'd always had great legs and never needed the extra sculpting.

Joe returned to his beer. This time he wrote *stilletto* in the condensation, not sure how to spell it. He tried to remember if he'd ever written the word before. He didn't think so. He couldn't remember writing *high heels*, either.

Joe took another long swallow of beer. He was about to draw a high heel, when a woman spoke behind him.

"It's only one *l*."

Joe turned and saw the blonde standing next to him. She offered a smile. He turned on his charm.

"Huh?"

She pointed to his mug. "*Stiletto* has one *l*. Why did you write that on your mug?"

Joe had an answer, but not one that made sense. Oh, hi. I noticed you weren't wearing stilettos, so I knew you weren't high-maintenance. Why, no, I'm not crazy. Why do you ask? Instead, he lied. "Reliving my fifth-grade spelling bee. I got it wrong then, too."

"You'd think you would have come to terms with that by now."

"Some losses are harder to get over than others."

"I'm sure." Their eyes locked for a moment. "I came over to thank you for the drink."

Joe searched out Mickey. The old bastard winked.

"Welcome to the neighborhood," Joe said. "Linda and Sue are a lot of fun." Lame.

"They are." She leaned in and whispered, "But they're so loud."

"Loud? I never noticed."

She laughed and held out her hand. "I'm Gillian."

"Joe. Nice to meet you."

"Would you like to join us?"

"No, I wouldn't be great company tonight. And besides, I have a failed geometry test from ninth grade I have to revisit. Still can't figure how I botched that one." He drew a triangle on his glass.

"You're funny." She turned and went back to her friends. Linda and Sue both looked over and waved. "Hi, Joe," they shouted almost in unison, but not quite. He waved back and placed his half-empty mug on the end of the counter. Mickey came over.

"She thanked me for the drink," Joe said.

"You're a real sweetheart."

"Yeah, I surprise myself sometimes."

"Another?"

"One more. I don't want to ruin my nice-guy impression by staggering out of here."

"Too late. Linda and Sue already know you. But I'll see what I can do with the new girl."

❖

C edro Bartolome swirled his glass of Chianti. He examined its legs, sniffed, and then took a sip. Plums and Mother Earth.

"*Excelente*," he said.

The waiter poured wine for the other three guests.

Tonight was special. For the last three weeks, he'd been courting a new client for the firm, a conglomerate with sizable holdings in both Mexico and the United States. A few hours earlier, the conglomerate's in-house counsel had notified him it had selected his firm, so he had called his wife, Daniela, and told her they would go out tonight to celebrate. Then he invited Ernesto and his wife. Ernesto was one of Cedro's five partners at the firm, and he rarely refused an opportunity to enjoy good food and spirits.

"Have you been following the news in America about Edgerton?" Ernesto asked in Spanish.

Almost two decades had passed since Cedro had last heard the name.

"It's not good," Ernesto said. "The authorities found his car. They could start asking you questions again, maybe put some pressure on the firm. We should be ready."

Cedro sipped his wine. He detected the pedestrian flavor of sour berries.

❖

SEPTEMBER 25
SATURDAY, 9:11 A.M.
JONES RANCH ROAD, CHI CHIL TAH (NAVAJO NATION),
NEW MEXICO

It took Joe a few minutes to find Bluehorse's trail, two tire tracks turning north off Jones Ranch Road. He got out and stuck a small orange flag into the clay by the path. Then he climbed back in his vehicle and drove into the tree line.

The way was rough. He switched to four-wheel drive. As he weaved around trees, he glanced occasionally in his rearview mirror, catching the brilliant rays of sunlight that penetrated the thin canopy and gave the clouds of dust behind him a surreal glow, as though he were passing through a magical gateway, a rift through worlds. Perhaps he was. Many have described the Navajo Nation as a mystical place, a place where superstition and the substantive world fuse into a new reality.

The trail ended in a small clearing, perhaps fifty feet at its widest. He parked next to Bluehorse's unit, then got out. They shook hands.

"The others are on their way," Joe said. "Should be here by ten."

"I called the chief a few minutes ago. He said he was upset I didn't know about this yesterday."

Joe had asked Bluehorse not to tell his chief the FBI would process the vehicle today. He hadn't wanted any press showing up at the road. He'd suspected the chief was the one behind leaking the story about the bullet holes.

"Don't worry. You'll have enough to update him on after we finish here."

"Did you tell your boss?" Bluehorse asked.

"We don't talk much."

❖

September 25
Saturday, 9:30 a.m.
The Constitution Room, Washington, D.C.

Kendall Holmes touched his lips to the gold-rimmed china cup and sipped the Earl Grey tea, letting it bathe his palate. The soft bergamot tang excited his mouth yet calmed his body. He relaxed into the oversized poppy-colored leather chair in the waiting lounge of the Constitution Room, an exclusive power dining spot in D.C. Anyone who was anyone kept this number on speed dial, and anyone who mattered had standing reservations. More legislation was finalized here than on the Senate and House floors combined. And, to be honest, the Constitution Room offered the proper atmosphere to run a country, rivaling the White House in elegance and grandeur—no, exceeding the White House. On his last visit to the home of the supposed most powerful man in the free world, he had noted how shabby the place looked. The radiators begging for paint, the plaster walls bulging and out of shape. Unacceptable. He might have an opportunity to do something about that in a couple of years. The Constitution

Room, however, was flawless. Even the silver and crystal chandeliers hanging from the twenty-foot ceiling gleamed with a perpetual polish. Never a speck of dust or the taint of tarnish. More important, these dangling islands of light cast the perfect illumination. As with every decision inside the Beltway, it was likely the product of a three-hundred-page report prepared by a consultant who had studied the exact number of lumens required to attract venerated statesmen— as well as the reviled.

Holmes looked over at the waiter, who stood off to the corner, visible to the eye yet distant to the ear. Eavesdropping does not attract politicians. Kendall held up his tea and nodded, indicating it was a fine cup. The young man returned the nod with a quick smile. The waiter was new. Holmes would develop him over time. Sources were important. A waiter at the Constitution Room was gold, maybe even platinum. A tidbit here, a morsel there. Holmes called it "mosaic intelligence." Individually, the pieces were meaningless, but together, they made a picture. That was the purpose of his meeting this morning. To gather intelligence. But with caution.

He checked his watch, a Blancpain. Nine-thirty-two. The roman numerals circling the face appeared blurry. He'd stayed up late last night, leaving in his contacts, something he rarely did because his eyes were sensitive. The Edgerton mess was not only disrupting his usual calm but also his sleep. His phone vibrated, a text from his head of security—and longtime bodyguard—who waited in the lobby. His guest had arrived.

A minute later, Helena Newridge, a journalist for the *Washington Post*, waddled through the lounge, her head bobbling about, no doubt spying for gossip. The bulky jewelry around her neck and wrists gave off a rattle as she walked.

Holmes hid his disgust. "Ms. Newridge, over here."

She sat down across from him. "I haven't been here in a while. Budget cuts—unlike the government."

He gave her his win-over laugh, one he'd perfected for his community-outreach meetings with constituents. "Allow me to grant you an appropriation. This will be my treat." He slipped on his D.C. smile.

"You're very smooth, Senator."

"I enjoy people."

She gave a smirk. "Uh-huh."

"But before we begin, we have to agree on the terms. Yes?"

"We covered that on the phone."

"We did, but for my own peace of mind, I would like to confirm our arrangement. You're new to certain circles, so I need to know if you can be trusted to keep a confidence."

"It's my bread and butter."

"I'm sure." He smiled, showing his laser-whitened dental work, and his slightly pointy canines. "So we agree to background only. No quotes and I am not to be mentioned in the piece, correct?"

"Correct."

"And no recording."

She looked disappointed. "Fine, no recording."

"Okay, shall we eat now?"

"Sure, as long as we talk, too."

Two midnight blue Suburbans pushed through the tree line. The first parked beside Joe's vehicle. Behind the wheel was Andi McBride. She burst from her vehicle and strode up to Joe like a hungry bear greeting a hiker.

"What do you have, Joe? And I hope we aren't parked in the scene."

"Hello to you, too, Andi. How have you been? How's the family? Go anywhere interesting on vacation this year?"

"Cut the crap. You know we've got all day to catch up. But if you want to know, I missed my jujitsu class this morning, so I haven't relieved all my stress"—she looked Joe up and down and cracked a knuckle—"yet. I got food poisoning on my cruise and was sick for three days. And if I don't get back to Albuquerque by six, my ex- is going to go apeshit, because I promised to take Pauly to the movies tonight. Other than that, I'm great."

Bluehorse, who was standing next to Joe, took a step back.

"Happy to hear it—I mean that you're great," Joe said, trying to suppress a smile.

"You doing all right?"

"My boss is on my ass, the job is telling me to retire, and there's a vehicle just over there"—he gestured to the east—"that's probably going to be a giant hemorrhoid. And I have another tuition payment due in two weeks. Other than that, I'm great."

"Happy to hear it—about you being great, I mean."

They shook hands.

"All right. Give me the nickel summary and skip the Edgerton part. I've been watching the news." She held her pen and clipboard at the ready.

Joe let Bluehorse tell about his find and the bullet holes. As he spoke, two more agents joined them, one male and one female. The female agent was reserved and stayed off to the side of the group, filling out what Joe guessed was a crime-scene form. He recognized the man.

"It's Joe, right?" said Mark Fisher, a young candlewick of a man constantly burning nervous energy. "We did the Lujan case together in Sandia."

Joe recalled the case. A fired railroad worker went home and lodged an ax in his son's head because the teen had left a carton of milk on the counter to spoil. The drunken father had wanted a bowl of cereal.

"It's been a while, Mark."

"I read the father got seventeen years. Good job."

"Thanks," Joe said. "We appreciated your help with it."

"Did they set a date for your retirement party?" Andi asked Joe.

"Not yet. Stretch is on it, though."

Andi assigned Mark to evidence collection, and the other agent to photos and sketching.

Before they started, Mark went back to the Suburban. He returned a few minutes later carrying a long black plastic case, a camera bag, a camo backpack, and a tripod. Then they all followed Bluehorse to the once-forgotten hunk of metal sitting a short distance in the woods.

The milky white paint of the Lincoln glowed rather than radiated from the morning sunlight, giving its edges a fuzziness that seemed to ripple as though alive. The group circled the plundered vehicle. Criminologists suggest that stripping a vehicle is an act of vandalism, representing a breakdown of law and order, society's failure at self-policing. Joe saw it as a symptom of social cancer. The doers, like mutated cells, ate away at a neighborhood, spreading, infecting others, until the mass got so large that the community collapsed. He was sure some of these cancerous cells lived nearby. They had taken what they could from this vehicle over the years, rather than reporting it to the police so a proper investigation could have been completed back when the congressman went missing. Now Joe had to deal with it.

Bluehorse showed them the bullet hole in the driver-side door and offered his theories.

"Let's see you work some magic, Mark," Joe said. He didn't feel hopeful, but he knew he had to cover every angle in order to uncover any possible clue.

"That's why I get paid the big bucks." Mark passed out breathing masks and gloves to Joe and Bluehorse as the other agent took photographs of the vehicle and the surrounding area. Over the next hour, they shoveled out the rat droppings from inside the vehicle and ran metal detectors over the piles, looking for slugs or shells or anything else out of place that might potentially be a clue. They found nothing other than nuts and bolts, bottle caps, and metal brackets.

When they finished, Mark climbed into the vehicle to examine the bullet holes in the windshield and door. He and the female agent photographed and measured them all. When they were done, Mark focused on the door, placing his left cheek to the hole. He peered through.

"Oh yeah. This is going to be fun."

Joe could hear a slight giddiness in his voice. He knew evidence guys—and gals—got excited by challenges at a scene.

"I feel pretty confident we can find this round," Mark said. "No guarantee, of course. But definitely possible."

Mark went to work. He opened the long black case and extracted a small box, a long metal rod, and a tiny tripod, all of which he handed to Bluehorse.

"Hold on to these until I get inside."

Mark slid back inside the vehicle.

Bluehorse handed Mark the equipment.

Mark placed it on the battered dashboard, opened it, and withdrew several small white plastic cones with holes running lengthwise through them. He held them to the bullet hole in the door, inserting each one gently, and then removing it to try the next, searching for a cone that fit snugly into the hole and was oriented in the direction the round would have traveled. He seemed to find the one he wanted and placed the others back in the box.

He grabbed the long rod and pushed it through the bottom of the cone, sliding the small white plastic halfway down its length. Angling the rod, he inserted it through the bullet hole until the cone seated. He wiggled the rod assembly a few times until he appeared satisfied. He looked up. The rod pierced the driver's door like a magician's sword through a magic box.

"Now for the angle finder," Mark said, more to himself than to the others.

Mark held a yellow plastic device at the back end of the rod. He read the dial and then made a notation on a small notepad he pulled from the cargo pocket of his pants.

Joe was absorbed by the process. He'd seen this technique used only once before, in an accidental shooting involving elk hunters.

Mark extended the legs of the tripod so they touched the now somewhat clean floorboard and then placed the rod in a small U-shaped clip at the tripod's top. After making a few adjustments, he leaned back and appraised his work.

"This is not going to be perfect, but it'll give us a good search vector."

"You got my attention," Joe said. "What's next?"

"Do you have any idea if the vehicle was moved over the last twenty years? Maybe pushed or towed? Even a few feet?"

Because of the car parts under and around the vehicle, they didn't believe it had been moved. It appeared to have been stripped in place.

"There are three unknowns we're dealing with here," Mark began. "First, was this vehicle parked here when the shot was fired? Second, was there anything on the outside of this door that could have intercepted the round and subsequently changed its direction, like a person or a tree that's been cut down since? And third, was the round an ice bullet and has it since melted away?"

Bluehorse looked surprised.

Joe laughed.

"Okay, we only have two unknowns. But one of these days someone will try something tricky like that, and I'll be ready."

"I pity the fool," Joe said in a poor imitation of Mr. T.

Mark and Bluehorse both looked at him, heads cocked.

"The *A-Team*?" Joe waited for a response. Nothing. He shook his head. "Young'uns."

Mark went on: "So we could do an entire three-part mathematical equation to calculate the round's time aloft, maximum height, and horizontal distance traveled, taking into account wind resistance and the Earth's rotation, but . . ."

Bluehorse bit. "But?"

"But we don't know the round's velocity, and without that, I can't do the calculations."

Dramatic pause.

Bluehorse bit again. "Oh."

"So we're left with one option. The string technique."

No one said anything.

Mark continued, possibly a little disappointed by the lack of response. "I connect a laser to the rod and shoot out a beam for about two hundred yards or until something stops it—something that could have stopped a round. That's our trajectory. Then we run a string from here to that point and use a metal detector along the string's path. If the shot was fired from this vehicle while it was sitting here, and if my angle of travel is correct, the round should be within five to ten feet on either side of that string."

Bluehorse clapped his hands together. "I'm game."

"Let me make two disclaimers. First, the car is at a lower angle because the tires are gone. Second, if my angle of travel through the door is off, or if the car shifted to the side over the years, that round may not be in our search area."

"Fair enough," Joe said.

"Let's find ourselves a bullet." Mark rifled through the little black box on the dash and pulled out a small penlike tube. He placed it at the back end of the rod and screwed it to the tip, making slow, careful twists, as though he were assembling a bomb. When it was connected, he checked the angle finder again and made an adjustment to the tripod.

"Bluehorse," Mark said. "In my backpack you'll find several sheets of white card stock. Grab a piece and hold it in front of the rod."

Bluehorse unzipped the bag.

A gunshot shattered the relative quiet of the woods.

William Tom dipped the last piece of wheat bread into the mixture of egg yolk and green chili. As he lifted the soaked morsel to his mouth, he felt the light patter of liquid on his shirt. He shoved what remained between his fingers into his mouth and used his forefinger to catch the runaways on his stretched and yellowed T-shirt, smearing them into a single large stain. He called out to his wife.

"Chllarrr!" Swallowing, he tried again. "Char!"

"*Ha'átíí?*" Charlene replied, annoyance apparent in her voice. She was sitting in the living room, watching cartoons.

"I need a new shirt."

"*Biniiyé?*"

"Because I got a stain on it."

"*Biniiyé?*"

"Damn it! I need a new shirt."

"*T'ah.*"

"Stop watching that shit and get me a shirt."

"*T'ah.*"

"You're a disgrace to your Navajo ancestors, woman. Don't speak the language if you can't live by the traditions."

"Go get it yourself, old man," she said, switching to English.

He pushed himself away from the kitchen table, his wheelchair sliding easily over the linoleum floor. He wheeled into the living room, looking at the back of Charlene's head as he went. At forty-two, she was twenty-five years his junior. Her liver was probably older than his, the way she drank, but that was probably all. She would surely outlive him.

He never touched alcohol and always ate well, but that hadn't made a difference. His whole body had given up on him a decade ago when he'd developed type 2 diabetes. He'd lost his right foot from a complication eight years ago. Then they took his lower leg. Last year, they took his thigh. Two months ago, a sharp tingling started to come and go in his left foot, but he kept that quiet. He'd lost most of the sight in his right eye and had been surprised that the doctors hadn't offered to cut that out, too.

In the bedroom, he maneuvered himself to the dresser and opened the middle drawer. The bottom three drawers were his, the top three hers. He pulled out a once-white T-shirt, now a sickly shade of piss.

William had left the Navajo reservation at the age of ten to attend boarding school in Vermont. He stayed there until he was eighteen, with few trips back home during those years. He went on to study archaeology at the University of Pennsylvania, and only after graduation did he return to the reservation. He wanted to bring his education back to his people. He was appointed as director of Navajo Antiquities, a department of government that safeguarded the Navajo Nation's cultural history, and a place where he tried to make a difference. But that position offered little opportunity. So, many years later, he ran for president of the Navajo Nation. One requirement for presidency was fluency in Navajo. Because he'd left the reservation so young, he'd never mastered the language. But when he wanted something, he did what was needed to attain it, so he'd studied hard for most of a year to gain fluency. He was elected in 1991, the same year he met Charlene, his third wife. His first two wives had become too traditional for him. Now, in his later, wiser years, he wished Charlene would become more traditional.

He pulled off his stained shirt and placed it on his lap. It took him a little time, but he put on the new shirt and adjusted it down around his back. His body had grown weak these last few years and simple tasks like getting dressed tired him quickly. He wheeled over to the laundry basket. The clothes were piled high, overflowing onto the floor. The pile would grow much larger before Char got around to doing the wash. He rolled up the soiled shirt and was about to toss it on the mound, when he saw a pair of her panties on top.

She had gone out the night before and hadn't returned home until after two, waking him up when she stumbled through the front door. She'd gone to Gallup, she'd said, with a few friends and had some drinks at the American Bar. When he asked her how she had gotten home, she said a friend drove her. She would not name the friend. He looked at the panties now, tempted to examine them for evidence of infidelity, to prove once again that she was cheating on him. But he realized it wouldn't do any good. He'd confronted her before, and she hadn't denied it.

"What do you want me to do?" she'd said. "I'm a woman. I'm young. You just want to sit home and read your stupid books. I can't do that." She hadn't spoken Navajo that time.

That was the first of a dozen arguments they'd had about her sleeping around. His family would tell him from time to time that they'd seen her here or there with this guy or that guy. He'd tell them to mind their own business. Once, he told his brother, "What am I supposed to do? I can't run after her." He'd stopped driving when he started to lose his sight, so he just sat at home like a good invalid. He still wielded some power on the reservation, still had some friends—still had some enemies, too. He could find someone to pay a visit to one of her *friends*, but that would imply he still cared. He didn't. Let her have her fun. He wouldn't be around much longer. Didn't *want* to be around much longer. Living was too much work now. Work and pain. As for him, they could put him in the ground tomorrow. A relic to be uncovered sometime in the future. A fitting end for an archaeologist.

He tossed his shirt on top of the pile and spun his chair around. He wheeled through the living room, out the front door, and onto the porch.

The *Navajo Times* lay there, wrapped with a rubber band. He bent and scooped it up, the effort making him breathe hard. He coughed. He smelled the air. The sage was strong and clean, energizing. As president, he had often told his constituents how much he loved the high desert and beautiful mesas, and how blessed the Navajo were to occupy their ancestral lands between the four sacred mountains. But after leaving office, he started telling the truth. He missed Vermont. He missed the deep greens and the vibrant colors of the Northeast. And more important, he missed the world-class hospitals there.

He sat for several moments, enjoying the warm sunshine. Then he pulled off the rubber band and unfolded the paper. He focused on the top story. "Clue to Congressman Edgerton's Disappearance Found on Reservation." His hands shook as he read.

❖

SEPTEMBER 25
SATURDAY, 11:43 A.M.
JONES RANCH ROAD, CHI CHIL TAH (NAVAJO NATION),
NEW MEXICO

Joe dropped to one knee, gun drawn. The sound of the shot had been close. Too close. He checked on the others. Bluehorse knelt by the fender. Mark's head eased up to the driver-side window from within the car.

Joe scanned the woods. Who the hell was shooting? And what were they shooting at?

"Police! Stop firing your weapon!"

Another gunshot roared.

It came from the east.

Joe and Bluehorse moved behind the vehicle.

"Police! Stop shooting!"

Silence.

"Get out of there, Mark." Joe said.

Mark crawled through the passenger door on his hands and knees, staying low, below the dash.

Bluehorse pointed in the direction of the shooter. "Maybe forty yards."

"Sounds like a shotgun," Mark said.

Joe swept his weapon across the tree line.

"Andi," Joe shouted over his shoulder. "You all right?"

Her voice came back immediately. "Right as rain!" She and the other agent were a little ways back, crouched behind trees. "Hunter?"

"Probably," Joe said.

Another gunshot.

"This is the police! Stop firing your weapon!"

"What do you want to do?" Mark asked.

"Let's move to contact before this asshole sends one our way," Joe said. They made a quick plan. He would head toward the shooter. Bluehorse and Mark would flank right. Andi would stay behind to secure the scene, along with the other agent.

He had worked with Andi many times over the years and would have preferred to go into the woods with her, but sometimes a situation dictated differently. Thankfully, Bluehorse and Mark both seemed more than capable of handling themselves. Some officers he'd encountered would have given him cause to worry. And he guessed his own squad may have felt that way about him.

Another gunshot went off.

"Let's go."

They sprinted for the tree line.

Joe's adrenaline surged. Twenty steps and his heart was already hammering. His thoughts turned dark. Would he have a heart attack or catch a stray bullet from some yokel shooting cans? With less than ninety days till retirement, what the hell was he doing out here? This was the type of story cops shared in the locker room. Hey, you remember old Joe from BIA. He was only ninety days out when . . .

He ran on, trying to clear his head. When was his last conversation with Melissa? Wednesday? Had he told her he loved her? He wasn't sure.

Another gun shot. Much louder. Closer. Like he was on the range without ear protection. He yelled for Bluehorse and Mark to hold up. He needed to get his bearings.

"See anything?" he asked.

Nothing.

He yelled again into the woods.

No answer.

Another gunshot. He zeroed in on the sound and rushed forward, jumping over sage and rabbitbrush. He smelled cordite in the air. That and freshly turned soil. Maybe a little burned wood, too.

He saw a figure no more than two dozen steps ahead of him. It appeared to be a man. He held a double-barreled shotgun, his back to Joe.

"Police! Stop firing!"

The man held the gun to his shoulder. It pointed down to the ground, to a fallen oak in front of him. Another round went off. Deafening. What the hell was he firing at?

Joe slowed, gun at his chest, muzzle lowered. He didn't expect to use force, but the man had a firearm. Bluehorse and Mark moved up from Joe's right. Good. Less chance of cross fire.

"Police! Stop firing!"

The man made no movement to indicate he'd heard the command. Instead, he broke the shotgun open and began to eject the two shells. Joe ran up behind him. With his left hand, he grabbed the man's wrist, disabling the hand that held the shotgun. The man turned and let out a startled yelp. Joe was glad the man hadn't dropped right there from fright. He was old enough. The warranty on his heart had surely expired a decade earlier. From the deep lines in his face and his urine-colored eyes, wide now from surprise, Joe guessed the old man had watched eighty pass him by a few years back. Hell, maybe even ninety, from the looks of his barren gum line. How had this decrepit old soul been firing a shotgun?

Bluehorse and Mark came to stand next to Joe.

They all looked down at the hole in the ground under the oak. A burrow.

The old man stared at Joe and then at Bluehorse. He gave Bluehorse's uniform the once-over.

"What are you shooting at, Grandpa?" Joe asked, his tone giving the title respect.

"Huh?" The old man cocked his head to the side, so his right ear faced Joe.

Louder: "What are you shooting at?"

The old man pointed to the other side of the oak. Joe leaned over for a view. A coyote lay dead on the ground, its body ripped apart from shotgun blasts.

"Why are you shooting at the hole?"

"Huh?"

Joe repeated himself, this time closer to the man's ear. Bluehorse and Mark covered their smiles.

"Pups."

The old man had been out to exterminate an entire den. Joe didn't agree with such wholesale slaughter of wildlife, but he knew how the Navajo viewed coyote: bad luck and a nuisance.

Mark spoke loudly, "Damn, old man, you gave us quite a scare."

The old man turned to Mark. "My English bad."

Bluehorse spoke to the old man in Navajo while Mark left to tell the others about the situation.

After a few minutes, Bluehorse filled Joe in on the grandpa.

"He lives a little east of here. The coyote killed two of his chickens and attacked one of his dogs, almost killed him, too."

"Ask him about the Lincoln."

Bluehorse spoke again in Navajo. His face was practically up against the side of the old man's head. Several more minutes passed as they talked.

"He says the car's been there a long time. Back when Peter Mac-Donald was president, before he was arrested by the FBI, before the riot. They called the police back then, but no one came out."

Joe knew the history. Every BIA agent did. Early in 1989, the then president of the Navajo Nation, Peter MacDonald, was suspended from office following allegations of corruption. On July 20 of that same year, MacDonald, unhappy with his own removal, led a group of supporters to take over the Navajo administration building in Window Rock, Arizona. The few Navajo police officers who responded to control the crowd and protect property were attacked by supporters; three lost their weapons, one of which was used in a shoot-out between supporters and the police. In the end, two people were killed and several officers wounded.

"He stays away from the car," Bluehorse said, "because evil spirits walk there."

"Why does he think that?"

Bluehorse translated. The old man's answer was long, his voice quiet, as though he didn't like the subject.

Bluehorse's voice had a touch of excitement. "There was blood on the seats when he found the car. The front seat, he thinks, but he's not sure because it was so long ago. That was why he called the police. He remembers the bullet hole in the door, but the ones in the windshield were from his son, Leon, years later, after the car had been stripped. His son had just been goofing around." Now his voice turned somber. "He thinks the car was bad luck for his son, who killed himself a few years later. The old man thinks it was because his son had disrespected the spirits."

❖

SEPTEMBER 25
SATURDAY, 12:51 P.M.
RESIDENCE OF HAWK RUSHINGWATER, CHINLE
(NAVAJO NATION), ARIZONA

Hawk Rushingwater, known as Dwight Henry before he broke ties with the American Indian Movement and founded Navajo NOW, tore open the envelope and extracted a handwritten letter and a check. He tossed the letter to Sleeping Bear, who sat across from him at the battered kitchen table. A small battery-powered radio sat on the counter behind them. A woman announcer reported the news in Navajo.

"Ten bucks." He flung the check to Sleeping Bear. It fluttered to a rest next to the bookkeeper's beer. "Donations are way down. We need publicity."

Sleeping Bear read the letter. "A Girl Scout in Green Bay held a cupcake sale."

"Write her back. Tell her to try selling magic brownies. Bigger profit margins."

Nightwind, who sat on the couch reading a comic book, laughed. Then he coughed. He took a hit from his bong, long and deep. He coughed again and went back to reading.

"We could do a podcast," Sleeping Bear said. "Maybe a video of you talking about the UN project."

"Yeah, I like that. Like our own news channel on the Internet. Maybe we can boycott something, too. Something controversial. Beer distributors." Rushingwater took a deep breath and pushed out his chest. "I call upon the righteous to take up our cause and put a stop to the annihilation of our people and the pervasion of capitalism. The beer industry has targeted Native American communities for genocide."

"Perversion," Sleeping Bear said.

Nightwind laughed. Rushingwater turned, lip curled, ready to attack, but Nightwind was laughing at his comic.

Sleeping Bear downed the rest of his warm beer, stood, and made his way to the bathroom, a five-gallon Home Depot bucket at the other end of the trailer. He stumbled only once.

Rushingwater watched Nightwind reading. Then something the radio announcer said caught his attention. Congressman Edgerton. Rushingwater tilted his head as though the idea formulating inside was too heavy for his neck. He grinned, a big toothy grin.

Mark was back inside the Lincoln, rechecking his bullet-trajectory rig, when Joe returned to the scene. Bluehorse had accompanied the old man home so he could talk with his wife. It was unlikely she had any additional information, but it was best to be thorough.

If the old man was telling the truth—and Joe had no reason to doubt him—then something had happened in this vehicle. Something bad. Blood put a whole different spin on this case, more than simply a congressman fleeing prosecution. Most people had assumed Edgerton had run. Others, however, including several prominent news personalities, had speculated Edgerton and his staffers had been killed to protect the people behind the corruption, but those theories never amounted to much because no bodies were ever recovered. In addition, there had been a number of alleged sightings over the intervening years, but none ever confirmed, and that folklore further cemented the idea Edgerton had simply fled. Mexico and South America had topped the list of possible destinations. The most outlandish had been a story connecting Edgerton to a secret cabal bent on world domination, operating on a Greek island in the Aegean Sea. This was supposedly the same island where John F. Kennedy had lived out the remainder of his life, confined to a wheelchair. Joe knew conspiracy theories abounded when prominent people were killed or went missing. Of course, being a New Mexican, Joe well knew the story of

Edgerton and even the tales of alleged sightings, which were often discussed on the evening news programs. But he never gave them much thought. He'd had his own cases. Wasting energy on gossip and speculation was something he never did.

And he didn't want to squander his time now considering tabloid scuttlebutt. Joe was still waiting for the case file, which he'd requested from the archives. Without it, the only information he had access to came from the publicized corruption probe, which estimated Edgerton had made off with as much as half a million dollars, possibly more. But the investigation was able to link him directly to only one small wire transfer made to a Mexico City bank. The money had been traced back to a lobbyist representing a group of casino developers interested in influencing the new Indian Gaming Regulatory Act. The lobbyist tried to ensure his clients would profit from exorbitant casino-management fees. Today, Indian gaming revenue was twice the size of that of Las Vegas and Atlantic City combined. A $27 billion industry. Half a million dollars in 1988 was now a stingy tip tossed to a cocktail waitress. He'd probably made off with a lot more than anyone had guessed. For all Joe knew, Edgerton was sitting on a beach somewhere, sipping a mojito, watching the news, and laughing his ass off that his car had finally been found. If he had run off alone, it could explain the blood. Edgerton could have killed the driver and that girl, the one the tabloids had labeled "the tramp with the movie star name." No witnesses. Edgerton as a killer didn't fit. There was nothing to indicate violence in the congressman's past. But Joe wasn't a fool. People did crazy things when money or sex was involved. Then again, there was another possibility. Edgerton had been killed to shut him up. Or one or both of his missing staffers had killed him and made off with the money. Or—

Mark was calling to him.

"Can you grab the card stock from my backpack?"

Joe searched the backpack and pulled out a sheet of the heavy paper.

"Now stand in front of the laser," Mark said, "and let the beam hit the center of the stock."

Joe moved into position and saw a bright red dot the diameter of a pencil hitting the paper. He shifted so the light rested in the center.

"The next part's easy. You walk backward, keeping the light on the sheet. If the light hits a tree, we'll just shoot an azimuth. It's not as accurate, but, oh well."

Joe began walking backward slowly, keeping the cardboard close to his body, head lowered, looking at the red dot as it danced up and down the sheet with each step. His progress was slow. And for some reason, Mark felt it necessary to offer encouragement.

"You're doing good. Nice and slow. Don't lose the beam. It's hard to find again."

Joe ignored him.

"Hey, watch out for the cactus."

Joe, a little annoyed, looked up at Mark. "I think I can—" His right foot landed on something flat and forgiving. Son of a bitch. He shifted to the side. When he looked down, the red dot was gone.

He looked behind him. The way seemed clear. It took him several minutes to find the red dot again. Then he continued moving backward.

Mark stayed silent.

Sixty paces later, Joe backed against a full-grown pine.

Joe yelled to Mark. "It stops here."

"Good work."

The beam was higher than the hole in the driver-side door by at least a foot, coming almost to his chest. Joe estimated the distance to the vehicle to be seventy-five yards. He checked the trunk for a questionable hole while Mark stretched yellow string along the ground from the Lincoln's door to the pine. He then created a triangle from two more lengths of string, the tip of the triangle at the vehicle's door, the base ending ten feet on each side of the tree.

Bluehorse returned, and they all broke for lunch.

◈

SEPTEMBER 25

SATURDAY, 1:46 P.M.

THE NEW MEXICO MUSEUM OF NATURAL HISTORY AND

SCIENCE, ALBUQUERQUE, NEW MEXICO

Sierra Hannaway knelt at the base of the *Coelophysis*, a dinosaur the size of a human, with a long, flat head and an impressive set of sharp carnivorous teeth. *Coelophysis* roamed New Mexico in the Triassic period, but several of the plants in the display were from the Carboniferous period. A major faux pas if another museum called them on it, but necessary if Sierra was to open the display on time. Paul, the director of acquisitions, had ordered an entire jungle of the wrong period, so Sierra was forced to use these plants until the correct period flora arrived, which might not be for several more weeks.

She jammed another handful of the fake flora into the display's painted foam base, and then started to cry. Her tears came freely. She looked around. A young couple with a little girl of maybe five paused on their way through the display room to stare at her.

"Why are you crying?" the little girl asked.

Her mother quickly hushed her.

Holding up the plants, Sierra said, "They're the wrong period."

The mother pushed the little girl forward, not giving her time to ask another question.

Sierra threw the plastic flora back into a cardboard box, stood, and ran to the restroom.

She splashed water on her face and took several deep breaths. She checked under the stalls. No feet.

She turned back and stared at herself in the mirror.

"It's been so long, Faye. I don't know if I can go through it again."

She walked into one of the empty stalls, sat down, and wept.

❖

SEPTEMBER 25

SATURDAY, 2:22 P.M.

JONES RANCH ROAD, CHI CHIL TAH (NAVAJO NATION),

NEW MEXICO

After lunch, Mark gathered them all by the Lincoln. He passed out ground-searching metal detectors, sifter trays, and shovels. After a quick how-to on using a detector, he assigned a plot in the triangle to each of them, passed out small marking flags, and set them to work. If a metal object was detected underground, they would plant a flag on the spot. After they searched the entire triangle, they would go back and dig up the hits.

Forty-five minutes and two planted flags later, Joe finished searching his plot. So did the others. They traded the detectors for hand-held versions and took up trowels and plastic sifting trays.

Joe went to his first flag and jammed the trowel deep into the clay soil. He removed a clump, placed it on his sifting tray, and ran the handheld metal detector over it. The detector beeped. He shook the tray, letting the loose dirt fall through the screen. Several rocks and a crushed green shotgun shell remained. Probably not related to the case, but it had to be collected.

"Shotgun shell."

Mark came over, carrying his backpack. He withdrew a camera, a GPS unit, a brown paper bag, and a black marker. Joe took the bag and marker and wrote out the date, time, location, description, and his name.

Mark photographed the shell. Then Joe dropped it in the bag. Mark pulled out a small stapler to seal it. They would tape it later.

That routine continued for the next twenty minutes, until Andi called, "I think I found it!"

Joe and Mark rushed over. On Andi's tray lay a black-colored chunk of metal: a deformed lead slug.

"Looks like a forty-five." Mark turned to look at Joe. "Could be your door slug. What do you think?"

"Luck of the Irish, Andi. I owe you a beer."

"One? You're insulting my ancestors."

They finished their treasure hunt a half hour later and compared notes on their finds: one lead slug, one shotgun shell, the rusty remains of a rifle trigger and trigger guard, one penny, fourteen bottle caps (mostly found near the vehicle), four pull-tabs (also mostly found near the vehicle), six nuts, two bolts, a three-inch piece of car trim, and one D battery. They bagged and tagged only the slug, shotgun shell, and trigger and guard. Mark pocketed the penny, saying it would be littering if they left it. He didn't seem to care about the other junk, though.

The tow truck arrived at four and hauled the vehicle back to the FBI's holding facility in Albuquerque. They cleared the site at five, which included taking exit photos of the area. Joe planned to catch a late dinner at Mickey's and then grab a nice long shower. Monday, he would brief Dale.

When he was on I-40, he called Melissa. It would be close to 7:30

New York time. After his stunt in the woods with the old man, he wanted to hear her voice. She answered on the third ring. In that instant, the tensions of the day—the tensions of the case—fell away.

❖

SEPTEMBER 27
MONDAY, 8:03 A.M.
PARKING GARAGE, HART SENATE OFFICE BUILDING,
WASHINGTON, D.C.

The back door to the Lincoln opened, but Kendall Holmes did not move. His bodyguard waited. In a way, the problem he was dealing with at that moment was partly of his bodyguard's making. But only partly. Edgerton was the real problem. Always had been.

Holmes finished typing out an e-mail to Chris Staples on his phone. He would have to meet with Grace Edgerton. A face-to-face would be good. He could promise her quiet support while protecting his public image. A win-win. Then if she survived, he could count on her later. After all, he would have his own campaign to worry about in two months. The big one. He was already getting calls from the party asking him what the fallout would be from the Edgerton debacle. He had to control it. Minimize collateral damage. If not, the party would stop him from running in the primary.

"Were you able to reach out to your friend?" he said to his bodyguard, whose dark, chiseled features reminded Kendall of the rocky formations found throughout the Navajo Nation.

"He will want a favor later."

"Of course."

Why didn't you call me Saturday?" Dale asked.

"I didn't want to bother you on the weekend," Joe said, lying.

"Goddamn it. Who knows about it?"

"Andi, two of her agents, and Bluehorse. Oh, and he briefed his chief."

"His chief knew before I did?" A vein stood out along Dale's temple.

Joe looked down to hide a smirk. One of Dale's model cars sat in the middle of the desk, a crumpled polishing rag next to it.

"Is that a Studebaker?"

Dale swatted away Joe's hand when he reached for the car. "Don't fuck around. If this hits the press before Washington knows about it, my ass becomes a target. And so does yours."

"Then you'd better make some calls. And while you're at it, why don't you give this case to Cordelli."

"Fine. I thought it was a fugitive case. You're not up to handling a high-profile murder. Go do your job-search bullshit. I don't care. Just get out of here."

On the way to his desk, Ginny called his name.

"Joe, there's a woman here about Edgerton."

"Tell Cordelli. It's his now."

"He's out."

"Who's on duty?"

"Tenny. He's out, too."

Joe sighed.

Ginny, who had been handling the squad's administrative matters for over twenty-three years, looked at him with her "Can you talk to this person?" eyes, which she always used when a walk-in came to the office and the duty agent wasn't available. Ginny was like a nanny to the squad, the one who always had a cookie and kind word for everyone. How could he refuse her?

"Who is it?"

"Sierra Hannaway."

Joe thought for a moment, trying to place the name. Nothing.

"Did she say why she's here?"

"Her sister, Faye Hannaway."

The tramp with the movie star name.

Ginny gave him a sly smile. "She's not wearing a wedding ring."

"Is everyone trying to set me up?"

"Everyone but you."

Joe rubbed his brow with his thumb and forefinger. He'd awakened with the usual headache this morning, but it had subsided on the drive in. Now it was returning.

Ginny winked. "Be a gentleman and turn on that Joe Evers charm."

Joe gave a fake smile.

To the right of Ginny's desk was the reception window, which provided a view of the waiting room. The woman wore a simple blue dress, the hem dropping below her knees. Conservative. There seemed nothing striking about this woman, except for her shoes: blue with shiny stones covering the toes. For some reason, the shoes seemed to say something about her, hinting at a hidden flair. Then he realized this was the second time he'd noticed a woman's shoes. First at

Mickey's and now here. But perhaps footwear wasn't really what drew his attention.

He stepped into the waiting room. The woman looked up. Runny mascara marred petite, elegant features. She was a few years younger than Joe, but only a few.

"Hello, I'm Joe Evers. How can I help you?"

The woman stood, and he saw her hair, all of it. He had seen it through the window but hadn't thought anything of it then. But now it was stunning, a shimmering ebony cascading down to the small of her back. The cheap fluorescent lamps in the room could not diminish its iridescent quality. When she moved, her hair glistened like dew running down fine blades of grass. Joe stared, captivated.

"Are you the agent handling the case?"

"Let's talk in here." He opened the door leading to the interview room. Devoid of decoration or warmth, the space contained only a desk, a phone, and three chairs. Its purpose was to obtain information from walk-ins, not entertain them.

He positioned one of the chairs for her, then sat behind the desk.

"It's about my sister." She brought a tissue to her cheek. "I'm sorry. I thought this was all behind me. It's been so many years."

"I understand. Some things are difficult. Take your time."

She looked up over her tissue, meeting his eyes. "Thank you."

He offered a smile.

"I've been following the news about Congressman Edgerton's car being found and . . ."

Joe waited.

"I want to know if you're going to be like the rest of those so-called investigators who worked on my sister's case. All they ever did was call her a conspirator and a gold digger."

Joe put a hand up. "Listen, I—"

"I'm not done. I need to get this out now, or I never will." She took a deep breath. "I accepted what they said twenty years ago because I was young and didn't know any better. But now I can't let you guys explain away her disappearance as though it were some ridiculous Bonnie and Clyde thing."

"I'm not—" He stopped himself. He was about to say he wasn't working the case anymore, but he thought that might get her even more upset. But stopping himself didn't make a difference.

"You're not *what*? Not interested?"

"Look, Ms. Hannaway, if you just came here to yell at me—"

"I'm not yelling. I just want someone to finally take her case seriously. My sister didn't run away. I know something happened to her. I just want closure. Our mother and father died never knowing what happened. Or why it happened. People said she ran off with Edgerton. People talked behind our backs, snickered, called her a tramp and a thief." She lowered her head. "My father had a small life-insurance policy taken out on us when we were young, only a thousand dollars. He didn't even put a claim in when my sister went missing, didn't even think about it. But do you know what they did, the Great American Insurance Company, with their billboards that read 'Take Comfort with Us'? A year after my sister went missing, they sent us a letter. They said they investigated and couldn't pay off on the policy because she was wanted in connection with congressional corruption, and it was their opinion she fled the country. No one even asked them to pay off the policy. And no one asked them for their opinion. My mother and father sat in the kitchen and cried over that letter, hugging each other. The rumors and tabloids didn't bother them half as much as that letter." She pulled out another tissue to soak up those painful memories.

Joe sat in silence, not sure what to say to comfort this woman, not sure if she even wanted him to try.

"Do you know what it's like to lose someone?" she asked. "Someone you love and care about. And then when they're gone, you realize

you can't move on. You're stuck. Stuck because you can't get closure. You can't understand why that person was taken. And you
somehow feel responsible. Do you know what that's like?"

Joe knew. He knew all too well. He looked at the woman in front of
him. He wanted to hug her and tell her he understood. Tell her that
was exactly how he'd felt ever since Christine died. Instead, he did
something he knew he shouldn't. Maybe something he couldn't.

"I'll do my best to find out what happened to your sister."

Her expression seemed to convey doubt, but she didn't voice her
feelings. Instead, she stood, shook his hand, turned, and walked out
without a backward glance.

Joe stayed in the room for another ten minutes, considered their
conversation. Then he went back into Dale's office.

Dale was on the phone, so Joe plopped in the seat in front of his
desk and waited. He listened to Dale tell the person on the other end
about the bullet holes and that the old man had remembered seeing
blood. He gave Joe a look that said, Get the hell out of my face. Joe
ignored it. He guessed this was Dale's third or fourth phone call. On
high-profile cases, the big bosses never wanted to wait to read the reports. They always demanded verbal updates. Everyone was afraid to
be caught outside the circle of knowledge. After a few minutes, Dale
hung up.

"I want the case back."

Dale said nothing, but his mouth moved a few times, as though
he were practicing what he would say, Joe had caught him off guard.
"Forget it. Not after that stunt. I'm giving it to Cordelli."

Joe tasted his own pride as it slipped down his throat. "I'm sorry. I
was wrong. I shouldn't have kept you out of the loop. It won't happen
again. I'll keep you updated from here on out."

"I can't trust you anymore. I should have known that when I gave
it to you. No way. Cordelli gets it."

"Dale, you were right. I need this. I do. I need it."

"No."

Joe had one last card to play.

"I'll rescind my retirement paperwork."

That caught Dale's attention. "You can't. It's too late."

"I called HR." He hadn't. "I can. And if you try to fight it, I'll file an appeal, which could take a good part of a year to settle."

Dale picked up his desk phone, probably to check with Human Resources.

Joe hurried on: "Or . . . you can let me run with the Edgerton case. Come three months, whatever happens, I leave. No problems. You don't even have to attend my retirement party."

Dale put down the phone. He didn't say anything for several moments. Then he leaned forward, his words slow, menacing.

"Okay. Run with it. But if you screw with me, I *will* file those negligence actions against you for the Longman case, retirement or no retirement. You got me?"

❖

SEPTEMBER 27
MONDAY, 10:10 A.M.
UNIVERSITY OF NEW MEXICO, ALBUQUERQUE,
NEW MEXICO

The yellow Post-it note stuck to Professor Lawrence Trudle's office door read "Larry, Congratulations. Meeting 10:30 conference room. RW." Professor Trudle peeled the note off the stained wood, crumpled it, and shoved it in his pocket. He unlocked the door, walked in, and went straight to his credenza, on which sat a four-cup electric teakettle. He dropped his bulging ostrich-skin briefcase, which his wife had given him the previous Christmas, to the floor and extracted a gallon jug of springwater from the bottom cabinet of the same credenza. Then he filled the kettle and turned it on. Next, he opened the top right drawer to his desk and reached all the way to the back, behind the selection of Bigelow teas, and pulled out a Folgers coffee single. He unwrapped the string and placed the small coffee bag in his *Who's Your Mummy?* coffee mug. Finished with his morning routine, he dropped into his desk chair to await the click of the kettle, a beautiful sound signaling the water had reached a boil and it was time to sin.

Professor Trudle was the only Mormon in the University of New Mexico's Anthropology Department, so one would have thought he wouldn't worry about his colleagues catching him drinking coffee, giving into the allure of the black nectar, which meant breaking his vow to abstain from caffeine. But one would have been wrong. Professor Trudle preferred to sin in private.

He removed his glasses and set them down on his desk. He massaged the bridge of his nose with his thumb and forefinger, closed his eyes, leaned back, and waited for the click.

"Knock! Knock!" a voice barked.

Professor Steve Mercado stood at the door, beaming.

"Good morning, Steve."

"And what a fine morning it is, Professor Trudle. Yes indeedy. A fine morning, made even finer by the good news of a grant. Am I the first to congratulate you?"

Steve walked in and plopped down on one of the chairs used by students during office hours.

"No. You are the second. I got a warm and friendly posty from our esteemed department head with, as I am sure you are aware, a rather surprising announcement of a meeting. I suspect he wants to share the good news with our fellow faculty. I was just contemplating his true motivation when you so crassly interrupted my somber meditation."

"I apologize, but your somber meditation looked curiously like napping." Steve withdrew a pen from his shirt pocket. Holding it lightly between his right thumb and forefinger, he tapped it against his left palm.

"Apology accepted. Any idea why Westerberry is having this meeting? And don't say he wants to celebrate my good news. That's horse pucky and you know it."

"Whoa, watch the language. No, I believe it's to gloat on one of your past misadventures—the Trudle Turkey."

On the bookcase beside Steve sat Lawrence's three published books. The second book, *Anasazi Lineage to the Aztec,* was the smallest of the three, but it had caused him the greatest chagrin in his career.

He planted both elbows on the desk and hung his head in his hands.

"I guess as an archaeologist you can never get away from the past." Steve grinned. "And with Edgerton all over the news, I guess Westerberry sees an opportunity to poke fun."

Lawrence rubbed his temples.

"What do you mean?"

"He's going to mention Edgerton, and you'll take the bait and say that Edgerton's disappearance is linked to your stolen artifacts. But you won't stop there. You'll say that those artifacts prove your theories and blah, blah, blah."

"But it's true."

"I'm not going to argue the history of the Anasazi with you. I'm just saying he's setting the stage for you to embarrass yourself . . . again."

Lawrence picked up his glasses and set them back on his face.

Steve continued. "If you go in there and react, our esteemed colleagues are going to laugh behind your back like they did when you published your book without proof."

"Did you laugh, too?"

"No. I did the 'I told you so' thing, remember? And if you go to this meeting and play into his hands, I'm going to do the 'I told you so' thing again."

"But if they find Edgerton, perhaps—"

"Look. You earned this grant. You put a lot of blood, sweat, and tears into getting the committee to approve it. Westerberry knows that and knows you deserve the recognition. But he would love to temper your success with a poke at your Anasazi fiasco. Don't give him the satisfaction. Don't let him bait you."

The kettle clicked off.

"Come on, sinner, grab your coffee and let's go."

Surprised, Lawrence turned to the teakettle. Next to the kettle sat his mug, the Folgers label dangling down the side.

❖

SEPTEMBER 27

MONDAY, 11:07 A.M.

BUREAU OF INDIAN AFFAIRS, OFFICE OF INVESTIGATIONS,

ALBUQUERQUE, NEW MEXICO

Joe was typing up a transfer document for one of his cases when he heard a commotion by the office entrance. He stepped out of his cubicle to see what was happening. Cordelli, Stretch, Sadi, and Tenny were guffawing as they passed Ginny's desk. They went silent when they saw Joe.

"What's up, tiger?" Cordelli asked.

Tenny snickered.

They were all wearing cargo pants. An op?

"Did I miss something this morning?" Joe asked.

Cordelli walked past Joe, close enough to brush elbows. "I had an arrest."

"We knew you were busy with the Edgerton thing," Stretch said.

"Yeah, busy. That's new." Sadi snorted.

Joe ignored her comment. She was the only female on the squad, and her attitude was as tightly wound as her hair, which she kept in a taut bun at the back of her head. She was a good agent, efficient and tough, never trying to prove herself, because she didn't have to. She'd spent nine years as a criminal investigator in the Pueblo of Zuni before joining the BIA.

"Fine," Joe said. He'd lost their respect.

Sadi and Tenny went to their desks. Stretch hung back.

"Come on," Stretch said. "Let's take a ride."

"Where?" But it really didn't matter. Joe didn't want to be in the office.

"Pueblo Pintado. I gotta find a guy."

"For Sadi?"

Stretch looked toward her cubicle. "Don't let her hear you say that."

On the way out, Ginny handed Joe a FedEx package. It was the case file on Arlen Edgerton. Joe took it with him.

❖

SEPTEMBER 27
MONDAY, 11:56 A.M.
STATE ROUTE 550, SANDOVAL COUNTY, NEW MEXICO

Route 550 cuts through Zia Pueblo, a small community northeast of Albuquerque. The brown and beige of the New Mexican desert turns slightly greener there, mostly due to the Jemez River, which borders the road to the east. But the scenery didn't interest Joe. He'd been reading the Edgerton file for the past thirty minutes, allowing Stretch to navigate the winding road in silence. But now, having skimmed most of the file and realizing there had been few leads developed back when the congressman went missing, he felt he needed a break.

"What's in Pueblo Pintado?"

"Shit, you're still here," Stretch said.

"Sorry, I needed to cool off."

"It's all right. We're going to see Eddie Begay. He's in front of the grand jury tomorrow, but he's not answering his phone."

"Sounds like he doesn't want to testify."

Stretch nodded. "Probably not. Thing is, he's the whole case. No physical evidence. I want to take him back to Albuquerque and stash him in a hotel. He likes the bottle. We can't depend on him to show."

"Like me?"

Stretch looked at Joe, then turned away.

"Is that why you guys didn't tell me about the arrest this morning? Am I undependable, too?"

"You know that's not—"

"Don't bullshit me."

Stretch didn't answer right away. Instead, he stared out the windshield at the barren desert to the west. Joe waited.

"They feel you're washed-up. Cordelli doesn't think you can do the job any longer. He's saying you've lost your edge."

"He's an asshole. And he's still wet behind the ears. I'm over the hill, yeah, but I haven't lost my edge."

"It's not just him. Tenny and Sadi agree. They don't trust you. They don't think your head's in the game anymore. Ever since the Longman trial. Maybe even before then."

"Screw Tenny. The guy never had a thought in his head unless Cordelli put it there."

"What about Sadi? She calls it straight."

Joe had no answer.

They were passing the southern edge of Fenton Lake State Park. Half a dozen crows circled over a wooded area to the east, perhaps planning to kill one of their own who lay injured on the ground below. They were known to do that. Was he projecting? Maybe. Joe had heard enough truth about himself. "So what's your case about?"

"Our guy got jammed up on a CSA and squealed. He told the FBI he sold a Navajo artifact to some collector in Santa Fe. They called us because they knew we tried to bust the same buyer a few years back."

"Who's that?"

"Arthur Othmann. He likes to spend his daddy's fortune on art."

"And the artifact?"

"Begay chiseled off a thousand-year-old petroglyph from Chaco Canyon."

"Bold little bastard. What's something like that go for?"

"He only got twenty-five hundred. He's a pedophile and an idiot."

They rode in silence for a little ways, the conversation seeming to have reached a natural ebb. Joe tried to appreciate the land around him. In a few months, he might never work in the field again. Almost all the jobs he'd responded to were deskbound. Except for one, an insurance adjuster for a small firm out of Rio Rancho. The pay sucked, but at least it wouldn't be all pushing paper. And he'd be able to do most of that from home, e-mailing in his reports. But they hadn't called him back. Maybe he should send them a follow-up letter. He supposed, if he had to, he could live just on his pension for a little while, but he wouldn't be able to help Melissa with college or pay off the rest of Christine's medical bills.

"So what did you get from Edgerton's file?" Stretch asked.

"A little, not much. It was worked pretty much as a fugitive case. Though they did track down one threat, a hate letter from an AIM member out of Crownpoint. But they really didn't follow up on it."

"Did they check out the wife? I prefer simple motives like jealousy." As usual, everything was black and white for Stretch, which was often the best approach for most investigations.

"I can see her taking out the husband and girlfriend, but the driver?"

"Just a witness she couldn't let live. She got his congressional seat, right? Did she get his money, too? Maybe a little jealousy, a little greed. Kind of like a tossed salad of motives."

"I thought you like to keep it simple. And anyway, she's got her own money."

"You're right. Keep it simple. Put me down for the jealousy angle. A woman scorned. Powerful shit."

"Speaking of scorned females, how's the wife?"

"She loves me."

"Taking the whole family to Italy helped, I'm sure."

"Didn't hurt." Stretch gave a sly smile.

Silence.

"So . . . do you need any help on the Edgerton case?" Stretch asked.

No doubt Stretch wanted to change the subject. Joe knew it was awkward talking about family to someone whose own family had fallen apart. But Stretch really did deserve the Best Dad award. He paid his dues every day. Did all the fatherly stuff. Spent time with his kids. Coaching, volunteering, attending all the crappy school plays, even a cool vacation every year. His kids were teenagers now, but he still seemed able to stay involved in their lives. Joe felt an ache in his chest.

Joe's phone rang. It was Bluehorse, reporting the latest development. When he finished, Joe provided a sage response.

"Shit."

Bluehorse responded in kind.

"Well, we knew it would get out fast," Joe said. "Forget about it. We got a dog team coming out from Albuquerque tomorrow at nine. Do me a favor, though. Hold off on telling your chief."

Joe clicked the phone off. "That was the NPD officer I'm working with. Apparently, the *Gallup Herald* put out a story about the bullet holes in Edgerton's vehicle. They're really hyping it up."

"What newspaper wouldn't?"

He didn't want to make the next call, but he had promised Dale he would keep him updated. Joe swallowed. He tasted pride again.

❖

SEPTEMBER 27
MONDAY 12:45 P.M.
RESIDENCE OF EDDIE BEGAY, PUEBLO PINTADO,
NEW MEXICO

L ooks abandoned," Joe said.

He and Stretch walked to the trailer. Several sheets of peeled aluminum sheathing exposed rotted plywood beneath. The trailer had once been painted yellow; now it was the whitish gray color of oxidization.

Stretch climbed the wooden steps that led to the front door. He placed each foot with care. Joe stayed a few paces back, watching the windows. Several were covered with trash bags.

Stretch knocked. They waited. An unpleasant smell tainted the air. Spoiled food maybe.

When no one answered, they walked around back. Cardboard covered another two windows.

"I'm guessing he didn't put any of that twenty-five hundred toward renovations," Joe said.

"More likely he pickled his liver with it."

Joe lifted a corner of the cardboard and peered inside. Empty, except for discarded beer cans and saved trash.

When they went around the other side, heading back to the front, Joe noticed an animal lying on the ground. A dog. He walked over. Its head had been crushed. Dry blood caked the animal's ear and jaw. From the degree of decay and the colony of insects, Joe guessed the animal had been there a few days, which explained the smell.

"Do you think he would have left his dog like this if he was staying here?" Joe asked.

Stretch shrugged. "The guy's a dirtbag. Who knows?"

Begay's trailer wasn't part of a community. It sat by itself in the open country, like so many of the residences on the reservation. No electric, no water, no paved driveways, just desert and sun. About a quarter mile to the south, there was a hogan, the traditional Navajo dwelling, a small, round wooden structure with an east-facing door. The Navajo believed in greeting the morning.

"Let's check out the neighbor," Joe said.

"Why bother? He got scared and ran off. I'm sure he'll turn up in a few weeks."

"We're already here."

"Fine." Stretch plodded back to his Suburban.

Joe looked down at the dog. It was a mutt, mostly Lab. He hated to leave it out there to rot, but he guessed that was nature's way. He checked the sky. No crows. Strange. A crow could smell decay for miles. Were they afraid of this place? Ridiculous. But Joe sensed that somehow this dog was wrong. Perhaps it was a harbinger of things to come.

Stop it, he told himself.

He didn't like thinking that way. Life was already chock-full of crap, no need to conjure up more.

"I'll walk. Stretch my legs a little." And clear my head, too, he thought.

Stretch nodded and climbed into his vehicle.

Joe started toward the hogan. He forced his mind back to his job search and the insurance adjuster position. He decided he wouldn't send out that follow-up letter. A desk job might be nice for a change.

❖

SEPTEMBER 27
MONDAY 1:04 P.M.
WASHINGTON POST **HEADQUARTERS, WASHINGTON, D.C.**

H elena Newridge had one unusual physical tic that she'd noticed in herself a number of years ago. She probably had others but never bothered to take inventory. It was during the time she studied mass media at UDC and had seen Bree Simpson talking to Barry. Bree was the typical buxom-beauty media darling. And Barry, whose last name she no longer remembered, was someone Helena wanted to trounce after a bar run. It was when she'd seen the two of them talking, and how easy it was for someone like Bree to attract the attention of a man, that she felt her right eyelid do a dance. And now, as she weaved through the pool of respected contributors granted cubicle space, her right eyelid performed the Macarena. It made her realize just how much she wanted to be one of the regulars, and not a gossip nobody.

"One day." She said those words quietly so as not to disturb anyone, but she knew no one would have paid her mind anyway. Her byline was more of an afterthought than a selling point for the *Post*.

She strode into the editor's office. Arvin, the manager of classifieds, slumped in one of the chairs before the desk of Ezra Gray, a managing editor at the paper.

"Morning, boss." She placed the printout of the article she'd found on Ezra's desk. She sniffed. Cherry. On the bookcase behind him lay his pipe. She'd never seen him smoke it, but rumor held that he celebrated putting a big story to bed with the pipe and a glass of Royal Lochnagar here in his office, door shut, and the journalist of the moment in company. He had a flair for the old traditions of journalism. That was one of the reasons he held on to the gossip column, while many other papers did away with theirs or went Web only, which was often where Helena's contributions ended up.

Ezra read the *Gallup Herald*'s article about bullet holes and blood in Edgerton's vehicle. He lifted an eyebrow.

Helena shifted her considerable weight from her right leg to her left.

He handed the single page back to her. "It's interesting."

"Interesting? Damn right it's interesting. I'd like to run with it. It's the trifecta: sex, money, and murder."

The managing editor laughed. "What about Senator Fordham falling down during the banquet last night? She may have a medical condition she's hiding."

"There's nothing there. She's fat. I'm fat. You should see me trying to walk in heels."

Arvin laughed behind her.

She leaned on Ezra's desk. "I want out of gossip. Give me a chance, please. And I'm smelling front-page serial." She sniffed. "Ahh, it smells like Pulitzer."

Ezra laughed. "Let's not get ahead of ourselves, Bernstein."

She lowered her voice to what she hoped was a sexy whisper. "Come on, Ezra. You give me seven days in the Land of Enchantment and in seven months you get to enjoy a free lunch at Columbia while I receive my award."

Ezra's laugh was worthy of imitation by any respectable archvillain.

Helena's stomach dropped. "Okay. How about I go out there on my own dime? If you like my angle, you approve my reimbursement."

"I like your spunk, Helena," Ezra said. "It's a deal."

❖

SEPTEMBER 27
MONDAY 1:15 P.M.
PUEBLO PINTADO, NEW MEXICO

Stretch was already talking to the occupant of the hogan when Joe walked up. They stood in front of the house, next to an older dark blue pickup, which clearly had earned the moniker Ford Tough. The resident was a middle-aged woman with a slight hunch to her back. She barely reached Stretch's chest and had to crane her head to talk to him.

"Eddie ain't been around for a few days," she said. "He usually asks me for a ride on Fridays to go into town. He don't drive no more because of his eye." She pointed to her own right eye, hesitated, then pointed to her left.

"When was the last time you saw him?" Stretch asked.

She looked over to Eddie's trailer. "Is he in trouble?"

"Nope. I just need to talk to him."

She studied Stretch's face. "Last week, maybe Wednesday . . . no, Thursday. He had a visitor. Pretty late. I only looked over because I heard his dog barking. I think they was fighting."

"Why do you think that?" Stretch asked.

"I heard Eddie yelling."

"Who was the visitor?"

"I don't know. I think he was a *bilagáana*—I mean a white guy. He drove a nice truck like yours, maybe gray. Hard to tell 'cause it was almost dark out."

"What'd the guy look like?"

She pulled up her baggy bright red Fire Rock Casino T-shirt. Its out-of-shape neck had been drifting downward. "I don't know. A white guy. Big. They was too far away."

"Since he hasn't come back, do you know where he might be now?"

"His mom lives in Shiprock. The trailer there was his dad's." She pushed out her lips and chin toward Eddie's home. Navajo often *lipped* directions rather than pointing a finger. "He died a few years back."

"Thank you, ma'am. If I leave you my card, will you call me if you see him?"

She nodded. Joe doubted she would. Stretch handed her his card.

"I have a question, ma'am," Joe said. "There's a dead dog by Eddie's house. Do you know how it was killed?"

"Killed? Someone killed it?" She lowered her head. "We get skin-walkers around these parts. They'll kill a dog if it keeps barking. And Eddie's dog liked to bark."

"Thank you, ma'am," Joe said.

❖

SEPTEMBER 27

MONDAY, 4:28 P.M.

MICKEY'S BAR & GRILL, ALBUQUERQUE, NEW MEXICO

The savory smell of roast beef welcomed Joe. The aroma was from the full steamboat cut of beef that Mickey roasted to make his signature sandwich, the Combo, chunks of tender beef on a kaiser roll with a thick slice of provolone cheese, and a wet, sloppy scoop of gravy. His stomach knocked to tell him it was ready. All he'd eaten today was a bean wrap, which he'd gotten that morning from the burrito lady who came by the office carrying a small cooler filled with chicken, beef, or bean. The burrito lady didn't know she'd been sustaining him for the past several months. Sometimes, he'd buy two or three, storing the extras in the office fridge for lunch or dinner, sometimes taking them home for the weekend.

Walking toward the bar, Joe noticed a solitary figure sitting at a table in the corner of the dining area, reading a book, sipping a drink. It was the woman from Friday. What was her name? Ginger? No, Gillian. Nice name. He hadn't thought about the sound of it before. *Gillian*. Smooth.

Mickey grinned and whipped out a frosted mug from under the counter. "Evening, Joe. What's the good word?"

"The guys will be around tonight. They had an arrest." Joe felt awkward attending the ritual, since he hadn't been invited that morning, but he didn't want to come off like an angry little brat, even though what he really wanted to do was break their toys and throw a tantrum.

"Anything I'll see in the paper?"

"No. Just the usual. Sex, lies, and video-streamed preliminary hearings." As heinous as some of the crimes were on the reservation, very little of it found its way into the newspapers or the evening news.

Mickey filled the mug from the tap. "Too bad. A good juicy case is just what you need. Get a little media attention and—boom. The job offers come pouring in. Everybody loves a celebrity. And you're probably due your fifteen minutes of fame."

Joe checked out the customers. A balding middle-aged man with glasses and a bad comb-over sat four stools over, reading from a binder and gnawing his pencil between sips of beer. In the dining area, a young couple worked on a pair of Combos. He glanced at Gillian's table. Serafina, a young Hispanic waitress who yelled at Mickey in Spanish when they fought, collected a glass and napkin and wiped down the surface. Gillian was no longer there.

He turned back, to see Mickey pushing a mug toward him, a perfect one-inch foam head fizzing quietly atop it. The beginning of a slow decompression. Exactly what he needed to do. Blow off some steam. Chill out. Relax. A fellow barfly had once shared a mantra with Joe: "Be the beer. Be the beer."

Joe stopped. What just happened? He'd thought of himself as a barfly. Was he? Had he fallen so low that he'd actually started to commune with drunks? Had he joined the Church of the Golden Barley? He didn't need this beer. He grabbed the handle and raised it chest-high, then told himself to put it down. He'd promised Melissa he'd cut back. He lowered it, so it hovered over the wood counter. Condensation coated the outside. Inside, tiny bubbles broke free, rising to the top, joining their brethren in an orgy of effervescent bliss. Just one sip. He licked his lips. And then regretted it. That was a sure sign of hunger. Craving. Need. A tug-of-war battled in his mind. Put it down versus take a sip.

"You all right, Joe?" Mickey picked up a dish towel and flipped it over his shoulder. The quintessential bartender, tools ready, senses sharp, prepared to offer sage advice at a moment's notice. It wasn't just the alcohol that kept Joe coming back. It was Mickey. He was one of the few friends he had left. One of the few he hadn't alienated since losing Christine.

"The usual," Joe said. He put the mug down and wrote *friends* in the condensation. Then a woman's voice came from behind him.

"They say the eyes are the windows to the soul." Gillian placed her purse and a book on the counter. "In your case, I think it's your beer mug. *Stilettos* and *friends*. Freud would love to get inside your head."

She knew how to wear a smile. He returned it, feeling a tingling in his stomach. Maybe it was because he hadn't eaten. Maybe. For a moment, he was at a loss for words. Surprise, he guessed. He started to tell her that he thought she had left but then decided not to. She might think him a stalker for noticing.

"Who needs Freud when I have Mickey here? He's held more therapy sessions than Dr. Phil. And he makes an incredible roast beef sandwich, too."

"You guys should open a PR firm. You sell each other so well. Last night, Mickey pitches you. Today, you do a commercial for him."

"Yeah, well, let me warn you that Mickey tends to color things a bit."

Mickey piped up: "I'll have you know I was a Boy Scout. And we never lie." He stood up straight, raised his right hand with two fingers extended, looked at it, and then added one more.

"He colors things, huh? By how much?"

"Think housepainter."

She laughed, and he realized he liked making her laugh.

"So, how is Joe the Despondent Spelling Bee Champ today?" She pointed to the mug. "Working on another missed win?"

"I guess spelling bee fame is not as fleeting as I once thought."

"Hey, everybody's entitled to their fifteen minutes."

"That's funny. Mickey just said the same thing. And he doesn't even know I'm a frustrated spelling bee runner-up."

"I think she's got the gift, Joe." Mickey said. "You know, can sense things like one of them psychics."

"No, I'm just an Andy Warhol fan," she said.

Mickey leaned in conspiratorially. "Well, I've been told I got the gift. And right now I'm sensing I need to order you two a couple of my one-of-a-kind, incredibly delicious roast beef Combos, some red wine, soft music, and put you in that quiet corner over there." He pointed to a small alcove.

Joe said nothing.

Gillian laughed. "I'll have to take a rain check. My sister is picking me up."

"Did I say my one-of-a-kind, incredibly delicious, *never refused* roast beef Combo?"

"I would love to, but I really do have to go."

Mickey was a war hero. No surrender. "I'll tell you what. Tomorrow, you two be here at five thirty and I'll make my wife's secret recipe for penne alla vodka." He put his fingers together, kissed them—*smack*—and flicked his wrist. "*Bellissimo.*"

"Mick, for an Irishman, your Italian sucks," Joe said.

"Hey." Mickey waved his hands around and spoke in a thick Italian-immigrant voice. "I look Irish, but I cook Italian."

Joe and Gillian both laughed.

"I don't know," Gillian said.

"Let me tell you. This recipe'll knock your socks off. . . ." Mickey leaned over the counter and looked at her feet. "I mean knock your pumps off."

"Well, if you're promising to knock my pumps off, Mickey." She gave him a mischievous grin. "How can a girl refuse?"

Mickey placed both hands over his heart. "You're making an old man very happy, missy." Then he pointed to Joe. "You keep quiet. I don't want you blowing this."

"You're right," Joe said. "He is a good PR man."

"Told you." Gillian picked up her book and purse. "I'm sure my sister's outside by now. I guess I'll see you both tomorrow. Toodles." She spun around and walked away. Joe thought he'd seen some redness in her cheeks. A blush? Excitement? He liked *toodles*. He liked a lot of things about her.

Joe turned back to Mickey. "Maybe I should take you along on my job interviews."

"Man, drop the funk. You need to wake up, smell the coffee, and mingle with some babes. I look at you and I feel like a teenager."

Joe was getting tired of hearing the same thing from everybody.

"What's getting old is that speech."

"Do yourself a favor. Reach for the life preserver, or else you're going to drown in your own self-pity."

Mickey limped off to check on the pencil chewer. Good riddance.

Joe took a sip from his mug, forgetting the battle that had waged in him only minutes earlier. He should be happy. Dinner with a beautiful woman. What's not to like? But it wasn't about not liking it. He was afraid. He hadn't been on a date in twenty-two years. So he told himself it wasn't a date. It was two adults having dinner. What was the big deal? They seemed to get along. And she was easy to talk to. It should be fun. Nothing to it. A fine meal, some chitchat, a little wine, talk about family, career, movies. Tomorrow would be a nice change.

Then why was he still afraid?

❖

SEPTEMBER 27

MONDAY, 5:00 P.M.

OTHMANN ESTATE, SANTA FE, NEW MEXICO

B ooks placed a small cardboard box on Othmann's desk.

"How much?"

"She wanted three thousand," Books said. "I gave her a grand."

Othmann opened the box and unwrapped a dirty hand towel, careful not to drop the item within. It was a mortar and pestle made of stone.

"Any problems?"

"She smelled. Maybe she'll bathe now that she's got some money."

Othmann took out several photographs from his top desk drawer. They were images taken at the Acoma Museum. They showed a four-hundred-year-old mortar and pestle used by the tribe to ground ceremonial corn. He smiled. Maybe he could use it to grind up some of his Christmas powder. Have his own sacred ceremony.

"When they find it missing, all the cleaners will be questioned," Books said.

"She knows I'm good pay. She'll keep quiet."

"Like Eddie?"

"No. Not like Eddie."

Othmann picked up the precious artifact and cradled it in his hands. He removed a small card from the printer by his desk. On it, he had documented the history of the item as well as the date he acquired it. He was a meticulous collector and record keeper. At the display cabinet closest to his desk, he pushed a tiny lever underneath the bottom shelf. *Click.*

Books pulled the display cabinet forward to reveal stairs, which led down to Othmann's private gallery.

❖

SEPTEMBER 27

MONDAY, 5:15 P.M.

MICKEY'S BAR & GRILL, ALBUQUERQUE, NEW MEXICO

A hand clasped Joe on the shoulder and squeezed.

"I see you beat us to the drinking hole," Tenny said. He took the seat next to Joe.

Cordelli parked himself on the other side of Tenny. "What a surprise."

"Cordelli," Joe said. "I didn't see you. I'll be right back. I left my hemorrhoid cream in the car."

Tenny laughed. "Zing."

"I'll give that to you, Joe," Cordelli said.

"Aren't you the philanthropist."

Tenny whooped. "That's two. What's gotten into you tonight?"

"You know"—Cordelli's voice went solemn, professorial—"they say people are most funny where they feel most at home. Is that it, Joe? This where you feel most at home?"

"You're an asshole."

"Hey, it's all in fun. Don't get mad. You look like you're running dry over there. Let me buy you another." Cordelli slapped the counter. "Hey, Mickey. You got some thirsty people over here."

The bar was starting to fill as professionals from nearby offices trickled in. Joe's squad would stay at the bar most of the night. There was something about sitting around a table that made a get-together more sober, more real. Maybe it was because people felt the need to control their volume, in order not to disturb the other diners. The bar kept it loose, allowed Joe to pick and choose his conversations. But it sometimes got tiring, avoiding getting cornered in a discussion, bobbing and weaving through the banter like a boxer working the ropes.

He was on his second beer, courtesy of Cordelli, when Stretch and Sadi showed up. Stretch plopped down on Joe's left; Sadi sat one seat over. She didn't look happy. Not so unusual. But she seemed more sullen than normal, if that was possible.

"What's wrong?" Joe asked.

Stretch spun on his stool to face him. "Sadi checked with Begay's family. No one's seen him since last week."

"That little prick better show tomorrow," Sadi said, anger oozing. "Or I'm gonna slam his ass so fast with charges, he'll be

Bubba's prison bitch by Halloween." She clobbered the counter with her fist.

Stretch gave Joe a sideways look. No one laughed. They knew better. She didn't see herself as funny, so if anyone laughed at one of her comments, she thought the person was laughing at her, not with her.

Joe and Stretch talked a little more about the case. Sadi remained silent, resting her jaw on her right hand, fist clenched, her pinkie tapping a beat on her chin to an unknown tune.

They placed their orders. Mickey returned a short time later with five Combos, and they all dug in. When they were done, each plate sat covered in used napkins.

Joe leaned back, his belly full and his spirits buoyed. A good meal had that effect on him. Christine was an excellent cook—had been an excellent cook. After a rotten day at work, he'd come home to a set table, his plate piled with whatever feast suited her fancy. Joe, Christine, and Melissa would sit around eating and talking, discussing the day's events, joking, laughing, enjoying one another's company and the time spent together. The grime from his job, which had built up throughout the day, would be washed away by the time they cleared the dishes. On the nights that Joe cooked, it was usually something thrown together. Looking back, he wished he had spent more time preparing those meals. He knew now that dinnertime had been important to her. To her, it had been family time. There was so much he would have done differently if he had known.

Tenny's loud voice brought Joe back to Mickey's. "What kept you? We already ate."

"The usual," Dale said. "Crime and politics."

"What's happening, cappy?" Mickey said. "You keepin' these miscreants you call a squad in line?"

"Twenty-three years in law enforcement, and I end up a zookeeper."

Mickey cleared away the plates. "Should I order you up a Combo?"

"Of course," Dale said. He grabbed an empty stool and wedged it between Joe and Tenny.

"Hey, Mickey," Stretch yelled. "Joe's promising to give me a date so we can start planning his retirement party. I'm thinking second week in December. That's when his daughter comes home."

"You tell me when and I'll have the back room available."

Mickey had a reception-size private dining area in the rear that he used for special events and meetings. The room easily accommodated a hundred people. Joe doubted his party would fill more than twenty seats.

"All I want is something private with the squad," Joe said.

"Too bad," Stretch said. "I already have people calling to attend. We're gonna give you a nice send-off."

"I say we give him a full-blown roast, dais and all," Cordelli said. "I'll write some material."

Stretch shook his head. "I heard your material. My gang informant would be embarrassed by it, let alone Joe's daughter."

Tenny came to Cordelli's aid. "I think a roast would be a blast. We'll keep it in good taste. What do you say, Joe?"

"I don't think I'm allowed to have much say in what you guys decide. But keep it small. I'm not into crowds much anymore."

Cordelli took the opportunity. "That's strange. You like happy hour."

The group laughed.

"Good one," Joe said. He was in a better mood now that he had eaten.

Cordelli stood up and moved to the center of their little group. They all turned in their seats to face him. He held up his beer. "Down a thug, down a mug." This was the squad's arrest ritual.

"You're a son of a bitch, Cordelli." Dale said, grinning, a full glass in his hand. Everyone else had half or less. The others quickly finished theirs and watched Dale chugging. He slowed at the halfway point.

The squad started chanting, "Down. Down. Down."

Dale drained the last gulp and put down the mug. Then he gave a slight bow.

Cordelli raised a hand. "Hey, Mickey. Another round on me."

Dale leaned into Joe. "I was late because I got a call from Chief Cornfield over at Navajo Nation. He's angry. He thinks you're cutting his office out of the case."

"That's because it goes from his ears to the front page of the paper."

Dale nodded knowingly.

"So how is the Edgerton case going?" Tenny asked. But before Joe could answer, Tenny turned to Dale. "And by the way, boss, why'd you give it to him? He's leaving. I'd have worked it."

"Yeah." Cordelli stood behind them. "Joe's on his way out. That could've been a high-profile case. Now it's as good as dead."

Stretch put his beer on the counter and turned to face Cordelli. "Why don't you back off." Sadi also turned, but she kept quiet.

Cordelli smirked. "Well, it's the—"

"Shut up, Cordelli," Dale ordered. "I assigned it to Joe. It's his. End of story."

Joe stood and walked off toward the restrooms. The talk was turning ugly.

Cordelli yelled, "Hey, if you need a real investigator to work that case, call me. My number's in the book."

"It's over the urinal, too," Joe shot back.

Tenny whooped.

When Joe returned to the bar, Cordelli was recounting the detention hearing for today's arrestee.

". . . so the marshals are shorthanded and they ask me to help take the perv back down to holding. We're on the elevator and he turns to me and says, 'I don't understand why the judge thought I was a flight risk. I don't even live near an airport.'" Everyone laughed, including Mickey.

Cordelli saw Joe. "Hey, seriously, why don't you give me the Edgerton case?"

"Put it to bed, Cordelli," Dale said.

Sadi, who had been twisting a napkin and tearing it to pieces, turned her attention to the argument. "I agree, dude. Give it a rest."

Cordelli looked around at everyone. "What? It's a good case. He'll just run it into the ground. No offense, Joe, but you ain't exactly sprintin' these days." He smiled. "I'm guessing some of the higher-ups don't want the Edgerton case going anywhere. That's the only reason that explains why they gave it to you."

Joe stepped up to Cordelli. "You're an asshole."

Stretch raised a hand. "I second that."

Dale stood up and grabbed Joe's elbow, steering him to the front door.

When they were outside, Joe said, "I was wondering the same thing. Why did you give me this case originally?"

Dale waited a few seconds before responding. "I told you. I thought it might be good for your career."

"Bullshit. If you were worried about my career, you wouldn't have told the board I was a drunk."

They moved to the side of the door to let a group of women enter. A blonde with thick green eye shadow looked over, probably drawn to the raised voices. Dale lowered his. "It's a big case, and I need someone who's going to move carefully on it."

"You mean slow or not at all."

"I know you're a good investigator. This case is delicate. A lot of important people involved. Edgerton's wife is running for governor, so we don't want to be used by the press to further some political agenda. Plus, BIA conducted the investigation twenty years ago. We don't want egg on our faces now. We need to control what gets released to the public."

Joe laughed. "You want to bury the truth."

"Don't put words in my mouth. I just don't want to lose control in the press and make BIA look bad." Dale pulled out a pack of Camels from his inside breast pocket and shook one out. He rarely smoked.

"So you assigned it to me, hoping it wouldn't go anywhere, right? No investigation. No bad news."

"I assigned it to you because you have the most experience on the squad, and you're careful." Dale patted his pockets. He didn't find what he was looking for.

Joe nodded toward the entrance of Mickey's. "They think it's bullshit."

"Why don't you go home. We'll talk about it in the morning." He returned the unlit cigarette to the pack and shoved it back inside his breast pocket. He hitched up his pants.

"I'll be out with the cadaver dogs tomorrow."

"Fine. We'll talk Wednesday."

Joe pulled out his wallet. He handed Dale some bills for his tab.

Dale shook his head. "I got it. And do me a favor. Don't let Cordelli get under your skin."

"That's too much to ask."

H elena Newridge yanked her oversize suitcase off the luggage carousel, gave a loud *tsk* to the geeky-looking guy next to her who hadn't offered to help or get out of her way, and headed to the Enterprise rental counter.

She pulled out her phone and punched in the number she had called only ten minutes earlier, when her plane landed.

"Hey, sweetie. This is Helena Newridge again. Did the chief get in yet?"

He had. She was transferred.

"Hello, Chief. I got your message. . . . Yes, thank you."

She listened as Chief Cornfield welcomed her to New Mexico.

"If you give me directions, I'll be fine. Unless you want to lend me one of your cute Navajo officers as a guide."

The chief gave her directions.

Y*a'at eeh,* my friend," Bluehorse said.

Joe nodded. "Sorry I'm late."

"They started about fifteen minutes ago."

"Why's Andi here?" Joe had recognized her Suburban parked with two other vehicles in the field.

"She's anticipating bodies."

They walked into the woods, heading to where Edgerton's vehicle had been found. Andi and Mark sat on folding chairs, drinking coffee and chatting. Starbucks in the woods. In the distance, two women worked, each with a dog. One of the dogs raced over to Joe to say hello. The second dog followed. They were both chocolate Labs. The cadaver dog team. Joe introduced himself to the handlers, and then the dog team returned to work. He didn't direct the handlers. He trusted that Bluehorse and Andi had already worked all that out with them. But really, it didn't matter. They had no leads that suggested any particular direction. It was a guessing game at this point. Educated guesses, but still guesses. In investigation parlance, this was called a "logical investigation." Looking for bodies near a bloody vehicle was the logical next step. Nothing brilliant. Nothing flashy. Nothing that would sound good in a book someday. And like most successful investigations, it would be the fundamentals that solved the case, not psychics, high-tech gadgets, satellite imagery, or any other fancy techniques shown in the movies. Joe had never been afraid to try something new, but it had always been the basics that had led him to the clues that solved a case. He hoped the basics would hold true again.

It was almost two hours later when the dogs hit on something. The elder of the two handlers called to Joe. She looked like a librarian in shorts, her platinum hair in a pseudobeehive and large red eyeglasses covering half her face.

"Hemingway found something," she said.

They were maybe thirty yards north of where the vehicle had been recovered. A juniper lay flat on the ground, its once-dark green needles now brown and scarce. Hemingway, the bigger of the two Labs, began whining. The handler went to the dog and stroked his back, which seemed to soothe the animal. Joe had learned over the years that some cadaver dogs became depressed after finding a body. Either they were traumatized by death or they picked up on the emotions of their handlers. Whatever the reason, Joe had seen the change in some dogs.

Joe surveyed the ground, not expecting it to reveal its decades-old secret, if it even held a secret. Withered grass, loose rocks, discarded piñon husks, orphaned weeds, and hard-packed clay refused to offer witness to what rested below. The oak nearby, strong and silent, said nothing. But it didn't have to. Buried remains usually spoke for themselves.

"It's all yours," Joe said.

Andi and Mark got to work. They took several photographs, then excavated the ground using trowels. The area the dog had identified showed a slight depression, which was consistent with a body decomposing and the soil sinking to fill the void. Not always, but sometimes. It depended on the depth and the soil composition.

The topsoil here was the color of sand. It became darker as Andi dug. One, two, three inches. She lifted a scoop of the deeper soil to her nose. It had a russet color. She sniffed.

She held it out to Joe. The soil had a slightly rancid odor, which was stronger than decaying vegetation. He recognized the odor from other recoveries. Not nearly as strong, but still present.

Mark was the first to hit bone. He had uncovered a two-square-foot area eighteen inches deep when he hit something hard. He brushed away soil to reveal fabric. Ten minutes later, he uncovered what appeared to be the upper thighbone of a person.

Joe bent down and gave Hemingway a vigorous neck rub. The dog enjoyed the attention and tried to lick Joe's face.

"Why Hemingway?" Joe asked.

"He's my favorite author," the handler said.

"Are you an English teacher?"

"No, a librarian, twenty-seven years. I still work part-time." Amused, Joe continued to give Hemingway attention.

Some handlers worked for police agencies, others for nonprofit groups. This group was out of Albuquerque and consisted of volunteers not directly associated with a specific law-enforcement agency. They survived through grants and occasional donations from the requesting department or the families of missing persons. He'd worked with this group before, but not these handlers. When he got back to the office tomorrow, he would put in a request for payment to the organization. Since they didn't invoice their services, Joe would have to work out a dollar amount to cover their travel expenses and incidentals. A few hundred dollars, maybe five if Dale wasn't penny-pinching this month.

Bluehorse came over and patted the dog's head. The officer wore a smile, which Joe knew didn't derive from the dog or the body. It was from the satisfaction of finding a lead. The young officer's instincts had initiated this investigation. Finding this body confirmed that Bluehorse's gut had been right. He would make a fine criminal investigator someday. Maybe a fine agent.

Andi took more photos, then started sketching the scene.

By noon, most of the body was excavated. Turned soil, stained from leeched human oils, encircled the small depression where the skeleton lay. The air was now heady with the smell of mild putrefaction, the miasma of death. Time had surely weakened its potency, but it was still present.

From the bits of clothing around the bones, it looked to be the skeletal remains of a man. Light-colored dress shirt, dress pants, and dress shoes.

Bluehorse stood several feet behind Joe, slipping his hands in and out of his pants pockets. Navajo do not like to look upon dead bodies. They believe evil spirits gravitate to onlookers.

"I appreciate your hanging in here," Joe said. "I know it goes against your traditions."

"You grow up hearing the stories and taboos and don't really believe all of it, and yet . . ."

Joe had heard much of the Navajo lore over the years, but he was always interested in learning more. "So, what are some of the taboos for a situation like this?"

"We believe evil spirits are everywhere, just waiting to bewitch you. They linger mostly in the dark and around dead bodies. Touching a bone will draw them to you. Saying the name of a dead person draws them to you. And walking over a grave will draw them to you—though that can also give you a sore leg. Dead bodies are never good."

"How do you protect yourself?"

Bluehorse grinned. He reached for his duty belt and removed a small leather satchel. He held it up. "A medicine bag. Corn pollen." He pulled a silver chain through the collar of his shirt. "And Saint Michael."

Joe grinned and touched his own medal around his neck, which Christine had given him their first year together. She'd said she wanted to make sure someone was looking out for him. He was about to ask Bluehorse if he was Catholic, when Andi spoke.

"Who the hell is she?" she asked.

Joe turned.

A short, heavyset woman strode toward them, snapping photos on her phone.

Joe advanced on the woman.

"Who are you, ma'am?" he said, putting himself between her and the remains. Bluehorse appeared next to Joe.

The woman offered a great big smile. "Is this where you all found Congressman Edgerton's vehicle?" She raised her hand to her mouth. "Oh my. Is that his body?"

Joe wasn't fooled.

"Who are you, ma'am?"

She held out a business card.

The card read *Helena Newridge, Journalist, Washington Post*. It looked like it had been printed at home.

Before he mentioned the cheap stock, she said, "I'm waiting for my new cards. Political desk reporter."

"Uh-huh," he said. "Do you have any other ID?"

She reached in a small purse that hung under her right arm and pulled out a driver's license and handed it to him.

It showed a D.C. address. He handed it back to her.

"I need to ask you to delete those photos," he said.

"Now you know I can't do that." She actually batted her eyes at him.

"Let's walk back to the road, ma'am."

"While I'm here," she said, trying to step around Joe, "I may as well—"

Joe moved his body in front of hers. "I can't let you do that, ma'am."

"Why? Is this a crime scene?"

"I can't answer that."

She lost her smile. "Then there's really no reason for me to walk back with you, is there?"

They stared at each other.

"Look, you can either cooperate and I can make sure you get all the information we give to the press, or you can be difficult and I make sure you're cut out. I'm really not that hard to work with, ma'am."

"Oh, stop with the 'ma'am' crap. My name's Helena." She held out a hand.

Joe shook it.

"So is this the site or not?"

Someone had already told her this was the place, or else she wouldn't have come.

"Let's start walking and I'll answer what I can."

Joe called to Andi. "I'm going to accompany this young lady back to her vehicle."

"Young lady?" Helena said. "Aren't you the charmer."

"Where did you park?"

"On the road."

Joe had Bluehorse lead them back through the woods to Jones Ranch Road.

"So, who are you?" she asked.

"Joe Evers, I'm with the BIA out of Albuquerque. If we talk, you can't quote me or reference me as a source with the BIA. Deal?"

"Deal. So is this where they found Edgerton's vehicle?"

"Yes. Will you delete those photos?"

"No. Whose body is that?"

"Can't say. How did you find this place?"

"Sorry, can't say. Did those dogs find the body?"

"Sorry, can't say. Are you working a particular angle for a story?"

"Good question," she said. "Not yet. Are you working a particular angle on your investigation?"

"Not yet. What do you plan to do with those photos?"

"Stupid question, Joe. You know I don't need your confirmation that you found a body to use them."

"I know. But like I said, if you want first crack at our information, then you need to play ball."

Her eyes narrowed. "And what does that mean?"

"I'd prefer not to have those pictures in the paper."

"Why?"

"They make us look stupid. You got too close to the scene. And photos are dangerous for undercover work."

"Undercover? Ain't that stretching it?"

"You asked. And it's a real concern."

"And what do I get if I hold back?"

"There's something you don't know about what you saw back there. Knowing that something won't make you look stupid. And I'll answer some questions as a bonus."

"I need a photo."

"What if I show you where the vehicle was found. No one's gotten that yet. We towed the vehicle, but you can get a location shot. There's some junk debris on the ground and oil stains. With the right lighting, it can be made to look quite grisly."

She thought about it a moment. "You know the way to a woman's heart, don't you? But I still have to write about the body."

"Fine, but without a photo of my team."

"Okay. Now what don't I know?"

"This is the Navajo Nation. They don't always bury their dead in cemeteries. That body may be totally unrelated to the Edgerton case. It might have been what we call a 'ceremonial burial.'"

"But you're going to call me first when you identify the body, right?"

Joe's head nodded even though his mind recoiled at the thought of tipping off a major newspaper.

SEPTEMBER 28

TUESDAY, 5:59 P.M.

MICKEY'S BAR & GRILL, ALBUQUERQUE, NEW MEXICO

Joe walked into Mickey's, still wearing the same clothes from the
body recovery. Not the best impression for a first date. Was this
a date? He wasn't sure. He considered the thought, then corrected
himself. Of course, it was a date. His stomach churned. Nerves. Guilt.
A little of both maybe.

They had cleared the scene by four o'clock and sent the remains to
the New Mexico Office of the Medical Investigator, referred to by law
enforcement as OMI. The body had no identification, but despite what
he'd told the reporter, it did not look in any way like a Navajo ceremonial burial. After a quick debrief with the team, Joe had raced back to
Albuquerque, knowing he would be late. He'd called ahead to Mickey.
Now, standing by the entryway, he wished he'd had time to go home
and change. A little aftershave would have been nice, too.

He made his way to the quiet rear of the dining area and saw
Gillian sitting at a table, a candle at its center, casting soft shadows
on the wall behind her. Had Mickey dimmed the lights more than
usual? He was, undeniably, a virtuoso at creating an uncomfortable
situation.

"Hi, Joe!" chimed two voices in unison.

Sue and Linda sat at the bar, waving, Mickey behind them at the
counter, also waving. All three were sporting big grins. Their watch-
ful eyes transported Joe back to fourth grade, to a field trip to Rocket's
Roller Rink, with its giant disco ball hanging from the ceiling, and the
overhead speakers delivering a mix of funk and love songs. But now a

slow song was playing. And he was that ten-year-old awkward boy again, hoping that Kristin, the girl he'd had a crush on since second grade, would allow him to hold her hand for the four laps it would take while the Jackson 5 promised "I'll be there." The memory was so real, he expected to see Mrs. Rubino, his fourth-grade homeroom teacher—and tonight's spiritual chaperone—sitting behind Gillian, telling him to sit up straight and stop daydreaming.

Gillian turned upon hearing her friends' greeting and now watched Joe approach. The look on her face made him think she might actually be glad to see him.

"Sorry I'm late. It really was unavoidable."

"No problem. I had Mickey to keep me company, as well as Linda and Sue, who kept telling me that I was being stood up." She said this with a gleam in her eye. Joe guessed she might have enjoyed the attention.

She continued, "Oh, and Mickey is quite your wingman. He told me you were in Gallup busting a terrorist cell and had to brief the president. He called you a 'man of duty.' Nice title. Is that on your business card?"

"No. But I did cut that briefing short. I told him I had a very important dinner engagement. The president tends to get a little testy, so he may try to call me back." Joe made a show of pressing the power button on his phone. "There. No interruptions . . . unless, of course, you'd like to say hi to him. If so, I'll call him back." He held up the phone, waiting for her reply.

She sat there a moment, a tiny smile frozen on her face. Had he gone too far with the joke? It'd been stupid, but he'd meant it to be playful. Now she'd be wondering if he was a moron.

Then she laughed. "You had me for a second." She held up her right hand, thumb and forefinger pinched together. "Just an itsy-bitsy second. You said it so seriously." She laughed again and raised her glass, holding it above the table. The red wine matched her ruby-colored dress. It covered her shoulders and contrasted nicely with her blond hair. He didn't know if she had tried for sexy, but she'd pulled it off.

Joe gave his drink order, a red wine, to the waitress. Then the expected get-to-know-each-other session started. They discussed their jobs and family. Joe avoided talking about Christine. When the topic arose, he simply said she'd died two years ago. He found himself bragging about Melissa. Gillian did the parent thing, too, and told Joe about her daughter and son, both at college. She spoke very little of her ex, though, which made Joe wonder if their breakup was still, in her mind, unsettled. Mickey came over, white towel draped over his forearm, and served warm bread and a Caesar salad. He also took a jab at the president for making Joe tardy. Gillian laughed. When he left, silence fell over the table for the first time.

Joe reached for his wineglass; his ring finger and pinkie shook. He looked at Gillian. She wasn't paying attention to his hand. He didn't feel nervous. Their banter had put him at ease. She'd been easy to talk to. Enjoyable, actually. Was he having the shakes? He couldn't tell. He wasn't an alcoholic, was he? At that moment, he didn't know the answer. He picked up his water glass instead.

"Did you grow up in Albuquerque?" Gillian asked.

"Air force brat. Moved around. Born in California. My father was stationed at Edwards. Later we moved to New Jersey, Kansas, Guam, then New Mexico, where he retired."

"Wow. All that moving around, experiencing all those new places." She sighed. "I've spent my entire life in Albuquerque."

"To be honest, they all seem the same to me now. Just school and regular kid stuff everywhere, except for Guam. A tropical island is pretty exciting to a kid. Lots of poverty, but incredible beaches. We'd go diving and grab a lobster and cook it up right there on the beach."

"Sounds like a little piece of paradise."

"It was. I really love the ocean. I'm surprised I stayed in New Mexico."

"Not me. I saw *Jaws* when I was a kid. Been afraid of the water ever since. We went to San Diego one year and my father carried me into the ocean and dropped me right into a wave. I screamed so loud, the lifeguard blew his whistle and told my father to take me out. Never been in it since."

Before Joe could reply, Mickey returned with their food. He laid out a family-style dish of penne alla vodka, a small bowl of grated Parmesan cheese, and a plate of Italian sausage.

"You're both gonna enjoy this. And even if you don't, *you're both gonna enjoy this*," Mickey said, his voice deep and slow.

Joe cringed. "Was that supposed to be the Godfather?"

Mickey lifted his head and rubbed the back of his hand under his chin. "*Someday, and that day may never come, I'll call upon you to do a service for me. But until that day—accept this meal as a gift.*"

"You outdid yourself tonight, Mickey," Joe said.

Gillian clapped; Joe followed. "Bravo!" she said.

"Now, this old man will get outta your hair so you two birds can create some beautiful magic together. Ciao."

Their host walked off to tend the bar.

Joe served the pasta.

A man's voice spoke. "And who is this lovely young lady?"

Joe held the pasta suspended over Gillian's plate. His jaw tightened, as did his hand holding the serving spoon. Cordelli approached the table, Tenny following like a good puppy. Joe emptied the spoon onto Gillian's plate before answering.

Joe introduced Gillian.

"You never mentioned you were seeing someone," Cordelli said.

Joe forced a jovial tone. "Sorry, Dad. I forgot to ask permission to borrow the car."

Tenny laughed.

Cordelli smiled. It actually looked good-natured.

"I only thought you might have mentioned her in the office."

Gillian spoke to Joe. "I'm glad this is our first time out; otherwise, you would've hurt my feelings. A woman likes to be thought about *and* talked about, nicely, of course."

"Joe's the quiet type," Cordelli said. "Strong and silent, just like in the movies."

She looked at Joe and smiled. "Well, he's not that quiet tonight. He's rather funny."

"We don't want to intrude on you two. Enjoy your dinner."

Cordelli and Tenny walked over to the bar.

"That seemed . . . odd," Gillian said.

"They are odd."

She blushed. "They brought something up that I wasn't quite sure how to talk about."

He felt a tingle in his stomach. It wasn't hunger. He reached for his wineglass, took a sip. A gulp. The first of the night.

She went on. "Back in June, after nineteen years of marriage, my husband told me he needed to find himself." She picked up her wine and sipped. Then she placed her glass back on the table and met his gaze. "He left, and now I'm lost. I'm not looking for another relationship. At least not right now." She lowered her head and spoke to the pasta. "You seem like a really nice guy, but I'm not ready for that yet."

He waited for her to continue, but she didn't.

"Is that all? I thought it was something serious, like you don't like vodka sauce."

She laughed and looked back up at him.

He continued, "I'm just glad not to be eating alone. Let's enjoy the evening. No pressure. No promises. No expectations. Fair enough?"

"Thank you." She picked up her fork. "And I love vodka sauce."

The morning seemed clear to Joe, everything sharp and defined. Feeling a little hokey, he thought of Johnny Nash. The man seemed to know a thing or two about bright sunshiny days.

After dinner the previous evening, Joe and Gillian had talked over coffee and cannoli—another one of Mickey's Italian surprises. At nine, Joe offered to drive her home, but she insisted she would be fine. She made it clear they should take things slow, very slow, but she kissed him on the cheek as she left.

Mickey had cornered him afterward, and Joe felt obligated to share with him her desire to set speed traps. Mickey nodded. "Smart girl," he said. "Hope she doesn't wait too long. You're not getting any younger, and neither am I." Joe went home soon after, getting to bed by eleven. When he woke this morning, he felt . . . different. One glass of wine with last night's meal. Not bad.

Now he sat in his cubicle, squad chatter the only background noise. In front of him sat several pages of his notes on the Edgerton case. He'd spent the last hour reading through the logs and interviews of the high-profile investigation from twenty years ago. It was starting to make sense. He began to understand why the original investigator felt Edgerton had run off. Jake Adderman, the lobbyist who had been charged in the subsequent federal investigation for congressional bribery, had been linked to several casino-development interests and two Indian tribes. One of his shell companies, Indigenous

Peoples Self-Governance Foundation, had been set up to promote Indian gaming. The investigation had uncovered a wire transfer of fifteen thousand dollars from the foundation to an account with Banamex, a large Mexican bank. According to the file, Special Agent Malcolm Tsosie, who had retired soon after Joe came on with the BIA in 1990, had tracked down the transfer and determined that the receiving account had been opened under Arlen Edgerton's name. The account also listed a Mexico City attorney by the name of Cedro Bartolome as the paymaster. Joe wasn't sure what that meant, but a report indicated that when Bartolome was contacted by the legal attaché at the U.S. embassy in Mexico City, he refused to discuss the account or Arlen Edgerton. Other wire transfers totaling more than $750,000 from the foundation had been made to two Cayman Islands accounts, neither of which was ever identified. It was apparent that after finding the account linked to Edgerton, the case had shifted from a missing-person investigation to a fugitive hunt.

Things were different now. Joe had found a body, and if it turned out to be linked to Edgerton's disappearance, then he was looking at a murder investigation. That might make things easier. It almost always did. Few cases were unsolvable. The absolute stranger crime was rare. When it came to murder, how the victim was killed often reflected the murderer's emotional state at the time of the crime and sometimes it indicated if the killer knew the victim or if he or she was a stranger. Anger. Revenge. Greed. Jealousy. Emotions help narrow the pool of suspects. If the victim was stabbed twenty-seven times, a likely suspect was a romantic partner—or Squeaky Fromme. When OMI shared their preliminary findings on the body, he might get a better direction for the case—maybe. A skeleton was not nearly as good at ratting out the culprit as a good old-fashioned flesh and blood body.

This morning, Joe's analytical skills seemed sharper, and it wasn't simply because of his reduced alcohol intake. There'd been chunks of time over the last two years that he wouldn't drink for days or weeks. No. It wasn't that. Last night, thanks to Mickey and Gillian, he'd let go of something . . . his stress? No, not stress. Work wasn't so taxing. He hadn't performed any heavy lifting in a while. Hell, that's why they wanted him packed up and sitting in a window seat on the express train to retirement. Perhaps it was the restful sleep he'd had last night. No dreams. No guilt. Or maybe it was that he'd awakened this morning without an overwhelming sense of responsibility. Responsibility for Melissa. For his wife.

As soon as these thoughts entered his mind, the fog moved in, mucking up the clarity he had so enjoyed the last few hours. Was he forgetting her? In that instant, the papers in front of him dimmed. That sunshiny-day thing winked out.

"Cordelli said you had a date last night." Stretch stood at the edge of Joe's cubicle, his lanky arm resting across the divider. "Heard she was quite a looker."

"You wanna swap stories in the locker room?"

Stretch raised both hands in front of him, palms out. "Whoa there, cowpoke. I'm only asking because I'm happy for you. I'm not trying to pry, but if you want to share, I'm all ears."

"Share? What is this, an AA meeting?"

"Take a breath, Joe. I'm just doing the friend thing here, okay?"

"Sorry," Joe said, realizing Stretch would have no idea why he was feeling defensive. "I know you're not screwing with me. And yes, I did have dinner last night. Her name's Gillian. She's very nice, but we're only friends."

"Good for you, buddy." Stretch gave him the attaboy nod. "I actually came over to ask about your cold case. Dale said you recovered a body yesterday and had a run-in with the press. He was pretty upset about the scene photos in the paper."

"He would have gone through the roof if he'd seen the originals. Us digging up the body." Joe picked up the reporter's business card from his desk. "Helena Newridge. *Washington Post.* Ever hear of her?"

Stretch shook his head.

"The few articles I could find seem to be D.C. gossip. I don't know what she's doing here." Joe tossed the card back down. "I'm heading over to OMI in an hour. Want to tag along?"

If this had been a standard autopsy, Joe, Stretch, and Bluehorse would have been standing behind the observation glass, watching the pathologist cut into the body, but since these were only bones, they were allowed inside the exam room. Everyone wore latex gloves and breathing masks. The masks were probably excellent at filtering bacteria and particles but did little for the smell. The air reeked, an effluvia of putrefaction and disinfectant from that morning's autopsies.

On the metal table before them rested the result of the previous day's cadaver dog search. The bones formed an almost complete human skeleton. Some were missing. Dirt, grime, and age had created a dark patchwork of muted colors that made the remains look more like tree branches than the bleached white bones found in displays or on television. In real life, death and decay were dirty work that marred the body as well as the soul.

The tattered clothing, which had dressed the bones in the shallow grave, had been separated and was now spread out on a second metal table to their right.

The pathologist stood on the other side of the bone-covered table wearing a head cover, goggles, mask, and layers of blue and white scrubs. A full-length blue apron covered his torso and legs.

When the man spoke, his voice had the tone of a high school teacher presenting biology to the football team. "This is the skeleton recovered yesterday. It will be sent down to the University of North Texas, to their Center for Human Identification. They'll do a complete workup on the bones, so understand that the findings I'm about to share with you are in no way official. Andi asked for a preliminary exam, so that's all I'm offering, preliminary findings based on my opinion and my opinion alone." The doctor looked at Joe as though waiting for some sort of acknowledgment.

Joe obliged. "I understand."

"Okay, so let's begin. It looks to be that of an adult male, between the ages of thirty to fifty-five, five five to five ten, one hundred and fifty to two hundred and seventy-five pounds, possibly Caucasian. Looks like it's been in the ground for more than fifteen years, but I can't be sure because New Mexico has such a unique climate. The dry conditions and clay soil can preserve bodies and clothing much better than other areas in the country, making it difficult for me to estimate how long it may have stayed underground. The center should be able to give a better time frame. We're missing three phalanges, the hallux and second toe on the right foot and the—"

"What's a hallux?" Stretch asked.

"Sorry. What's missing is the big toe and the second toe on the right foot, and the pinkie toe on the left foot. I think the disappearance was due to animals, because there appears to be some gnaw marks on the sesamoid bo—I mean the bones connecting the toe to the foot. The right tibia and fibula are also missing. Don't know if we have all the vertebrae. I didn't count them. A few teeth, but I don't know if they were lost postmortem or perimortem. And the only fingers recovered on the left hand were the thumb and forefinger. About eight ribs are broken, some missing but the breaks look postmortem. One rib is of interest. Fourth rib, right side." The pathologist lifted three bone fragments from the table and attempted to connect them together. "The second break, here." He pointed. "The bones don't fit together. The edges seem shattered, not broken. Possible gunshot."

"What makes you think gunshot?" Stretch said.

"The shattered bone appears to be the result of a projectile. A bullet is my best guess, but it's only a guess."

"I don't have much more to tell you on the bones." The pathologist moved to stand behind the table where the clothing lay. He pointed to a piece of dark blue fabric. "Dress pants. Synthetic material, possibly polyester blend, which helps explain why it held up so well. No wallet. No pocket litter."

"No pocket litter?" Bluehorse asked. "Is that strange? I mean, that's one of the things we look for when we try to determine if a ceremonial burial took place. That and the cheap suit makes me think it might be ceremonial."

"The grave was shallow," Joe said, "which isn't consistent with a family burial."

Joe was well aware of ceremonial burials. He'd investigated several suspected body dumps over the years, only to determine the sites were simply noncemetery graves. Native Americans often buried loved ones outside of cemeteries, sometimes without grave markers so no one could come along and dig them up to steal belongings—or body parts. Human bones are still part of Native American witchcraft rituals. Noncemetery burials were more common fifty years ago, but today, to bury someone outside of a cemetery within the Navajo Nation, the family would need the approval of the Navajo Land Board, which maintained records of present-day burial sites as well as known ancient ones.

The pathologist pointed to the shirt.

"Eighteen neck, thirty sleeves, manufacturer tag is unreadable. Most of the shirt is rotted. Some looks like it's been eaten, or more likely carried off for nesting. The suit jacket protected a lot of it from decay."

Joe could make out the collar and shoulders. The left sleeve was missing; the right retained most of its length. The stomach area of the shirt was gone. The chest was tattered with dark stains the color of soot. The back was completely intact, with only a few small holes.

"The area on the shirt where I suspect the bullet punctured the flesh has been eaten away. Blood draws insects and small animals, so those areas are often attacked first. Overall, your body and clothing are in remarkable condition. If they are part of the Edgerton disappearance, then that would put them underground over twenty years. I'm surprised you were able to recover an almost-intact skeleton. Was the grave covered by stones? That might explain why the animals left it alone."

Joe shook his head, "Just dirt, but a neighbor seemed pretty efficient at killing coyotes."

The pathologist raised an eyebrow.

Joe went on. "You said the body was one fifty to two seventy-five. Why such a wide range?"

"The lower range is based on his height. The upper range I guesstimated from the size of his clothing. If the clothing belonged to this man, he was obese. The center will be able to give you a better weight range."

"Edgerton was pretty fit, but I recall the driver was heavy," Joe said. "I have a report saying that our office sent OMI the dental records of all three people back when they went missing. Are they still on file here?"

"They were digitized and added to NamUs three years ago. I pulled them this morning." NamUs was the National Missing and Unidentified Persons System, a database used by medical examiners and investigators to identify remains.

Joe sensed a break in the case. "And?"

"Our odontologist has not done a comparison yet, but I think you're looking at the remains of Nicholas Garcia."

⬥

SEPTEMBER 29

WEDNESDAY, 3:08 P.M.

EDGERTON FOR GOVERNOR HEADQUARTERS, SANTA FE, NEW MEXICO

Joe and Bluehorse parked in the lot next to Grace Edgerton's campaign office. Joe thought about having Bluehorse park his marked unit elsewhere to avoid attention, but when they pulled up, there were no news vans or cameramen hanging around outside.

Edgerton's campaign office was situated in an art district, surrounded by galleries and bistros and money. It had all the elegance of a weed in a finely manicured garden. A banner across the front showed a giant picture of the possible future governor looking proud and determined, and next to her were the words BELIEVE NEW MEXICO.

"You think they're going to circle the wagons?" Bluehorse asked.

"Probably."

"My people are used to that tactic."

"Let's be straight on something," Joe said. "Grace Edgerton is a possible suspect so we're here to get information, not give it, okay?"

Bluehorse nodded in agreement.

Inside, Joe found the receptionist, an older, friendly-looking woman with gray hair, metal-rimmed glasses, and a cookie baker's face. She was on the phone, asking the person on the other end whom he or she would vote for in November.

They waited only a minute for the woman to hang up. "Hello, how may I help you?"

"We're here to see Mrs. Edgerton."

"You need to speak with Cassie. She's Grace's secretary." She pointed to a young woman sitting behind a desk at the back of the large, open room. Behind the young woman, along the back wall, were office doors, all closed.

As they walked over, Bluehorse leaned in and whispered, "Things are changing, Joe. The oldest person in the room is not always the one in charge."

"I thought the Navajo believed in respecting their elders?"

"We do. We also believe Sa, Old Age Woman, keeps her promise and lets the old die off so the young can take their place. That's how we learn patience. So don't worry, I can wait."

Cassie was in her midtwenties, no older. Her warm smile gave her a country-girl look, but Joe doubted there was any naïveté when it came to this woman. She held a phone to her right ear and a pen in her left hand, jotting notes in a calendar book, alternately looking at her computer screen and typing. When she hung up, Joe identified himself.

"Yes, they're expecting you," she said. "I'll let Mr. Staples know you're here. Please have a seat." She waved toward several chairs that sat along the wall.

So *they* were expecting him. A private meeting with Grace Edgerton seemed unlikely now.

The door to the office directly behind Cassie opened and two men exited. The first was a tall Native American who looked Navajo, but Joe couldn't be sure.

Next came Senator Kendall Holmes. Joe knew him instantly. He'd been a fixture of New Mexico politics for many years. Holmes was also mentioned in the Edgerton case file.

Joe approached the politician. "Excuse me, Senator Holmes."

The Native American placed a hand roughly on Joe's chest, stopping him in mid-stride. Up close, the man looked Navajo.

"It's going to be tough wiping your ass without that hand," Joe said in a low voice, so only the tall man could hear him.

The Navajo neither blinked nor budged.

"It's okay," Senator Holmes said.

Joe stepped past the bodyguard, who continued to scrutinize his every move.

"Senator Holmes, I'm Special Agent Joe Evers with the BIA. I'm following up on Arlen Edgerton's vehicle. I'd like to speak with you today, if that's possible?"

"I'm sorry, Agent. I'm due back in D.C. this evening. Perhaps you can call my office and set up an appointment. But to be honest, I'm not sure what more I can offer other than what I told the investigator back when Arlen went missing."

"I just have a few follow-up questions. It won't take long."

"Sorry, I need to catch a flight." He strode away. His Navajo muscle followed.

A portly gentleman with thick eyebrows and bouncing jowls came out of the same office from which the senator had emerged. He wore a look on his face that said everything was peachy and even if it wasn't, he could make it so.

"Mr. Evers," the man said. "Pleasure to meet you. I'm Christopher Staples, Mrs. Edgerton's campaign manager."

He yanked on Joe's arm as they shook hands. Each jolt released aftershave from Staples's body. Joe blinked from the burn as he introduced Bluehorse. More aftershave mingled with oxygen.

"Thanks for coming in today," Staples said. "We appreciate your giving us an update."

Joe had spoken to Staples earlier that morning, asking to speak to the congresswoman. He never said he would be giving an update on the investigation. Apparently, Chris Staples liked to play with words.

"Come this way, gentlemen. The future governor is anxious to meet you both."

Joe glanced toward the street entrance. The tall Indian stared at him as he and the senator exited the building.

Mrs. Edgerton's eyes were puffy, as though she'd been crying. She stood in the center of the room, talking to an attractive middle-aged woman dressed in a simple neutral-colored dress that reached below her knees. The woman wore little makeup. Joe guessed she was an adviser and knew better than to draw attention away from the person she was working for. The congresswoman wore a tailored red pantsuit that probably turned a few heads in the Capitol Building. It would have turned his. Joe guessed he and Mrs. Edgerton were close in age, she only a few years older.

Staples made the introductions. The woman was Paige Rousseau. French. They shook hands and exchanged smiles. Joe liked a few things French. Baguettes. Croissants. Women in berets. And now Paige. She appeared serious but geniune.

"Pleased to meet you, Agent Evers," Grace Edgerton said. "And you, Officer Bluehorse. I appreciate your finding the time to give us an update on the case."

More word games.

They all sat down, Mrs. Edgerton moving to the chair behind her desk, Staples and Paige taking the two seats in front, leaving Joe and Bluehorse to sit on the sofa.

"Sorry for the confusion," Joe said, "but I'm not here to give you an update on the case. I'm here to talk to you because you're part of my investigation."

Edgerton glanced at Staples.

Joe continued. "I was hoping to speak to you in private because I have to ask you some questions about your husband, which may be . . . very sensitive."

"Years ago, when I decided to run for my husband's seat, I accepted that my life would be an open book." She looked directly at Joe as she spoke, her posture straight and her tone even straighter. "I'm in a gubernational race right now and cannot afford to keep anything from my team. I trust them, and I appreciate your concern and sensitivity. I have nothing to hide, and neither did my husband, so you can speak freely in front of Paige and Chris."

"Fine." Joe paused, ordering his thoughts. "I'm sure this whole matter has come as somewhat of a shock after all these years, and—"

"Of course it's a shock," Staples said. "Look at the damn timing. After twenty years, you find the car only weeks before the biggest election of her life. And now a body. Grace was upset all morning. You couldn't have given us a heads-up about the body? She had to read about it in the paper. It all seems a little too much. A little too staged."

"If you're trying to imply that we're conducting this investigation based on some sort of political agenda, then you're way out of line," Joe said. "The congressman's car was found in the woods while Navajo PD was investigating an entirely unrelated case."

Staples opened his mouth and then closed it again. Paige pursed her lips, but the corners raised ever so slightly, betraying a smile.

Bluehorse shifted next to Joe. "Ma'am, I'm the officer who found you husband's vehicle, and I can assure you it's just as Agent Evers

said. I have no interest in politics, especially politics off the reservation."

"I never thought otherwise," Grace Edgerton said. "I think Chris is
only being protective of me and the campaign. I don't think he was
trying to imply any sort of impropriety on anyone's part."

Staples gave a dismissive laugh, as though he found such an idea a
joke. "Not at all. I thought the vehicle might have been found after a
tip from an anonymous caller or something like that. I wasn't trying
to imply you two were . . . were involved in something." He gave another awkward laugh. Laughing seemed uncomfortable for him.

Joe shifted into interrogation mode. After a few basic questions to
gauge her response, he moved to the meat of the interview. "At the
time of his disappearance, what was going on in his personal and
political life?"

"That's a very broad question, Agent Evers. And also very difficult. It's been a long time." She looked away, seeming to stare off
toward nothing. "As to his personal life, that was basically me. We
didn't have kids, but we had talked about having them. He wanted
two. A boy and a girl." She hesitated. "But I guess that wasn't meant to
be, was it? Politics was who he was. From the minute he woke up till
his head hit the pillow, which was usually past midnight, he was being the statesman. We did have our 'us' time, not a lot, mind you, but
we had it. Arlen was a good man. He loved me, but he also loved the
people of New Mexico. He wanted to take care of his constituents,
and that meant bringing jobs here, bringing federal money, and in-
creasing federal support to the tribes. I'm sure you're most interested
in knowing whether he took the payoffs they accused him of, and if
he had an affair with his secretary. Am I right?"

"Yes," Joe said. "But that's not all."

She took a breath and leaned back in her chair. "No on both counts.
He would never have taken that money. He didn't need it. We both

came from wealthy families. We weren't rich ourselves, but we were never concerned about our finances."

"Maybe your husband didn't take the money for himself. Maybe he was hoping to use it for something else. Something good."

"He would never have jeopardized his seat. He loved our system of government too much. And, even if the idea of the end justifying the means ever did cross his mind, he would have shared those thoughts with me. We had no secrets. He respected my counsel. He did not take that money." She paused, pressing out imaginary wrinkles on her red slacks. "He was a good man."

Joe picked up on her change in demeanor. "I think there's something you're not telling me, Mrs. Edgerton. If you want me to find out what happened to Arlen, I need to know what you know."

"I think she told you what she knows," Staples said.

Joe's tone softened. "I know there's something you want to tell me. I don't know if it's important or not, but I do know that in a cold case sometimes the smallest thing can make the biggest difference. Everything we talk about is confidential, Mrs. Edgerton. All we want to do is find out what happened to your husband."

"So do the papers," Staples said, his voice thundering in the room, which had just gone quiet.

The congresswoman looked up, but her gaze fell on Paige.

"Grace," Paige began. "I think Agent Evers is right. Do you remember how we wrestled with the Patriot Act? In the end, we agreed that law enforcement needed access to the tools and information to investigate national threats. It's the same here. He needs information to do his investigation. I know you don't have anything to hide." Paige turned and looked at Joe and Bluehorse. "And I believe they will respect your confidence."

The congresswoman looked down at her desk.

"In Navajo, words are magical," Bluehorse said. "They can give you power over a person or situation. A Navajo will not reveal his Indian name to just anyone, only to someone he trusts. Your words right now may help us find out what happened to your husband. I've known Joe only a few days now, since we've been working this case, but I believe he's a good man. Someone you can trust."

"What about you, Mr. Bluehorse?" Staples asked. "Can she trust you?"

The congresswoman raised her head and looked at each of them in turn, ending with Joe. "I don't want you to read too much into what I'm going to say, because it's really . . . I don't know. When the investigators asked me about Arlen and Faye back then, they wanted to know if they often traveled together. I said they did, but . . . but that wasn't necessarily true."

Staples raised his right hand, cutting the congresswoman off. "Grace, if you're about to say you . . . *misspoke* back then, I think we should have Ed in here just to be on the safe side. We're moving into his territory now."

"I'm not concerned about whether she lied twenty years ago," Joe said. "I'm only interested in having all the information now, so I can do my job. And besides, the statute of limitations ran out a long, long time ago."

"The press doesn't have a statute of limitations," Staples said. "Most of the time, they respect no limits."

"All I care about right now is what happened to your husband. What didn't you tell the investigators?"

"It was true that he sometimes took Faye around with him, but only to meet and greets and things like that. He always told me when he would be taking her, and I would go along, if I could."

"Why was that?"

"We were very conscious about his image. I don't believe anything ever would have happened. I trusted my husband. I wasn't foolish then, and I'm not foolish now. We were in love, plain and simple. He would not have done anything to ruin our marriage." She wiped at her eyes.

"I could see why he loved you," Joe said. "You've proven yourself an amazing woman."

"No offense, Mr. Evers, but I don't need to be charmed or cajoled. I'm going to tell you everything."

Staples shifted in his seat.

"Ken Holmes was my husband's chief of staff back then. He felt that people might question Faye's role because she was an attractive young woman. Rumors might circulate about them—or any woman around Arlen. He was very handsome."

"It's Senator Holmes now, correct?" Joe asked.

"Yes, Ken was very ambitious. Still is. I heard he might be planning a run for the White House soon." She laughed. "The day Arlen went missing, Ellery Gates was flying in to meet with him. Gates held a seat in Oklahoma. They had planned two days of fishing. Arlen loved fishing and was taking Ellery to Farmington. He used to say he was going to make fly-fishing the state sport because New Mexico had some of the best rivers in the country."

Staples lowered his head, either embarrassed by the touching remembrance or annoyed. Paige pulled a tissue from a box on the credenza beside her and handed it to the congresswoman. After a few moments, Mrs. Edgerton continued.

"Arlen was working on two bills impacting Native Americans. He loved their culture, but he also wanted their votes. Arlen and Ellery were sponsoring an Indian gaming bill together, but they disagreed on a few points. That's why they were meeting." She took a deep breath. "Arlen's second bill was to protect Native American artifacts from a growing black-market trade. He went to the Navajo Nation that day to visit a site where a number of ancient artifacts had been stolen. What I didn't tell the investigators was that Arlen hadn't told me he was taking Faye with him. I don't know why, but I just blurted out that it was normal for him to take Faye along. And once it was out there, I couldn't take it back. But it wasn't true. He would never take Faye without me, but I couldn't go that day because I was in Las Cruces, meeting with the University Hispanic League. I so wish I had canceled that trip."

"Do you know where they went that day?" Joe asked.

"He was meeting with an archaeologist at the Navajo Nation dig site, but I didn't know precisely where. Arlen was looking for anecdotal stories to bring to the floor." She shook her head. "Both bills were eventually passed, but they removed Arlen's name because of the scandal."

Joe took out a pad and jotted a few notes. "What were the bills?"

"The Indian Gaming Regulatory Bill and the Native American Graves and Repatriation Bill."

"Do you remember the archaeologist?"

"No, but I remember Arlen saying he was from UNM. He asked if I knew him, but I didn't. Arlen and I both attended UNM. We met there."

"What can you tell me about your husband's driver?"

"Nick?" She grinned. "He was very loyal to my husband. He'd worked on his first campaign. After getting elected, Arlen gave Nick whatever work he could. Nick helped write some speeches and also drove Arlen around. That might sound like a strange combination, speechwriter and driver, but Nick was an aspiring novelist. He wrote mostly short stories—fantasy, I think. He appreciated the odd jobs. It let him focus on his writing. He had just finished his novel when he went missing. I'd told him I wanted to read it." She put her tissue to use.

"Did anyone ever threaten your husband? Any enemies?"

"Of course. It comes with the office."

"Any threats that stand out? Odd letters or messages? Anything strange around the time of his disappearance?"

"Nothing really. He received the usual threatening letters. The investigators asked about them. They did seem interested in one, though. A letter from someone on the Navajo reservation. I think . . . I think the person who sent the letter was a member of AIM, or some other movement. I don't remember his name, but I'm sure it will be in your file. I gave permission to the investigators to search Arlen's office as well as Faye's desk. They found the threat letters. Oh, and they were also looking for Faye's calendar book. It was gone, but that wasn't unusual, because she always had it with her, even took it home."

"Tell me about Cedro Bartolome," Joe said.

"I don't know a Cedro Bartolome." She hesitated. "At least I don't think I do. Who is he?"

"He's the lawyer in Mexico City your husband used to set up a bank account."

"I remember now. Not his name, but that a lawyer was involved. I am sure he will tell you my husband did not set up that account. When do you plan to speak to him?"

"Yeah," Staples said. "When? If he says it wasn't Arlen, we can feed that to the press."

"Nothing is going to be fed to the press," Joe said. "This is an investigation, not a campaign stunt."

"I understand," Mrs. Edgerton said. "But you will be speaking to him, right?"

"I don't know. He's an attorney and outside U.S. jurisdiction. There's not much reason for him to speak to me."

"Well, that sucks," Staples said.

"Have you ever owned a gun, Mrs. Edgerton?"

"I really think Ed should be here," Staples said.

She raised her hand, gesturing for Staples to be quiet. "No, I never owned a gun."

Joe asked a few more questions, but none that revealed any new information.

"Okay, Mr. Evers. I answered your questions. Now, please answer mine. Was the body you recovered yesterday my husband's?"

"I'm sorry, but it's an ongoing inv—"

"Damn you, Mr. Evers. Don't treat me like a suspect. It's my husband's disappearance you're investigating. *My* husband. Not just a name in your case file."

Joe was surprised by her directness, but he wouldn't be bullied.

"We haven't identified the remains yet. OMI will do the identification. Hopefully, we'll know in a few days."

They asked Joe and Bluehorse several more probing questions, which Joe wouldn't answer. Then Paige asked to end the meeting so the congresswoman could have some alone time before her next appointment. Paige stayed with her while Staples walked Joe and Bluehorse out.

"Why was Senator Holmes here?" Joe asked.

"Arlen's car is a headache for everyone," Staples said. "I have a pack of reporters waiting for my press release," he added. "We go to the polls in three weeks. What you release to the press can change the outcome of this election. You know that. So I hope you don't have a political ax to grind. Grace is the real deal. And I'm not saying that because I'm paid to. She wants the best for this state. Bad press can kill her chances. From what I understand, you're no stranger to bad press."

"I'm not following you," Joe said.

"I read about the Longman case."

Joe didn't reply.

"So please keep us updated on what you find out. I'd appreciate it, and so would Grace."

"That's a hell of a way to get me on your side."

"I'm not trying to get you on my side. I don't want anyone saying we tried to influence your investigation. I just want you to know I'll be watching. I know she's not involved. As long as the truth comes out, she'll win this election. I'm confident of that. But if someone decides to play games with the truth and drags her into this mess . . . well, some members of the press who support her might not like it. And I'll be sure to point them to the person responsible." Staples reached into his pants pocket. "Here. It'll be a collector's item when she's president." He handed Joe and Bluehorse each a small white-and-blue Edgerton for Governor button. "Don't forget to vote."

SEPTEMBER 29

WEDNESDAY, 4:40 P.M.

EDGERTON FOR GOVERNOR HEADQUARTERS, SANTA FE,

NEW MEXICO

Helena Newridge, arms crossed, large purse dangling, leaned against Joe's Tahoe like a thug taking ownership of a corner.

"I didn't hear from you, Joe."

"I'll talk to you later," Bluehorse said as he walked on to his own unit, leaving Joe to deal with her by himself. The young officer displayed much wisdom.

"What are you doing here, Helena?"

"Same as you. Came to talk to her. I was hoping you came to arrest her, but I guess that was wishful thinking."

"Why would I arrest her?"

"Because she killed her husband."

Joe waited for the bomb.

"I lied to you yesterday," Helena said. "You asked what my angle was. Well, I think little Miss Oh I Love New Mexico is a vindictive, cheated-on wife who took revenge on her rotten, philandering husband."

Joe unlocked the door to his Tahoe. "And you base this on . . ."

"The fact I was a vindictive, cheated-on wife who wanted revenge on my rotten, philandering husband."

Joe smiled. "So where were you the day Arlen Edgerton went missing?"

She gave a full belly laugh. "Joey, you do have a sense of humor. I wasn't so sure of that yesterday."

He didn't care for Joey, but coming from her it seemed friendly, almost endearing. "How do you know Edgerton's even dead?"

"I don't, but I was hoping that the body you recovered would be his."

"That wouldn't prove she killed him."

"No, but a source tells me she knew about his affair with Faye and they argued about it. There may even have been talk of Arlen leaving her to marry Faye. His bullet-riddled body would go a long way in supporting my theory."

"Who's your source?"

"Oh, Joey. You know better than that."

"What else did he tell you?"

"Good try, but I never said *he*. And the source said Mrs. Edgerton was mean enough to do it."

"Anything else?"

"I thought this was a two-way street."

"What's your question?"

"Did she own a gun?"

"I'm told no," Joe said. He climbed in behind the wheel.

"Did she tell you that?"

"Can't say." He started the engine.

"Did Arlen own a gun?"

"Probably, but I haven't checked yet."

"Hmmm. I'll be checking on that, too."

"Good, let me know what you find." He tried to close the door. She held it open.

"Not so fast, Joey. Whose body is it?"

"When I get an ID, I'll call you."

"That's it? I give you good stuff, and you give me nothing."

"I'll tell you what. Check into that gun angle. Find me a gun and I'll tell you if it's involved. How's that?"

She thought about that. "Is there anything I should know before I talk to the wannabe governor?"

"Yeah, watch out for her campaign manager. He bites."

❖

SEPTEMBER 29

WEDNESDAY, 5:05 P.M.

INTERSTATE HIGHWAY 25 SOUTH, OUTSIDE OF SANTA FE,

NEW MEXICO

Cruising along 25 on his way home, Joe's mind filtered out the rush-hour traffic around him and instead replayed the interview with Grace Edgerton. She'd proved to be of little value. In a cold case, it was often hard to read a person's emotions so many years after a crime. Witnesses and subjects, even victims, find it easy to hide behind faulty memories. In this case, Joe felt the congresswoman had been honest with him. Hell, he wanted to believe she'd been honest with him. But he couldn't be sure. She made a living by telling people what they wanted to hear.

She'd mentioned three people Joe planned on interviewing. Kendall Holmes, now Senator Holmes, with whom an interview seemed unlikely. Dwight Henry, whose name she hadn't been able to recall, referring to him only as the AIM member who had sent the threatening letter. Joe had found a copy of the letter in the case file, as well as an interview with Dwight by the original case agent. And finally, she had mentioned an archaeologist, who seemed to be the last person to have seen Arlen and his group alive, Professor Lawrence Trudle. Joe had read the professor's interview and found it light, their meeting the day the congressman had disappeared amounting to nothing more than a few minutes staring at a dig site. At least that's how the report read, but Joe felt there had been more to it. He planned on talking to the professor sooner rather than later. Actually, tomorrow. Joe had searched his name on the Internet that morning and found him still listed as a faculty member at UNM. His posted office hours were nine to eleven o'clock on Thursdays.

Joe also planned to call upon Senator Holmes tomorrow, or at least schedule an appointment for an interview. But that would depend on the BIA. It was the agency's protocol to get approval before interviewing any state or federal politician. Joe had requested approval from Dale just that morning to interview Grace Edgerton. The request had gone up to D.C. Two hours later, the approval came down. He wondered how long it would take for approval to interview Senator Holmes, who sat on the Senate Committee on Indian Affairs, overseers of the BIA. Joe might retire before that approval was granted. So only Dwight Henry was left. He decided he would let Bluehorse track down that lead.

He called Bluehorse. They rehashed Grace Edgerton's interview first and then talked about Dwight Henry and recent AIM activity on the reservation, which turned out to be virtually nonexistent, at least to Bluehorse's knowledge, but he said he would check into it. The young officer agreed to locate the activist and try to set up an interview, which Joe warned might not be easy. AIM had a long-standing distrust of the government and law enforcement, including tribal law enforcement.

After disconnecting with Bluehorse, and still driving, Joe took out his notebook and wrote down "Gun" at the bottom of his notes on Grace Edgerton. Next to it he wrote "Helena Newridge." She might prove useful after all. Who was her source? Someone who must have known Grace and Arlen well, unless it was all a lie. Was the source someone on Grace's staff? A family member? Someone from the other candidate's team trying to plant suspicion right before the election? Exactly what Staples had warned about. For now, he'd have to weigh Helena's information very carefully. He hated reporters. Even when they were helping, they were a pain in the ass. Her source could be anyone, perhaps even Grace's running mate. He wasn't exactly sure how politics worked in New Mexico, but he recalled that the candidates for governor and lieutenant governor ran on separate tickets in the primary. If Grace was dirtied up, would the running mate get a shot at the governor's ticket? He didn't know. He tried to recall the name of her running mate. Jackson Adler. The owner of Adler Advanced Materials, a New Mexico defense and aerospace company. A big player. Rich. Probably ambitious, too. Joe would consider the angle, but it was a little too far-fetched. KISS—keep it simple, stupid. A touchstone for investigators. And Stretch's recommendation. He needed to focus on probabilities, not possibilities. Another maxim. Besides, Joe hated politics.

He turned his attention to driving. Traffic was somewhat heavy heading back to Albuquerque. It would take at least another forty minutes.

He picked up his phone again and punched in his daughter's number. He loved talking to her, loved learning what was new in her life, loved hearing her say she was happy and her grades were great. They always were. She was smart. Her mother's genes, no doubt. The "Radiant Book Worms" he would call them both. That and "Brainy Bugs." But there were days when he would avoid talking to her. The days he had difficulty accepting that Christine was gone. He would avoid Melissa then because he knew he would bring her down, make her worry about him. Even when he put on a happy front, she sensed his depression somehow.

She answered this time. He could hear voices and music in the background.

"Hey, Brainy Bug. How's the semester shaping up?" he asked.

"Would you be upset if I dropped out and returned home to start a broccoli farm?"

"You can always come home, but I know you're lying."

"And how do you know that?"

"'Cause you hate broccoli."

"Damn, I should have said cauliflower."

"I'm sure Columbia's too easy for you. Maybe you should have chosen Harvard."

She laughed. "Yeah, too easy. I study all night, every night."

"Doesn't sound like you're studying tonight. You at a party?"

"Why, you worried?"

"Of course. New York. Big city, big worries."

"There's a filmmaker here who's showing his latest documentary. They're playing music."

He listened. "Mexican?"

"Mexican folk-festival music. That's what his film's about."

"Okay, now I feel better. I know you're not mixing with the wrong crowd if you're going to events like that. So, anything new?"

Only the Mexican folk music came through the phone.

"Melissa?"

"No, nothing new."

"What is it?"

"Dad, you're interrogating me."

"Only because I love you. Now spill." He held his breath, waiting for the worst.

"Well, it's really good news, but I don't know how you'll take it."

"Honey, I never want you to be afraid to talk to me or tell me anything. What is it?"

"Well . . . I told you my grades were really good, and . . . well . . . I got invited to do a student exchange at Cambridge for next semester. It's really a once-in-a-lifetime opportunity and I don't know if I'll ever get the chance again and it's really a big deal and I really want to go and I hope you're okay with it."

Several things ran through his mind. First and foremost was how far away she would be and that he wouldn't be there if she needed him. But then he realized he wasn't there for her now. She was two thousand miles away.

"Honey, that's great."

"No it's not. I can hear it in your voice."

"Now you're interrogating me."

"I know you're worried, but I'll be all right. You know you can trust me."

"Honey, I always trust you. It's the guys I don't trust. And of course I'm happy for you. I don't want you to pass up such a great opportunity."

"I'm so happy you're okay with it, Dad. I have to put in my name next week, and I was worried about asking you. When I get home, I'll tell you all about it."

"Just make sure you get me some pictures of Stonehenge, and maybe a little piece of it, too, if nobody's looking. Nothing big. A chip will do."

"You got it. So what's new in Albuquerque?"

"Nothing. Except your over-the-hill father had a date last night." He'd gotten caught up in her good mood and tossed it out without thinking. He hadn't intended on mentioning it at all. And never like that.

Only the Mexican folk music came through the line.

Idiot, he thought.

"Melissa?"

Folk music.

"I'm sorry. I didn't mean to throw it out there like that. It wasn't a date. Just dinner."

"Dad, it's okay. You caught me off guard. I wasn't expecting it. I'm happy. Who is she?"

"Her name is Gillian and she works in Albuquerque at a big construction company."

"She's a construction worker?"

"Yep, operates a jackhammer and rips cast-iron pipes out of the ground with her teeth. They call her Gillian the Giant."

"Wow, a keeper. So, how did you meet her?"

"Hey, what's with the twenty questions? You're at your Mexican folk thing. How about we talk about this later?"

"It sounds like you're avoiding me."

"I am."

"Okay, but before you hang up, tell me how your job interview went."

"Went great. Knocked the guy's socks off. Literally. He had to pick them up in between questions. Now get back to your fiesta. We'll talk later."

"Love you, Dad."

"Not as much as I love you, Brainy Bug."

He pressed the disconnect key, not wanting to end the conversation but knowing she would start digging if he didn't. She worried about him probably as much as he worried about her.

Ellery Gates thumbed the television remote. Every station had news about the body. Talking heads spouted all kinds of nonsense and conspiracy theories. One idiot even suggested Ellery was somehow involved, explaining that it might have been an attempt to cover up his own corruption. "Everyone knows," the moron had said, "Ellery was in New Mexico that day. He would be at the top of my suspect list." Of course no one mentioned Ellery had not arrived in Albuquerque till after Edgerton had been reported missing. So, like any newsworthy item that held the nation's attention, lies and speculation took center stage over logic and reason. Ellery was being dragged back into the spotlight of political corruption. Joy.

But he supposed he couldn't complain. The last ten years had been peaceful for him. He'd left Oklahoma, his birth state, the state where two libraries, a section of highway, a federal building, and an overpass were named for Samson Gates, his father and the longest-serving United States senator to represent the Sooners. His father had left big shoes for his only son to fill. But Congressman Ellery Gates had given it his best. He had believed he was doing the right thing for the state. Thought he was even on the side of the angels. So what if he catered to the old-boy network? He used that very same network to do good, too. Some folks might even have considered his accomplishments *great,* but not anymore. Not after a fall. Never after a plunge from Mount Olympus.

He never took the money because he needed it—or even wanted it.

It was just the way that sort of thing worked. The money was only so the other side felt comfortable about the arrangement, less chance of a double cross. And Ellery never sold his conscience. He always did what he felt was right, even when money was involved. If it wasn't right, no deal. The news had labeled his actions the result of greed. But Ellery was wealthy, very wealthy. His grandfather had been one of the largest wheat producers in Oklahoma, and later, when natural gas was found under his fields, owner of the largest gas reserve in the eastern part of the state. That same wealth had financed Samson Gates's run for the Senate and kept him in office for almost three decades. But it couldn't keep Ellery there. After Casinogate—CNN's coinage—Ellery became the old-boy whipping boy.

"Do you need anything else before I turn in?" Mariana stood in the doorway to the television room, where Ellery found himself most nights now. She wiped her hands on a dish towel.

Ellery looked at his almost-empty glass of Johnnie Walker Red, cradled, forgotten, in his left hand.

"No, I'm fine."

"You shouldn't watch that, Mr. Gates. It's not healthy."

"When you reach my age, you care less and less about what people think of you. Any visitors today?"

"A few, but Gustavo chased them off."

"Sorry. It's been a lot for both of you. Why don't you and Gustavo take off this weekend. On me. Somewhere nice."

"Thank you, but we should stay. Those news folks are loco. Gustavo caught one climbing the fence."

"No. I insist. I'll get Ernesto to stay the weekend."

She didn't look happy. "Thank you, sir."

You old fox," Cordelli said when Joe walked into the office. "I didn't know you were stepping out with the ladies. Where'd you meet that hot little number? Gillian, right?"

"Drop it," Joe said, heading for his desk, not turning around.

"Hey, I'm trying to pay you a compliment. She seemed nice."

"Glad you approve."

Half a dozen "While You Were Out" notes rested on his keyboard. Ginny could easily have transferred all those calls to his voice mail, but she was old-fashioned and liked taking messages. The top one read "Sierra Hannaway—again!" He closed his eyes. Damn. She'd seen the news about the body. And he hadn't thought to call her. He let out a breath. Maybe the squad was right. Maybe he had lost his edge. Maybe a person's edge was simply staying on top of cases. Sierra deserved to find things out from him, not the evening news. He'd decided he would give that courtesy to her and to Grace Edgerton. And he'd do the same for the driver's family, too.

"You know your problem, Joe?" Cordelli said. He stood at the end of Joe's cubicle, his forearm on the filing cabinet. "You ain't part of the team. It's Team Joe or nothing. You're a dinosaur, man. You somehow survived the meteor, but now the world's a different place and you don't quite fit in, do you?"

"You're right. The world is different. I used to run with meat eaters.

Now I'm stuck with toads like you." Joe walked forward, shoulder-
ing past Cordelli.

Stretch and Sadi stood at the end of their cubicles, watching. Ginny
looked up from a telephone call. Joe had an audience. A reality show
free of commercials. *Joe Evers: A Life Faded.* He knew they were waiting for him to explode or fall apart like he had last year. Cordelli was
still talking as Joe made his way to Ginny's desk. She hung up the
phone as he approached.

"Ignore him, Joe," Ginny said, her eyes expressing sympathy. Another person butting into his life. He didn't need her pity.

"Did you notify Nick Garcia's parents that we were reopening the
case?" Joe asked. Ginny mailed out all the victim notifications.

"No," Ginny said. "His parents died some years ago. He doesn't
have any siblings. I even looked—"

"You didn't think to tell me that sooner?" Joe raised his voice. "I'm
the case agent, Ginny. I need to know those things." She cringed,
but Joe continued anyway. "You don't think I can handle my cases,
either, do you?"

"No . . . I never . . ." She looked around for help.

Cordelli's voice: "Now you're going off on Ginny. What the hell's
wrong with you, man?"

Joe's jaw tightened. "Back off."

Stretch whispered something to Cordelli that Joe couldn't hear.
Et tu, my friend.

Cordelli raised his voice. "You lost your wife, Joe. Bad shit happens, but you have to move on and take care of what's in your life
now, because that's all—"

"Shut your mouth, Cordelli," Joe said, spinning around, advancing
on him. "Don't you ever mention my wife again, you arrogant little
prick."

Cordelli fell silent, a look of uncertainty on his face. He took a step back. "Joe, all I'm trying to say is—"

"You've said enough already." Joe was ten feet from him and closing, intent on smashing a fist into the little prick's smug face. Maybe two or three times. He wouldn't count.

A hand grabbed Joe's left shoulder. Stretch's voice: "Take it easy."

He shrugged it off. Only two strides separated Joe and Cordelli. Joe's hands balled into fists. Cordelli took another step back. Joe smiled.

"You better watch yourself, old man." Cordelli's voice wavered. "You come at me, I'm going to put you down."

"Maybe."

Sadi stepped between them, her back to Joe. "You need to back off, asshole, before Joe beats your half-Mediterranean ass back to Italy."

Stretch grabbed Joe's arm. "You don't need this. Don't bring more shit down on yourself."

Joe turned to Stretch. "I have only three months left. And I'm KMA, remember." Stretch had kidded Joe about being kiss my ass–eligible, meaning that if Joe got in trouble now, the process to sanction him would take longer than his time left in the bureau. He had a total of twenty-two years in government service and could retire at any time.

"What the hell is going on?" Dale bellowed from his office doorway.

"Nothing," Stretch said. "We're good."

"Good my ass. Get in here, Joe!"

"I need to get out of here," Joe said, turning to go.

"I'm not asking."

"We're good, Dale." Joe's anger waned. Cordelli's being afraid of him had been therapy enough.

"Get in here or go home . . . for good."

Joe walked back but paused at Ginny's desk. "Sorry for snapping. It wasn't meant for you."

"I know." But she leaned back when she said it.

Dale stepped aside. Joe entered. Dale followed, closing the door. "What the hell was that all about?"

"Wonder Boy talks shit sometimes."

"Toughen up. Life's a bitch. You, of all people, know that."

"Cordelli was pushing my buttons. He thinks he's God's gift to the BIA."

"Yeah, he may be full of himself, but you're a pain in the ass. You drag your sorry ass around here every day crying, *Woe is me.* Even Stretch has to work to be your friend."

"Me and Stretch are fine."

"Damn it, Joe. We were never close, but even I can see how you've changed."

Joe stood up and faced Dale. "Is that all you wanted me in here for? To tell me I'm miserable? Mission accomplished. Can I go?"

Dale walked behind his desk. "You're incredible." He sat down. "People are reaching out to help, and you push them away."

Joe felt his anger returning. "Yeah, you're a big help. You and that review board. Thanks. You're a peach."

"I called that board because you became unfit. You stopped caring about your cases. You even stopped caring about yourself. Our victims deserve more than that. Longman's family deserved better than you gave them."

"You don't think I know that? You don't think I regret what happened? But it was a mistake. I screwed up. We all screw up. No one's perfect doing this job, even your golden boy Cordelli. But I don't deserve to be canned over it."

"You weren't canned. They asked you to retire. You agreed."

Joe pursed his lips. "Are we done? You need anything else, *boss*?" He looked over at the bookcase full of model cars. Dale's pride and joy. One good shove would send the whole miserable collection to the floor.

"What's the status of the Edgerton case?"

"I'm working follow-ups. I want to interview Senator Holmes. He was Edgerton's chief of staff."

"Forget it. I'm not calling Washington on that one. You're not fishing around in his pond. Not with the press watching our every move."

"You want me to solve this case, or just run it into the ground?"

"Funny. I got a call from a Chris Staples. He was concerned about the same thing. He was afraid you would try and run Grace Edgerton's campaign into the ground."

"What do you think?"

"Any other time, I'd say I know you better than that. But now, with what just happened, I'm not so sure."

"What do you want to do?"

"I gave it to you. Run with it. Sink or swim, it's yours."

Part of Joe was relieved. But only a part. He wanted to work the case. Perhaps he could figure out what happened to Edgerton and go out on a high. But another part of him knew cold cases were often unsolvable. There was a better chance he would go out on a low. Even lower than he was right at that moment, which, honestly, seemed impossible.

"Then let me do my job."

"Doing your job is what I've been asking you to do for a year now."

Special Agent?" the girl behind the reception desk said. "What makes you special?" She tilted her head and smiled up at Joe. Too bad she was Melissa's age.

Joe put away his credentials. He returned the smile. He hoped he wasn't blushing. "I like to think it's my personality."

"You carry handcuffs?"

"I do." Joe was looking around now, hoping no one was over-hearing their conversation. Students and faculty moved through the hallway behind him, oblivious to the bold flirting by this nubile teen. He didn't know if she was a teen. She could be twenty-five. Wishful thinking. Thankfully, the university had cranked up the air-conditioning.

"I've never been handcuffed."

Time to put an end to this before he needed a shower. "That's because you're a good girl. And I hope you stay one."

She wasn't deterred. "Maybe I'm not a good girl."

Maybe he should test her convictions. "Professor Trudle?"

She actually pouted, but she pointed down the hall. "Last door on the left."

He got out of there—quick.

The girl had put him in a better mood. A different mood. After he finished with the professor, he planned to grab some lunch, then head over to the New Mexico Museum of Natural History and Science, where Sierra Hannaway worked. He had called her during the drive to the university, and she'd agreed to meet him at two.

The doors along the hall listed names and titles. The one the girl had indicated bore Professor Lawrence Trudle's name on a small plastic plaque. The door was open. A balding man, quite a few years older than Joe, with big, round professorial eyeglasses, sat behind a desk.

"Professor Trudle?"

"Yes. What can I do for you?"

"I'm here about Congressman Edgerton." Joe threw the name out there, watching the man closely for a reaction, but there was no need for scrutiny. The man wore his emotions on his sleeve.

"I've been following the news. I was hoping someone would come talk to me. Are you an investigator or with the press?"

Joe showed his credentials. The professor didn't ask him why he was *special.*

"The Bureau of Indian Affairs. I remember speaking to an agent from there back when all this occurred."

The professor stood and shook hands. Joe eased into a chair in front of the desk and took out his notepad.

"I appreciate your time, Professor."

"Yes, of course. Anything I can do. I was told I was the last person to see the congressman and Faye that day."

Faye? Joe felt a tingle of suspicion creep up the back of his neck.

"What do you remember?"

"Oh, I remember everything. That day changed my life. Well, actually, finding those artifacts changed my life."

"Go on."

"I'd been contacted by Faye Hannaway, Congressman Edgerton's secretary. She said the congressman was working on a piece of legislation to protect Native American antiquities. He wanted to come out and talk with me and visit my site, where a number of artifacts had been stolen. I said of course. I mean, I wanted those artifacts back. I thought that if a congressman could throw some of his weight around, perhaps the police would actually take the case seriously."

"What do you mean, take it seriously?"

"I'd reported the theft to the Navajo Nation police, but I'm not even sure they made a report. It happened a week before the congressman visited the site. I made the report the night of the theft, and when I followed up a few days later, they couldn't find the original report. I think William Tom squashed the whole investigation."

"William Tom? The president of Navajo Nation?" Joe groaned inside. Not another conspiracy theory. He jotted the name down anyway.

"The same. But he wasn't president back then. At that time, he was the director of Navajo Antiquities. Smart man, very ambitious. He always talked like he knew what was best for the Navajo people. His words, not mine. He always said 'my people' when he spoke about the tribe. A little grandiose, if you ask me."

"Help me understand," Joe said, somewhat incredulous. "Why would the director of Navajo Antiquities want to stop an investigation into stolen Navajo artifacts?"

"Because I think he stole them."

Joe closed his notepad.

Trudle continued: "William visited my site the morning of the theft. I was required to call his office after a find, so that they could inventory the items with us. He arrived alone, made his inventory, and then left. He was amazed at what we'd found, as was I. Later that day, I ran into Gallup to purchase more packing material. We'd found much more than we'd expected. Massive pots. Preserved bones. What looked like painted stones with pictographs that seemed to tell a story. We never got to examine them, though. When I returned that night, everything was gone."

"Why do you suspect William Tom?"

"Because I saw him driving back on six oh two when I was returning to the site. It was about nine o'clock at night. I saw his truck, a Suburban."

"He could have been working late."

"When I confronted him the next day, he denied it was his truck. But I knew his truck. It had Department of Navajo Antiquities printed on the side."

Joe opened his notepad again.

"When I got back to camp," the professor continued, "our most important finds were gone. My two assistants had been in their tents. One had fallen asleep and the other had been listening to music. Neither heard or saw anything. William Tom was the only one outside my group who knew of the find and knew what those artifacts were worth."

"Worth to whom? It seems like a big risk for someone like him. How much are we talking?"

"Artifacts are worth whatever a collector is willing to pay for them. Maybe a few thousand dollars, maybe some financial help for a presidential run. I later found out that he was very close to Arthur Othmann, who was one of his campaign's biggest supporters. A lot of Santa Fe money. Do you know who he is? Arthur Othmann?"

The name sounded familiar. Joe shrugged.

"He's somewhat known in archaeology circles as a collector of Native American art and antiquities. He's tried to finance several of our digs. The Othmann Gallery in Santa Fe sells legitimate art, but I'm told he also sells to the black market. At least that's the rumor. I think that was who Tom sold the artifacts to."

Now Joe placed the name. Arthur Othmann was the subject in Stretch and Sadi's investigation.

"You said these artifacts changed your life. How?"

Professor Trudle stood and walked over to his bookcase, where he pulled a slim volume off the middle shelf.

"This is what is known as the 'Trudle Turkey,' " the professor said as he handed Joe the book.

Joe read the title, *Anasazi Lineage to the Aztec*. He recalled his own knowledge of the ancient ruins in New Mexico and Arizona and the people who supposedly built them. "You believe the Anasazi were connected with the Aztec Empire?"

Professor Trudle removed his glasses and rubbed at the bridge of his nose. "Most mainstream archaeologists don't believe that, but some items found at El Morro and Chaco Canyon point to that lineage. What I found were two massive pots that had residue inside consistent with the boiling of humans, a common ritual in Aztec ceremonies."

"That's very interesting." Joe wondered how the interview had gone so far off topic.

The professor put his glasses back on and beamed. "Yes, it is. But I lost the proof when the artifacts were stolen. All I had was a scraping of the residue. The actual pots would have supported my theory. Luckily, my assistant had taken some very good photographs. I used them in the book. As a matter of fact, she was the reason Congressman Edgerton visited the site."

"Who was your assistant?"

"Sierra Hannaway, Faye's younger sister."

Joe took in the information. Why wasn't that in the file? It would have explained why Edgerton went out to visit the professor and why Faye went with him. It would have punched a crater-size hole in the illicit affair angle.

"Was Sierra there when you met with Edgerton?"

"Yes, but only in the beginning. She left soon after they arrived, for a supply run to Gallup. She was with Steve. Steve Mercado. He's a professor here now, in this department. And he's a friend."

"So what happened at the meeting?"

"Nothing. We talked about protecting Native American antiquities and he told me he wanted to use the theft as an example. He was working on what would become the Native American Graves and Repatriation Act, NAGPRA. We spoke for about an hour, I showed him the site, and he left."

"Who was there that day?"

"The congressman, Faye, a man who stayed with the car, and Sierra and Steve. But as I said, Sierra and Steve left soon after."

"Anyone else? Perhaps someone visited the site that day, a passerby? Anyone?"

"No. No one."

"Any vehicles? Anything out of the ordinary?"

The professor said no. Joe tried several variations of the question, but there seemed nothing otherwise unusual that day or during the visit.

"I'm sure you know about the supposed affair between Edgerton and Faye," Joe said. "Did you notice anything between them?"

"No. Not at all. They seemed friendly, but professional. After all that stuff about them came out, Sierra came to talk to me. She asked about the same thing, thinking that because I'm a man, I might have picked up on something. I didn't. The whole story didn't make sense. Why would he have stopped to talk with me and visit the site, only to skip town? He even took photos. Why do all that?"

They talked some more. Then the professor checked his watch. "I'm sorry, I have to get to my class. Can we continue this later?"

"Sure, but one last question. Where was your site?"

"Jones Ranch. It's in the book."

Joe looked down.

Trudle continued. "There's a map inside. I didn't give the exact location, but it's within a football field of the actual site. We try to protect dig locations. Keep it. I have boxes of them in my garage. It wasn't a big seller."

They walked into the hall.

Joe saw the receptionist. She waved. Trudle glanced at Joe but said nothing.

"Thanks for your time, Professor. I may have another agent from my office come out to talk to you about Arthur Othmann."

The professor seemed pleased.

❖

SEPTEMBER 30

THURSDAY, 1:48 P.M.

CENTRAL AVENUE NW, ALBUQUERQUE, NEW MEXICO

Hey, Brainy Bug," Joe said into his phone, surprised to hear from his daughter this early in the afternoon on a weekday. He was in his vehicle, on his way to the New Mexico Museum of Natural History and Science in Albuquerque.

"Hi, Dad."

He heard the stress in her voice.

"What's wrong, Lissa? Where are you?"

"I'm . . ." She paused. "Don't get upset. I'm okay. I'm at the apartment. There's a policeman with me."

"What happened?" Joe's hand clenched the steering wheel. The Tahoe drifted into the right lane. A car horn blared, and he swerved back left.

"The landlord's here, too," she said.

Joe remembered the man from his trip to New York to find Melissa an apartment for her second year at Columbia. Rudy. It took him a moment, but his last name came to him. Palmieri. Rudy Palmieri, an old Italian. A nice man. The kind of older gentleman who would look after two young girls on their own. Joe had approved of him and the apartment.

"I got back from school about a half hour ago, and when I walked in . . . the place was a wreck. The TV's missing and Shana's laptop. They even took the router box for the Internet. I can't believe it. I think they ate here, too. There was food left out on the counter. I didn't check all of Shana's stuff, but I'm missing my perfume and—"

"Don't worry about that. Are you okay?"

"Yeah, I'm fine. But I'm mad as hell."

"Where's Shana?" Joe asked.

"She's on her way. She's with her boyfriend."

"She's okay, too?"

"Yeah. She's okay."

"Let me speak to the officer," Joe said.

He heard his daughter talking to someone, but he couldn't make out what she was saying. There was a muffled sound, then a man's voice came on the line.

"This is Officer O'Brien."

Joe introduced himself and let the officer know he, too, was on the job. Then he asked for his take on the burglary.

"The best I can tell, the perp jimmied the doorknob. Apparently, the dead bolt wasn't set."

"Any damage to the place. Any sicko stuff? Anything I need to be worried about for my daughter and her roommate?"

"No. Looks like a simple burglary," the officer said. "There've been a few on the block the past month." He gave Joe the log number for the report. Officer O'Brien wasn't going to lift prints. Most big cities didn't process burglary scenes unless it was a major theft or a burglary linked to something else, like murder or rape or arson. "I'll give your daughter my cell number. If she has any more problems, she can call me."

"Thanks. If I can ever do you a good turn down here in Albuquerque, let me know." Joe gave the officer his cell phone number. That was how it often worked in law enforcement. A favor for a favor. This guy might call a year or two from now looking for some help, never mentioning the original favor, only saying how they knew each other, or how their paths had crossed a few years back.

Joe had parked in the lot in front of the museum and was walking through the main doors when Melissa got back on the phone.

"Did Shana get there yet?" Joe asked.

"No."

"Ask Mr. Palmieri if he can stay with you until she gets home." More mumbled voices.

"He will."

"You have a chain on the door, right?"

"Yeah," she said.

"Tonight, set the chain and the dead bolt. The officer said the perp must've jimmied the doorknob lock. Did you or Shana set the bolt today?"

"No, we haven't been."

He walked to the counter where visitors purchase tickets.

"Hold on a second, honey," Joe said into the phone. He lowered it and spoke to the woman behind the counter.

"I'm here to see Ms. Hannaway. She's expecting me."

She picked up a phone and dialed a number.

Joe spoke into his cell phone again. "Did either of you lose a set of keys recently?"

"No."

"Double-check with Shana."

"She's waiting for you by the security desk," the woman behind the counter said. "Right through those doors."

Joe nodded but continued speaking into his phone.

"You're getting a security system installed. I'll arrange it."

On his right, large glass partitions separated a gift store from the main corridor, which led into the museum proper. A round information counter was tucked up against the glass wall. Behind it sat a disinterested middle-aged security guard, a copy of the *Albuquerque Journal* opened to the crossword puzzle.

"Dad, we don't need a security system. We'll lock the dead bolt. I promise."

Sierra Hannaway stood beside the security desk, talking to a man with a ponytail and a goatee. He wore a white thigh-length lab coat, bell-bottoms, and sandals. A bohemian.

"Don't argue, Lissa. This guy could be a wacko. Either you let me install the alarm or I fly out there, lift prints, and investigate. What do you want to do?"

No response. Joe knew Melissa was getting angry.

The security guard handed Joe a pen and pointed to the visitors' log. Before signing, Joe looked over at Sierra. She and the man were watching him. She turned and said something to the man, but Joe couldn't hear what she said. He seemed to size up Joe. Then he walked away. The man was younger than Sierra, perhaps by ten years, but the way he'd stood next to her made Joe think they knew each other well, maybe intimately.

"I'm sure Shana would prefer an alarm system over my poking around the apartment and interviewing her boyfriend," Joe said. "What's his name?"

"Fine," Melissa said, her frustration obvious. "We'll do the alarm."

Joe didn't care if Melissa was upset with him. He didn't know what he would do if something happened to her. What he wanted to do was hop on a plane and check out the situation himself, but he knew that was overreacting. Or was it?

"How about I fly out there and spend a few days with you. Maybe we—"

"Dad. Stop it. You're doing it again. You're smothering me. I'm fine. We're fine. The alarm will be more than fine. No more. Please. I called you because I wanted you to know. Don't make me not want to call you when something happens."

Joe took a deep breath. "Okay. We'll do the alarm. I'll call you later. And get me the boyfriend's name."

"Dad!"

"I'll call you later." Then, in a low voice, he said, "I love you."

"You seem busy," Sierra said once he'd pocketed the phone. "Should I expect to be told you don't have time to work on my sister's case?" She was obviously still mad that he hadn't called her about the body. She'd been testy when they'd spoken earlier.

"That wasn't a case. It was my daughter. She's in New York, at college by herself. Her apartment was broken into. Couldn't wait. Sorry." He wasn't sorry.

He noticed something change in Sierra. Perhaps it was a shift in her stance or maybe her face softened. He wasn't sure.

"I apologize," she said. "I shouldn't have attacked you. I'm not used to anyone paying attention to my sister's case, and I want to yell at someone about it. I guess you're that someone."

They talked as they walked.

"I can understand your frustration," he said.

"I'm not sure you can," she replied, but her voice was soft, almost apologetic. "Hearing people give you lip service when you're trying to deal with your grief is difficult."

Joe thought about Christine. "I had a lot of doctors and specialists talking about hope and new advances when my wife got sick. In the end, I think the truth would have been easier."

She stopped walking and turned to face him. "I'm sorry again. I didn't mean . . . of course other people have loss. I wasn't—"

"It's okay," he said. "You're allowed to feel the way you do. There's no right way to deal with these things. Believe me, I know."

She looked into his eyes. "Thank you."

They were in the grand room of the museum now, the ceiling at least three stories high. A twenty-foot-tall *Tyrannosaurus rex* turned its head to Joe and opened its mouth, revealing two rows of massive teeth. An elephant-size *Triceratops* ignored the apparently hungry meat eater next to it and bobbed its head up and down, grazing on a mound of plastic foliage.

"Pretty neat, huh?" she said. "It's animatronics. The same engineers who design robotics for Disney built that."

"Kids must love it."

"When we have visiting classes, we have to post a guard next to the display to keep them from climbing on top of them or putting their arms in the *T. rex*'s mouth."

She led Joe around the left side of the two dinosaurs, into an alcove, and then down another corridor. They passed a set of double doors.

"What do you do here?" he asked.

"I'm the chief preparator. I actually work in the building next door, which is where we do our skeletal restorations and assembly. I also oversee our volunteer restorations and sometimes help set up displays. That's the fun part." They stopped at a glass-enclosed room, which allowed visitors a full view of the workers beyond. A sign read FOSSIL-WORKS. "This is where our volunteer preparators work."

An assortment of various-size metal tables lined the walls of the work space beyond. Three people sat at different stations, all of them hunched over, focused on the items on their individual tables. An older gentleman, possibly in his sixties, sat at the table closest to where Joe stood looking in. He wore a T-shirt showing a squatting dinosaur; it read COPROLITE HAPPENS! Joe grinned. In front of the man was a mound of soil and rock sitting in what looked like half of an egg the size of a baby's cradle.

"What's that?"

"The white part is a plaster mold, called a 'jacket.' We pour it over a fossil deposit out in the field and then dig down below the mold to scoop up that portion of sediment. He's extracting the jaw of a phytosaur," she said, pointing to an oar-shaped fossil next to the man. "A giant crocodile that prowled the floodplains in New Mexico in the late Triassic period. About five hundred fragments so far, all glued together."

An old woman sat at another table. She squinted through a large round magnifying glass that articulated on a mechanical arm attached to the edge of the table. She appeared to be working on a collection of small vertebrae. She held one of the tiny bones between her gloved thumb and forefinger and probed it with a dental pick.

Next to her sat another older gentleman. He rubbed a small animal's skull with a bright green-and-yellow toothbrush.

"I'll be right back," Sierra said. She walked through a door at the end of the glass wall.

Joe watched her through the glass, her white lab coat swishing this way and that. He appreciated her slim figure beneath, which swayed from side to side against the material, outlining her hips and legs.

The little pixie back at UNM had warmed his blood.

Joe turned his attention back to the volunteers. The old woman was looking at him. Their eyes met, and she smiled.

Sierra now stood at the center of the room. The three occupants turned to look at her. She said something that Joe couldn't hear, and the two men nodded and returned to their work. The old woman waved Sierra over. They exchanged a few words, and at one point the old woman stole a glance at Joe. Sierra shook her head. The old woman nodded. Sierra walked away, exiting through the same far door.

"Did she guess I was a cop?" Joe asked.

"No," she said.

He waited, but she didn't offer any further explanation.

"There's a conference room upstairs we can use," she said, and walked off.

Joe glanced back into the volunteer preparators' room. The old woman smiled and waved. He waved back, then turned and hurried after Sierra.

The conference room consisted of eight chairs arranged around an oval table. Sierra took a seat at the end closest to the door. An accordion folder already sat on the table. Joe chose the seat opposite hers. When he'd called to arrange this interview, they'd spoken about the recovered skeleton, so he felt comfortable starting with a different topic now.

"I spoke with Professor Trudle at UNM," he said. "He told me about the dig at Jones Ranch and that you were there when the congressman and your sister visited. Tell me what you remember about that day."

"I've played it over in my mind so many times. Down to the clothes I wore. Nothing stands out."

He flipped open his notepad and took out a pen. "Tell me what you remember."

She took a deep breath. "I have to go back about two months before the visit. That's when my sister called me. At the time, I was doing graduate work in anthropology at UNM; only later did I get into paleontology. She told me about a bill Arlen was working on to protect Native American artifacts and asked if there was someone at the university he could talk to for some background on the issue. I gave her Professor Trudle's name. Two months later, we had the theft at our dig site, and Professor Trudle asked me to tell Arlen. I called my sister. The next day, he and my sister came out to look at the site." Sierra paused. "She surprised me. I didn't know she'd be with him."

She stared at his notepad.

"You okay?" he asked.

"You're the first person in twenty years to take what I'm saying seriously."

"What do you mean?"

"I don't remember any of the other agents taking notes. All they did was ask about Arlen and Faye, and how they got along, if she ever talked to me about him."

"Some investigators don't take notes during an interview, but make them afterward," Joe said.

"No, that wasn't it. They were so damn convinced that he was guilty and my sister was his lover. You'd think we were talking about Bonnie and Clyde."

Joe wasn't about to argue with her. He'd started to feel the same way about the investigation. Over lunch, he'd reviewed Sierra's statement from back then and had not seen any mention of the dig site or Sierra's contact with Faye about the theft. Sierra had been mentioned only as Faye's sister. But the omission didn't mean the original agents were unaware of the connection. During an investigation, a lot of work is performed and a lot of people interviewed, but not everything makes it into a report.

"You're sure they visited the site the next day?"

"Yes."

"What time?"

"Early. Ten o'clock maybe."

If their disappearance had been planned, it had been planned the day before.

"How did she know where to go? The dig site doesn't sound like it was easy to get to."

"I gave her directions over the phone. We didn't have e-mail back then, and I didn't have access to a fax to send her a map."

"Where did you call her from?" Joe asked, looking for some clue as to who might have known about the visit.

"I drove to Gallup and used a pay phone in front of the courthouse. No cell phones back then, either."

"Who knew about the congressman's visit?"

"Hmmm. I never thought about that. I guess it was me, Lawrence, of course, Arlen, Faye, and Steve Mercado. He was another grad student working at the site. He's a professor now at UNM. Oh, and Nick, Arlen's driver."

"I notice your refer to the congressman as Arlen."

"I worked on his campaign. Even danced with him at his election party. He was a nice man. Not a bad dancer, either. I knew Nick, too."

Another omission from the file.

"Don't get offended, but I need to ask. Was the congressman a womanizer? Did you get any sense of that when you danced with him?"

"You're starting to sound like the others."

"All I'm asking for is the truth. You're an attractive woman." Joe realized belatedly what he'd just said, but he continued on without a pause. "When you danced with him, or spent time with him, did he ever make a pass, or in any way indicate he was—"

"No. Even when we danced, it was at a distance. You never met him, I'm sure, because if you had, you would know better. He was always a gentleman."

"I know you don't like the question, but I need to explore the possibility of another woman, and I don't mean Faye."

"I never saw anything that made me think he was stepping out on his wife. And Faye never said anything like that."

"Let's go back to the dig site. They arrive. Then what?"

"Then Steve and I head into Gallup to get water and supplies."

"What kind of supplies?"

"Is that important?"

"I don't know."

"I think it was gas for the generator," she said. "Yeah, I remember now. After the theft, Professor Trudle kept the site lights running all night, and that meant that the generator ran all night, too, so we needed gas. Also, I wanted to clean up. We used the showers at UNM-Gallup."

"So, when you and Steve went to Gallup, Professor Trudle was left alone with the congressman and Faye?"

"And Nick."

"And Nick. What do you know about Nick?"

"I think Faye said he was a writer. I didn't know him well. Only to say hi. His father called me after they went missing. He accused me of knowing where Nick was. He said that my sister was involved in the scandal with Edgerton and that they had pulled Nick into it. He was an old man and wanted to blame someone."

"How did he get your number?"

"You don't have any idea how big the media coverage was back then, do you? That was my fifteen minutes of fame."

He thought about his conversation with Gillian only the week before. "What were your fifteen minutes like?"

"The first two weeks, I had reporters camped outside my apartment. They were at my parents' house, too. And I received so many phone calls. Some threats, some support, mostly crazy people. My parents received calls, too. And some letters."

"Did any of the calls or letters have details about the disappearance?"

"My sister was either sunbathing on some South American beach or she was abducted by aliens. One person said that Edgerton was secretly an intergalactic ambassador. I don't know if people like that ever realize how much their foolishness hurts." She wiped at her brimming eye with the back of her hand and then picked up the accordion folder next to her and placed it in front of Joe. "Here are the letters and some newspaper clippings. I thought they might help."

He took his time going through the material. She waited patiently. He asked more questions about the case, about her sister, and about the congressman. When he felt he had covered everything, he asked for her opinion on what had happened. An opinion often provided good insight into how that person's mind worked. If she mentioned the Illuminati, he was out of here.

"I think someone killed them. I don't know why. Maybe because of that casino bill he was working on. Maybe because of some other bill. Maybe it was random. I don't know. But I do know my sister is dead, because there is no way she would just run away and cause me and my parents to worry all these years."

"Is there anyone you suspect?"

She didn't answer right away. "I always thought Faye's boyfriend, Bobby Lopez, could have done something to her. He always seemed a little . . . controlling. The jealous type. He works for the Albuquerque Police Department now. I saw him last year. We had some vandalism here. The creep actually hit on me."

Joe asked a few more questions about the boyfriend. When he'd finished, she asked, "Will you call me when you identify the body?"

"Yes."

She dabbed at her eyes with a tissue. "Please find my sister, Agent Evers."

"Sierra," a man's voice said.

They both turned. In the doorway stood the ponytailed man Sierra had been talking to at the security desk. Joe had pegged him as a bohemian. But now, he got a better look. Not bohemian. Ponytail was the guy on the cover of every romance novel, only he didn't have a torn shirt—yet.

Ponytail spoke. "I'm sorry to interrupt, but if we don't leave now, we're going to be late." He stared at Joe.

Joe thought the guy was going to lift his leg and mark his territory right then and there.

"That's fine, Ms. Hannaway," Joe said. "I have enough here to work on." He shoved the letters and envelopes back into the accordion folder. "I'll make copies and get the originals back to you."

❖

SEPTEMBER 30
THURSDAY, 8:35 P.M.
JOE EVERS'S APARTMENT, ALBUQUERQUE, NEW MEXICO

Joe reclined on the couch, feet up, a beer within easy reach. The Edgerton file was spread out around him, along with an empty bean burrito wrapper.

Sierra suspected Faye's boyfriend, Bobby Lopez, so he started with him. Lopez had served six years with the 101st Airborne Division and was part of Operation Urgent Fury, the U.S. invasion of Grenada in 1983. In June 1987, he received an honorable discharge and returned

to Albuquerque, his hometown. According to his interview, he'd met
Faye at a Veterans of Foreign Wars event. They started dating. Three
months later, he moved in with her. He was unemployed at the time.
The day Faye disappeared, he was at home watching soap operas and
The People's Court. Not much of an alibi. He was familiar with fire-
arms and had tactical training. Joe wrote "Bobby Lopez" on his legal
pad and jotted a few notes.

He spent the next hour going through the file, identifying everyone of interest to the investigation. He added their names to his list.
He planned to conduct a follow-up interview with each of them. He
hoped they were all alive. Time had a way of thinning out witness
lists in a cold case.

By his third beer, he had eight names written on his sheet. Not
many. All of them had been interviewed by the BIA agent who'd
headed the case, Malcolm Tsosie.

Joe had transferred to BIA from the old Immigration and Natu-
ralization Service, INS, long before it was rolled into Homeland Security after 9/11. During Joe's first year with BIA, Malcolm had
been put on suspension, so they'd never met. Back then, Joe had
been assigned to the Mescalero Apache reservation and was living
in Roswell. He'd spent little time in Albuquerque, where Malcolm
worked. Like Joe, Malcolm had also left under a cloud. If he remembered correctly, Malcolm had been investigated for excessive force.
He'd been on the Laguna reservation, interviewing a victim, when
the victim's neighbors began fighting. A domestic. Malcolm and another agent attempted to break it up. The irate husband punched
Malcolm, so Malcolm hit the man on the head with an expandable
baton, putting him in a coma for eight days. When the man came to,
he had no recollection of the incident, but Malcolm had already come
under investigation by then. Apparently, it wasn't his first violent

encounter. Rather than face a review board, Malcolm had quit. No retirement. Nothing. Malcolm was roughly Joe's age, so he was likely still working. Dale might know how to find him. They'd been partners at one time.

Reading the original investigation reports proved disappointing. All the interviews seemed to focus on Edgerton's affair and the investigation of casino gaming corruption. The day Edgerton went missing was the same day the Committee on Standards of Official Conduct, later renamed the House Committee on Ethics, announced it was opening a probe into allegations of bribery and corruption by Edgerton and Ellery Gates, a congressman from Oklahoma. Gates was mentioned in a number of the news stories about Edgerton. The congressional probe had focused on their joint sponsorship of the Indian Gaming Regulatory Bill and a number of significant money transfers to offshore accounts and to Gates's reelection campaign fund. As Joe had learned the day before, the source of the money was the nonprofit group Indigenous Peoples Self-Governance Foundation, which turned out to be a front funded by three international gaming corporations and two Oklahoma tribes. The corporations wanted favorable access to gaming on tribal lands. The tribes wanted less oversight. Both goals were compatible. A three-year investigation resulted in an opinion of corruption against Edgerton, but he was never found, so he never responded to the charges and never faced punishment. Ellery Gates, however, did face his peers. He was expelled from the House and fined by the IRS for failing to pay taxes on the income. No prison. Lucky bastard. The evidence against him was solid.

But now, after finding Edgerton's vehicle and a skeleton, Joe wasn't so sure the congressman had run off with the money. The case appeared much more sinister.

Joe read over his notes.

1. Bobby Lopez: boyfriend of Faye, former military, unemployed at time of disappearance, now police officer (jealousy?)
2. Grace Edgerton: wife (jealousy?)
3. Kendall Holmes: Edgerton's chief of staff, now senator (congressional inquiry? involved in bribery?)
4. Ellery Gates: traveled to New Mexico day of disappearance, involved in bribery, powerful, now living in Texas (protect himself in bribery inquiry?)
5. William Tom: director of Navajo Antiquities, later president of Navajo Nation (theft at archaeology site?)
6. Hawk Rushingwater: real name Dwight Henry, American Indian Movement, radical, sent vague threats (make example of Edgerton? prove himself?)
7. Dr. Lawrence Trudle: UNM archaeologist, last to meet with Edgerton, had artifacts stolen (motive unknown)
8. Sierra Hannaway: younger sister of Faye Hannaway (motive unknown)

The list was interesting but incomplete. He added another name.

9. Indigenous Peoples Self-Governance Foundation: bribed Edgerton and Gates, any one of the corporations or tribes (protect themselves in the investigation?)

He looked at his list again. Several good leads, but Stretch was right: Look for the simple motive. Bobby Lopez fit that nicely. Jealousy.

Joe sat in Captain Carmen Chavez's corner office at police headquarters. Their friendship went back years. They'd first met at a regional police shooting competition. Joe was good, but Chavez had proven better. She'd won four of the seven revolver matches, becoming the first female officer to ever achieve that honor. Several National Police Shooting plaques hung on her walls. "Good guy?" Joe asked. Chavez oversaw personnel, including Bobby Lopez.

"He's a sexist pig with a bad attitude and a worse temper," Chavez said. "He's had so many excessive-force complaints made against him that I keep his file in my desk. It saves time when I need to send it to IA." She shook her head. "Somehow he gets out of them."

A knock at the door.

"That's the prick now." She stood and came around the desk. "I'll let you talk to him in here while I grab a cup of coffee."

She called Lopez in and made the introductions. Joe showed his credentials and gave him a business card. They shook hands. Lopez's grip was a little too firm, his eye contact a little too long.

"I guess you can have a union rep if you want," Chavez said. "But Joe's questions concern a matter prior to your employment. It's your call."

When he learned it was about Faye Hannaway, Bobby agreed to talk.

Chavez nodded to Joe on her way out. He got the message: Good luck.

Lopez's gaze followed the captain's backside out the door. Chavez had this guy pegged.

"Thanks for talking to me. Can I call you Bobby?"

"That's my name."

Bobby dropped into the seat across from Joe and reclined as though not having a care. He was intimidating, with his tightly cropped blond hair slicked back, his compact frame, no neck, and powerful arms. Joe guessed steroids. The man before him looked like a G.I. Joe action figure. His name tag read B. LOPEZ.

"Is Bobby short for Robert?"

"Nope. Bobby Joe."

"Where're you from, Bobby?"

"I'm from Grants, *Joe.*"

Joe decided that trying to build rapport with this asshole would only waste time. "What can you tell me about Faye?"

"She ran off with that Edgerton fuck and left me on the hook for her apartment. She's a whore. Did you find her?"

"No, but I hope to."

"Drag her ass back here to New Mexico so everyone can see what a cunt she is."

Bobby had charm. "I take it you didn't care for her?"

"You must be a college boy."

Joe smiled. "Everyone seems to think Faye was having an affair with Edgerton. What do you think?"

"She'd spread her legs for anybody. I screwed her the night we met. That's why I moved in with her. Easy. Not someone you would take home to Mom, but okay in the sack."

Joe leaned forward, moving into Bobby's space. "I read in the file that when you met her you were unemployed and living at a veterans shelter. Then you moved in with her. I guess she was a free ride in every sense, right?"

Bobby was silent for several seconds. "Yeah, I got out of the army and was having difficulty finding a job."

"Discharged after Grenada. Did you suffer from PTSD when you got back?"

"Is that important, or are you just a nosy prick?"

Joe waited.

"I wasn't nuts. I had problems finding a job. So what? So did other guys. Grenada was a big cluster fuck." He rubbed the back of his forefinger over one eyebrow, then rubbed again. "Our friggin' commander ordered us to jump at seven hundred feet. No point in carrying a reserve, 'cause you don't have time to deploy it. So we carried extra ammo instead. We came in low and hot. The drop zone was an airfield. Do you know what it's like to hit asphalt and concrete coming in that low with extra weight? More than half my unit took leg injuries on landing. A big fucking cluster. All to get out a bunch of Commie students. Most didn't even wanna leave."

"That piss you off?"

"Hell yeah. A big fucking waste."

"Did Faye's affair with Edgerton piss you off, too?"

Bobby's nostrils flared. "Is that supposed to be your big interview technique? Surprise questions? Catch me off guard?"

"Wanted to see how you'd react."

"Do you have any real questions, or are you going to waste my time with bullshit?"

"Tell me what you were doing the day Faye went missing."

"It's in the file. Read it. You got a degree."

Joe embraced the silence; it was often an ally during interviews.

"I don't remember," Bobby said. "It was over twenty years ago."

"Everyone else seems to remember that day."

"I don't care about anyone else. I don't remember."

"Why are you different?"

"I said, I don't remember." Bobby's attention drifted to the desk. He seemed to find Captain Chavez's files interesting.

"Why?"

"I don't know."

"It's a simple question."

"I was drinking back then. And doing weed. I don't remember."

"Convenient."

"It's the fucking truth."

"Unemployed. Drinking. Drugs. A real catch."

"What?"

"Did you beat her, too? Offer her the deluxe package?"

"Fuck you." Bobby got up, yanked the door open, and walked out.

Joe silently chastised himself. He'd allowed the creep to get to him. Joe wasn't a tenderfoot. He knew better.

❖

OCTOBER 1

FRIDAY, 11:11 A.M.

GALLUP DISTRIBUTION, ROUTE 66, GALLUP, NEW MEXICO

A crowd of about seventy Native Americans milled along the sidewalk of Gallup Distribution. The facility, a small warehouse, distributed beer to regional bars and liquor stores. A few nonnatives also joined in the milling. It had rained earlier, so the ground was still wet. Some of the people carried umbrellas. They looked bored.

Cars passed by, tooting their horns in response to the hand-painted signs the protesters carried: HONK! TO STOP THE GENOCIDE;

ALCOHOL IS KILLING OUR NATIVE SONS & DAUGHTERS; STOP THE CON-
SPIRACY, JOIN NAVAJO NOW.

Bluehorse wasn't sure if the honkers agreed or were making fun of
the group. While he watched from his unit, which was parked at a
gas station a little ways down Route 66, a metallic blue Toyota with
extended chrome rims and tinted windows swerved close to the sidewalk where the protesters circled. The Toyota hit a small puddle along
the curb. Water sprayed, people jumped back, and cries of anger followed. An empty soda or beer can flew from the Toyota's passenger
side. The sound of it bouncing along the roadway carried all the way
to Bluehorse. The officer in the Gallup PD patrol car parked next to
his vehicle also had been watching the protesters and turned on his
flashers and took off after the troublemakers. Bluehorse put his Tahoe
in drive and headed over to the now partially wet group.

He pulled into the lot beside Gallup Distribution. Two employees
standing by the front door waved to him, probably hoping he would
move the group along.

Curious faces looked over from the protest group—unfriendly
faces. Before getting out, Bluehorse checked the driver's license photo
for Dwight Henry, aka Hawk Rushingwater. He spotted him.
Dwight stood to the edge of the crowd, drinking from a bottle of water,
carrying a red bullhorn, and staring at Bluehorse. Dwight's was one
of the unfriendly faces. So was the big heavyset man's next to him.
The big man wore a black T-shirt that read MY ANCESTORS SURVIVED
THE LONG WALK.

Bluehorse approached Dwight. The big man stepped forward,
standing in front of his little leader.

"Dwight Henry?" Bluehorse asked.

"This isn't the rez," the big man said.

"I wasn't talking to you."

"You don't have any authority off the rez, Mr. Police Officer. The white man makes sure of that."

"I thought your group was about protecting people's rights. Who needs authority to talk to someone?"

A skinny Navajo walked over. He wore thin wire-rim glasses and a polo shirt. "Hello, Officer. How can we be of help?"

"I need to talk to Dwight. Who are you?"

"I'm Sleeping Bear. And if you would, please refer to Dwight as Hawk. We use our spiritual names."

"Fine," Bluehorse said. He looked around the big man to Dwight. "Can we talk for a few minutes, Hawk?"

People started to drift over. Eavesdroppers.

"Can't you see I'm in the middle of a protest?"

"When would be a good time?"

The horn blasts from passing vehicles diminished now that the sign holders had left the sidewalk to gather around Bluehorse's little party.

Rushingwater stepped forward to stand beside his bodyguard. "What's it about?"

"I don't think you want to discuss it in front of all these people."

Rushingwater raised his hands. He still held the bullhorn. "I have nothing to hide from my oppressed brothers and sisters. We are all used to the white man's government trampling our rights as the great herds of buffalo once trampled these lands. We're mere cattle to the white man, and the reservation is our range."

Sleeping Bear said. "Buffalo? This isn't the—"

"I have no secrets," Rushingwater repeated, raising his voice, playing to the crowd. "What is this about?"

"It's about Arlen Edgerton," Bluehorse said.

The eavesdroppers seemed impressed. Heads turned to Rushingwater.

"Tell that reporter to get back here," Rushingwater said to Sleeping Bear. "Tell him the NPD wants to interrogate me regarding Congressman Arlen Edgerton's disappearance."

Sleeping Bear shook his head. "Hold on. Let's—"

"I didn't say that," Bluehorse said. The honking from passersby had entirely stopped. All seventy or so protesters formed a shoulder-to-shoulder ring around Bluehorse and Rushingwater.

"I heard you say it," a woman in her sixties said. "I'm a witness." She bore a mound of turquoise necklaces around her neck.

The heads around Bluehorse bobbed up and down like chickens at feed time.

The hair on the back of Bluehorse's neck jumped up and tried to get his attention, yelled at him to get the hell out of there. "Look, I just want contact information for you." Where was that Gallup officer? Was he still ticketing that knucklehead in the Toyota? He glanced over at the two employees by the front door. They were watching the show. Why didn't they call the police? Because they thought he was the police, that's why. If things went bad, Bluehorse would be on his own.

"Why do you want to know how to find him?" the old woman said. "So you can get him alone? Make him disappear?"

What was she talking about?

"Ask your questions here," Rushingwater said. "In front of my people. The people you sold out."

Someone bumped Bluehorse from behind. He moved his hand to cover his holster and turned to the threat. A wall of faces stared back.

"Okay, everyone, move back," Bluehorse ordered, his voice loud but slightly high-pitched.

"Are you afraid of your own people, officer man?" Rushingwater said.

Another bump. Bluehorse spun around and drew his Taser, afraid to draw his gun. *Get out of there!* his neck hair screamed.

"Whoa! Whoa!" Sleeping Bear yelled, arms raised, moving to stand beside Bluehorse. "This is a peaceful demonstration. Let's not get carried away. This officer only came to talk." He stepped forward, pushing his hands out toward the people. They moved back—slowly.

"Everyone just back up," Bluehorse said. He turned, showing the Taser to those around him. When the Taser moved in the direction of Rushingwater, the old woman reacted.

"He's going to shoot him!"

A fist caught Bluehorse on the left side of his head. His vision blurred. He staggered. Another blow glanced off the back of his head. He fought the reflex to fire the Taser. An arm wrapped around him.

"Stop! Back up! Back up!" It was Sleeping Bear standing next to Bluehorse, holding him up.

"What are you doing?" It was the same woman. "He tried to shoot Rushingwater!"

"Shut up, old woman!" Sleeping Bear started moving Bluehorse backward toward the vehicle. "Nightwind!"

A hand grabbed onto Bluehorse's right arm. He was turned around, walking forward now, his head clearing, his left ear ringing.

"That was stupid, man," Sleeping Bear whispered. "Never mess around with a crowd. Some of these people are crazy."

"Yeah," Bluehorse said, holstering his Taser. "Lesson learned." He shrugged off the helping hands. The crowd was moving back toward the road. "Which one hit me?"

"Come on. You know I can't say. I got you out of there. Be grateful."

Bluehorse looked from Sleeping Bear to the other man who'd helped him. It was the big guy with the Long Walk T-shirt. Nightwind. He didn't look pleased to have saved a cop.

"All right," Bluehorse said. "Thanks for your help. But I still need to talk to him."

"No one's stopping you. Just not here. We stay in a trailer three miles northeast of Chinle Chapter House."

"Why so helpful now?"

"Our supporters aren't around now," Sleeping Bear pointed with his lips toward Rushingwater, who was getting attaboys from the other protesters. "He can't look weak before the man."

"And I'm the man?"

Sleeping Bear grinned. "Today, you were the man."

❖

OCTOBER 1

FRIDAY, 11:31 A.M.

ALBUQUERQUE POLICE HEADQUARTERS, 400 ROMA

AVENUE NW, ALBUQUERQUE, NEW MEXICO

It was raining when Joe stepped outside onto the sidewalk. The clouds came in from the west, the smell of ozone strong. He had a pang of nostalgia and stopped to let the feeling manifest. The rain fell on him with a gentle patter. The memory took hold. The first time he'd met Christine. Twenty-two years ago. When he worked for INS. He'd traveled down to Roswell to interview an Iranian teacher on a work visa who taught math at Eastern New Mexico State University. It had rained that day. When he'd parked in the lot, he'd noticed a woman trying to lift a large box of papers out of her trunk. He'd offered her a hand and followed her inside. They'd dried themselves off with napkins from the cafeteria over a cup of coffee. She'd told him she taught English. That cup of coffee had lasted nearly an hour. Two years later, they were married. The following year, Joe took a transfer to BIA to stay in Roswell. Later, they moved to Albuquerque.

His phone rang.

The memory slipped away, and so did the feeling.

"This is Dr. Lineman with OMI," a female voice said when he answered. "I'm the forensic odontologist. I examined the jaw on the skull you brought in earlier this week. Sorry, I couldn't get to it sooner. I was at a seminar in St. Paul. I got back yesterday."

"Nice city. I'm sure you enjoyed it." Joe gave the response out of courtesy. He was anxious to hear what the doctor had found.

"Anyway, I called to tell you that I compared the skull to the dental records of Nicholas Garcia and I consider them a match. I'll have a report out to you in a couple of days."

No surprise there. Joe thanked her and clicked off.

By the time he reached his car, which was parked two blocks from the police headquarters, he was soaked. He hung his sport coat up on a hanger in the backseat to let it dry. Christine would have yelled at him for not taking an umbrella, and she would have sent his sports coat to the dry cleaner's the next day.

On the trip back to the office, he ticked off the list of people he had to notify about the identification. But there was one call he didn't have to make. Nick Garcia had no living relatives. No loved ones. No friends, except maybe Grace Edgerton—if she wasn't the one who'd killed him. What a way to leave this world. Remembered only as an entry in a cold case.

Joe decided to grab lunch instead of heading back to the office. He hadn't yet made any of the notification calls regarding Nicholas Garcia. Whether it was his encounter with Bobby Lopez or the rain, he didn't know, but he wasn't in the mood to call people and tell them someone they knew was dead. He supposed it shouldn't be that hard considering it had been over twenty years, but nevertheless.

No one had needed to notify Joe when Christine died. He'd been at her bedside all night. Melissa had been there, too. The doctors had told them that would be best. Christine had looked so thin, so pale, none of the rich Latin color that he found so sensual when they'd first met. She wore the Mickey Mouse head wrap. Joe had promised to take her and Melissa to Disneyland when she recovered, so Melissa had bought her mother the scarf soon after the chemo treatments began. When she'd first been diagnosed with pancreatic cancer, she'd been in stage 3, which meant it had spread to her lymphatic system. The doctors had been so quick to give them hope, but slow to render a prognosis. Cowards. Joe soon learned that stage 3 was a death sentence.

Now, as he sat at the bar, making his way through a solitary lunch, he realized it had rained the day Christine died. Rain served as bookends to their love.

"So you do lunch and dinner here?"

Gillian stood behind him. Her hair was pulled up, revealing a slender neck. Her beauty made him wince. Christine's neck had been slender as she lay dying, starving from a lack of appetite, a lack of will, worn out from her battle with a vicious and ruthless enemy, an enemy that gave no quarter. He put down his sandwich and grabbed a napkin, covering his mouth while he finished chewing. Then he swallowed. It stuck in his throat. He sipped his iced tea, trying to wash it—push it—down.

"Hi," he said.

"Hi."

Mickey waved to her from the other end of the counter. She waved back.

"I wanted to call you," Joe said. "I thought you might like to see a show tomorrow at a little theater in North Valley."

Her smile faltered. "I'm glad you're here. I wanted to talk to you, too."

His chest tingled. The bar wasn't full, yet he felt crowded.

"I got a call from my ex Wednesday. He broke up with his midlife hottie." She looked away, seeming to have an interest in the other customers.

Joe pushed out the stool next to him, moving it close to Gillian. "Do you want to sit and talk?"

"I have to get back with Sue and Linda."

Her two coworkers sat at a table in the dining area. They weren't their usual smiling selves.

"He wants to come back. We went to dinner last night. . . . I don't know . . . it's all so confusing. I mean, not you. We just met. But with him. It's confusing with him. We were together nineteen years. I feel I owe him at least a chance. At least that."

Joe wasn't sure what to say. He barely knew this woman. He had hoped to get to know her better, perhaps a lot better, but they were nothing more than acquaintances right now. She wasn't upset about their relationship, of course. He'd been around victims long enough to recognize confusion, and the emotions associated with it. Her ex had sprung a surprise on her, and she didn't know how to handle it.

"I think you should do whatever you feel is right. I would've liked an opportunity to get to know you better, I won't lie about that, but I also think nineteen years is a lot of history. I know if it was me, I'd be kicking myself right now, mad that I ever let you go."

She didn't say anything.

"Your friends are waiting for you," he said. "I have a feeling they're eager to give you advice."

She looked back at Sue and Linda. "They are."

"I'm glad you have someone to talk to," he said. "Let me know how things go."

"Thanks, Joe." She stood there a moment, awkward, her eyes searching, meeting his, lingering. Then she walked away.

He turned back to his plate, no longer hungry. He hadn't known Gillian except for a single dinner date, a friendly meal, but he had liked her, and had really wanted to see her again.

Mickey came over. "You look like you just lost the big game. What's up?"

"Give me a beer."

❖

OCTOBER 1
FRIDAY, 2:10 P.M.
BUREAU OF INDIAN AFFAIRS, OFFICE OF INVESTIGATIONS,
ALBUQUERQUE, NEW MEXICO

After lunch, Joe had stopped at a Walgreens and picked up a pack of Life Savers. He used to call them "Job Savers" back when he worried about Dale finding out he'd tipped one back midday.

But he didn't care anymore. What could Dale do now? Joe would be out by Christmas. Ho ho ho.

When Joe told him about Nick Garcia, Dale said to hold off releasing the news for an hour, until he notified D.C. So Joe waited. He was playing the game, keeping Dale happy.

Work proved to be good therapy. It helped push Gillian from his mind. He hadn't considered before now what finding Nick Garcia's body would mean to the investigation. It made the theory that Edgerton and Faye had run away together that much more feasible. If either one of them had been found, it would have changed things considerably. But that wasn't the case. The dogs had combed the area around the vehicle. Only one body.

Joe pulled out a photo of Nick from the file. The driver/would-be writer wore a tux and stood next to a woman in a pink fluffy dress. A wedding photo? Joe hadn't found any mention of Nick's friends in the file. Malcolm, the lead investigator at the time, had sure done a real bang-up job. So much for a thorough investigation. Joe studied the picture, trying to get a feel for the dead man. Nick looked happy. He was big and round, and he fit the stereotype of the jolly fat guy. He also wore glasses, which hadn't been found with the body. Joe stared at the photo. He was missing something. He could feel it. Why would Edgerton kill this man? A friend. It would have been much easier for the congressman simply to drive himself that day. Give Nick the day off. No, Edgerton hadn't killed him. He was sure of it now. What about Faye? Could Faye have killed Nick and Edgerton? If so, then where was Edgerton's body? And how could Faye have dragged Nick so far from the vehicle to bury him? And how did she get out of there? She'd left the vehicle, so she would have needed a ride, someone to pick her up. She could have stashed a car nearby, but she would still have needed someone to get her back to Albuquerque. Bobby Lopez? It didn't make sense.

Then it hit him. *Drag the body.* Nick was big. Too heavy to drag too far. No, they hadn't found the others because they were buried much farther away. The killer would have figured that someday the vehicle would be found, so he or she would have wanted to drag the bodies as far as possible so they wouldn't be found. But Nick had been too big. Too heavy. He checked Nick's driver's license. Five nine, 285 pounds. The others were out there. Joe felt certain of it. He would get the dogs out again and expand the search area. The killer had been careful. Thorough. Had taken the vehicle to a desolate location, a place that had been even more desolate twenty years ago. The person had known Edgerton was at Professor Trudle's dig site that day and had probably known the area, or at least had scoped out the dump site. Who knew the area? Joe checked his list of suspects. The AIM member, Hawk Rushingwater. He was from the reservation. Joe pulled his interview. Rushingwater had been living in Mentmore twenty years ago, which was on the west side of Gallup. Not far from the dump location, maybe fifteen miles. Rushingwater probably would have known the area. Joe grabbed his list of suspects and wrote "From Mentmore" next to Rushingwater's name. Wait. Rushingwater wouldn't have known Edgerton would be out there that day, would he?

He flipped through his case notes. Rushingwater seemed the most likely suspect right now, but Arthur Othmann was also an interesting lead. The art collector might have found out about Edgerton's visit if he were connected with William Tom and had been following other digs around the state. Joe still needed to work out the whole Othmann angle. Joe tried to plug everyone into their own little hole on his game board. Othmann just wasn't fitting. Yet.

Stretch's advice came back to him, and he reminded himself to keep it simple. He needed more on Othmann before he could even theorize about his involvement. And if he did decide to talk to him, he would need something more concrete than an accusation from a slightly animated professor.

William Tom was also a good suspect. Very good. He knew the area and could have known about Edgerton's visit. He might even give Joe something more on Othmann. Professor Trudle had been passionate about the connection between William Tom and Othmann's black-market art dealings. He decided to talk to the former president of the Navajo Nation next.

Joe checked the time. Dale's one hour was up.

He called Sierra.

She took the news well at first, but when he asked if she knew of any of Nick's friends, she started to cry. She said she needed to call him back later.

Next, he phoned Grace Edgerton. She took his call while in a meeting. When he told her the body was that of Nick Garcia, she said, "I see." He thought he picked up disappointment in her voice, which he supposed was appropriate. She probably wanted it to be her husband's body. It would mean for certain that he hadn't run off with Faye.

She asked what he planned to do next.

He didn't hesitate. "Continue my investigation."

"Thank you," she said, her voice warm, genuine.

The next call, he liked least of all. But he'd promised.

"Joey," Helena Newridge said. "I thought you'd forgotten about me."

"I don't think you let anyone ever forget about you."

She laughed. "You're right. I'm guessing you identified the body."

"Nicholas Garcia. OMI identified him from dental records."

"Damn." That made two people who were disappointed.

"Is Garcia's dead body not good enough for you?"

"No. Of course not. That's not it. But finding Edgerton or Faye would have changed the whole case."

Joe agreed but didn't say anything.

She continued: "When I spoke to the wife, she said an AIM member had sent her husband some threatening letters. I'm guessing she wants to throw suspicion elsewhere. Anywhere but on her. It's a good lead, but she doesn't remember the name of the person. What do you say?"

He contemplated giving it to her.

"You still there?"

"Hold on. I'm thinking."

"About his name?"

"About giving it to you."

"Oh, come on. I thought we were gumbas. I scratch your back. You scratch mine. Kind of like bathtub buddies."

"I'm thinking how I want to be scratched."

"Are you flirtin'?"

Joe didn't answer. He was still weighing the pros and cons of telling her.

"Here's the deal," he said. "I give you the name and you run a search for any news reports on the guy and then check it with your source. You also run anything you have about AIM on the Navajo reservation."

"No prob—"

"I'm not done. You hold off on the story till I say when."

There was a pause on the other end. Then she said, "I'll hold off a week."

"I still need to interview him. We're trying to find him."

"Okay, but don't take too long, Joey," she said. "I need something for my editor." There was a hint of desperation in her voice.

He told her about Dwight Henry, aka Hawk Rushingwater.

Officer Bobby Joe Lopez sipped from his large McDonald's Coke as he cruised down Central Avenue. He should switch to diet. The sodas were costing him an extra hour in the gym each week. He had put in a request to transfer to the bike unit for the summer, but it had been denied. That bitch Chavez had probably squashed it. She had it in for him. He could tell by the way she spoke to him. She knew he didn't go for old Mexican chicks. He'd caught her staring at him once. It wasn't his problem she was ass-ugly and looked like an overstuffed burrito. He made exceptions for mature women who took care of themselves, like his sergeant's wife, Vicky. They'd met at the police barbecue last summer. Now, every time Sarge fucked with him, he fucked her. She'd been so exhausted after their last rodeo together, she hadn't known he'd snapped a few photos of her sprawled out on the bed—Sarge's bed—naked and covered in Bobby Joe's sweat. Vicky had smelled of rough sex and cheating. Just like that bitch Faye. He'd loved Faye, and she'd broken his heart with that prick Edgerton. They were all cheats. All of them. Nothing but sluts. And that's how he used them, too, *slut machines*. Like the nickel slots at a casino, only good for deposits, never a worthwhile jackpot or a lifetime payout. He took out his phone and pulled up the photos of Vicky. A little loose around the middle, but she had a nice can. Maybe he'd text her later. When he got tired of her, he might send the images to Sarge, anonymously of course. He knew she was banging other guys, probably other cops. She'd never know he sent them. Woman just couldn't lock it up. He had suspected Faye was fucking more than just Edgerton. She'd been a little too friendly with the other guy in her office. He was a senator now. Bobby Joe had seen his campaign ads and recognized him. The guy hadn't looked like he did when he'd worked with her. He'd worn tinted glasses then, to hide his two different-colored eyes. Bobby Joe had joked, calling him "The Crayola Kid." Faye hadn't laughed. That's how he'd known. The guy belonged in a circus, not Congress. Bobby Joe grinned. Congress was a circus.

His radio squawked. "Ten-ten, Pine and Gold Avenue."

Bobby took the call. He flicked on his lights and sirens and accelerated to forty-five on Central Avenue, weaving through midafternoon traffic. He blasted through a red light at University Boulevard, almost getting T-boned by a FedEx truck. At Pine Street, he turned left and raced one block to Gold. He hung another left and stopped in the middle of the street. Two men in their twenties, both in white tank tops, were fighting in front of a tricked-out gold Cadillac. The skinnier of the two looked to be losing. Blood covered his face and the front of his shirt. A small group of onlookers watched, doing nothing. A girl screamed and stood crying by the car. Probably the skinny guy's girlfriend. She had a nice rack. Big and round.

Bobby got out, stretched his neck left, then right, flicked his expandable steel baton to its full length, and ran over to break it up—or break some heads. He felt pumped. He hoped one of them would resist. Then he'd pretend it was that BIA asshole and break his fucking skull.

Joe called Bluehorse, but before he could tell him about OMI's identification of Nick Garcia, Bluehorse told him about his encounter with Rushingwater.

"He was smiling when I got hit," Bluehorse said.

"Did you arrest anyone? Gallup PD help?"

"No," Bluehorse said, regret in his voice. "There was another guy. He was pretty levelheaded. He got me out of there and said I shouldn't ramp it up because Rushingwater might not talk to us if I did. His name is Sleeping Bear. He's Rushingwater's deputy or lieutenant. Something like that."

"Rushingwater. Sleeping Bear. These guys sound like a bad Western." Joe was familiar with family names on the Navajo reservation. These were clearly meant for impact.

"They're into native revival. Going back to their roots. Shedding the white man's influence."

"They sound more like a *National Geographic* special than a native movement." Joe bit his lip as soon as he'd said it. He hadn't meant to be insensitive. He was simply frustrated for Bluehorse and angry at the protesters. A crowd mentality was dangerous. The young officer could have been hurt.

"Anyway," Bluehorse said, seeming to ignore the comment, "Sleeping Bear told me where they stay in Chinle. This weekend, they

have rallies at a few beer distributors in Gallup and Holbrook, but I
don't think we should try that again."

"We'll catch them in Chinle next week." Joe told him about
OMI's identification of Nick Garcia.

"Does that help us?" Bluehorse asked.

"I don't know. But I want to get the dogs out there again and widen
the search area. Also, I spoke to that professor at UNM, the archaeologist." Joe gave Bluehorse a summary of what Professor Trudle had told
him, but he played down William Tom's suspected involvement in
the theft of the artifacts, saying only that the former president might
know something about Edgerton's visit to the site. "Do you want to
be there when I talk to him?"

Silence. Joe waited. He knew it could be a political minefield for
Bluehorse, but he wanted to give him the chance to be part of the
interview.

"What information is he supposed to have?" Bluehorse asked.

"I don't know."

More silence.

"I take it you don't want me asking permission."

"You are correct, sir," Joe said, imitating Ed McMahon from his
Tonight Show days. He thought the humor might lighten a heavy decision for the Navajo officer.

Bluehorse didn't respond. Joe wondered if Bluehorse even knew
who Johnny Carson was.

Bluehorse had a difficult decision. Even though Tom was out of
office, he probably still had a few chits owed to him, and he could
use them to cause Bluehorse trouble, maybe even his job. Navajo
politics suffered from favoritism and protectionism and plain old
bullshitism. Doing the right thing on the reservation didn't matter
much if it made someone in power look bad.

"I'm in," the young officer said.

He'd judged him right. "You're okay in my book, Bluehorse."

"I hope your book has a help wanted section for when they fire my crazy Indian ass."

"When the shit hits the fan, tell them I dragged you along to translate."

"You think I don't know about the white man's defense. I plan to toss you under the wagon wheel at the first sign of trouble."

❖

Arthur Othmann popped up in my investigation." Joe said, his notepad flipped open in his hand.

Stretch, who was sitting at his desk, turned to face him. "What do you mean?"

"A professor named him as a possible person of interest. What's the dirt on him?"

Stretch looked confused, but he answered. "He's from Santa Fe. Rich. I'm told he has the largest collection of Indian art outside of the Smithsonian."

"And he might be a murderer," Sadi said as she came out from her cubicle, which adjoined Stretch's.

"That's all conjecture," Stretch said. "We don't have anything solid on him. A lot of rumors, that's all."

Sadi moved closer to Joe. "And one missing person."

"Your grand jury witness?" Joe asked.

"Eddie's facing at least five on the child rap even if he flips on Othmann," Stretch said. "I'm betting he ran."

"We checked his house," Sadi said, incredulity in her voice. "He left everything. His clothes. His money. Even his pot. You think he just up and left? Bullshit."

Joe asked, "What do you have on his black-market activities?"

"Oh, no, no, no." Sadi shook her head. "You first. Othmann is our case. Spill. How's he tied to Edgerton?"

"I spoke to an archaeologist at UNM. He thinks Othmann bought artifacts that were stolen from the dig site that Edgerton visited the day he disappeared."

Stretch asked, "How did your archaeologist come up with his name?"

"Not real clear. He says Othmann is a big-time dealer in native art and artifacts. Retail and black market."

"That's pretty weak," Stretch said. "Anyone in the state who deals in native art would know him. He's local and he has money."

"Maybe," Sadi said, "but that sounds like our guy's MO."

Joe turned his attention to her. "Tell me about him."

Sadi's eyes narrowed, but she filled him in. "He was probably just getting started when Edgerton went missing. We don't have much on him from back then. He's a collector. Loves native art. If he touches antiquities, it's usually art items. Pottery, drawings, rugs. He's rich, probably ten or twenty million. Family money. Dad owned a number of mines—silver, nickel, and coal. He went off to school to learn business but came back an art snob and liking white powder."

Joe made some notes.

Sadi continued: "He has a private fortress in Santa Fe, complete with bodyguard."

"David Drud, aka Books," Stretch said. "Interesting story there.

When Books was in juvie, he was molested by one of the counselors. One night, while he was being counseled in the library, David grabs a *Webster's Unabridged Dictionary,* one of the big ones that you can use as a step stool, and bashes the guy over the head with it. Repeatedly. They find the guy's brains under *M,* for *mush.* After that, people called him Books. It stuck. He's been a suspect in several murders over the years and spent six inside for agg assault."

"Was Books with Othmann twenty years ago?"

"No," Sadi said. "Othmann's had a string of muscle over the years. Books is the latest. I don't know who he had back then." She looked at Stretch. "You?"

Stretch shook his head.

"You think Othmann is capable of murder?" Joe asked.

"Hell yeah," Sadi said. "But what's the motive for Edgerton? How do you tie him to Othmann?"

"NAGPRA."

Stretch laughed. "NAGPRA wasn't passed until 1990. Edgerton went missing in '88."

"Edgerton was an original cosponsor. The bill was making its way around Congress in '88."

"That's pretty far out there," Sadi said. "He's smart, but that's way too forward-thinking even for him. Kill a congressman to kill a piece of legislation? I don't buy it."

Joe wasn't surprised. "Neither do I, but the connection is interesting. And I think it's worth checking out."

"Why don't you let us run it down?" Stretch asked.

"No, I'll check it out. I might pay him a visit."

"The hell you will." Sadi stabbed a finger at Joe. "He's ours. Check him out all you want, but don't go talking to him and tipping him off."

"Relax, Sadi," Stretch said. "He's only following a lead. We may not even have a case if our guy doesn't show up soon."

"You get anything, you give it to us," Sadi said. "He's been on our radar for the past three years, and we haven't been able to get shit on him."

"Three years? I have less than three months. If he's involved in Edgerton's disappearance, he's mine."

"No fucking way." Her face was red.

"Sorry, Sadi, but I'm short on time. If I need to talk to him, I will." She turned and stormed into her cubicle. "Asshole."

The office bespoke statesmanship. The navy-and-gold-striped settee, blue leather wing chair, polished wood tables and bookshelves, and the many photos of Holmes with the who's who of Washington, as well as a few favorable Hollywood personalities, were all appropriate for a true statesman, a leader of the free world. Not *the* leader. Not yet. But one of its leaders. He'd solidified that position when he took his post on the Appropriations Committee six years ago. He would soon be appointed to the Foreign Relations Committee, which would give him the necessary international credentials to make a viable run in the presidential primary in five years. That is, if this whole Edgerton drama didn't derail his plans before he could deposit his first campaign contribution.

So far, the press hadn't set their sights on him. There had been some comments on a few political blogs referring to him as Edgerton's policy guru, which were both a compliment and a slight, because

they implied he had a lot of influence on the Indian gaming legislation. The other knocks came from a few comedians. One particularly
popular political satirist had made a sly comment that Senator Holmes
brought a lot of professional experience to the Appropriations Committee with his gambling and corruption background. Then he followed that with a joke about appointing a cat as head of security in a
tuna factory. Something smells fishy. *Ba dum bum.*

Holmes looked up from his computer when his head of security
walked into the office. He'd been reading through articles sent to him
by his news-clipping service, which gave him a daily accounting of all
items mentioning his name. He needed to stay on top of the Edgerton
debacle, so he'd been diligently reading every word of every write-up.
The number of blogs had become overwhelming, and those authors
were more willing to voice opinions based on nothing but conjecture. That was troubling.

"Helena Newridge called again," Malcolm Tsosie said. He stood
almost at attention, shoulders back, hands at his sides, but with the
relaxed posture of a person who had no need to impress and no
desire to be subservient.

Senator Holmes imagined that was how proud Indian chiefs had
stood when they first met representatives of the United States government centuries back. They thought they were on equal footing, but
they weren't. Malcolm had grown a little too comfortable over the
years. A little too in the know. Holmes might have to deal with him
someday. But not now. Not with the Edgerton mess mucking up the
works. Malcolm had a talent for those things. A talent for dealing with
law enforcement and for getting information.

"Did she say what she wanted?"

"What do you think?"

And a little too cocky, too.

Holmes debated if he should call her back. He believed in Sun

Tzu's advice: Keep your enemies closer. Newridge could be his enemy one day. All journalists were potential enemies to a politician. He wanted to know what she knew. He pulled out her business card, which she'd given to him over breakfast. Thin card stock. Cheap. It had her cell phone number on the back, written in purple ink. He dialed, then waved for Malcolm to take a seat.

"Hello, Helena." He used her first name. Make her feel like a friend. Her abrasive voice came through the earpiece, and he rubbed his brow as though his brain ached.

"Threats from an AIM member on the Navajo reservation?" he said, more for Malcolm's ears than to infer thoughtfulness. "Yes, I do remember something about that."

His brain didn't ache so much now.

❖

OCTOBER 1
FRIDAY, 5:14 P.M.
BUREAU OF INDIAN AFFAIRS, OFFICE OF INVESTIGATIONS,
ALBUQUERQUE, NEW MEXICO

On his way out of the office, Joe stopped at Stretch's desk. Sadi was in her cubicle, on the phone.

Joe whispered, "Send me what you have on Othmann and Books."

"Man, you're messing with fire. She will kick your ass."

Joe grinned.

"I'm serious," Stretch said. "She's taking this whole grand jury thing personal. And anyway, Sadi's right. We know these characters. Let us run it down."

"I need it. I need to climb back on the horse."

"What is this, a Western? You get back up on the horse and what? You ride off into the sunset?"

"Something like that."

"You're losing it, cowboy."

"Maybe. Or maybe I want to get a little justice for the skeleton we found in the woods."

"Wow. That's not just any horse you're riding. That there's a high horse."

❖

OCTOBER 1
FRIDAY, 5:32 P.M.
MICKEY'S BAR & GRILL, ALBUQUERQUE, NEW MEXICO

Mickey stood behind the counter, filling two pints of draft. The bar was full, the Friday-night crowd packed in tight. Joe got lucky and found a seat at the counter, behind the beer taps, Mickey's post during happy hour. Throughout the night, the other two bartenders would give Mickey their draft orders, and he would fill them, giving each pint a perfect head.

"What's the good word, Joe?"

"I need new coworkers and a new boss."

"Ever think it was you?"

Joe didn't answer.

"Dale's not so bad," Mickey said. "But I guess everyone hates their boss."

"You're a boss."

"Yeah, but I'm the exception."

"I don't think Serafina would agree."

"Serafina," Mickey yelled. "Am I a good boss?"

She carried several plates of Combos on her way to the dining room. "Pretty good, except when you're here."

A group of patrons at the bar laughed.

"Remember that when you ask for a raise."

She launched into fast Spanish, which did not sound complimentary.

Mickey walked to the end of the counter, his limp not so noticeable tonight. He grabbed the white towel that he kept draped over his shoulder and tossed it into a metal bucket that sat on the floor. He picked up a fresh one from the folded pile on the back shelf and whipped it into place on the same shoulder. Joe watched in a seeming trance. Maybe he could leave BIA, start fresh like that towel.

Mickey returned to his post.

"You hiring?" Joe asked.

"For what, kitchen help?"

"Behind the bar."

"You?"

"Yeah, I'm looking for a change."

"My patrons have enough of their own troubles. You think they wanna hear yours?"

Mickey was joking, but Joe figured there was an element of truth lurking in the comment.

"And besides, you have to go to bartending school. That and tight buns get you good tips. Customers like tight buns."

"Explains your success."

One of the two female bartenders called an order to Mickey. Joe noticed she did indeed have tight buns.

"Has Gillian been in tonight?"

"No, but Linda and Sue are here." Mickey pointed. "They're entertaining a couple of attorneys."

Joe looked. Linda and Sue were putting on a show, laughing and shouting. He could hear them now. He wondered why he hadn't noticed them before. The two men looked like corporate types, dark suits, ties pulled down.

"You want a soda? I saw you taking it easy with Gillian."

No need to impress her anymore.

But there was Melissa.

"Soda sounds fine."

❖

OCTOBER 2
SATURDAY, 9:07 A.M.
RESIDENCE OF WILLIAM TOM, FORT DEFIANCE
(NAVAJO NATION), ARIZONA

Joe pressed the doorbell beside William Tom's front door. An extravagance for the rez. Most houses didn't have electricity. And the owners of those that did were unlikely to waste money on such trivialities as a doorbell.

The house, a single-story adobe structure with a gravel driveway, was not a mansion in any sense of the word, even for the reservation, but it was nice, secluded at the base of a red mesa in the westernmost corner of Fort Defiance, Arizona. A wooden ramp led up to the front door. At the bottom of the ramp, a mutt sat on his haunches, watching Joe and Bluehorse. The dog had been friendly enough, and Joe had given him a treat, which he kept in his vehicle for just such an occasion. The vast majority of the dogs on the rez were not house dogs and not chained. Knocking on a strange door was often risky business. If a dog ignored a treat, Joe took that as fair warning not to step out of his vehicle.

From inside the house came a muffled male voice, angry—someone yelling about the door.

Officer Bluehorse stood next to Joe on the porch. He leaned over and whispered. "You know about his leg?"

Joe's bewildered look was answer enough.

"He lost it a few years back," Bluehorse said, "Diabetes, I think."

Joe looked at the wooden ramp. "Is he going to play sick?"

"He spoke at the county fair last year. He seemed okay then."

A woman's voice shouted from behind the door. "Shut up, old man."

The door swung open, revealing a fortyish Navajo woman with long hair, a too-slim body, and a face that seemed rubbed raw by rough living. Joe suspected alcohol, but she also had the premature aging of a meth user. The top three buttons of her denim shirt were undone, revealing the slopes of two sagging breasts. He guessed she had been pretty once upon a time, but now it was just a fairy tale. Life had been hard on her, or she'd been hard on life.

"*Yah-ta-hey*," Bluehorse greeted the woman. "We're here to see Mr. Tom?"

The woman smiled, showing off her meth mouth. "Is he in trouble? Are you here to arrest him?"

"No." Bluehorse said. "Only to talk."

Her smile dissipated. "About what?"

"Is he home, ma'am?" Joe asked.

"What's it about?"

"He can share that with you if he wants," Joe said. "But that'll be his decision."

A male voice called from inside. "Char! Who is it?"

The woman, who Joe guessed was Char, looked from Joe to Bluehorse, then back to Joe.

"Is it about me?"

"Is there something about you we should know?" Joe asked.

That seemed to stop her. She turned and yelled into the house. "It's the men in blue. They're here to see you, old man." She looked back to Joe. "If you take him, take his wheels, too." She disappeared inside, leaving the door open.

Bluehorse walked in. Joe followed, shutting the door behind him.

The interior was dark and smelled of left-out food and sickness. They walked down a short hallway that opened into a kitchen on the left and a living room on the right. The rooms were decorated in a southwestern motif, with Navajo rugs adorning the walls and wood beams crossing the ceiling. Beyond the living room, another hallway led to several closed doors—bedrooms most likely. The last door along the hallway slammed closed: Char's disappearing act.

The occupants of this house did not appear concerned with housekeeping. Balled-up blankets and discarded clothing ornamented the furniture. Opened and unopened mail littered every flat surface. And a haphazard stack of newspapers, more than a foot high, teetered in the corner.

"What can I do for you, Officers? And please pardon my appearance. I was not expecting company." The voice was that of an old man, and it betrayed some annoyance. William Tom rolled forward in a wheelchair from the kitchen. He wore plaid pajama bottoms and a white T-shirt, though *white* was generous. His right pajama leg dangled from the chair's seat in acknowledgment of his missing extremity.

"Mr. Tom, my name is Randall Bluehorse. I'm out of Window Rock. This is Joe Evers. He's an agent with BIA."

"An agent? What brings you to my home, Agent?"

William Tom's voice was cultured. He articulated every word slowly and clearly, as though speaking to someone who might have difficulty understanding him.

"I'm investigating the disappearance of Arlen Edgerton."

"Arlen Edgerton?" The old man rolled the name around in his mouth as though savoring the syllables. "The name sounds familiar. My memory is not what it used to be."

"Congressman Edgerton," Joe said. "He went missing about twenty years ago. Officer Bluehorse recently found his car."

"Oh, yes. Congressman Edgerton. I recall his disappearance." William Tom looked at Bluehorse. "What's so urgent that NPD and BIA couldn't call first? Your visit has upset my wife."

"That was your wife?" Joe said without thinking.

"Is there a problem?"

Joe thought it was obvious, but he said nothing.

"So what is so important that you had to show up unannounced?"

"Officer Bluehorse is only accompanying me today. He's not conducting this interview."

"Well, speak. What is this all about?"

"Perhaps it would be better if we talk in the kitchen."

"Here is fine."

People who tried to make the police feel uncomfortable usually had something to hide or were simply ignorant. Joe doubted that the man before him was the latter.

"I don't think you want your wife to hear our discussion."

William Tom looked past Joe, toward the bedroom door. "Fine," he said. He wheeled himself around and back into the kitchen.

Joe and Bluehorse each took a seat at a wooden table. William Tom tucked himself under the other side, a half-eaten green chili burrito between them.

"Sorry if we interrupted your breakfast," Joe said.

William Tom pushed the plate to the side without answering.

"Please tell us what you know about Congressman Edgerton."

"I'm sure this will be a short discussion. I don't know anything about him. I never met him. I never voted for him. I never spoke to him. Are we done?"

"Mr. Tom, I don't understand why you're being so short with us. We're following up on a lead concerning his disappearance. I'm sure you would want to help if you could, right?"

"What I don't understand is why you are here. What fresh lead?"

"What was your position with the Navajo Nation in 1988?"

"Agent Evers, I already told you my memory is not what it used to be."

"Were you the director of Navajo Antiquities back then?"

William Tom was thoughtful. "Yes. What does that have to do with the congressman's disappearance?"

So William Tom was going to play along. The old man wanted to know what Joe knew. But there was something else. Something the old man didn't want Joe to know.

"Tell me about Professor Lawrence Trudle."

William Tom's eyebrows dropped low and his eyes darkened. "What about him?"

"I understand he was conducting an excavation that you were overseeing for the Navajo Nation."

"I oversaw many excavations while I was director."

"The one I'm asking about was the last place the congressman was seen before his disappearance."

"Just because I oversaw all the archaeological sites on the reservation doesn't mean I spent much time at them. I conducted inspections and audited all recovered items, logging them in our artifacts inventory. That was how we kept track of everything found. We lost too much of our culture over the last century through self-proclaimed do-good museums and universities. They raped our history."

"That was why the congressman visited Professor Trudle's site." Joe watched the old man as he spoke. "He was working on legislation to protect Indian culture. He was looking into the theft of a number of artifacts, which the professor had unearthed."

William Tom leaned back in his seat. "Yes, now I remember. We had several thefts at different sites that year, and the following year, too. I believe the professor wrote a book on those missing artifacts. I read it years ago. He tried to link the Anasazi to the Aztecs. A lot of theory but no evidence. Shameful research. Rather pathetic."

Bluehorse stayed silent, but Joe saw that he was watching William Tom intently.

"What did you do at Professor Trudle's site?"

"Are you accusing me of something?"

"I'm investigating the congressman's disappearance. I'm talking to everyone and anyone related to the case. You were overseeing the site the congressman visited. And I have people telling me you might know something about the theft of the artifacts."

The old man put both of his hands flat on the kitchen table, as if to push himself to a standing position.

"Have you forgotten who you're talking to, Special Agent? I am the former president of the Navajo Nation. And I would think that title would grant me a little courtesy and perhaps a little protocol, too. How dare you come to my home and accuse me of being involved in some theft of trinkets from two decades ago."

"I don't think we're talking about trinkets, Mr. Tom. And I wouldn't be here if I didn't have a reason to talk to you." As Joe said this, he started to doubt his position. After all, this visit was based solely on the professor's suspicion.

"I think we're done here, Agent." William Tom turned to Blue-horse. "And I will have a discussion with your commander about why you brought this man to my home. It is Officer Bluehorse, right?"

"Yes, sir," Bluehorse said, his voice a tad shaky.

Joe had one card to play. "Tell me about Arthur Othmann, Mr. Tom."

That seemed to curb the old man's anger. The lines on his face deepened into shadowed crevices of age and defeat. He looked at Joe and then down at his own hands. The old man had spent what little energy he had on that display of indignation. Joe had called his bluff, and the old man's resolve had faltered.

"I am a sick man. I don't understand why you're doing this to me. Trying to tarnish what I've done for my people. I—"

Now Joe simply needed to make the old man feel safe in revealing his secrets. "Mr. Tom, I'm just trying to find out what happened to the congressman, that's all. I'm not trying to tarnish your reputation or that of the Navajo presidency. Help me. Tell me what you know about Arthur Othmann."

"He's a collector. And a powerful man. His money has helped many Navajo."

Joe chose his words carefully. "Did he collect the items from Professor Trudle's site?"

The former president of the largest Indian reservation in the world hung his head like a schoolkid caught cheating on a test. "You don't understand what it was like on the reservation back then. The corruption. Our people discarded by the world. We needed change. We needed unity. We needed vision. I did that. I gave hope to my people. I went off and learned in your schools and brought back that knowledge to make us stronger. And we are better for it."

"I know that, Mr. Tom. You led the Navajo Nation into a new century of prosperity. My guess is that Othmann took advantage of the situation back then. Is that what he did? Did he try to profit from the misery of your people while pretending to help them? Pretending to help you?"

The old man's head moved up, then down. Affirmation.

"What happened at the site?" Joe asked, his voice soft, encouraging. He looked at Bluehorse. The officer sat motionless, not taking his eyes from his former leader.

"I went to the site to do the audit. When I—" William Tom began.

A door banged.

Joe turned. From his seat at the table, he had a view of the length of the house and saw Char walking toward the living room from the bedroom.

"I'm going out, old man. I'll be back whenever."

She jangled a set of keys in her hand.

"I'm sure law and order can see themselves out." Char disappeared down the short hallway to the front entrance. The front door opened and closed. Joe turned back to William Tom.

The old man no longer looked so old.

"I don't have any more to say. I'm not feeling well, so you are both going to have to leave. As my wife said, you can see yourselves out."

"Mr. Tom, why don't we—"

William Tom pushed his chair back from the table. He wheeled himself into the living room. "I said we're done."

They had been close, but Joe knew they would get no closer. Not now. He stood. So did Bluehorse.

"Mr. Tom, this matter isn't going away. I will find out what happened to the congressman and what happened at that site. I think we both know it's better if you help us get to the truth. Otherwise, I can't help you."

William Tom did not slow down. He rolled toward the bedroom hallway. "I need to rest now."

The old man opened the first door along the hallway and wheeled himself through it.

Joe and Bluehorse started toward the front door.

"Hold on," Joe said. He walked to the pile of newspapers and rifled through the stack. He found it: a *Navajo Times* from the week before. The front page had a section cut out.

"Any guesses on what the article was about?" Joe asked, handing the dissected paper to Bluehorse.

❖

OCTOBER 3

SUNDAY, 10:40 A.M.

JOE EVERS'S APARTMENT, ALBUQUERQUE, NEW MEXICO

Joe slept in on Sunday morning. Christine had paid him a visit the night before. He'd dreamed they were having breakfast at some pancake house, discussing what Joe would do after retirement. It was as if she'd never left. They talked about moving to Florida to be by the water. He said they should consider Jersey to be closer to Melissa. Christine had laughed at the suggestion.

"Give her some space," she said. "You're smothering her."

"Someone broke into her apartment."

"I know. But you need to let *her* deal with it. You won't always be there for her. And neither will I. She has to be able to take care of herself. And she will, if you let her."

"I—"

"*Let her.*" She put her hand over his.

And at her touch, he awoke.

He didn't know how long he had lain in bed after that, stroking her pillow, talking to her, asking her questions she never answered. Eventually, he fell back asleep.

Now he showered. Afterward, he would go in search of an IHOP or some other restaurant like the one in his dream.

You wanted to see me?" Joe said.

Dale sat behind his desk, a cotton swab in one hand and a dark blue model car in the other. "I got a call about you," Dale said.

"A fan?"

"Chief Cornfield."

"Not a fan?"

"Definitely not a fan."

Dale pushed the swab through the car's opened doors. It was a Mercedes. Joe didn't know the model.

"He said you were out to see William Tom. Tom's the former president of the Navajo Nation, in case you didn't know who you interviewed Saturday."

"My interview had nothing to do with his presidency."

Dale put down the car and leaned back in his seat, his hands on the armrests.

"You never thought to . . . oh, I don't know . . . maybe tell your supervisor you might be interviewing the former head of the largest Indian reservation in the country?"

"I was going to tell you today. Sorry you caught shit about it. What's his gripe?"

"Chief Cornfield doesn't want you talking to Tom again without one of their senior investigators present."

"Did you tell him he's interfering with a federal investigation?"

"Perhaps I would have had you kept me informed. But since you decided to leave me out there hanging again, I returned the favor. I told him okay."

"Bullshit."

"What's bullshit is your running around like a martyred prima donna, thinking you can do whatever you want, and then when someone calls you on it, you cry that everyone's on your back."

"You're just a big ol' teddy bear, aren't you?"

"I'm sure you're going to stub your toe a few more times before you're out of here. Give the case to Cordelli. Enjoy your last few months."

Dale watched, waiting for a response. Did he expect Joe just to roll over? Give the case to Wonder Boy? Walk away from the headaches and battles? It sounded good. Real good. And easy, too. All he had to do was agree and he could be out there job hunting again. But Sierra was counting on him to do right by her sister. And Christine would've wanted him to see this through. Any family would want closure. He thought of Melissa and his stomach tightened.

"No. I got it."

"Do your job, don't cause any problems, and I'll be happy."

"We done?"

"One last thing. I've got reporters calling me daily on this case. I'm handling them, but I don't want to start getting updates from them or other departments. Understand?"

When Joe got to his desk, he found Othmann's file waiting for him. He read through it. Nothing much. Suspected of this. Suspected of that. Not a nice guy, but he knew that already. At the back of the folder was a rap sheet on David "Books" Drud. Six years in Marion for putting a pipe wrench to the legs of a plumber in Philadelphia. The plumber had liked the Broncos a little more than he could afford. Books had worked for the bank.

Joe closed the file and logged into his computer. The only unread message was from Atlantic Technologies. The invoice for Melissa's security system and new locks. He closed his eyes when he saw the amount. New York prices.

After a few minutes, he got up and walked over to Stretch's cubicle.

"I'm talking to Othmann," Joe said.

Stretch stopped typing. "Is that a good idea?"

"He's a viable suspect. I need to get a line on him. See if he's good for this."

"He's not. He was just starting his art empire when Edgerton went missing. There's no way he had the balls back then to snuff a congressman. Today? Maybe. But not back then. You're chasing your tail."

"I only have a few leads. This is one."

Stretch lowered his voice. "Don't stir up more shit, especially with Sadi. Let Dale give it to someone else. Focus on getting a new job."

This wasn't like Stretch. Usually, he did the life-coach thing, pushing Joe into action, telling him to grab life in a headlock. Even Stretch had lost faith in Joe's ability to do the job.

"I won't discuss your case," Joe said.

"Othmann's not someone to mess with. He's got money, and that gives him some pull in the state. If he takes it personal, he could make it difficult for you to find a job."

"I doubt it. My job prospects right now are so far below his level of influence that the only way our paths might cross is if he drives through an intersection where I'm hawking oranges."

"Sadi's going to be pissed. Hell, I'm pissed."

"I'll let you know how it goes," Joe said. He had expected Stretch to be more supportive.

He walked away. Back at his desk, Joe picked up the phone and called Professor Trudle.

The massive oak front door at Othmann's estate was probably meant to intimidate visitors. Rising to almost eight feet, and more than wide enough to allow a small car to pass through, it communicated money and security. Below a small etched-glass window in the center of the door hung a large, brass Indian head. Joe lifted its swinging brass thumper and let it fall. A dull clank rang out.

"You think he'll talk to us?" Professor Trudle asked.

"I don't see why not. He'll be curious to know what we want."

"Can we do good cop, bad cop?" the professor asked, eyebrows raised.

"I left my rubber hose in the car," Joe said. "Maybe next time." The professor had been joking, but there'd been a twang of desire in his voice.

Metal clinked and the massive door opened, revealing a blocky blond bull. David "Books" Drud. Joe recognized him from his mug shot in the file.

Books studied Joe and Trudle and then looked past them to the two cars in the circular driveway. The Tahoe would speak *cop*, but the professor's Saab had only one language, and *cop* wasn't part of its vernacular.

"Yeah?" Books's voice was deep but not menacing.

Joe showed his credentials. "I'd like to talk with Mr. Othmann."

"And who are you?" the bull said, looking at Trudle.

Joe answered for him. "He's with me."

Books met Joe's eyes. A stare-down.

"Wait here."

Joe pressed his palm against the closing door. "How about we wait inside?"

"No." The door closed.

"Are people always so rude to cops?" Trudle asked.

"This guy's not so much rude as he is smart. He knows we have no right to enter without a warrant. He's letting us know that he knows."

While they waited for the big man to return, Joe's phone rang: Sadi. Stretch must have told her. Joe powered off the phone. He knew she wouldn't stop calling.

The door opened. "Come in."

They followed Books through a huge grand room decorated with sculptures, pottery, and wall-hung rugs. Joe knew nothing about what he saw. That was Trudle's department. The reason Joe had brought him.

Books opened a door and stood to the side, waiting for Joe and the professor to enter.

"After you," Joe said.

Another stare-down.

Books grinned. Either way, he had won. If he had gotten behind Joe, he would have been in a dominant position if things went bad. Since Joe made a fuss about having him go first, he knew he made Joe uncomfortable.

A trim man in a light, flowing shirt and breezy pants approached Joe, hand outstretched. He looked more like a Jimmy Buffett disciple than a desert art collector.

"I'm Arthur Othmann. Welcome to my own little Xanadu."

"Thank you for meeting with us," Joe said.

Trudle walked around, inspecting the contents of the museum-quality cabinets that lined the room.

"You have an incredible collection," Joe said. "Perhaps we can have a tour when we finish?"

"Absolutely. I'll have my assistant, David, show you around."

Books offered Joe a cocky grin, like a hunter spotting a lame buck.

"Now, what's this all about? What can I do for the BIA?"

"If it's the same with you, it would be better if we spoke alone."

Othmann angled his body to face Trudle. "Does the same go for the professor?"

"He's helping me with a case," Joe said. "How did you know he was a professor?"

Othmann turned away, walking toward his desk. "Well, for one, he doesn't look like a cop."

"But how did you know he was a professor?"

Trudle became interested and stopped examining the cabinets.

Books took another step into the room.

Othmann stood behind his desk, his hands resting on the back of his chair.

"I believe I've seen Professor Trudle at one or two events over the years." He turned to the professor. "And I've read one of your books."

"Which one?" Trudle asked.

Othmann waved his hand toward the two upholstered chairs in front of his desk. "Not one of your better ones, I'm sure."

"And him?" Joe said.

"David, I'll call you when we're done."

Books left, closing the door behind him.

As Joe and Trudle approached the desk to take a seat, the professor nodded toward the cabinets on the opposite wall. Joe had no idea what the professor was trying to tell him, but now wasn't the time to ask.

Joe had debated trying to build rapport, the first step in most interviews. Get the person comfortable. Help him to drop his guard. But he'd decided that would be a waste of time. By all accounts, Othmann was smart. Joe would simply try to interpret the art collector's responses and hope for him to slip up. A confession would be unlikely, especially if he was innocent.

"I'd like to talk to you about Congressman Arlen Edgerton."

Othmann tilted his head, his attention flickering from Joe to Trudle and back to Joe. "What makes you think I know anything about the congressman?"

"That's what I'd like to know. Do you?"

Othmann's gaze still wandered; the man was refusing to look directly at Joe. Perhaps he, too, had expected some rapport building.

"I read the papers, Agent Evers," Othmann said. "I know his vehicle was recently found on the reservation. Of course, I also know Grace Edgerton is running for governor. I hope you're not here because I'm supporting her opponent?"

Othmann liked to answer questions with questions.

"Your politics are your politics," Joe said, then stopped. "How did you know my name?"

The easy self-confidence the art collector had conveyed earlier faltered. "You introduced yourself when you came in."

"Did you know I was coming today?"

"Agent, I don't know anything about any of this. I'm sure you introduced yourself when you came in here."

"No, he didn't," Professor Trudle said. "I remember. He didn't."

"My assistant must have told me the agent's name." He looked again at Joe. "And if I'm not mistaken, I believe you made the news last year."

Joe *had* made the news last year, but it wasn't headlines. A Metro D-2 filler. Joe and his squad had found the story, but they'd been looking for it. At the time, it had seemed like breaking news to Joe. But now, on reflection, it had amounted to little more than a classified ad, and the notoriety lasted only slightly longer.

"How could you possibly remember that?"

"I have an exceptional memory. It was something about a case being thrown out because of an issue with key evidence. Am I right?"

"Something like that. But it wasn't thrown out. We lost." In his peripheral vision, Joe saw Trudle looking at him. "I don't believe you just happened to remember my name from a blurb in a newspaper almost a year ago. I think you knew I was coming here to talk to you." William Tom must have called ahead.

Othmann didn't reply. Joe had made a mistake. Othmann had been a little loose with his talk earlier, obviously judging Joe to be a little inept, maybe even an idiot. By challenging the arrogant bastard, he'd given him pause and put him on guard. But maybe it wasn't too late to play the bumbling detective.

"Sorry, I'm a little defensive about that whole fiasco last year. That case wasn't my best moment."

The corner of Othmann's lip curled into a smile. Joe had humbled himself. "No, I'm sure it wasn't. You were asking how I knew Arlen Edgerton. In answer to that, I didn't. I never met him. Never spoke to him. Never shared a scotch with him. Never voted for him."

"How did you feel about the bill he was working on before he disappeared? A bill to protect Native American antiquities."

"I didn't know he was working on such a bill." Othmann raised his hands to his chest and interlaced his fingers. His face brightened as though a lightbulb were shining over it. "Oh, I understand now. You thought because I collect native art that I had something to do with his disappearance. Is that it? I was protecting my interests?"

"Something like that," Joe said.

"Well, if that is all you want to know, then let me save you some time. I had nothing to do with his disappearance. I think the papers said he disappeared in 1988. Back then, I had no idea what the government was doing to regulate native antiquities. And, frankly, I wasn't interested. And I'm still not. I buy from artists and other collectors. I never give the government a second thought . . . except for the taxes, of course."

"Did you ever buy anything from William Tom?" Professor Trudle asked.

"President of the Navajo Nation?"

"Former president," Joe said.

"Why would I buy anything from him?" Othmann asked.

"That wasn't the question. The professor asked if you ever did."

"No. Not that I can recall."

A qualified answer.

"So you might have?" Joe said.

Othmann licked his lips before answering. "I've purchased lots of things over the years. Many, many things. I cannot be sure who I bought them all from."

Joe wanted to remind him of his exceptional memory but didn't.

Professor Trudle shifted in his seat. "So, you're telling me you can't remember if you bought something from the president of the Navajo Nation?"

"He wasn't always the president. And who's asking the questions? Is UNM now doing investigations into missing congressmen? I'm getting a little annoyed at the accusations. Should I have a lawyer present, Agent Evers?"

"Mr. Othmann, I'm looking into Edgerton's disappearance. Professor Trudle is assisting me with the antiquities-protection angle." Joe looked at the professor. "I'm the one asking the questions." He let his gaze linger so Trudle would get the message.

"Then ask," Othmann said.

"I came across information that you had purchased a number of items from William Tom some years ago. I would like to talk to you about those items and about William Tom."

"If you say you know I bought some items from him, then why don't you tell me what they are and maybe that will jog my memory."

Othmann was testing Joe. No doubt he wanted to see what Joe knew. "Perhaps we can look through some purchase records."

"I don't keep records going back too many years. How long ago was this supposed purchase?"

Trudle leaned forward. "Oh, come on. Every collector keeps records. You own a gallery. That's how you prove provenance."

"Professor," Joe said.

"Half of your collection would be worthless without a record of the artist," Trudle said. "You couldn't even prove it was Native American."

Joe put a hand on Trudle's shoulder. "Professor!"

Trudle relaxed. He folded his hands in his lap. "Sorry."

"We're interested in some old pottery," Joe said. "Eight or nine hundred years old. Purchased from William Tom in 1988."

Othmann lifted his gaze toward the ceiling: a good imitation of a man thinking.

A few moments earlier, when Trudle had started his tirade, Joe had watched the art collector. What he'd seen was a composed face, somewhat like that of a patient father allowing a young child to vent, but below that was something nebulous, something dark, a soul void of virtue. Joe could see it in his eyes. Othmann was mentally disturbed. Most cops knew the look. It almost always came through in the eyes. A crazy person might be able to hide it, even act rationally most of the time, but given a stressful situation, the pressure builds and the craziness surfaces. Any decent investigator could spot it instantly, a mental problem peeking through sanity's curtained windows. Othmann was a sociopath. On the surface, he acted like any other person, but below that facade of normalcy, he was an emotionless creature concerned only with his own needs and desires. Compassion and humanity were foreign to him. Joe did not get all this from these few moments of observation. Mostly it came from his file. Between that and what he had just seen, there was no doubt Othmann was dangerous.

"I'm sorry, Agent Evers, I don't recall buying anything like that from William Tom," Othmann said. "But I will see if I have any records from back then. If there's nothing else, I am scheduled for a phone conference in a few minutes."

"That will be fine. I'll stop by later this week to see if you found anything."

"I'll call you." Othmann pressed a button on his phone, and a moment later Books walked into the room. "David will see you out."

They stood and made their way to the door.

"One last question," Joe said. "How often do you travel down to Mexico?"

"Rarely. Why do you ask?"

"Do you know a Cedro Bartolome?"

"Should I?"

"That's what I'm asking."

"Doesn't sound familiar."

"Thank you for your time, Mr. Othmann," Joe said. "Do you think we can have that tour now?"

"Maybe next time."

"I couldn't help noticing the Navajo Yei mask," Professor Trudle said.

Joe and Othmann both turned to face the professor, who stood before a display case, holding his phone. He pointed to an object behind the glass. "It's beautiful. Is it authentic?"

"I wouldn't waste shelf space on a fake."

"That's what I thought."

'm sorry, Joe," Trudle said. "I couldn't help it. He was lying. There is no way he doesn't have records. No collector neglects his record keeping."

They stood by their vehicles, in front of the Othmann mansion, discussing what had just happened. Joe surveyed the residence. The structure was Pueblo Revival style, with a flat roof and projecting wooden beams known as vigas, which, most of the time, were only decorative and served no structural purpose. The tan adobe of the building blended nicely with the surrounding desert tones. The grounds around the residence were well kept. Othmann surely used landscapers. But they wouldn't know what went on inside.

"Othmann's got a pretty big place," Joe said. "He must have a maid or a cook, right?"

Trudle's expression showed his confusion. "I'm sure he does, but there's no way they live here."

"Why not?"

"Would you want to be locked up in a house with those two?"

Trudle had a point. Joe changed the subject. "Did you see any of the items from your dig?"

"I don't think so. I can't be sure. Some of the stuff we saw is old enough to be from the same time period, but I didn't recognize any of the designs."

"It's okay. I wasn't expecting to find anything."

"Then why bring me along?"

"It was worth a shot. You know what you're looking at. To me, all that stuff was just old pottery and artwork."

"There was something." Trudle took out his phone. "The Navajo Yei mask." He brought up the picture, then handed it to Joe.

On the screen was the image of a black-and-white over-the-head mask, leather, hand-sewn stitching, padded eye holes, ragged edges. A fringe of dangling thin leather strips circled the head like a lion's mane.

"What is it?" Joe asked.

"One of the most powerful objects in Navajo ceremonial magic."

"Oh," Joe said, losing interest. He offered the phone back.

"It's a Yei mask. They're used in Yeibichai ceremonies. Very sacred."

"I'm not following you. Why should this interest me?"

"NAGPRA protects them. After the act was passed, universities, museums, and even private collectors had to return articles like this to the tribes."

Stretch and Sadi might be interested, but Joe wasn't. "Come on. I owe you lunch."

❖

OCTOBER 4

MONDAY, 1:18 P.M.

OTHMANN ESTATE, SANTA FE, NEW MEXICO

Othmann and Books stood in front of two large computer monitors mounted on the wall, below which sat a bank of digital recorders. They were downstairs in the environmentally controlled room beneath the study. The screen on the left showed the study. The screen on the right was segmented into sixteen squares, showing views of all the hidden cameras on the property. One of the views was of the driveway in front of the house. Agent Evers and the professor stood by their cars, talking. They were too far to be picked up by the camera's mike. Othmann rewound the dedicated DVR that monitored the study. He stopped it at the point just before Professor Trudle asked about the Yei mask.

"There!" Othmann paused the video. "He took a photo of it."

The frozen image showed Othmann and Joe engaged in conversation in the foreground. In the background, the professor held his phone in front of the glass cabinet.

Othmann pointed to Joe's figure. "He brought the professor here to get something on me."

"Can that photo cause you trouble?" Books asked.

Othmann didn't answer right away. "I don't know."

"Well, you'd better find out."

"Don't tell me what to do. Of course I'm going to find out."

Books grunted. Othmann didn't know what that meant, either.

"Did you hear what that asshole said to me? 'How did you know he was a professor? How did you know my name?' Everything I said, he challenged. Did you hear him?"

"I wasn't in the room."

"It doesn't matter. He's a fucking asshole." Othmann flicked the screen with his finger. "The BIA's getting rid of him. He's a total wreck. A drunk. They don't trust him."

"I think you should be careful around him," Books said.

"Fuck him."

Books showed no emotion. "Don't underestimate him. He's been around. He may be off his game now, but don't discount experience."

"What am I, an idiot? It's covered. I'll know what the son of a bitch is doing before he does."

Othmann rewound the video to the beginning of the interview. As he watched, he chewed the inside of his lip. Thinking. Hating.

Three rewinds later, he tasted blood.

❖

OCTOBER 4

MONDAY, 2:23 P.M.

DOWNTOWN SANTA FE, NEW MEXICO

Over lunch at a small Mexican restaurant in downtown Santa Fe, the professor shared his theories. He believed that prior to and during the rise of the Aztec Empire, when war waged among many of the tiny city-states in MesoAmerica, a few of the tribes migrated north, settling in Chaco Canyon. They organized the local nomadic and pueblo peoples in the area and established a highly sophisticated community. They introduced new ceremonies and the science of astronomy to the region, which explained the commonalities between the civilizations. While many archaeologists had speculated about trade between the groups, there had never been any physical evidence of a migration. That was until Professor Trudle found the pots. According to him, the large pots stolen from his dig site were proof. They were decorated with MesoAmerican imagery, but that wasn't nearly as important as what was found inside: organic residue. He'd taken several scrapings and later had them tested. Human remains. The pots were used to boil people, a common Aztec practice of sacrifice.

Toward the end of lunch, Trudle changed the subject and asked Joe about the court case Othmann had mentioned. Joe swallowed his pride and told the story. Felix Longman had been stabbed to death by his neighbor in his own house. Joe had been on duty and caught the case. He'd been hungover. The neighbor was arrested and the evidence collected. Joe cleared the scene and headed home in record time. Felix's mother called him an hour later and told him he'd left an evidence bag behind. It was the knife. He'd gone back quickly and recovered it. Later, when defense counsel had learned of Joe's sloppiness, they had rushed the case to trial. Joe took the stand in the afternoon and the defense attorney hammered him for hours on every detail of the case, especially on his handling of the evidence. By the end of the day, the defense was still not finished their cross-examination. The judge ordered Joe back the following morning to finish. That night, Joe drank himself into a stupor. The next morning, he didn't make it into court. When he did, it was too late. The damage had been done. The jury decided Joe was unreliable, so Felix Longman never got justice.

While Joe was baring his soul about Felix Longman, Chris Staples called. He said he wanted to talk. Joe told him he would stop by the campaign office after lunch.

Now, he was heading over to Grace Edgerton's headquarters. Back in Albuquerque, Stretch would be waiting for an update. This little detour would give Joe time to get his thoughts in order. Othmann had given him little. The Yei mask was interesting, but he wasn't sure how that helped him. Perhaps Stretch could run with it. No doubt Sadi would want to deliver her own gentle rebuke, perhaps battery acid in his face. Maybe he deserved it. He didn't have many leads left. He checked his notes. He still needed to interview Senator Holmes and the AIM character, Dwight Henry, aka Hawk Rushingwater. What he really needed was to talk to the agent who had worked the investigation back in '88: Malcolm Tsosie. Only he could tell Joe how these folks had reacted when they were first interviewed as part of the initial investigation. A person's first reaction was one of the best indicators of involvement or guilt. Maybe Dale could help him find Malcolm.

He texted Stretch a message to meet him at Mickey's at five.

❖

OCTOBER 4

MONDAY, 2:23 P.M.

EDGERTON FOR GOVERNOR HEADQUARTERS, SANTA FE,

NEW MEXICO

Joe sat in Chris Staples's office, listening to the fat man's problems.

Staples held up a stack of computer printouts. "Her polls are tanking. People think she was involved."

"I can't help her polls."

"I'm not asking you to." He dropped the stack on his desk. A wave of cheap aftershave washed over Joe. It was tinged with the odor of sweaty desperation.

"Then why am I here?"

"Helena Newridge is looking into those threats from that AIM guy."

"It isn't AIM. The guy started his own group. He called it Navajo NOW. It's a splinter group."

"Who cares? The threat was real. If the public learns about those threats, they would have something else to hang their suspicions on. A lone terrorist. A fringe group. Take your pick."

"That's stretching it. His letters were ominous, but no direct threats. They warned about unrest on the reservation."

"And a year later, during the Peter MacDonald riots, two people were killed. It was civil war on the rez."

Staples was right: There had been a riot and people had been killed, but in no way had it been related to Edgerton.

"I asked Ms. Newridge to hold off for a few days while I checked into it," Joe said. "If you release that information to another paper now, you're interfering with my investigation."

"And if you *don't* release it, you're interfering with my campaign."

❖

OCTOBER 4
MONDAY, 4:54 P.M.
MICKEY'S BAR & GRILL, ALBUQUERQUE, NEW MEXICO

G illian been around?" Joe asked when Mickey appeared at the tap to fill mugs.

"Haven't seen her."

Joe wanted to be happy for her, happy she was getting back with her husband, happy her family was healing, happy to be happy for her. But a little part of him—maybe a not so little part—wanted to hear they'd been unable to work it out, and that she was unencumbered again and willing to reexplore the whole friend thing.

"Hey, Joe," Tenny said as he sat on the stool to Joe's right, the only empty seat at the counter. Cordelli stood behind him.

"Peace?" Cordelli held out his hand.

Joe shook it, not too disappointed to see them.

He waved to get Mickey's attention.

"You guys eating, drinking, or both?" Mickey said.

"I'm in the mood for a hot dog," Cordelli said.

"You'd pass up my Combo for a wiener?"

"I saw the Isotopes practicing at the field. It brought me back to when I was a kid and my pops took me to see the Reading Phillies, a double-A farm team out of Pennsylvania. We got a Coke and a hot dog on some sort of weird split white-bread bun. Man, it was the best thing ever."

"You oughta try a Chicago dog," Tenny said. He made a smacking sound with his lips. "Relish, pickles, tomatoes, peppers, onions, mustard, and a kitchen sink thrown in for good measure."

"I can't believe you guys," Mickey said. "I give you the best roast beef sandwich this side of the Mississippi, probably the other side, too, and you want a bologna tube. You believe them, Joe?"

"I'm with the guys on this. A hot dog has a special place in a man's heart. I took Christine and Melissa to New York when Melissa was about eight. We ice-skated at Rockefeller Center and then had a dirty-water dog from a street vendor. Just mustard and sauerkraut. Best ever."

Mickey waved them away. "You guys have no taste. How about it, Sadi? You got a special place in your heart for a hot dog?"

Joe turned. Sadi and Stretch stood behind him.

"Not for this hot dog," Sadi said, her eyes focused on Joe, her face deadpan.

Cordelli and Tenny both chortled like little kids about to see a school-yard brawl.

Sadi started in. "What the hell are you doing screwing around in our case?"

"Let's not do this here," Joe said.

Stretch put a hand on Sadi's shoulder. She shrugged it off. "You're an asshole, Joe. Cordelli was right. You ain't part of the team."

"Don't drag me into this," Cordelli said, hands up, grinning.

Joe was getting tired of people attacking him.

Sadi looked down at Joe's hands. "You wanna hit me, Joe? You wanna go after me like you went after Cordelli?"

Joe unclenched his fists and spun back to the counter, surprised by his own reaction. The bar was watching their exchange. Watching him. He reached into his pocket, pulled out some bills, threw them down. "See you later, Mickey." He stood and shouldered his way past Sadi.

"You're an asshole, Joe," she said to his back, her voice loud. It carried over the music coming through the speakers. People in the dining area turned to look.

Joe faced her. He wanted to tell her to shut her trap and get out of his face. He wanted to call her a bitch and tell her that's why no one liked her. He wanted to tell her to get laid. But instead, he restrained himself and offered a reluctant "Sorry."

"Sorry?" Sadi said. "Why be sorry? You're going to solve the big case. Be the big hero, right?" Her voice turned cold. "The sad thing is, you'll screw it up because you can't help yourself. You're a walking mess, Joe. Do yourself a favor and leave the investigating to people who still care about the cases and who don't bury themselves in a bottle."

Stretch moved closer to Sadi. Joe expected him to say something, anything. It wasn't only her case; it was his, too. But his friend stood silent, not meeting Joe's gaze.

Joe turned.

At the entrance stood Linda and Sue. Next to them was Gillian.

All three had watched the show.

He gave an embarrassed smile and got the hell out of there.

The next morning was akin to a midlife circumcision, except the pain was in Joe's other brain. It took him an hour and four aspirin before he could crawl out from his cubicle to give Stretch an update on the Othmann interview and attempt to repair the damage to his manhood. Sadi joined them. Surprisingly, she was in a good mood.

"You look like shit," she said.

"Good," Joe said. "That's better than I feel."

She crossed her arms. "Well?"

"I didn't get much," Joe said.

"You always seem to know the right words to make a girl feel good, don't you?"

"No, that's not—"

She held up a hand. "Save it. All I want to know is if you tipped him off to our investigation."

He didn't bother answering. Instead, he gave an account of the interview. Sadi and Stretch listened, dropping comments here and there when they didn't like what they heard.

"I think he knew I was coming," Joe said.

"How?" Stretch asked. "From the newspapers?"

"I don't know. But he knew me. He said he remembered my name from when I was in the paper last year."

Sadi laughed. "Your reputation precedes you. You'd better hope the people you're sending résumés to don't read the papers."

"Was there a lot of coverage last year?" Joe asked. "I only remember the one article. And it was buried."

"I don't know." Sadi said. "I wasn't following the Joe Saga last year."

"I didn't follow the papers much, just the talk on the squad," Stretch said. "Dale tracked it, though. I recall he mentioned a couple articles." He paused a moment and then said, "Maybe someone you interviewed tipped him off."

"My thought was William Tom," Joe said. "But to bring up a newspaper article from last year?"

"You're a dinosaur, Joe," Sadi said. "The *Internet?* You know, that magical box on your desk." She shook her head. "You're immortal and don't even know it."

Of course. Othmann had found the articles on the Net. Joe had never searched himself, but they had to be out there. That was probably why he hadn't received many replies from the companies where he had sent his résumé. They did their due diligence.

"So what you're telling us," she continued "is that Othmann is on his guard."

"I may have something for you." He told them about the Yei mask. "The professor's e-mailing me the photo."

Sadi actually seemed somewhat mollified.

"I don't see how we can use it," Stretch said.

"You might be able to get a search warrant."

"Maybe," Sadi said, her mollification exhausted. "A single Yei mask isn't much."

"I need to talk to the boss. I'll send you the photo when I get it."

He walked over to Dale's door and knocked. An unintelligible grunt invited him in.

Dale looked annoyed. "What?"

Joe gave him a summary of the Othmann interview.

"So it's another dead end."

"I need to talk to Malcolm Tsosie," Joe said. "He was a buddy of yours, wasn't he? Where can I find him?"

"Why do you need to talk to him?"

"You're not seriously asking me that, are you?"

Dale didn't respond right away. "Tell me why."

Joe couldn't believe his ears. "Why do you think? He was the primary on Edgerton."

Another pause. "Are you doing an end run to interview Senator Holmes?"

"What are you talking about? I need—" Then Joe got it. "Wait . . . Malcolm works for Senator Holmes?"

Dale didn't answer.

"You shittin' me?"

Dale just looked at him.

"You're not shittin' me."

Dale wasn't.

"You didn't think that was important to tell me?" Joe didn't know how to feel. What was it? Betrayal. No, not betrayal. What, then? He didn't know. There was no word for this. No way to describe how he felt. But that wasn't true. There was a word. He felt *screwed*. He sat back and smiled. The revelation wasn't as big as the fact that Dale had held back that little tidbit.

"You were going off in all different directions. I didn't want you pissing off a senator unless you had something solid."

"You mean pissing off a senator on the Indian Affairs Committee?"

"Exactly."

"Are you letting politics dictate our investigations now?"

"Grow up. Get me something solid. Otherwise, you don't go near the senator."

"That's bullshit."

"That's how it is."

Joe walked out. The stench was too much.

D avid!" blared from the intercom speakers mounted throughout the house. It was particularly loud in the kitchen, where
Books sat at the breakfast bar, eating his second bowl of Cap'n
Crunch cereal and reading a *Forbes* article about the ten best places
to retire outside the United States. Tendons in his neck tightened.

The Cap'n seemed to laugh at him.

He'd been with Mr. O. seven years. He wasn't sure if there would be
an eighth. Before coming to work for him, he'd spent six years in
lockup. When he got out, he had asked the parole board to allow him
to go to Albuquerque to try to make a fresh start. He'd been at a halfway house for only a day when Ernie, the house daddy, told him about
a gig in Santa Fe.

"There's a rich dude up there. He takes on a few of my guys from
time to time, doing security and stuff around his gallery. Pays good,
but he don't take no thieves, only honest felons."

Books almost laughed. Honest felons? Was this guy for real?

Ernie went on: "You honest? Good, 'cause he'll like you. Big and
mean. I guess art's a tough business. You interested?"

The next day, Ernie gave him a ride up to Santa Fe to meet
Mr. O. "That's what he likes being called: Mr. O. I guess it's because

his last name is Othmann. You know, that begins with an *O*," Ernie said.

Several smart remarks came to Books, but he kept quiet. He was good at keeping quiet. And anyway, Ernie was doing him a favor.

After a quarter-mile drive from the front gate, Ernie parked the halfway house's ten-year-old passenger van in front of a huge Southwest-style home. The place was peaceful, tucked away in its own little part of the desert. This was somewhere Books could make a fresh start. Not like the big city. Not like city life anywhere. This is what he needed. No matter what, he wanted this job.

His interview had taken place in the study, where Books was heading now. It had been short.

"I hear you worked for some people in Philadelphia."

Books nodded. He'd learned years earlier that the less he spoke, the better.

"People tell me you understand loyalty. Is that true?"

He wondered, What people? but only nodded.

"I have a special job that recently opened up. I need someone I can count on. Someone I can trust. A bodyguard. You interested?"

Books held back a smile. Another nod. It seemed the proper response for a bodyguard.

"Okay, we'll give it a go for a few weeks, see if we get along. How's that? If we do, you stay here and live in the house. The pay's good. Two a week, plus room and board."

At first, Books thought two hundred a week was chump money, even with room and board, but it was better than living at the halfway house. A week later, he got his first paycheck and realized that Mr. O.'s two was followed by three zeros. He decided he would be staying on as long as Mr. O. would have him.

But now, Mr. O. was no longer that cool dude he'd met seven years ago. The crazy had set in. He constantly talked about his father, who had died long before Books came along. And he was hitting the powder more and more. Just the year before, he and some artist tramp had spent a Bolivian weekend together in his room. Come Monday, she wouldn't wake up, so Books spent the rest of that day finding a safe place to dump her. He also spent two hours bleaching her—in and out—after Mr. O. admitted to having had sex with her that morning, thinking she had only passed out. The police had come around looking for her, hearing that Mr. O. had been with her on Friday, but they went away. Mr. O. never skimped on spreading his money around. He had several officers he could reach out to throughout the state—not to mention lawyers.

Books had been frugal over the years, saved up most of his salary. He thought it was a good time to leave. Cut out before his boss lost it altogether and brought Books down with him. But Ernie had been right: Books was honest, and he was loyal. He would see his boss through this mess before he left. It was a matter of honor for Books. But afterward, he would be heading for Ecuador.

When he walked into Mr. O.'s study, he was daydreaming about opening a little coastal restaurant catering to tourists, maybe calling it Rick's Café, like in *Casablanca*. They'd shown the movie in prison.

"That motherfucker Evers isn't letting this shit go!"

Books debated whether he should serve French or Italian food.

Mr. O. paced the room, powder on his upper lip like a Hitler mustache. "Motherfucker. Who does he think he is? He comes in my fucking house and accuses me. Fuck him! And fuck that William Tom. That son of a bitch should have died ten years ago." He stopped pacing and looked at Books, eyes wide, finger pointing. "David, you need to take care of this. You need to take care of it now. He's coming after you, too. For Eddie." He spun around and jacked a finger at the painting of his father. "And you shut the fuck up. I can handle my own shit."

Books decided on an American menu for Rick's Café.

The interview was going well. Joe had the answers, and Samuel Becenti seemed to have the interest.

"You'd be working here in Window Rock," Samuel said. "Do you plan to commute, or would you move out this way?"

"I'm in an apartment right now, but if I got the job, I'd move to Gallup." He picked at a piece of lint on his pressed pant leg. The crease was sharp. Yes, he felt good about the interview. "There's nothing holding me there. I'm actually looking forward to a move."

Samuel appeared pleased. He wrote something on his notepad.

A knock at the door. Samuel gave a perturbed "Come in."

A man in a Navajo police uniform entered. Joe didn't recognize the face, but he recognized the name on the name tag. Calvert Cornfield. Chief Cornfield of the Navajo Nation Police Department.

"Hello, Samuel. I stopped by to say hi to your guest here." He walked into the room and held out his hand. "Hello, Joe. I heard you were interviewing today. I spoke to your supervisor last week. I hope you got the message."

Joe stood and shook hands. "I did. Nice to meet you, Chief."

"I'm sure." Cornfield turned to Samuel. "Well, as I said, I wanted to stop by and say hi. Didn't mean to interrupt." He turned to go, then stopped. "Samuel, if you can, call me later. I'd like to talk to you about something."

"Sure thing."

Joe could only smile, a goofy, good-for-nothing smile. The kind that surfaces when you're too stunned to think of anything else to do.

"Well, let's see. Where were we?" Samuel looked up from his notepad. "What's funny?"

"Nothing," Joe said. "Nothing at all." Exactly what this interview would amount to now.

❖

OCTOBER 6

WEDNESDAY, 11:38 A.M.

INTERSTATE HIGHWAY 40 EAST, MCKINLEY COUNTY,

NEW MEXICO

The phone number came up as blocked, which made Joe anxious. He was still concerned about Melissa and the break-in.

"Hello?"

"Are you investigating Congressman Edgerton's disappearance?" a male voice said, the words delivered low, methodically.

"Who's this?"

"Someone with information."

"Okay," Joe said. He clicked off the Tahoe's radio. "What's your name?"

"No names. I don't want anyone to know I'm helping you."

Joe scrambled for something to write on. "I need to call you something."

A pause. "Call me Eddie."

"Okay, Eddie. What's the information?"

"Is there a reward?"

"That depends on the information."

"Can we meet? I don't want to talk over the phone."

"Why not?"

"I'm scared. And I want to know I can trust you."

Eddie didn't sound scared.

"How did you get my number?"

Another pause. "We met once. You gave it to me."

"If we met, why won't you give me your name?"

This time, no pause. "I told you, I'm scared."

"Come to my office. It's safe there."

"No, it's not. I live in Jones Ranch. Can we meet there?"

"First, you need to tell me what the information is."

"I know who killed that driver."

"How do you know?"

"The person who did it told me."

"Who told you?"

"Uh-uh. Only in person."

"So far, nothing you've said makes me think you know anything about the case."

"Forty-five-caliber."

It was Joe's turn to pause. That hadn't been released.

"When do you want to meet?"

"Tomorrow."

Joe would be with Bluehorse tomorrow, taking a crack at Rushing-water and his troupe of afternoon freedom fighters.

"How about we meet now?"

"Tomorrow."

Eddie was too smooth. Too sure of himself. Tomorrow would be better for Joe, too. Tomorrow he would have Bluehorse for backup, perhaps the squad.

"Okay, four o'clock. Where?"

"Jones Ranch Road. Where you found the vehicle."

"Why there?"

"Because I need to show you something. Something buried."

"Okay, Eddie. We'll meet on the road. How will—"

Click.

At the very least, this guy knew next to nothing and was playing him. At the most, he had information to identify a killer. And at worst, it was a setup. Eddie was a player. But what was his game?

❖

OCTOBER 7

THURSDAY, 2:00 A.M.

RESIDENCE OF WILLIAM TOM, FORT DEFIANCE

(NAVAJO NATION), ARIZONA

Books had been watching the house since midnight. A light at the back had stayed on till one o'clock. It was now two. He'd taken care of the dog that ran free about the place by sprinkling sleeping pills on ground meat. He liked dogs and never hurt one unnecessarily. He felt bad about that kid-diddler's dog the other week, but the damn thing had felt obliged to protect its owner, which was too bad. And *owner* was probably too generous a description of that arrangement. The dog obviously hadn't been cared for; it simply existed in close proximity to that jerk. Books rarely felt regret. And never for people. But animals were different.

A car pulled up. A woman got out, swaying. Books couldn't see her face from that distance, but she appeared young from the way she moved and from her high-pitched giggles. The driver pinched her ass, then drove off amid shushed hoots and hollers from the other occupants. When the vehicle passed the spot where Books hid, concealed

behind a sagging juniper, the moonlight penetrated the car's darkened interior and he could make out the silhouettes of three men. He
turned his attention back to the woman.

She remained where she'd been pinched for another minute or
so, seeming to gather herself. Her swaying slowed like a metronome
winding down, as did her fits of giggles. She turned slowly toward the
house, as though the simple effort had required significant concen-
tration and even more deliberation. The woman made her way to the
front door, albeit in a not so straight path. She stumbled once and
cursed before making it inside. The lights in the house stayed off.

He waited.

An hour passed. All was quiet.

Now it was time.

He put on his gloves, then made his way to the front door. He had
to step over the snoring dog, which lay across the narrow stone path
at the bottom of the wheelchair ramp and was probably what had
tripped the woman.

He had his lock-pick gun out, but he found the door slightly ajar.
Drunks often made things easy for people like Books.

He crept inside and surveyed the darkened room. The woman was
passed out on the couch, snoring louder than the dog. She stank of
alcohol and sex. The room was empty.

He pulled out a plastic bag and headed down the hall to the
bedrooms.

Joe took 7 to Chinle, then turned north on 64.

"What do you think about our mysterious Eddie?" Joe asked.

Bluehorse didn't answer right away. "If Eddie's Navajo, I can see him being scared. We don't like getting involved with outsiders."

"He didn't sound Navajo."

Bluehorse shrugged but said nothing.

Joe pulled to the side of the road. They were about a mile from Rushingwater's turnoff. He got out and put on his bulletproof vest under his shirt. Most investigators rarely wore them on interviews, unlike police officers, who never knew when they might arrive at a gunfight. Joe didn't want to take chances with Rushingwater's group.

He got back in the vehicle and they continued on 64 in silence until Bluehorse told him to turn left.

The road needed grading. The Tahoe bounced along, slipping in and out of well-traveled ruts. About a half mile in, they came to a double-wide with smoke rising from a narrow metal chimney jutting from the roof. The trailer looked a lot like Eddie Begay's: crappy.

Two men lounged out front on green plastic lawn chairs. Joe pulled to a stop twenty feet from the trailer and thought of two Eddies: Stretch and Sadi's Eddie Begay, and his own mysterious Eddie. But he didn't have time to ponder the coincidence. The two men sitting outside stood and walked into the trailer. Were they retreating because they didn't like visitors, or because they wanted to get their guns?

Joe and Bluehorse climbed out of the Tahoe, but they kept their doors open in front of them. Bluehorse wore his uniform. The people inside would know they were law and order.

Joe reached under the steering wheel and pushed the release button to unlock the roof rack above the front seats. It held a loaded M4 assault rifle with penetrator rounds.

A man wearing a red bandanna around his head, a black T-shirt, and a pair of well-worn jeans appeared at the trailer's entrance. Joe recognized him from the mug shot taken in 1989 for assaulting an officer. The name on that photo read Dwight Henry. He looked the same, only older, and now with two long braids, one coming down over each shoulder.

"You are trespassing on my land, the land of my ancestors," Rushingwater called.

Joe wanted to laugh. Who spoke like that?

Bluehorse said, "*Ya'at eeh*, Rushingwater. We only want to talk."

"I have no business with a *bilagáana*."

Joe noticed that while Rushingwater spoke, his body stayed motionless. Physically, he wasn't conveying a threat. He was acting for the others inside the trailer.

Movement at one of the windows.

Joe put his hand to his gun. He whispered, "Ten o'clock."

"I see it," Bluehorse said. "Rushingwater, this is Joe Evers. He's a BIA agent. We won't take—"

One of the men who had been sitting in a lawn chair came around from the left side of the trailer. A big guy. He held a rifle in his right hand, barrel up, the butt resting on his hip. The trailer had a back door. Not good. Someone else could flank them if they weren't careful.

Joe drew his weapon and held it by his thigh. Bluehorse did the same.

"Mr. Rushingwater," Joe said. "We didn't come looking for trouble.

I understand you're doing some important work for your people. Work with the United Nations. Is that true?"

"Yes, I petitioned with the United Nations. What is your point?"

Joe kept his eyes on the man with the rifle. "My point is, I am a federal agent. If this situation escalates, I know, and you know, that it would end your work with the UN. Neither of us wants that to happen."

Rushingwater was silent a moment. "Nightwind is my war chief. There is no need to be concerned of him if you came here intending me no harm."

Joe looked directly at the man called Nightwind. "No matter his position in your organization, I'm still a federal agent. He needs to put down his rifle."

Rushingwater said, "Let me see some ID."

Joe took out his credentials and held them up. The large blue BIA letters would be visible from a distance.

"Nightwind, put down your rifle," Rushingwater said.

The war chief placed his weapon on the ground.

Joe advanced.

"I'm securing the rifle," he said. "You'll get it back when we leave." When he was ten paces from Nightwind, he ordered, "Step back."

Nightwind obeyed, but he didn't look happy. Nor did he look relieved. Joe was sure that if Rushingwater had given the command, Nightwind would have opened fire. Joe picked up the rifle, keeping his Glock pointed at the ground. He didn't want to appear threatening to the person or persons behind the window.

The rifle was a Remington .22-caliber Apache rifle with a fourteen-cartridge clip, a common firearm in the area. Joe moved back to the vehicle, holstered his weapon, dropped the rifle clip, and ejected the round in the barrel. He put the clip in his pocket, then laid the rifle on the front seat.

"Do you want to talk in our car or inside your trailer?" Joe said to Rushingwater, not giving him the option to talk outside.

"What do you think?" Rushingwater said.

"We need to do a security sweep first. I'd feel more comfortable, and it would lessen the likelihood of an accident or a misunderstanding."

"You mean search the house? No."

Another man stepped into the doorway behind Rushingwater and whispered something into his ear.

"That's Sleeping Bear," Bluehorse said.

Rushingwater spoke again: "Fine, you can come inside. But Nightwind will accompany you on your security sweep."

Joe and Bluehorse approached the trailer cautiously. Rushingwater and Sleeping Bear stepped outside. Bluehorse stayed with them while Joe conducted a sweep of the trailer with Nightwind.

The interior was surprisingly neat, though it smelled like marijuana. But he wasn't the pot police. Besides, it usually made people mellow, which was good.

In the living room, three men sat squeezed together on the couch like hellish lovebirds. In the corner sat a cheap assemble-it-yourself desk with a hutch, the cubbyholes stuffed with papers. Above the desk was a map of the Navajo Nation, with colored pins stuck at various locations.

"I need to check the couch," Joe said.

The lovebirds stood and walked to the other side of the room.

"You gentlemen have any weapons on you?"

They said they didn't.

He asked to check. They agreed. He did. Nothing.

Even so, this was foolish. He and Bluehorse should have hightailed it as soon as the rifle came out. But Joe was tired of being pushed around in this case. Too many other people seemed to be calling the shots. He'd had enough. He wasn't about to let these two-bit freedom fighters kick him in the balls, too.

He checked the sofa and found a shotgun under the cushions. He removed the shells.

"Any other guns?"

They all shrugged. That meant yes.

"Where?"

Again all three men shrugged.

Joe did a walk-through of the trailer, which consisted of a kitchen, living room, three bedrooms, and a nonfunctioning bathroom with a five-gallon bucket on the floor. He found another shotgun behind the door of the middle bedroom. It was unloaded.

When Joe finished, Bluehorse, Rushingwater, and Sleeping Bear came inside. Rushingwater nodded to the front door, and Nightwind and the other three men moved outside to wait. An obedient bunch.

Joe led Rushingwater into the kitchen. Bluehorse followed. Sleeping Bear sat down on the couch.

Joe placed the shotguns on the floor in the kitchen. Then he removed the rifle clip and shells from his pocket and placed them next to the shotguns. He took out his notepad.

"Is your real name Dwight Henry?" Joe asked.

"Not anymore. It is the white man's label. My name is Hawk Rushingwater."

"Okay, but is Dwight Henry printed on your CIB?" Joe asked, referring to his Navajo Certificate of Indian Blood, which was used by the tribe to establish membership.

"Yes."

Joe asked for Rushingwater's date of birth and other identifiers. Rushingwater responded readily. When Joe asked his employment, Rushingwater smiled.

"I am president of Navajo NOW and tribal chief of the Peoples of Diné."

"Is Navajo NOW a chapter of AIM?"

"No. They have lost their way. They no longer represent the will of our people."

"Tell me about the Peoples of Diné."

Rushingwater's chest puffed out. "In 2007, the United Nations adopted a Declaration on the Rights of Indigenous Peoples. Based on that and the Vienna Convention on the Law of Treaties, it's clear the United States has consistently violated its treaties with Native American tribes. I have petitioned the United Nations to formally recognize the Peoples of Diné as an independent country."

Joe wanted to ask how that was working out for him, but he rephrased his question. "Has the Peoples of Diné been recognized?"

"Not yet, but we are confident. Our sister tribe, the Lakota, are also seeking independence. My brother Russell Means was leading that effort before his death."

"Where is headquarters for the Peoples of Diné?" Bluehorse asked.

"Here," Rushingwater said. "All great accomplishments start from humble beginnings. Did not the United States start from the whisperings of men meeting in backrooms and dreaming of independence?"

"I guess," Joe said. "But we're here on a different matter. What do you know about Congressman Edgerton?"

"His vehicle was found. I figure that is why you came."

"If you knew, then why did you have your war chief out there with a rifle?"

"I believe it was one of your country's forefathers, Samuel Adams, who said 'No people will tamely surrender their Liberties, nor can any be easily subdued, when knowledge is diffused and virtue is preserved.' I have to stay vigilant of those who try to stop my work."

Joe was growing weary of the freedom-fighter rhetoric. "So you believe the Navajo Nation should be an independent country. Did you feel that way in '88?"

"I was not as politically savvy those early years."

"So your actions spoke louder than your words back then."

"I wasn't afraid to force change, no. I wanted to see my brothers and sisters break free of the slavery we call reservation life."

"Was Edgerton part of the problem? He was a member of Congress. The same Congress that set up the reservations."

"He was only one of many."

"You wrote letters to him, right?"

"I spoke to BIA agents back then about those letters. My answers satisfied them. Do they not satisfy you now?"

"Your letters concern me." Joe pulled copies from his inside jacket pocket. Three letters, two pages each. "Are these the letters you sent him?" Joe did not hand them over, but instead held them up for Rushingwater to see.

"It has been many years."

"Well, let's see if we can jog your memory." Joe turned to a page he had marked up. "You wrote, 'Your government has consistently treated Native Americans as animals. You force us to live on reservations like cattle slowly dying on barren lands. You force us to submit to a blood quantum for membership. The only other uses for a blood quantum are the tracking of Thoroughbred and dog pedigrees. Are we dogs? Are we not eligible for inclusion under the belief that all men are created equal?'" Joe looked up. "And here you quote the Declaration of Independence. I liked that part. 'When in the course of human events, it becomes necessary for one people to dissolve the political bands which have connected them with another . . .' You go on quoting, and then you write, 'Those who support our cause are our brothers. Those who oppose our cause are our enemies. Where do you stand, Congressman Edgerton?'" Joe paused. "Did you write those words?"

"I did. And I am proud of them. Those words were from my heart, the heart of every oppressed Navajo."

"So was Congressman Edgerton an enemy?"

"There is no threat in that letter. It was a warning that the American government was creating an oppressed population that someday might rise up against its oppressors."

"You're right: Your threat was veiled. But you asked him what side he was on. Did he side with the American government? Was he the first casualty of your uprising?"

"Is the congressman missing or is he dead?"

Rushingwater was no dummy.

"I'm exploring the possibility that he's dead, since we found his driver."

"What would I have gained from killing him secretly? Movements need attention. If I had done anything like that, I would have announced it and garnished the attention of the press—"

"Garnered," a voice from the living room said. It was Sleeping Bear. He sat on the couch, bored.

Rushingwater seemed unruffled. "I would have garnered the attention of the nation to our cause. But I did not know if Edgerton was an enemy or not. He never answered the letter."

"He was working on legislation to protect Native American history and also to allow casinos on the reservations."

"Casinos. I guess that has proven beneficial to my people. The white man gave us reservations, but we gave them casinos. Over time, we shall see who the losers are. In that sense, we are the house."

They talked for another twenty minutes, but Joe got nowhere. He would read a passage from a letter, even mock it to see if Rushingwater would rise to the bait and show his anger, but he remained calm, responding to each quote with a call to end the oppression. He had twenty years of rhetoric at his disposal. Joe tired. He asked Rushing-water to submit to a polygraph.

"No, Mr. BIA. Believe my words or don't. I will not play the *bilagáana*s game of technology."

"When was the last time you traveled down to Mexico?"

"I've never been outside the United States, and I try not to pass beyond our four sacred mountains."

Joe ended the interview a few minutes later. Rushingwater agreed to talk again if Joe had additional questions. He also agreed not to have his war chief on alert should Joe return.

"What do the pins in your map represent?" Bluehorse asked.

"Supporters. We are growing in membership every day."

Joe looked at the map again. There were maybe a hundred pins. He had been about to say good luck, but he stopped himself. He wasn't going to wish someone success in seceding from the United States. Too many people had given their lives to hold the country together, including Native Americans.

Outside, Sleeping Bear followed them to the Tahoe.

"Why are you with this crowd?" Bluehorse asked.

"I believe in the cause," Sleeping Bear said.

"To break away from America?" Bluehorse asked.

"To see our people return to our traditions. And that requires greater independence."

Bluehorse seemed thoughtful.

Joe took Nightwind's rifle from his front seat. He handed it to Sleep-ing Bear. "Do you think your leader could kill someone?"

"Words are his only weapon."

"You were there when my partner was attacked because of his

words. And I'm sure you know your leader was arrested for assaulting an officer. He's no Gandhi."

"That was during the MacDonald riots," Sleeping Bear said. "He threw white paint on a Navajo officer. Symbolic. Not violent."

❖

OCTOBER 7

THURSDAY, 2:31 P.M.

NEAR JONES RANCH ROAD, CHI CHIL TAH

(NAVAJO NATION), NEW MEXICO

The Yamaha YZ250 bounced over the ground, ripping through rabbitbrush and patchy brown grass. Books followed no trail. The bike's skinny tires blazed their own path, leaving behind ragged furrows in the clay and torn flora. He took his time, focused on what was before him, and paid particular attention to avoiding the flat cacti, whose thorns could easily cause a puncture and strand him out here. If that happened, he'd rethink his plan. His getaway didn't include pushing his bike for miles. He checked the GPS.

Two minutes later, he arrived.

Edgerton's vehicle was no longer there, of course. The FBI had towed it away. At least that's what the news had reported, which was a shame. He would have liked to have laid eyes on the cause of Mr. O.'s troubles, which now were his troubles, since he'd been recruited as the cleanup team. How his boss was connected to the whole missing congressman thing was a mystery to Books. And he really didn't care. If Mr. O. didn't want to say, that was fine with him. He would be gone soon enough. Only last night, after he'd gotten back from his visit with William Tom, he'd found Mr. O. lying on the bathroom floor, naked, crying, begging his daddy not to take away his dolls, white powder on the counter, a puddle of his own urine next to him. Books knew it was time to beat feet. He'd seen guys in Philadelphia, a successful business-man, a shortstop for the Phillies, a city councilman, the wife of a big developer, all of them, each of them, take the sleigh ride straight down. And Mr. O. was zipping down that same mountain right now. No con-trols and no brakes. The crash would be ugly, and Books hoped not to be around for the aftermath.

After the phone call the previous day, his boss had not stopped talking about the agent.

"That son of a bitch isn't going to let it drop." They were standing in the study. Mr. O. went to the cabinet and took out a Navajo mask, the same one the professor had photographed.

"That fat worm Trudle is going to pay, too. But first we take care of Evers." Othmann gave Books the look: the *This is why I pay you so well* look. "I want him dead."

"How?"

"I don't care. But as far from here as possible."

"What's he got on you?"

His boss didn't reply at first, and Books could almost see the paranoia swirling around in the crazy bastard's head.

Mr. O. held up the mask. "It's against the law to own one, and apparently Evers wants to get a search warrant to look around."

"Just turn it over to him. Why take on the trouble?"

"That's why I don't pay you to think. I don't let anyone take from me. Not that little fuck Eddie or this big fuck Evers. No one takes from me."

Books hadn't liked the agent from the start, so taking him out was almost a perk. Most people, even cops, were intimidated by Books's size. But not Evers. Books had wanted to knock that arrogant look off his face when he'd first met him at the door, but he wasn't an idiot. You never messed with a cop unless you knew you'd get away with it. And in a little more than an hour from now, he would get away with it.

He turned the bike's engine off.

Mr. O. had made one call and had gotten the coordinates to where Edgerton's vehicle had been found. He also learned the caliber of the round, so that Books could use it to pique Evers's interest.

Books walked to the road. He picked a spot ten feet into the tree line, knelt down, opened his backpack, and took out the barrel and then the stock of a Browning .30-06 lever-action takedown rifle. He slid the barrel in place, listening for the click. He checked the scope. Clean. He liked a lever action on his rifles. It had a nice cowboy feel to it, like in the old Westerns.

Jones Ranch Road was clear. No cars, but there was life. Across from his position, a prairie dog stood on its hind legs. It, too, seemed to be watching the road for vehicles. Books lowered the weapon and sighted on the animal. Its head filled the target ring of the lens.

"Bang," he whispered.

❖

OCTOBER 7
THURSDAY, 3:44 P.M.
JONES RANCH ROAD, CHI CHIL TAH (NAVAJO NATION),
NEW MEXICO

They'd left the asphalt about a mile back and were now traveling along a gravel road. It stretched out before them, seemingly endless, disappearing into a horizon of trees and blue sky. No vehicles around. No witnesses, either. The same road Edgerton and his party had traveled all those years ago when they vanished.

"It feels wrong," Joe said. "He knows us, but we don't know him."

He slowed to a stop a little more than a hundred feet from the turnoff they had used to get to Edgerton's vehicle.

"It's the rez," Bluehorse said. "People do strange stuff here."

"Yeah, but his voice didn't sound native."

"What do you want to do?"

Joe had thought about having Stretch and Sadi come out to provide backup for the meet, but the incident at Mickey's with Sadi was still too raw. He didn't want her or Stretch out here judging how he was running this case. And besides, meeting sources on the rez was pretty common, even with those who wanted to stay anonymous and didn't trust cops. Neighbors often ratted on one another and were afraid to be found out. Then why did this meet bother him? Because of the voice. It had seemed disguised, yet he'd thought he'd recognized it. When—

"What do you want to do, Joe?" Bluehorse asked, this time his tone more insistent.

Joe didn't know.

❖

OCTOBER 7

THURSDAY, 3:48 P.M.

JONES RANCH ROAD, CHI CHIL TAH (NAVAJO NATION),

NEW MEXICO

Books was prone on the ground, not moving, when the sound of tires on gravel came from the east. He waited.

Minutes passed.

No vehicle.

He crawled forward, careful not to disturb the brush around him. He saw the vehicle, Joe Evers's Tahoe, but he couldn't make out the occupants. He edged forward another foot and peered through his rifle's scope. The reflection of sun and sky on windshield made it impossible to see inside. Was Evers alone? Perhaps he'd brought the professor with him. If so, Books could be tossing back Pacíficos in La Libertad by Monday, maybe scouting café sites by Tuesday.

It felt good to have a plan. A goal. The only time Books had ever truly felt good about life was a year after he came out of juvie. He'd gotten a job at a coffee shop, a quaint little place in Doylestown, Pennsylvania, run by an old Italian named Cosimo. The old man had treated him well, given him respect even before Books had earned it. Trusted him. Let him open and close the place, even tally the register. Books stayed on for more than a year, even dated a local girl, a transcriptionist at the courthouse, Clair. Cosimo called her "Clairabelle." Things were good.

And then the landlord refused to renew the old man's lease; Cosimo had been there thirty years.

Books paid a visit to the landlord, hoping to somehow change his mind. But the daughter answered the door. Turned out the landlord was eighty-three, bedridden, and senile. The daughter ran things. So Books tried to talk to her, tried to get her to see reason, explaining that the café was Cosimo's whole life. But all she kept saying was that he had to leave or she'd call the cops. She went for the phone. He stopped her. That's when she told him about unloading her father's properties. She had a buyer for the café, but it needed to be vacant. She explained all this while begging him not to hurt her. He hadn't gone there to hurt anyone. The next day, he quit, telling Cosimo simply that it was time he moved on. Cosimo died later that same year, heart attack. The police never found the woman's body. And no one ever questioned Books about her.

He liked the name Rick's Café, but maybe he would call it Cosimo's. That sounded nice. And he would offer Italian food.

Lying there on the red clay with the odor of sage strong, too strong, all around him, he promised himself this was his last gig. He wasn't going to die in prison, take a shiv in the face while he sat on the shitter. He wanted to go out like the old man, in the kitchen, brewing coffee and stuffing cannoli. Peaceful. Maybe even find a lady along the way. Another Clairabelle.

It was 4:02 and he couldn't see into the bastard's vehicle. The son of a bitch was screwing things up. Now Books would have to move to get a clean shot.

❖

OCTOBER 7
THURSDAY, 4:08 P.M.
JONES RANCH ROAD, CHI CHIL TAH (NAVAJO NATION),
NEW MEXICO

There he is," Bluehorse said.

At first, Joe saw only a scraggly forest. Then he caught movement. A man walking along the tree line, appearing from behind one juniper, then just as quickly disappearing behind the next. He wore a brown jacket, baseball cap, and sunglasses. Bluehorse opened his door.

Joe didn't like it. "Hold on. Let's—"

Bluehorse wasn't listening. "Eddie!" He stood by his open door.

Joe got out and moved behind the engine compartment.

The man, perhaps twenty yards from the road, knelt.

Joe drew his weapon.

The man brought up a rifle.

"Gun!" Joe fired his Glock: one, two, three rounds.

In his periphery, he saw Bluehorse fall against the rear passenger door. Joe's ears rang from the Glock's loud reports. He called out to his partner.

No answer.

Bluehorse had on his vest, Joe repeated to himself.

The man in the tree line moved to his left, behind a thick oak. The rifle's barrel peeked around the tree. It barked.

Air rushed past Joe's head. He returned three rounds.

Another rifle shot.

The round punched into the engine compartment.

He called again to Bluehorse.

No answer. Gurgling sounds.

Joe dropped to the hard-packed clay and peered beneath the truck.

Bluehorse lay on his back on the ground. Blood stained the left side of his neck and shoulder. He stared straight up, struggling to breathe, blood leaking from his mouth.

"Hold on, buddy," Joe said.

He stood up. A rifle round smashed into the windshield to his right.

Joe emptied his magazine, shooting into the tree line, spacing the rounds in and around the oak. No targeting. Keeping the shooter's head down so Joe could acquire better firepower. At this distance, a rifle had the advantage. When his Glock locked back, Joe hunkered down, dropped the mag, and reloaded with the extra on his hip. As he did this, he moved around the driver's door, staying low.

The front passenger tire exploded; the Tahoe lurched.

Joe stood and put another three shots over the windshield. Again ɔ target. The shooter wasn't exposing himself. Joe hit the rifle rack's release button, reached up, and pulled the M4 from its cradle above the front seat.

Another rifle round came through the passenger window and smashed into the seat belt fixture on the driver's side. He felt sharp, stabbing pain in his right cheek. He didn't have time to worry about it. He charged the M4 and stood, delivering a volley of rounds: five, ten, fifteen. Jolts of pain ran down the side of his face.

A round sailed through the windshield, creasing the dashboard above Joe's head as he reached inside and grabbed the handset of the car radio. "Officer down! Officer down!" He yelled their location, his voice high and breaking.

A round slammed into the outside corner of the driver's seat, to the right of his head. The dispatcher was talking, but Joe wasn't listening. He couldn't stay where he was; it offered too little protection. He calculated the location of the shooter from the trajectory of the last round. The man was moving to his left, Joe's right. He grabbed three M4 magazines from the pocket of the driver's door. Then he stood and delivered the M4's remaining rounds as he moved back behind the engine block and front tire.

When the M4's bolt locked back, Joe dropped the mag and rammed another home. His heart raced, the sound hammering in his ears. Blood dripped from his cheek onto the stock of the rifle. He made a mental inventory of his ammunition. Two M4 mags, plus the one he'd loaded. Ninety rounds. Plus twelve left in the pistol. All this quick, mechanical. Two decades of rote training on the firing range.

The radio was chattering now. Officers en route. Voices and sirens blared through the radio speakers. The dispatcher cleared the channel for Joe.

"Help's on the way, buddy," he called to Bluehorse, shouting to be heard over the radio. Another shot thudded into the front fender.

He needed to move. If not, the shooter would gain more of an advantage. Worse yet, he might put another round into Bluehorse.

Thoughts crowded Joe's mind. He pushed back the fear. Time pressed down on him. Adrenaline raced through his limbs. He shook. Fight-or-flight tremors. Anticipation. Readiness. The shooter knew exactly where Joe was. Joe had only a vague idea where the shooter was.

Time to change that.

He held his hand out and willed the tremors to stop. He took a deep breath, then rose to his feet. He put five rounds in the shooter's direction directly across from the front passenger door. Still firing, he ran into the tree line, to the left of where he thought the shooter waited. He dropped to the ground behind a juniper tree and fired several more rounds. Released the mag. Loaded a fresh one. Put the now-partial mag in his right pocket.

He studied his target area. A bush shook. He delivered three rounds.

A second later, the man stood and ran deeper into the woods. Joe fired. He got up, moved forward at a trot, the M4 up, locked into his shoulder. Ready.

He glimpsed the brown jacket and dispatched another two rounds. He kept moving forward.

Another glimpse. Another two rounds. Then two more.

The man found cover behind a tree. Fired back.

Pain ripped into Joe's left bicep. He ignored it, firing off a volley. The M4 locked back. He took a knee, changed mags, quick and fluid despite the burning in his left arm. He slammed the charging handle forward, rose to his feet, and advanced, putting multiple rounds down range.

The man was running now, disappearing into the woods.

Sirens in the distance. Joe pressed forward.

He heard a small engine start up ahead and to his left. He ran in that direction.

A dirt bike with the man atop it tore across the woods forty yards in front of him. Joe took aim. The bike was moving fast. Too fast. One, two, three. He fired off four rounds before the bike and driver vanished.

When the sound of the engine grew too distant to hear, Joe ran back to the road, back to Bluehorse.

❖

OCTOBER 7

THURSDAY, 7:51 P.M.

OTHMANN ESTATE, SANTA FE, NEW MEXICO

Mr. O. was pacing when Books walked into the study. Neither spoke. Books waited. The throb in his right arm was beginning to subside, the pain still intense. He was popping ibuprofen every half hour. It wasn't helping. The drive back to Santa Fe had been excruciating. When Mr. O. finally looked at him, saw the blood, he freaked.

After Books told his story, Mr. O. yelled and carried on. He snorted three lines while Books waited, holding bath towels under his arm so the blood wouldn't drip on Mr. O.'s precious carpet. The coke seemed to have the opposite of its usual effect on his boss. It calmed him.

"Okay. Okay. We need to think. Let's be cool. Okay." He sat down behind his desk. "Evers is probably alive, right?"

"I think so."

"You think so. You fucked this whole thing up, and you *think* so?"

"I'll fix it," Books said.

"You better."

Books had planned to come back, tell his boss the good news, and then quit. He would have been in his room that very minute, packing instead of standing here, soaking up blood with his boss's designer bath towels. But the situation had changed. He would take care of it, of course. He'd given his word. And, on top of that, he owed Evers.

"I need antibiotics for my arm," he said. "I can't go to the hospital."

"Jesus Christ, you're worried about your fucking arm. Did he see you?"

Books shook his head.

Mr. O. got him antibiotics and Percocet that night. Not out of personal concern, Books was sure. His boss wanted him healthy enough to fix the problem.

Back in his room, Books locked his door, set his gun on the nightstand, and tried to relax. He cleaned the wound with peroxide and then packed it with gauze. Later, when his hand steadied, he stitched his arm the best he could, having learned how during his time in Philly. He'd been lucky. No arteries severed, no broken bones. He drifted off into restless sleep and dreamed of Ecuador, a little coastal town called La Libertad, and of his café. Then an El Niño hit the shore and swept it out to sea. He tried to swim out to get it all back.

He woke drenched in sweat, his arm throbbing.

◈

OCTOBER 8
FRIDAY, 9:13 A.M.
GALLUP INDIAN MEDICAL CENTER, GALLUP,
NEW MEXICO

Joe opened his eyes. A low, repetitive beep emanated from somewhere behind him. Tubes connected him to intravenous bags. The room smelled of disinfectant and urine. Sunlight streamed in through the windows, catching tiny dust motes floating in the air, giving them an iridescent glow.

The events at Jones Ranch Road flooded his mind, though the images were jumbled. Pieces really. Eventually, they organized themselves into one coherent memory. After chasing the shooter, he'd raced back to the Tahoe, sat next to Bluehorse, and held a hand on his bleeding neck wound. He told him everything would be okay. Bluehorse never spoke, only stared into Joe's eyes. He didn't know if his friend saw anything, but he spoke to him just the same. He tried to say the right thing, just as he had tried to say the right thing to Christine in his last minutes with her, never wanting the time to end, no matter how painful. He went through that again, sitting there by the Tahoe, watching his friend's life seep through his fingers.

The young officer struggled with each breath, spitting blood. The bullet had entered through the top of his chest, at the clavicle.

So much blood.

"It's going to be okay," Joe kept saying. "The EMTs are almost here. You're going to be fine. We'll be laughing about it next week. You'll see. Just hang in there." He found himself repeating *hang in there* over and over again as he searched for the right words, any words.

Two sheriff's deputies arrived first. After Joe told them what direction the shooter had gone when he fled the scene, one deputy stood guard, securing the tree line; the other brought over a trauma kit and applied compresses to Bluehorse's injuries, pulling away the wadded-up cloth that had once been Joe's shirt.

When the EMTs arrived, Joe insisted they treat Bluehorse first, threatening the one EMT who wanted to look at Joe's wounds. Everything after that blurred. His last clear memory was of fluorescent lights passing overhead and a woman's voice asking him if he knew his name. He couldn't remember if he'd answered her.

Now he checked himself over, wanting to know his injuries. He tried to sit up, but a bolt of pain electrified his left arm and shoulder. For a moment, he couldn't move. Tremors coursed through his body. His upper arm was wrapped in a bandage, preventing him from assessing the injury. He remembered very little from the previous evening in the ER and then later in surgery. He touched his cheek. His fingers caressed gauze and medical tape. He pressed the call button on the side rail of his bed. A few moments later, a nurse entered his room.

A sheriff's deputy standing outside the door looked in.

"Glad to see you're awake, Agent."

Joe nodded cautiously, anticipating another jolt of pain. Not too bad. A little soreness in the neck, but that was all.

The nurse told him she, too, was glad he was awake. She checked his vitals and gave him some water. His cheek hurt with each gulp. She said the doctor would be in soon. He asked about Bluehorse. His cheek protested, but he got the words out. She told him again that the doctor would be in shortly, then left.

A few minutes later, the doctor arrived. A squat Hispanic man whose smile seemed larger than his face.

"Welcome back, Agent Evers. How are you feeling?"

Joe told him it hurt like a son of a bitch. And then he told him it hurt like a son of a bitch to tell him it hurt like a son of a bitch.

The doctor found that amusing, which hadn't been Joe's intention.

"How's Randall, Doc? The other officer?"

The doctor's smile disappeared. "I'm sorry. He didn't make it. He died early this morning. Lost too much blood."

Joe's breath caught. He turned away, ignoring the pain in his cheek.

The doctor checked his patient's chart, made some notes.

Joe used the time to get his mind right. He felt new pain, a throb in his chest. And it wasn't from any physical injury. Twenty-two years, he'd never lost another agent—or another officer. Why now, so close to retirement? Why couldn't it have been him? That would have been so much easier. All his miseries, over. All his time away from Christine, over. All his failures as a husband, a father, an agent . . . over.

But what about Melissa? How would she feel if he were gone? She would be alone.

Selfish bastard.

The doctor was talking.

". . . guessing a ricochet?" He waited for a response. When Joe didn't answer, he continued. "We found a fragment on your vest." He stabbed a finger at the right side of his own chest. "We removed several fragments from your cheek. There will be some scarring." He pointed to the right side of his own face, an inch or two below his temple. "There was combined soft-tissue damage, mostly to your zygomaticus muscle, which some folks call the 'smile muscle.' Some nerve damage, too, but I don't think that's as serious. The puncture wound to your left arm nicked your humerus and tore your bicep and tricep. With appropriate wound care and some restrictions for a few weeks, it should be fine. Not bad, considering. I'm actually more concerned about your cheek. We'll give it some time, but you might consider consulting a plastic surgeon."

Joe nodded, half-listening.

The doctor removed the bandage on Joe's cheek and had him perform what he called a 'facial animation test,' requiring Joe to make expressions: a big smile and a little smile, a look of surprise and a frown, an open mouth, a closed mouth.

When he finished, the doctor said, "Some people are waiting to see you. Are you up for company?"

H ey, buddy," Stretch said. "How you feeling?"

The entire squad stood around the bed.

"Is that a smile?" Cordelli said. "You look like you're trying to take a shit."

Tenny laughed.

Ginny shoved a motherly elbow into Cordelli's gut.

Cordelli pretended to double over. "What? He does."

"The FBI sent a shooting review team out there," Dale said. "I called and let them know you were awake. They're sending someone over to talk to you." Joe had never been involved in a shoot-out before, but he knew the shooting review team would consist of investigators and evidence technicians who would try to reconstruct what happened.

Joe nodded.

"Don't take this the wrong way, but do you need a lawyer?"

Joe met Dale's eyes. "What for?"

"You were involved in a shooting. I need to ask."

"Do you think I did something wrong?"

"I don't know. I wasn't there."

Tenny shook his head. "That's kinda rude, boss. The man's been shot."

"I wasn't implying anything," Dale said. "An officer lost his life out there. I'm only covering the bases."

Joe felt a pang in his stomach. He had screwed up. Eddie had felt wrong to him. He should have called it off. Or had more backup. They'd walked into an ambush. He needed answers.

"Is Andi out there?"

"Been out there all night. Said she won't go home until they get every trace of the shooter collected."

"What'd they find?" Stretch asked.

"They followed the bike tracks for several miles to truck-tire impressions. They took molds. They also collected all the shell casings and some blood. Looks like you hit the son of a bitch. Maybe you killed him. But all that may be unnecessary if you can ID the shooter." Dale paused. "Can you?"

"He called himself Eddie. Male. Wore a cap and sunglasses." He felt the room deflate. The squad had been hoping he could finger the shooter.

Sadi said, "Eddie? You're not saying it was Eddie Begay, are you?"

"The guy didn't sound native, but it was hard to tell," Joe said. "I don't think so."

Sadi visibly relaxed.

"Where's my phone?"

Everyone but Joe looked around the room. Ginny found it in the drawer of the bedside table.

Joe scrolled through the call history. He found the private number and showed it to Dale. "The guy called to set the meet."

Dale handed the phone to Cordelli. "Get his incoming calls. Let the FBI know what you're doing. Make sure they get copies."

"Got it, boss," Cordelli said. He took out a notepad and jotted down the call information.

"You made CNN," Tenny said.

"Yeah, big news," Dale said. "I got a call from that Chris Staples guy again. Apparently, the shooting is stirring up more conspiracy theories. I like the one about Edgerton trying to bump you off so you won't find him. Staples's worried. He asked me to put out a press release saying Grace Edgerton wasn't involved."

"Did he at least ask how I was doing?"

"Eventually."

"Did anyone call Melissa?" Joe said in panic. "If she saw it on CNN, she's probably freaking out. Where's—"

"Calm down." Stretch put a hand on his shoulder. "I spoke to her last night and this morning. The doctor assured us you would be fine, and I told her that. She wanted to fly out right then, but I told her to wait until she spoke to you. She wants to come home. You can't blame her, Joe."

No, he couldn't. "How about Bluehorse's family?"

Several pairs of eyes avoided Joe's.

"They were here last night," Dale said. "They're taking it pretty hard, of course."

Of course.

They spoke for another half hour. Joe gave them an account of the incident. When breakfast arrived, they agreed to let him eat in peace.

"What's up with the guard on my room?"

"The sheriff's department offered. I accepted," Dale said. "We didn't know what happened and didn't want to take chances." He followed the others to the door. "The doctor told me you're being released tomorrow. Stretch will pick you up."

They filed out of the room. Stretch hung back.

"I got a call from a woman this morning. Said she was concerned about you."

"Gillian? Did she want me to call her?"

"No. Not her. She said her name was Sierra."

"Sierra Hannaway?"

Stretch nodded.

"Let me guess. She wanted to know who was going to work her sister's case while I was laid up in bed."

"Actually, she didn't talk about the case. She asked how you were and if she could visit you."

"Really?"

"Yeah, really."

"What did you tell her?"

"I told her yes."

Joe said nothing.

"From that stupid look on your face, I take it I made the right decision."

"I have to call Melissa. I'll see you tomorrow."

"Yeah, I thought so. See you tomorrow."

❖

OCTOBER 8

FRIDAY, 1:24 P.M.

GALLUP INDIAN MEDICAL CENTER, GALLUP,

NEW MEXICO

s it okay to come in?"

A woman's soft voice brought Joe out of a light sleep.

Sierra Hannaway stood at the door.

"Sure." He used the bed control to raise himself to a sitting position. His pain meds were working.

She held a small bouquet of flowers set in a *Get Well* coffee mug. "Sorry, they didn't have much of a selection."

She placed it on the end table next to his bed.

"Thank you," he said. "For the flowers . . . and for coming."

"I'm sorry about the other officer."

Joe didn't want condolences. He wanted to give them. To Blue-horse's family. He wasn't sure if the young officer had been married. He didn't think so, but maybe he'd had a girlfriend. He should know that.

"I feel bad," Sierra said, her voice gentle, almost inaudible.

"So do I."

"No, not about him—I mean, I do feel bad about him, of course, but I feel bad about you. About the way I treated you when I first met you. I accused you of not doing anything, and . . . and I don't want to repeat some of the things I said about you to other people."

Joe had no idea where this was going.

"I don't mean I was bad-mouthing you specifically," she said. Her hands wrestled each other almost as much as she seemed to wrestle with her words. "I mean, I was talking about the police in general. You know, how sometimes they don't care about victims or the families."

"Wow. Thanks for coming and making me feel good about my job."

"That wasn't what I meant." She looked around. "I'm not good at this."

"At what?"

"This." She gestured toward him and the nightstand. "All this."

"The flowers? They're great. I really appreciate them." He motioned to the empty room. "They're my first."

She gave an embarrassed smile. "I mean talking to people. I'm not good at talking to people. I work with old bones, so I don't have to talk to people. I didn't want to be the chief preparator at the museum, because I knew that then I'd have to talk to the volunteers. And that's not me. But they pushed me to take the position. And I hate it."

"I see."

"So, every time we've met, I came off . . ." She searched for the words. "I came off mean. And I'm really not. But I did it again today. I'm sorry."

"I don't think you came off mean. I appreciate your visit. I really do. I'm surprised and pleased by it. Believe me. There's no reason to apologize. And besides, you've perked me up. I was starting to feel sorry for myself, lying here in bed, shot, not knowing if I was going to make it. I'm glad you set me straight." He smiled, or tried to. He hoped Cordelli had been joking about what the effort looked like. "I'm a good-for-nothing cop."

She giggled, then broke into a genuine laugh. "I know you're making fun of me, and I deserve it. You really were shot, and I come in here insulting you. Then tell you about my own troubles. And there you are in pain, and yet . . . so nice."

Joe started to laugh and then stopped, clutching his cheek.

"Are you okay?" She started to move to the door. "Should I get the nurse?"

He laughed harder, pressing against the bandage, trying to push down the pain. "No. No. I'm fine. Laughing hurts. Go back to insulting me. Please."

She covered her mouth. He guessed part of the reason they were laughing was due not to the humor, but to the awkwardness of the situation. She was innocent. And so vulnerable.

"I never knew anyone who was shot," she said. "Is it bad?"

"The doctor said I'll be fine. A little rest. Some rehabilitation. I'll be good as new. They're releasing me tomorrow."

"So, you'll be off from work for a while?"

"Yes, but another agent will be assigned to your sister's case."

"No. No. That wasn't what I meant. I was wondering if you

would like to stop by the museum. It's very relaxing, and I can show you around. We even have wheelchairs, if you can't walk."

Joe met her eyes. "Yes, I'd like that. Though not the wheelchair part."

❖

October 8

Friday, 4:37 p.m.

Denny's Restaurant, Albuquerque, New Mexico

Officer Lopez sat at the counter. He liked this Denny's because it gave cops half off. He was eating a T-bone steak and shrimp platter and reading the paper. Actually, he was rereading the article about Joe Evers's getting shot. It was his third time through and he couldn't stop smiling.

Damn his steak tasted good. Actually, everything tasted good. It was funny how good news made everything seem right in the world.

He looked for his overworked waitress. She was carrying a milk shake over to a trucker at the other end of the counter. There was a little junk in that trunk, but even she was looking all right to him today.

"Hey, sweetie. I'll take one of them shakes from you. Vanilla." He winked at her. "With a cherry, please."

Yeah, life was good.

He watched her butt jiggle as she scooped his ice cream.

Real good.

OCTOBER 8

FRIDAY, 6:37 P.M.

GALLUP INDIAN MEDICAL CENTER, GALLUP,

NEW MEXICO

J esus, Mary, and Joseph!" Helena's voice came through the
phone, loud and brassy. "What the hell happened, Joey?"

"You've been scooped. I was shot."

"Well, it must not be that bad, 'cause you still got that sexy dry
humor. And now you have a kinda cowboy drawl. I like it."

"I'm drawling because I got shot in the face."

"Are you going to be okay?" She sounded concerned.

"A few scars."

"Don't worry about that. You'll wear them well, I'm sure."

Helena had called the hospital. Other reporters were trying to talk
to him and visit him, but they were all being screened by the hospital
staff and the deputy. Helena had told a nurse at the nurses' station
that she was a friend. The nurse gave Joe her name and he said to
put the call through. Helena Newridge had a perky charm about her
that he liked.

"My boss pulls me back to D.C. to cover an old broad with low
blood sugar who's tripping all over the place, and then you go and get
shot. And I have to read about it in that Gallup rag."

"I'll tell you what. I'll wait for you to be in town the next time I get
shot, how's that?"

"Deal. By the way, I searched through some archives and found
out that Grace Edgerton does own a gun." She let her words hang in
the air.

"You know I'm lying in a hospital bed, shot, hooked up to machines, right? Are you trying to kill me with suspense?"

"Sorry, I can't help it. I deliver news like doctors deliver babies. And it's a . . . boy!"

Joe waited.

"Okay. Okay. Don't get your catheter in a bunch. I found an article in the *Albuquerque Journal* from a year before Edgerton went missing. The Veterans of Foreign Wars had honored him for getting them funding to build a new hall. They gave him an engraved Colt 1911 pistol. There was a photo of him receiving it."

Joe's mind went into overdrive. 1911s were .45-caliber. Had Grace Edgerton lied to him about the gun? Did she still have it? And hadn't Bobby Joe Lopez met Faye Hannaway at a veterans' function?

"Where's the gun now?"

She let out a sigh. "You need to start pulling your own weight around here, Joey."

"I was shot."

"Yeah, and I got corns, but I'm working."

❖

OCTOBER 9
SATURDAY, 9:20 A.M.
OTHMANN ESTATE, SANTA FE, NEW MEXICO

W hat did you find out?" Books asked. He cradled his arm. He'd stopped taking Percocet today, gone back on ibuprofen. The heavy drug had fogged his brain, and he couldn't afford that handicap right now.

"He was shot, but he's okay," Othmann said. "He's going to be just *super* in a couple days."

"I'll take care of it."

"Maybe we don't need to. He's retiring soon, and this may put him on medical leave."

There'd been another bathroom episode last night, and while Books was helping him back to bed, a promise to cut back on the white powder had been uttered. Books thought nothing of it then, but today Mr. O. seemed more lucid. And that made two of them, which was good. Clear heads were less likely to screw up and land them in jail— or dead.

"I still owe him," Books said. He rubbed the wound on his arm.

"This was all William Tom's fault. That crooked jackass."

Books remained silent, knowing Othmann would continue. He could tell his boss needed to talk about it, to bitch about it and blame someone else.

"He got greedy and took some items from that fat worm Trudle. I can't even show them because Trudle published photos in his book."

"What does that have to do with Edgerton?"

"Trudle told him about the theft."

"Is that why he disappeared?"

"Why are you so interested in history all of a sudden?"

"Forget it," Books said, disgusted by his boss's paranoia.

"What?"

"Did you get the address?"

Mr. O. pulled a sheet of paper from his shirt pocket. He held it just out of reach of Books's outstretched hand.

"Not until I give the okay."

Books nodded and took the paper. He smiled when he read what was written on it. It was the smile several people had seen before their lives abruptly ended.

OCTOBER 9

SATURDAY, 10:20 A.M.

GALLUP INDIAN MEDICAL CENTER, GALLUP,

NEW MEXICO

After the doctor signed the discharge paperwork, the nurse wheeled Joe downstairs, Stretch following. Several journalists stood by the front doors, so Stretch pulled his car around to the emergency entrance at the rear of the hospital, where Joe and the nurse waited. A journalist came running around the corner as Joe got into the passenger seat.

"Agent Evers!" The young man made it to the car before the nurse could shut the door. "Agent Evers, can I talk to you a minute?" A camera with a telephoto lens hung from his neck.

Stretch came around the car to close Joe's door. "Sorry, you need to contact the Albuquerque BIA office. Ask for Dale Warren. He likes talking to the press."

The man looked at Joe. "Were you investigating William Tom?"

Joe moved his foot against the door, stopping Stretch from closing it. The way the man said that last sentence got Joe's attention. "Why would you ask that?"

"His wife told me a BIA agent was out to interview him. Chief Cornfield with NPD confirmed it."

"But why did you say *were*?"

"He's dead." The man looked surprised. "You didn't know?"

"When? How?"

"Come on, Joe," Stretch said. "We need to leave."

Joe blocked the door again with his foot.

"His wife found him dead the morning you were shot," the reporter said. "She thinks your visit caused him stress and killed him. She wants to sue the BIA. What did you talk to him about?"

Joe moved his foot.

Stretch shut the door.

The journalist took a photograph of Joe through the passenger window.

What the hell was happening? People were dying all around him.

❖

OCTOBER 9

SATURDAY, 3:33 P.M.

JOE EVERS'S APARTMENT, ALBUQUERQUE, NEW MEXICO

The front door opened. Joe tried to sit up. Stretch had dropped him off a few hours earlier and then had gone to pick up Melissa. Joe had been on the sofa, watching back-to-back shark movies on the SyFy channel, dozing off from the pain medication.

"Dad!" Melissa came around the couch. "Are you okay?" She kissed him on the forehead, as though he were the child and she the parent. Then she examined his cheek, her hand a few inches from the gauze.

Stretch stood in the entryway of the apartment, holding a suitcase.

"I'm fine, Brainy Bug," Joe said, trying to sit up. "You didn't need to come home. Stretch made it sound worse than it is." He gave his friend the stink eye.

She straightened and put her hands on her hips. "Are you nuts? You get shot and you think I'm not going to come home?" She waited for a reply, but he kept silent. "I came home to take care of you, because, God knows, you can't take care of yourself."

"Amen" Stretch said.

Joe tossed another stink eye toward his friend.

"You want this in the bedroom?" Stretch asked.

"Leave it there; I'll get it."

"I'll let you two do your father-daughter thing. And don't let him push you around, Melissa." He gave her a peck on the cheek. "The doctor said nothing strenuous. So keep an eye on him." He returned the stink eye to Joe and then left.

Melissa went to the kitchen. A few seconds later, she gasped.

"Is this all you've been eating?" She held up two tinfoil-wrapped bean burritos. The refrigerator stood open. "You don't have anything else in here." She pulled out four more and tossed all of them in the trash can.

"Leave that alone, and come here," Joe said.

"What?"

"Come here."

She walked to the couch. He stood. She looked so much like Christine. And she had her fire, too, which warmed his heart and stung his eyes. For any father, a daughter was perfect beauty. He wrapped his good arm around her, holding her close, then wrapped his injured arm around her, too, ignoring the pain to pull her even closer.

"Dad, be careful. Don't hurt yourself."

"It only hurts if I don't hug you."

What do you think?" Sierra said.

Beside her, a dinosaur, shorter than she was, with a long, narrow head, prowled through foliage from 200 million years ago.

"Wow." Joe read the plaque: *Coelophysis*. "How do you pronounce it?"

"See-low-fy-sis."

He repeated the name.

"I finished it last night," she said, pride in her voice.

He looked directly into her eyes. "I'm impressed." He really was.

The color rose in her face. "Thank you, Joe."

He walked around the exhibit. "Lot of teeth. Meat eater?"

"Yes. And a cannibal, too. We found fossilized remains of a young *Coelophysis* in its stomach."

"Thank you for getting me out of my apartment. My daughter's been smothering me. Now I know what I do to her." He made small rotations with his shoulder. "Do you mind if we walk. I'm a little stiff."

They moved through the exhibits, taking it slow, Sierra the tour guide, Joe the interested visitor. Even though a part of him was attentive to the history, or the science, or whatever one would call the stories behind dinosaur displays, he was more attentive to her, simply enjoying hearing her speak. He smiled when she smiled. He laughed when she laughed. And he showed appropriate fascination when her voice took on that dreamy quality people have when talking about something they love.

When they arrived at the FossilWorks, she asked if he remembered it from their last visit. He wanted to tell her that of course he did. This was where he had first noticed her figure beneath that lab coat. But he only nodded.

Behind the glass, the same group of volunteers toiled away. The old woman in the center of the room looked up and waved to Sierra. When she saw Joe, she broke into a large, full-faced grin. She gave Sierra a thumbs-up. Sierra seemed to blush.

"So what's the thumbs-up for?" he asked, not letting the opportunity pass.

"Oh, that's Trixie. She's a real spitfire. Been volunteering here for fifteen years. She's almost ninety, but her mind and attitude are no older than nineteen."

She was being coy. He was about to press her for the real meaning of Trixie's gesture, when a man spoke.

"Excuse me, Sierra."

It was the ponytail guy, the same one who had interrupted their last meeting. Joe could smell the man's testosterone even from this distance.

"Hello, Paul." She turned to Joe. "This is Paul Drake, our director of acquisitions. Paul, this is Joe Evers. He's . . . he's a friend."

Joe picked up on Sierra's hesitation. Was she trying to hide he was a cop, or was she explaining their relationship to Paul?

They shook hands and stared at each other a moment. Paul seemed to be sizing him up.

"We're about to open the crates for the *Seismosaurus*," Paul said. "You said you wanted to be there."

"Why are we doing them now? I thought we planned it for this afternoon."

"We did, but I saw you finished the *Coelophysis* exhibit, so I thought we might get a jump on the crates. Unless you're otherwise tied up." Paul looked at Joe.

"Well, I was planning on this afternoon."

"That's fine. I thought I'd stop by to see if you wanted to do it now, that's all. We can do it later."

Joe sensed a relationship here, a slight tension between them. Past or present?

"Actually," Joe said, "I have to go anyway. I need to stop by the office."

"Are you going back to work already? I thought—" She stopped herself, clasping her hands together.

"No. I'm taking the week off. I just need to check on something."

Paul said good-bye. Sierra walked Joe out.

Their time together had been nice, but Joe worried he'd misinterpreted her invitation. "I'll be back on the case next week, so I may need to talk with you again about Bobby Lopez. I met him. I didn't know your sister, but he didn't seem like the kind of guy she would have been involved with."

"She was going to change the world one stray dog at a time. Bobby was broken. She met him at some veterans' event. Congressman Edgerton was there receiving an award, and she went along."

"Was it the Veterans of Foreign Wars?"

"It could have been. I may have photos. Faye often took photos at the congressman's events. When I cleaned her apartment, I took all of her things, or at least whatever Bobby didn't steal. I still have them all in my attic."

Joe thanked her for the tour and left. Joe wondered what Sierra's relationship was with Paul Drake. Obviously more than coworkers, but how much more, he didn't know. Ex-lover? Maybe. Hopeful suitor? He hoped not. But he knew he shouldn't be jealous. He'd had twenty-two amazing years with Christine. He shouldn't begrudge another man that same happiness.

Ｈow are you feeling?" Tenny asked.

"Been better." The drive to the office from the museum had been painful. "Are you the only one here?"

"Cordelli and Ginny went to lunch. I'm heading out, too. Sadi and Stretch are in Dale's office."

Joe did an about-face. Something was up. Dale wasn't into pow-wows around his desk.

At the door, he knocked once, then entered.

Dale looked up from a folder he held in his hand. "Come in, Joe. How're you feeling?"

Stretch stood up, offered Joe his chair. "What the hell're you doing in the office? You're supposed to be resting."

Joe waved off the seat. "I needed to get out of the apartment. So what's going on?"

"We were talking about Othmann." Dale said.

"What about him?"

"We think he was behind the shooting." Sadi said. No attitude.

"Okay." Joe decided to take Stretch's seat. "Explain."

"Cordelli ran your incoming numbers and ID'd the caller," Stretch said. "A cell phone belonging to Eddie Begay. The call to your phone was made in Santa Fe. Cordelli requested a cell-tower trace, and Othmann's estate was in the call zone."

"Why would Eddie try to take us out?" Joe said. "How is he connected to the Edgerton case?"

"We don't know," Sadi said. "Maybe he thought you were working his CSA case or investigating the stolen petroglyph."

That was a lot of maybes. Joe was having difficulty keeping it straight. "I thought you said Eddie was a drunken loser. The guy who shot at me was cool, levelheaded. It wasn't his first time. And where did he get the high-powered rifle and the dirt bike?"

"Yeah, that doesn't sound like our Eddie," Sadi said. "But we put a lookout for him in NCIC and notified the FBI and Navajo PD. When he turns up, we'll get him. His phone's been inactive since he called you."

"What if Othmann financed the op?" Joe said. "He brings in someone or uses that Books character to pull it off. Maybe uses Eddie's phone to set it up, and set up Eddie. That I'll buy. Eddie as a patsy. Let's get a search warrant for Othmann's house."

"With what?" Stretch said. "We have nothing. A theory. No proof. We can't place Eddie's phone. All we have is a phone call made in the vicinity of Othmann's house."

Joe knew Stretch was right. "So what's the plan?"

"We were about to go out there and talk to him," Sadi said.

"All you're going to do is tip him off. Isn't that exactly why you didn't want me to talk to him? You were afraid he would get wind of your damn cave-drawing investigation."

"Petroglyph," she said. No fire. No anger.

"Well, now it's my turn to say it." Joe looked directly at Sadi. "Bullshit! He's not going to give you consent to search his house. He's not stupid enough to leave the evidence right out in the open, so you can—" He stopped himself, his mind quickly working through a scenario to see if it made sense.

"What?" Dale said. "You're thinking of something. What is it?"

"We get a search warrant," Joe said.

Dale sighed. "We can't."

"We can. We can get a search warrant for the Yei mask." Joe explained his meeting with Othmann and what Trudle had noticed. "He told us it was authentic. It's in my report. We put that in the affidavit and add Eddie Begay's statement that he sold him the cave drawing, or whatever it is, and we have more than enough probable cause."

"Why add the petroglyph?" Stretch said. "We have enough with the mask."

"We know where the mask is. Once we get it, we have to stop the search. My guess is that the petroglyph is hidden or sold. Either way, we get to tear his place apart."

"Let's get the warrant," Dale said. "We'll hit his place tomorrow."

"No, Friday," Joe said. "Tomorrow's the funeral."

❖

OCTOBER 14
THURSDAY 9:47 A.M.
ROLLIE'S FUNERAL HOME, GALLUP, NEW MEXICO

Cars spilled over from the parking lot and lined Mesquite Drive, starting from Nizhoni Boulevard and extending almost two blocks. A Gallup PD officer directed traffic while two funeral home employees handled parking. Attendance was in the hundreds. More would show up, no doubt. Family, friends, and officers formed groups outside, waiting to go inside to say their good-byes.

Reporters and photographers flitted about. Someone, probably Chief Cornfield, had leaked that Joe and Bluehorse had been following up on a lead in the Edgerton case when Bluehorse was shot. The papers did not have all the facts of the shooting, but that didn't limit the number of articles. Some of them gave a short accounting of Joe's career, not failing to mention the Felix Longman trial. But this time it was not a D-2 story. Now it had front-page prominence because of the Edgerton connection.

Every night since Bluehorse's death, after sunset, family and friends had gathered at the family home to share meals and take part in ceremonies. Joe had not been invited. But now he walked with Melissa through the parking lot to pay his respects to Bluehorse's loved ones, and to privately ask forgiveness from his young partner. He spotted his squad, Andi McBride with them. She wore a black pantsuit. It had been a while since he'd seen her in anything other than 511's and FBI polos.

"Hey, hero," she said, her voice somber. She gave him a hug.

They all wore their shields on metal chains, a thin black cloth band around each to honor the fallen officer.

He introduced Andi to Melissa. Then small talk began: the weather, the drive, other officers and agents who had fallen over the years, where they would eat after.

A funeral home employee told a large group next to them that they could go in. Several FBI agents were in that group. Joe spotted Mark. They nodded to each other. Joe's squad would probably be part of the next group called. His stomach recoiled at the thought of meeting the family.

"Let's talk," Andi said. The anguish on her face told him she didn't want to say her final farewell yet, either.

They walked away from the group.

"McKinley Country Search and Rescue agreed to help out. I also have three dogs coming in. We're set for Saturday. If there are more bodies out there, we'll find them."

He nodded. "I have another favor to ask."

"Anything."

"I got a lead on a forty-five." He told her about Edgerton's engraved

Colt 1911. "I'm guessing his wife should still have it. Can you get it from her and send it in for comparison?"

She pointed. "Why don't we both ask her?"

Grace Edgerton stepped from a black Lincoln Town Car parked on Nizhoni. A reporter and photographer darted over as she and Chris Staples walked into the funeral home. The press hounds were stopped at the door.

Joe and Andi rejoined their group. A few minutes later, a funeral home employee told them they could pay their respects. Joe took Melissa's hand.

Inside, they were directed to the main viewing room. It seated maybe 150 people. All the seats were taken. Grace Edgerton stood by the casket, praying, Staples behind her. After a few moments, she turned and walked over to a group of people Joe assumed to be the family. Maybe a dozen in all. Some old, some young, some very old, and a baby. Jesus, a baby. Don't let it be Bluehorse's. Joe didn't want to be responsible for leaving a child fatherless. Please.

"Are you okay, Dad?" Melissa asked.

He relaxed his grip on her hand. "Yeah. Fine."

No, he definitely wasn't. He was about to say good-bye to a partner. When he'd come in, he'd made sure to look at everything but the coffin. Even now, he avoided it. He couldn't catch his breath. This was a bad idea.

She looked for an empty pew. "Let's sit down."

Stretch found a folding chair and brought it over. Joe sat. His squad gathered around him. People stared, whispered.

"I'm fine," he said in between deep breaths. "Go. Go and pay your respects. I need a moment. I'll be fine." The others went up. Melissa and Stretch stayed with him.

Faces stared at him—some sad, some disinterested, a few angry. The family stared, too. Chief Cornfield was with them.

"How are you, Agent Evers?" a woman said.

It broke his trance.

Grace Edgerton looked down at him.

He told her he was fine. Fine was the flavor of the day.

Melissa introduced herself.

"I don't know what to say," Edgerton said. "You and Officer Bluehorse were shot because of my husband's case. I'm humbled. I want you to know I'm sorry it happened. I'm so very sorry Officer Bluehorse lost his life. And I'm sorry you were shot. I never imagined anything like this would happen. And I don't understand how it happened. When you are feeling better, I would like to talk."

He didn't trust himself to speak. He nodded. Then he looked at Andi. He wasn't up to talking about the handgun. Andi understood. She gestured with her hand that she would handle it.

Grace Edgerton said good-bye. Chris Staples looked as though he wanted to say something, but he must have sensed it was the wrong time. He left without speaking.

Joe sat there another minute. When he stood, his legs wanted to betray him, but he willed them to keep him upright. He took Melissa's hand and walked to the front of the viewing room, she on one side, Stretch on the other.

Bluehorse was flanked by two Navajo policemen in honor-guard uniforms, one at the head of the coffin and the other at the foot.

The coffin was closed, which was not uncommon among the more traditional Navajo families. The dead were dead. From what Joe had learned over the years, working with Navajo and other Native American officers, death was not something to be feared and should not be mourned, though who could not mourn the passing of a loved one? As was Navajo tradition, Bluehorse's family would have selected several men to prepare his body, and then others to dig a grave and carry his coffin. The Navajo have many traditions to protect the living from the dead. But it had been Joe's job to protect his partner from the living. He wished he had been smart enough and brave enough on that road in Jones Ranch to protect his friend. Instead, he had been too proud and too stupid and had led this young man to his death.

Joe wiped at his eyes.

Off to the side of the coffin, a small table displayed several large framed photographs of Bluehorse. One drew Joe's attention: Bluehorse in his Navajo policeman's uniform. A new uniform. Neat, pressed, sharp creases. Just like at their first meeting. Bluehorse standing by his cruiser, gleaming in the New Mexican sun. A spit-shined rookie. Joe smiled. His chest hitched. He knelt by the coffin and prayed. Knelt because he didn't trust his cowardly legs.

Our father, who art in heaven . . . The words came easily enough, even though he hadn't said the prayer since Christine's death. When he finished, he whispered, "I'm sure we'll meet again, buddy." Then he forced a smile. A smile only Bluehorse could see, for it was meant only for him.

After a bit, he stood and made his way over to the family. In his pocket was his Saint Michael's medal, Christine's gift. He'd brought it to ask the family if they would place it in the coffin with Bluehorse.

A funeral employee, possibly the director, made introductions. "This is the mother and father of Officer Bluehorse." His voice was soft, as though he wanted to be sure not to wake the dead.

His mother looked sad, his father impassive.

"I'm so . . . I'm so sorry. He was my friend. And a fine . . . a fine officer."

The mother began to cry. The father said nothing, did nothing.

"Were you drunk?" a man asked. He stood amongst the family members. In his twenties, dressed in a shirt, tie, black jeans, he resembled Bluehorse. "Were you drunk?" he repeated.

The mother said something sharp in Navajo to the man.

"No. I need to know," the man said. "Were you drunk when my brother was killed? The papers say you're a drunk cop who should have been thrown out years ago. So I'm asking. Were you drunk?"

"My father—" Melissa began.

Joe squeezed her hand. "No, I wasn't drunk."

Stretch put a hand on his shoulder. "Come on. Let's go."

Cornfield stepped up to Joe. "Yes, I think you'd better leave." His face set. "And the truth will come out eventually."

"What are you talking about?" Joe asked, confused but not angry.

"Your antics. They caused the deaths of two people. Officer Blue-horse and William Tom."

Joe looked around. A dozen sets of eyes stared back at him. Pushed at him. Wished him gone. Cornfield had fed these people his own hate. Joe felt that hate now. Not from all of them, but from enough to know he should leave. He understood their need to blame someone, anyone. Losing a loved one, especially one so young, made no sense. To blame someone was to bring order to chaos. Bringing anger into focus blurred the grief. Joe had been there. He understood.

"I'm sorry," Joe said, looking only at the parents. He let Stretch and Melissa lead him away.

They were almost to the door, almost out of the funeral home, away from the family and their rightful anger, when a voice called after him.

"*T'ah*." A soft voice. "*T'ah*." An old voice. Strong, yet frail.

He stopped.

An old woman hobbled toward him. He expected a stern look, an angry word, perhaps. He'd readied himself. Part of him wanted to be blamed. To be labeled. To be punished for not preventing what had happened. This was good. The old woman would give him what he needed most: penance.

He braced himself. She would slap him. He was sure.

As she drew close, the old woman gave a gentle smile, causing the lines on her cheeks to curve and deepen.

He felt the sting of that smile. Worse than a slap.

She held something wrapped in a small Pendleton blanket. Her English was not good. "My grandson want this for you."

She unwrapped the blanket. Cradled at its center was a carved wooden kachina: a ceremonial dancer with a feathered head, winged arms like an eagle, a multicolored body. It held a tiny chanting rattle in one hand.

She held it out to him. "He say he see in you a heavy weight. This help you."

"I don't think I can take it."

"You take." She pushed it at him. "You must take."

He lifted the carving from the blanket. It was heavy. Oak. Bluehorse had told him his grandfather carved special kachinas from oak because it was strong and could bear great burdens.

He reached in his pocket and removed the Saint Michael's medal. Then he handed it to the old woman. She let him place it on her open palm. "It was an honor to know your grandson and to work with him," Joe said, the words difficult to get out. "And I wish I could have worked with him longer." His chest tightened. "On . . . on the day he was killed, he was working with me, helping me. He didn't want me to go alone to a meeting with someone I didn't know. He was trying to keep me safe." He took a deep breath. "I should have been more aware. I should have known it was a setup. But I didn't, and it cost your grandson his life." His eyes welled. "And I can't change that. I can't bring him back. And I'm sorry." A tear spilled. He felt it roll down his cheek. "I am so, so sorry."

The old woman began to cry.

He lowered his head, too ashamed to witness her grief.

Melissa stood at the end of the couch, arms folded. "Look at you. You're in pain. You need to rest. Whatever is happening tomorrow, they can do it without you."

They hadn't gone to the cemetery. He hadn't wanted to upset the family further, so they'd come back home and he'd fallen asleep on the couch. Now his body was stiff. He'd asked for his pain medication and mentioned he was going into work the next day, just for a few hours.

"You look so much like your mother," he said, regretting the words as soon as they left his mouth.

Her arms dropped to her sides. "I know you miss Mom, but burying yourself in work isn't the answer."

"I've barely put in a full day since that damn trial last year. Too much work is not my problem. Finding out who shot Bluehorse—that's my problem. And that's what I'm doing tomorrow."

She started to cry. "You were shot, Dad. I'm worried about you. I'm worried because you're all alone, and I'm worried because you might get hurt again, or worse."

"Honey, I know you're worried, but I promise nothing is going to happen to me tomorrow. The whole squad will be there."

Melissa sat down. He put his arm around her and pulled her close.

"Everything is going to be fine," he said. "And as for being alone, your old man still has a little game."

She pulled away. "I forgot. When do I meet her?"

"Actually, she dumped me. She got back together with her ex. I think he was a rock star or an astronaut or something."

"Her loss."

G ot it," Andi said.
        "Which one?" Joe asked.

They walked through the house, looking for Dale.

"The Ram. Left rear tire. It has a unique striation in the tread. A perfect match to the impression. Did you get the mask?"

"He says he threw it out. Says after Trudle called attention to it, he looked at it again and realized it was a fake."

"Does that make any sense?" Andi asked.

"No one's buying it. We're tearing the place apart, looking for hidden safes or rooms. He called his attorney."

"And Eddie Begay? Any indication he was staying here?"

"Nothing."

They passed the great room, where Sadi and Stretch were moving a couch, and headed into the study. Dale was there, as was Othmann. Cordelli and Tenny were lifting a picture off the wall: the portrait of Othmann's father.

"Be careful with that," Othmann said. "The frame alone cost more than both of you make in a year." He sat behind his desk, smiling. The son of a bitch was amused.

"I think you got robbed," Cordelli said. "Maybe we should be investigating that."

Tenny snickered.

"Like I said, more than both of you make in a year." Othmann turned to Books, who stood off to the right side of the desk. "Keep an eye on these baboons. Make sure they don't break anything."

Books did not reply, nor did he shift his gaze from Joe. The big man had been watching him since he'd entered the room.

Joe motioned for Dale to follow him and Andi into the hall.

"You pulling security?" Joe said to Dale in a low voice.

"I don't trust that Books character," Dale said. "Looks like he might snap any minute."

"Did you find anything?"

Dale shook his head. "We're almost done in here. All we have left is the kitchen and the bedrooms. And the two outbuildings." He said to Andi, "Did you check the garage yet?"

She smiled. "Don't need to."

"You got a match?"

"The Ram out front. Rear tire."

They all looked toward Othmann. He must have sensed something because the look of amusement left his face.

"Between that and the phone call, we have enough to get a search warrant for the shooting," Andi said. "I'll have my whole team out here in an hour. We'll be looking for the rifle and bike. Dale, get me a list of anything else you think we should include in the warrant. We'll also ask authority to obtain DNA samples and examine these assholes for injuries." She said to Joe, "You know you can't be here for our search, right?"

"Yeah."

Dale, Cordelli, and Tenny left to work on the bedrooms. Andi went to follow up on her warrant. Joe stayed back to keep an eye on Othmann and Books. He sized up the big man, a soulless knight at the side of an evil king, or maybe a spoiled prince. The man who had attacked

Joe and Bluehorse had been thickset, although it had been difficult to judge his size from a distance. No one would dispute Books was thickset.

"You know you're making a mistake, Joe," Othmann said. "I could be a much better friend than an enemy."

"What's that supposed to mean?"

"It means you should think twice about what you're doing here. A Yei mask? Pathetic."

Joe said nothing.

"How's your arm?" Othmann asked.

Joe felt his neck muscles tighten.

"You're retiring in a few months, and I hear you haven't found a job yet."

"How do you know that?"

"Joe, I told you before. I know a lot of things. Like I know you have a daughter at Columbia University. Tuition must be hell."

Joe took a step toward Othmann's desk. Books also took a step forward.

"Shut your mouth, Othmann, before you say something you'll regret."

"Why do you insist on making me your enemy? All I want to do is help."

"Like you did last week?"

"I don't know what you mean."

Joe balled his hands into fists. He so wanted to put a hurtin' on this smug bastard. And his Neanderthal.

Othmann glanced at the door. Joe guessed one of his squad mates had returned.

Othmann put on a wide smile. "Why aren't you home with your daughter, Joe? She traveled all this way to see you. To see her daddy."

Joe advanced on Othmann. Books stepped in front of the desk, moving to intercept him. Joe reached for his gun.

"What is going on in here?" a voice boomed. "Are you threatening my client?"

Joe turned. Behind Dale stood a silver-haired gentleman in a tailored suit, carrying a leather attaché case.

"I asked you a question, Agent?" the well-dressed man said. He turned to Dale. "You're his supervisor, are you not?"

Dale nodded. "I don't see a problem here. Everyone's a little hot, that's all. Let's—"

"I want to file a complaint," the man said. "And I want him out of this room right now."

"Your client threatened my daughter."

The man strode into the room to stand beside Othmann's desk.

"I didn't hear a threat. I heard him ask about your daughter's visit."

Joe took a deep breath. "That's not what he meant."

"I don't care what you think he meant. I know what he said, as does everyone else who was present. You need to leave. Now."

Joe looked to Dale, who nodded toward the door.

Joe marched out of the room, fingers clenching and unclenching. He followed the hall to the great room. The room lived up to the name. Twenty-foot ceilings, skylights, and a massive stone fireplace. He needed to be alone. But he wasn't. Stretch and Sadi were still searching, removing books from shelves along the wall.

He blew out a long breath. How did that bastard know about Melissa? How? Joe knew, but he didn't want to visit the idea. No. He tried to push it out of his mind. He didn't want to believe it. Couldn't believe it.

"What's up?" Stretch asked.

"That son of bitch threatened Melissa."

A book thudded to the tiled floor.

"What did he say?" Sadi asked.

"Damn it, Joe." Dale's voice came sharp and insistent. "What the hell happened in there?"

"He knew Melissa attended Columbia and that she'd come home to visit me."

"He's an asshole, yeah," Dale said. "But why did you react? You played right into his hands. And with his lawyer standing right there."

"Who cares about his lawyer? The point is, he knew about Melissa. How? Either he's getting information from someone or he has someone watching me. How else would he have known she came to visit?"

"The shooting was in the news," Stretch said. "Maybe he guessed you had a daughter."

"He also knew I haven't found a job yet."

"You're not exactly hiring material right now. Bad press does that."

"And when I interviewed him, he knew Trudle was a professor, and he knew my name before I introduced myself." Joe shook his head, disgusted with himself. "I thought William Tom gave him the heads-up, but . . ."

"What are you saying?" Dale asked.

Joe's mind was spinning. He needed time to get his thoughts in order. He needed to be alone. He needed to think.

"Forget it," Joe said. "Just forget it."

Then Andi entered the room, followed by Cordelli and Tenny.

"We got the warrant," she said. "My team's on the way, but we can start with the body search and DNA collection. You need to leave. Joe."

Dale looked at Cordelli and Tenny. "Give her a hand." They followed Andi to the study.

Dale and Joe moved to the hallway to talk.

"You were thinking hard about Othmann a few moments ago," Dale said. "Where were you going with it?"

"All I know is that he has information he shouldn't."

"Someone on the squad?" Dale's voice took on an edge. A challenge.

"I don't know." Joe considered the implications of Dale's words. The implications of his own suspicions. Hearing the idea spoken out loud gave it more weight. "Why? Do you suspect someone?"

Dale hesitated. "I thought it was you."

"*Me?*" Joe said. "Why the hell would you think it was me?"

"Keep your voice down." He looked around. "Why do you think? You had financial problems after Christine's death. You lost the house. Melissa's in college. And we're retiring you."

"You thought I was selling out to Othmann? I didn't even know him. And how did you know Othmann was even buying?"

"We've been trying to put a case together on him for years, and every time he's one step ahead."

"Why didn't—"

A commotion erupted from the study.

"Drop the gun!"

Joe drew his Glock and started down the hall.

Books came through the study door, walking backward.

Andi yelled, "Drop the gun!"

Joe took aim.

Books turned. In his right hand, he held a gun—a Glock. Under his left arm was Cordelli's neck. He jammed the gun into the side of Cordelli's head.

Joe yelled, "Let him go!"

Books spun Cordelli under his arm and pushed him down the hall toward Joe.

Joe took a step to the side to get a clear shot.

Books fired.

Cordelli grunted.

A round slammed into the wall beside Joe's head. He dropped to a knee. Took aim. Cordelli fell into him, obstructing his view and knocking him off balance. Joe wrestled Cordelli aside, trying to get a bead on Books, wanting to eliminate the threat. Cordelli seemed wooden, unresponsive, an expression of surprise frozen on his face. Then it was Bluehorse Joe was holding. He was back on Jones Ranch Road, watching—

Stop it. He forced his mind to return to the present. Using his left arm, his injured arm, he eased Cordelli to the floor, his tricep screaming under the weight. Joe scrambled to his feet.

Now Joe could see Books. He was at the end of the hall, heading to the back of the house. Joe raised his gun, finger on trigger—

"Moving!" Andi shouted, and buttonhooked into the hall from the study's doorway, right into Joe's target area.

Tenny followed. They both had their guns trained down the hall.

Books turned the corner and was gone.

"Cordelli's down!" Joe said, rushing past Andi and Tenny. "Andi, on me."

Joe ran down the hall, Andi right behind him. They stopped short at the turn. He went to a knee and darted his head forward, beyond the outside corner of the wall, a quick peek, then pulled it back. In that fraction of a second, he saw the door at the end of this second hallway swing closed.

"Clear!" Joe was up and running. "Rear door!"

At the door, he stopped and moved to the right, pressing up against the wall on the strike-plate side of the frame. Andi and Tenny hugged the wall on the other side. Joe signaled, using his fingers and hand, indicating he wanted to clear the door quick and with a purpose, criss-crossing through the entryway. Joe would go through first, moving diagonally to cover everything beyond the door to the left. Andi would then move to cover everything beyond the door on the right. Tenny would follow to support either side. But the signals weren't necessary. They had all trained for this. Whoever goes through first is always right. Whichever way number one goes, number two adapts and goes the other way. Clearings were dynamic and fluid and strong. They would address, engage, and overwhelm whatever threat was on the other side of that door.

He raised his left fist.

His arm shook.

His heart pounded.

Finger count.

One, two, three.

He shoved the door open and took three quick steps, assessing everything in his field of fire: trees, dirt path, lawn furniture, shed.

His quarry, twenty yards past the shed, heading out into open country.

"Got him!" Joe took aim, but Books was running hard, bobbing and weaving along the path into the woods beyond.

Joe ran. Andi with him.

The door slammed open behind them.

Feet pounding.

He looked back. Tenny and Dale.

As he ran, Joe recalled his conversation with Melissa, telling her nothing would happen, promising her. There would be a whole team of agents there, he'd said.

Books fired two rounds at his pursuers. Joe instinctively ducked. A round whizzed close by. He took a knee and returned three rounds. Andi fired another three.

They took off again, running hard, running in a pack.

He gasped for air. They'd covered almost a hundred yards. Peering through sparsely spaced junipers, Joe could see Books fifty yards ahead and still running. Books stopped out in the open; the high desert here offered little cover or concealment. The scraggly trees were spaced too far apart.

"Down!" Joe took a knee.

Books fired two rounds. One round sailed overhead. The second hit the dirt twenty feet in front of Joe, kicking up a spray of earth.

Joe felt his vision focusing. He was hypersensitive to Books, his gun, and the agents behind him, but everything else was melting away into a black fog. A part of his mind recognized it. He'd experienced it at Jones Ranch Road. This was what officers who'd told him about firefights called "tunnel vision." When threatened, a person develops an acuity of the senses to address the threat and only the threat. A survival mechanism.

Joe fired off three more rounds. His chest was heaving and he knew his rounds were landing everywhere but on Books.

Books was off and running.

A volley of shots came from around him.

Joe started running again. The son of a bitch was not getting away. He counted Books's shots. Six rounds fired. Nine left. Joe had fired six rounds, too. They both had nine left.

Joe kept his eyes focused on Books. One moment Books was cutting past a tree; the next he was gone.

"Where did he go? Is he down?"

Tenny pointed. "He's in the arroyo!"

A small engine started up. Then the sound of a dirt bike as it took off. They raced to the arroyo. Too late.

"Shit!" Tenny stomped his foot. "Shit! Shit! Shit!"

Joe said nothing, unable to speak. He bent over, hands on knees, drawing in deep breaths. Finally, he managed to ask, "How's Cordelli?"

One second I'm listening to Andi tell Othmann's lawyer about the search warrant, the next I have the gorilla's arm around my neck." Cordelli moved his right hand from his chest to his throat. His hand shook. "I don't know how the hell he got my gun. It all happened so fast."

Cordelli sat on a chair in Othmann's study, his bulletproof vest discarded on the floor. The squad formed a semicircle around him. Dale was on his cell by the door, contacting the locals to be on the lookout for Books.

"Then he drags me into the hallway. The bastard was strong. Man, when he pushed me down and I heard the shot, I thought I was done. It felt like I'd gotten whacked with a baseball bat. I couldn't breathe."

Cordelli's shirt hung unbuttoned. He lifted his white T-shirt beneath to reveal a dark red welt over his left nipple. He rubbed at it with a still-shaking hand.

Joe felt dizzy, his arm on fire. Even his cheek, which hadn't bothered him the last couple days, felt like someone had shoved a hot coal under the bandage. His adrenaline was dissipating and the realization of what had just happened began to dawn. He needed to sit down or he'd surely fall down.

Joe walked away from the others. They kept talking. He leaned against a display cabinet and slid to the floor, sitting with his back to the glass.

Stretch looked over. "You okay?"

Joe waved him off.

Ten minutes later, Andi's search team arrived. He tried to stand, putting his weight against the cabinet. It gave a little and seemed to spring back when he stepped away. He climbed to his feet and examined the cabinet. He called Andi over. There was something behind it. She would have her team pull it.

Othmann walked into the room with his attorney. Joe had nothing to lose. He spoke loudly to attract the attention of his squad. "I'm sure we will find your bodyguard. And when we do, you can bet he'll want to make a deal." He watched Othmann. "How did you know about my daughter?"

"You have got to be kidding," the attorney said.

But Joe already had his answer. Othmann had glanced over at his squad. He had looked at someone. Joe didn't know who, but at least his suspicion was confirmed. The rat was real. Sooner or later, they would figure it out. But not today. Too much had already happened. He started for the door but stopped when he heard Sadi's voice.

"Why did he look at you?"

Who was she talking to? He looked at Othmann. The collector's self-assuredness crumbled. Even after Books had run, Othmann had somehow held his composure. Now, realizing Joe had tricked him, his veneer broke.

"He didn't look at me."

Joe stopped moving. Stopped breathing. Stopped thinking. No. No way. He couldn't believe it. Didn't want to believe it. He closed his eyes, but it changed nothing.

"Don't give me that shit." Sadi's voice rose in anger. "He looked right at you."

There was a pause, then Stretch said, "It's not what you think."

A tremor moved through Joe. His mind roiled. His senses numbed. If conversation continued in the room, he did not hear it. If there had been a fire at that moment, he would have burned. And, in a way, there was a fire. Everything he believed to be real and true was ablaze, and there was nothing he could do to put it out. *It's not what you think.* Nothing good could come from those words. He did not want to know the full extent of his best friend's betrayal.

When Joe opened his eyes, Stretch was leaving the study with Dale behind him. Sadi followed.

She looked back at Othmann. "That's my partner, you son of a bitch. What the hell did you do to him?"

Othmann had recovered. His face revealed nothing.

Sadi continued toward the door, but Dale raised his hand, blocking her way. "I need to talk to him."

"But—"

"Alone."

Sadi's face contorted into a patchwork of emotion.

Joe pushed past her. He followed Dale down the hall

Dale saw him. "No."

"Save it."

Joe sidestepped Dale and rushed into the great room. Two agents from Andi's team followed them in. Stretch turned only in time to look surprised. Joe grabbed the front of Stretch's shirt and pushed the tall man into the room, all the way to the fireplace wall. He ignored the throb in his injured arm. The two FBI agents started toward them. From the corner of his eye, Joe saw Dale wave them off.

"Stretch, I'm going to ask you one time, and if our friendship ever meant anything to you, then you need to tell me the truth. Did you tell him about Melissa?"

Stretch said nothing, tears welling up in his eyes.

"You attended every one of her birthday parties." Joe's voice broke. "You went to her graduation. You told Christine on her death-bed that we were your family."

Stretch said nothing. But the tear that slid down his cheek said everything.

Joe lowered his head.

"How could you? How could you? You knew what Othmann was capable of." Joe looked up, anger replacing sorrow. "You told him about the mask and about my wanting to go after him, didn't you? You set me up. Because of you, Bluehorse is dead."

Joe slammed Stretch against the stone wall. "Because of you!" He slammed him again. "I trusted you!"

Dale came up and tried to pull him away.

"I trusted you!" Joe struggled to hold on to his best friend. Once he let go, Stretch would be gone. Gone forever. Like Christine. Another part of his life gone. Like Bluehorse, gone. Like his job, gone. He was losing everything. And he could have lost Melissa because of his best friend's betrayal.

The two FBI agents grabbed Joe.

With a burst of strength, he threw Stretch back against the fireplace. His head smacked against stone. The agents dragged Joe away.

Dale snatched Stretch's weapon.

Stretch bent over and put his hand to the back of his head. When he took it away, blood spotted his fingers.

Bluehorse was just a kid," Joe said. "A goddamn kid, and you killed him!" Joe couldn't talk anymore. The image of Bluehorse on the ground, struggling to breathe, flashed into his mind and wouldn't leave. Pressure built in his throat. He wanted to scream, to let it out, but he couldn't. It was stuck, and he didn't know how to get it unstuck. His body slumped. The agents must have felt the change, because they relaxed their grip on his arms and let him go.

Stretch slid to the floor, crying. "I'm sorry."

Professor Trudle had been in the middle of presenting the arcaeo-logical implications of Coronado's 1540 expedition in search of the Seven Cities of Gold to his two o'clock Ancient New Mexico class when two FBI agents walked into the lecture hall. They quietly identified themselves and asked him to accompany them to Santa Fe to assist with an investigation. Class dismissed.

Now the agents led him through Othmann's house to the same study he had been in less than two weeks earlier. Other agents milled about the various rooms, taking photos and bagging evidence. One of the large display cabinets had been pulled away from the wall and agents disappeared behind it.

"I'm Agent Andi McBride," a redheaded woman said to Trudle. "Agent Evers gave me your name and said you could assist us with inventorying some items."

"Yes, of course," Trudle said.

She led Trudle down a flight of stairs behind the display case and into a temperature-controlled room larger than a three-car garage. Glass cabinets filled the space. Half a dozen people who looked like agents were already there, spread throughout the space, some photo-graphing, some taking notes, some simply staring in awe at the items there, just like Trudle.

Andi stood next to one of the displays. "Over here, Professor."

"That's the Yei mask I told Joe about," he said, looking through the glass beside her. "It was upstairs in the study the last time we were here." In front of the mask was a white card with printed information.

"I need you to look around and see if you can identify any other items that might have been stolen. I have a feeling all the stuff down here fits that bill."

Trudle moved slowly through the room. The items in the cabinets captivated him: pottery, bones, ancient tools, petroglyphs and pictographs. He listened to the conversations among the agents, who also were amazed by the collection.

"Andi," a female agent called. She wore her dark hair in a tight bun and her jacket had BIA emblazoned in large yellow letters on the back. "This belonged to Eddie Begay." Trudle looked. She held a beautiful turquoise and silver necklace "The son of a bitch even wrote down the date: September twenty-third. The same day he disappeared."

"Hey, Matt," Andi said. "Pull up that date."

Matt stood by a tall metal server rack. Two monitors were mounted on the wall above. The screen on the right showed various camera angles around the house. The monitor on the left displayed Othmann's study.

On the screen, Othmann was alone in the room until two men entered. Trudle recognized Othmann's bodyguard. The other man, he did not know. A few minutes later, the bodyguard hit the other man, who fell to the floor. Trudle stopped watching when the bodyguard looped his belt around the other man's neck.

Trudle returned to examining the cabinets. One item after another told a significant story about Native American history. He made his way slowly down the aisles, taking his time, reading all the cards associated with the objects. It was obvious Othmann had had no intention of anyone ever seeing these items or reading the cards. They were detailed accounts of how he'd come by the items, sometimes even documenting if they'd been stolen and when.

Oversize cabinets populated the last aisle. He began his methodical perusal and then stopped.

"Oh my . . ."

He dropped to his knees and leaned against the cabinet before him. Joy filled his being. He had finally found his artifacts. The Trudle Turkey would be no more.

❖

OCTOBER 15

FRIDAY, 8:48 P.M.

JOE EVERS'S APARTMENT, ALBUQUERQUE, NEW MEXICO

When Joe returned home, he told Melissa about Stretch. Afterward, they sat next to each other on the couch, neither of them speaking. He appreciated the silence, and her company.

His mind turned to Christine. Since her death, he hadn't seen any of their couples friends. They, of course, had tried to reach out to him, perhaps in a sincere effort to continue the relationship, but he'd avoided their contact. He didn't want to be a third, fifth, or seventh wheel at get-togethers. He thought of their attempts as sympathy invites. Maybe he'd been wrong. Maybe they had recognized something he was only now beginning to understand. That it was time for him to move forward. To live again. Not to forget her, no. He would never do that. But maybe to share her life with others. Share her through his memories of her love and their time together.

"Would you like to see a *Coelophysis*?" Joe said.

"A what? It sounds like something you grow in a petri dish."

"Come on, everyone knows what a *Coelophysis* is. It's the state dinosaur."

like your *Coel . . . Coelophysis* display," Melissa said.

Sierra beamed.

Joe had not called ahead to see if Sierra was working today, but he was happy when he saw her by the *Coelophysis* display, changing out the plastic plants.

Sierra asked a volunteer to finish replacing the flora, and then she accompanied Joe and Melissa around the museum. Joe noticed she did not take them to the same displays that she had taken him to, but to others, new to him.

Despite his efforts, he found it hard to concentrate. His mind kept returning to the case and the body search going on at Jones Ranch. He sneaked into the bathroom and called Andi.

"I missed Pauly's soccer game for this," Andi said. "But it's better than being at Othmann's house. I put Mark in charge of the art recovery. He's going to be there at least a week cataloging that tomb below the study. And your professor is quite the character. He wanted to sleep there last night. Was going to have his wife drive over his toothbrush and pillow."

Joe laughed. It felt good. Even his cheek enjoyed it.

"Have you found anything in the woods?"

"Nothing. I'm telling you now, if it turns out Edgerton's been sunning himself on a beach somewhere, I'm going to drag his ass out here and bury him myself."

"I'll bring the shovel."

"What are you doing with your time off?"

"Learning about dinosaurs."

"Yeah, that's nice. You're a real catch, Joe. Pure adventure. Well, let me go see what the mutts are up to."

They disconnected. He felt better after talking to Andi and returned to the museum tour with renewed interest.

An hour later, it seemed an appropriate time for a break. He felt a tickle in his chest. Nerves?

"Would you like to join us for lunch?" he asked Sierra.

Melissa glanced at him. He hadn't mentioned Sierra to her, but he suspected she now realized his wanting to go to the museum had been a cheap trick.

"Sure," Sierra said. She looked at Melissa. "If that's okay."

They ate lunch at the museum's café. Sierra seemed to take a real interest in Melissa and Columbia. When Sierra told her that she, too, had been selected to take part in an exchange program with Cambridge, Melissa was sold. They seemed like new best friends. Joe quickly became the interloper at the table as they discussed England. Then the conversation took an abrupt shift.

"Can you go to dinner with us tonight?" Melissa asked. "My father promised a nice restaurant before I fly back tomorrow. And we could talk more about Cambridge."

Sierra looked at him.

Caught off guard, all he could think to do was smile and nod, his best impression of an imbecile.

"I would love to," Sierra said.

A lucky imbecile.

Melissa had insisted he take a platter home from the restaurant, an elegant hibachi grill on San Mateo, and made him promise to lay off burritos. When Sierra learned about the burrito lady diet, she invited him to her house the following week for a home-cooked meal. Only then did it become clear: His daughter had set him up. Afterward, they took Sierra home and called it a night.

Joe carried the food container as he and Melissa walked from the car to the front door of his apartment building. He took out his phone and turned it on.

Seven missed calls and three text messages. Before he could check them, his phone rang in his hand.

He glanced at Melissa.

"Don't answer it," she said.

"Sorry, Brainy Bug."

"Damn, Joe." Andi's voice blared through the earpiece. "I've been calling you all night."

"What's up?"

"We found him."

"Books?"

"Edgerton. And not just him. We've got two bodies. A man and a woman."

Everyone talked about finding Edgerton. He wanted to find Edgerton, of course. But finding Sierra's sister had become personal for him.

"Could it have been a ceremonial burial?" He wanted to pull back the words as soon as they passed his lips. Of course it was Edgerton.

"It's a shallow grave and the condition of the clothing and the bones are similar to our other body. It's gotta be them."

"You still out there?"

"We'll be here all night."

"Give me a couple hours."

He hung up.

Melissa glared at him.

He didn't say anything. She couldn't understand what it was like to be an investigator. To take on a case, a murder, and feel responsible for the victim. To be driven by something greater than yourself, an unstoppable compulsion to find the truth, to restore balance, to hold someone accountable for a wrong committed. Some called it "closure." Others, like Joe, could not put a label on something so nebulous. He never tried to name it. He had simply let it drive him throughout his career.

He inserted his key in the apartment door's top lock. It turned, then stopped. Already unlocked. Melissa had been the last one out and hadn't set the dead bolt. Even after the break-in at her apartment. She had to get out of the habit of locking only the knob. But now was not the time to go into that. He was about to break his promise.

"Melissa, I'm sorry. I have—"

"Save it, Dad. I don't want to hear it. You're going to do what you want to do regardless of what I say."

Her words pierced his soul. That was what Christine used to say when they argued and he went against her wishes.

Melissa rushed past him into the apartment.

He closed the door and threw the dead bolt. And then he knew something was wrong. Very wrong. The sixth sense that most cops developed after experiencing so many bad situations kicked in. He bent down to pull the gun from his ankle holster.

"Don't." The voice was calm but firm.

He looked up and saw Melissa was straight ahead, a mask of fear on her face. She stood by the counter that separated the kitchen on the right from the living room on the left.

Books stood in the hallway leading to the bedrooms. He held Cordelli's Glock.

Joe's stomach clenched.

"Lissa, come and stand by me." If he could get her to the door, he would take the first bullet, give her time to run. He kept his eyes on Books.

Melissa started forward.

Books raised the gun. "Stay."

"Point the gun at me, Books, please." He'd added *please* to make Books feel in control. He wanted him calm. Calm would buy time. He hoped.

"We're going to do this nice and slow," Books said, his voice devoid of emotion. He sounded like a man in control, someone who didn't make mistakes. But he had made a mistake. He'd killed Bluehorse instead of Joe, and he had fled Othmann's. Why? Because he knew if Andi had taken his DNA, it would match the blood at the scene of the shoot-out.

Melissa had her arms raised, eyes wide.

Books walked to the center of the living room.

Joe needed his hands free, so he leaned to his right to place the food container on the thin table that sat against the wall next to the door, the same table where Bluehorse's oak kachina now rested.

"Don't put it down." Books was on to Joe's tactic, and he probably guessed Joe wore an ankle holster. He waved the gun toward the kitchen. "Walk."

As Joe moved, Books also moved, placing himself by the door.

Joe stopped in front of Melissa. Fear paid him a visit. Not the fear he would be killed, but the fear he wouldn't be able to protect her.

"Why did you come back? Why didn't you run?"

Books shook his head. The gesture meant nothing.

"I'm retiring," Joe said. "I'm not coming after you. You can still get away."

"That's funny. I was retiring, too. Made all my plans. Had all the money I needed. And then you came along investigating Eddie and ruined everything."

"I wasn't interested in Eddie. I was looking into Congressman Edgerton's disappearance."

"No. Mr. O. said you were investigating Eddie, too."

"I wasn't. Another agent was. The one Othmann was paying off. He lied to you. I wasn't interested in Eddie. Just Edgerton. So you had nothing to worry about. You weren't even with Othmann when Edgerton went missing."

"You were investigating Eddie. Mr. O. didn't have anything to do with the missing congressman."

"How do you know he didn't have anything to do with it?"

"He's coking all the time now, doesn't know what he says anymore." Books held his gun in his left hand. It seemed unsteady, as though he wasn't used to the motion. His right hand hung down by his side, motionless. "That's why I'm retiring. He's flaking out. I asked him when he was floatin' if he killed the congressman. He said no. I believe him. He's crazy. He likes to tell his dead father the shit he does. If he had anything to do with your guy, he would have told me."

"You don't have to do this. You can still leave. Run. Retire." Joe watched Books's right arm. It was unnatural. He suspected Books had injured it. Perhaps the blood at the shooting scene in Jones Ranch was from that arm. He was probably right-handed and that's why his left appeared choppy. That could be a weakness Joe could exploit.

"It's too late now. You fucked everything up. Eddie fucked things up, too. I can't hurt him anymore, but I can hurt you."

"Let my daughter go. She has nothing to do with this."

Books looked directly at Melissa. "Come here."

In that instant, Joe knew what Books intended. He would hurt her in front of Joe. Make him suffer the ultimate pain. Books had come back not because he wanted to stop Joe from going after him. No. That had probably been Othmann's foolish idea. Books wanted revenge.

Joe sensed her moving. He reacted, stepped to the side, making sure his body was between Melissa and the gun, and launched himself at Books, throwing the food container first.

Seared beef and grilled vegetables exploded on the big man's face and upper chest even as he raised his arms to stop it, the gun still in his hand.

A deafening blast. Another.

Joe felt nothing. He crashed into Books, driving him back with his shoulder, both his hands on the Glock. He grasped the top of the weapon, pressing on the slide, pushing it back so it would unseat the firing pin, twisting it down and to the side so it would face away from Melissa.

Something hit the back of his head. His vision went white.

"Run, Lissa! Run!"

Another crack to his head. He knew he would lose consciousness soon.

Books punched at him again and again with his right fist. Joe had been wrong. His right arm may have been injured, but it wasn't incapacitated. Books had simply been favoring it. His one advantage was now gone. Anger welled up inside him. Anger and desperation. He struck at Books with all his strength, trying to give this monster pause, a break in the attack to get clear of him so he could draw his own weapon.

Books roared, emitting an inhuman sound, and Joe was driven back, turning, Books's gun turning with them, sweeping in the direction of Melissa.

Click. The Glock's firing pin unseated, stopping short of the round's primer.

Another *click.*

"Run!"

Joe fell backward, crashing to the floor by the entryway, Books on top of him. He felt a sharp, almost paralyzing pain course up his left arm and through his shoulder. For a crazy moment, the short Hispanic doctor from GIMC flashed into his mind, reprimanding him for not taking it easy. Then he felt something like a hammer on his forehead. Books punching again. Blood on Books's fist. Through a white haze, he saw his daughter. She was screaming.

He shouted. Told her to run. Fought to stay conscious, his grip weakening on the gun.

He knew he couldn't overpower this animal on top of him. He had only one chance left. His weapon. He hadn't tried for it before, because he'd needed both hands to control Books's gun. He brought his leg back, took his right hand off Books's Glock, and reached for his ankle holster.

Another blow struck him, this time on his right cheek. Fire ripped through his head. Blood filled his mouth. Joe grasped the handle of his own Glock. He pulled. For a second, he thought it was free, but then his hand wouldn't move.

Books smiled down at him. He had his hand on Joe's Glock, trying to wrench it away.

Joe glimpsed Melissa again. Why hadn't she run? Now Books would kill them both. He felt a cry of rage rising from deep inside. Hopeless rage. Powerless rage.

Then a loud *thunk.*

Another.

He heard a distant voice yelling, "Get off him!"

For a fraction of a second, Books's hold on Joe's gun weakened.

Without hesitation, Joe yanked his right hand up, breaking Books's grasp. Then he pushed the gun forward into the big man's side. He pulled the trigger. Pulled again.

He blinked through his own blood, through the white haze. Books fell forward, pinning him to the floor. Off to the side, his daughter stood, arms raised, Bluehorse's kachina held high with both hands.

❖

They sat on the bed, not saying anything. Joe held her close, wrapped tightly in his good arm. He hadn't let the EMTs take him to the hospital. He'd go later. Right now, Melissa needed him. She'd just seen her father almost killed, and she had been forced to do something that might haunt her for years. A man was dead, deservedly so, but still dead. He knew the way of the haunted. Not only at night, when he closed his eyes, but during the day, too. The terror of what had just happened and of that day on Jones Ranch Road would linger. It would visit him in his dreams. Bluehorse would visit him. Worst, the knowledge that he had been the cause of his friend's death would be the most unwelcome caller.

He didn't want any of that for Melissa. But how could he stop it? All he could do was try to be there for her. Here and now. As long as he could.

She'd shut down when the police had arrived and hadn't spoken since. Joe comforted his daughter while only yards away officers processed the crime scene. He felt worlds away, lost in his own thoughts of fatherhood and his concerns for his daughter. He would be there for her for as long as she needed him to be there, for as long as it took for her to feel safe again.

Over a week had passed since Joe's confrontation with Books. The doctors had checked his injuries and restitched his cheek. His arm had significant bruising, but in the end they gave it a clean bill. He'd been sent home with strict orders to rest. The remainder of that week, he spent with Melissa. For the first few days, reporters hung around outside the apartment building, waiting for an interview or at least a photo. But they got neither. Joe and Melissa stayed inside, not feeling up to facing the world, even if that meant a simple trip for groceries. So he found a store that delivered, and they watched TV and talked, played board games and talked some more. A lot of talking. By Friday, cabin fever had set in, and the reporters had given up, so they ventured outside to Sierra's house for a chicken cordon bleu dinner.

Today, Melissa was on a plane back to New York. He had taken her to the airport two hours ago and then waited to see her flight take off.

Now he sat at his desk, the Edgerton file spread out. The case file had been copied and sent to the FBI. Murder on the reservation was officially their territory. When Nick Garcia's body had been found, Andi had opened a murder investigation, but she'd never pushed the issue and had let Joe run with it. But now, with three bodies, it had clearly moved into their jurisdiction. BIA could assist, but the FBI would be lead. And Joe was off the case. On paid leave because of the shooting. But he needed to do something.

So he reviewed photos from the search of the congressman's office.

Technically, it was Cordelli's case. He was BIA's point agent for the Edgerton murder investigation, as it was now called in the news. But Wonder Boy had taken some time off himself. Joe guessed the young agent would need that time to decide if he really wanted to be in law enforcement. Being shot in the chest and surviving would alter anyone's perspective. Sadi had also taken this week off, but for a different reason. And Joe understood that, too.

He pulled Ellery Gates's interview from the file: a half-page memo documenting that the congressman had lawyered up and refused to talk to the agents. That was two days after Edgerton went missing. Gates had still been in Albuquerque, having come to meet with Edgerton and then staying in the state, even after Edgerton hadn't shown. What was strange was that Gates had traveled alone. No aid. No wife. He hadn't wanted witnesses to the meeting. Grace had said Gates came to New Mexico to go fly-fishing with Edgerton. If that were true, then it was an amazing coincidence that the supposed fishing trip was the same day Congress had announced their probe into allegations of bribery and corruption against Edgerton and Gates. No doubt Gates had come to New Mexico to talk about the probe. He or Edgerton had gotten advance warning, and they were getting together to work out a strategy.

But Edgerton had been killed that day.

The two bodies had been identified as those of Edgerton and Faye Hannaway. They'd been buried next to each other almost two hundred yards from the vehicle. Joe and Andi surmised the only reason

Nick, the driver, had been found so close was because he'd been too heavy to drag far.

Another piece of evidence was the result of the Colt 1911 ballistic examination. Andi had collected the gun from Grace Edgerton's home after Bluehorse's funeral and sent it to Quantico for an expedited comparison. She'd phoned him earlier this morning with the result: The round recovered near the vehicle had been fired from Edgerton's gun. That piece of information had not hit the news. Andi would play that one close. Nothing to the press.

A week ago, he'd thought Othmann could have been behind Edgerton's disappearance. He would have been okay with allowing Cordelli and the FBI to sort it out. But the ballistic report changed all that.

When he'd told Sierra about the bodies, she cried in joy and in sorrow. For Sierra, the fact she would no longer have to defend her sister was enough. But he felt the need to give her more. The answers to the *who* and *why* of every investigation. Only then would true closure be possible.

He picked up a photo of Edgerton's office taken during the BIA's search in the days following his disappearance. The gun Andi had collected from Mrs. Edgerton had been a gift to her husband from the Veterans of Foreign Wars. Something a politician would keep visible. In the photo was a bookcase, and on the second shelf from the top sat a wooden display frame the size of a shoe box. Through a magnifying glass, he could see a nickel-plated Colt 1911 inside. The only two people of Edgerton's inner circle who had access to that gun—and could have put it back afterward—were Grace Edgerton and Kendall Holmes.

Joe's plane had been scheduled to leave at 3:05, but the flight information board by the gate now flashed DELAYED. The new departure time was 3:45.

He made a phone call.

Helena answered on the first ring.

"Hey, cowboy. I don't think I ever thanked you for the heads-up on the two bodies."

"You didn't, but maybe you can pay me back. Are we off the record?"

"Ooh, pillow talk." She may have purred. "Shoot."

"Tell me everything you know about Senator Kendall Holmes."

Joe reached out the car window and pressed the intercom button. A few seconds later, a woman's voice came through the speaker.

"¡Hola!"

He held his credentials in front of the tiny camera lens poking through the intercom housing.

"Joe Evers, BIA."

"Okay," the voice said with a thick Mexican accent. "Come up to the main house."

The ten-foot-high wrought-iron gate swung inward, the huge *G* at its center splitting in half. An arch straddling the road read: GATES RANCH.

He drove up to the large timber and stone house. Joe guessed the term *lodge* would be a better description. He parked behind a navy Land Rover. A woman waited on the front porch. She gestured for him to come in—or maybe hurry up. He did both.

They walked inside, where the woman led him into a huge room constructed of massive timber beams. At the room's center sat an impressive stone fireplace. The woman glanced at the bandage on his cheek. She gave a look of displeasure but did not comment.

"Mr. Gates wants you to join him for dinner." She did not wait for his reply, but instead started walking.

He followed.

They came to what he guessed was the dining room, but he would have been just as comfortable calling it a dining hall. Ellery Gates sat at the far end of the long table. A second place setting was arranged next to his seat. At least they wouldn't be shouting.

"Welcome, Agent Evers." Gates stood and walked to Joe, hand outstretched. "I hope you don't mind. I took the liberty of holding dinner for you. When you said you were flying down so late in the day, I thought you might enjoy a good meal. And I don't get much company out here, so entertaining a guest has become an infrequent joy for me."

They shook hands.

"I learned about the shooting incident on the news and am sorry about the officer's death. Please accept my condolences for you and the officer's family."

Joe nodded, unsure how to respond.

"Now please, come and sit down," Gates said, walking back to his seat at the table. "Mariana cooks up one of the finest T-bones you'll ever have, I guarantee it. So for the next hour or so, if you don't mind, I'll treat you to some fine food, good spirits, and some straight talking. I'll do my best to answer any questions you might have. Sound good?"

Joe sat down and admired the elegant dinner service and expensive crystal. "I would be a total heel if I turned down such an offer, Mr. Gates."

"And cut the mister crap. It's Ellery." Gates clapped him on the back. "Mariana, bring out a bottle of red. Something he can brag about tryin'."

Mariana started them off with a salad and a small bowl of posole. The T-bone followed and was as good as Gates had promised. Over the next hour, they talked about Texas, Oklahoma, and the BIA. They talked about everything but the Edgerton case. And Joe didn't mind. Gates was enjoyable company. A gentleman, a history buff, and an entertaining storyteller.

After dinner, they retired to what his host called the "smoking room." It smelled of whiskey and leather, just as Joe imagined every smoking room should. Gates poured them each a glass of Johnnie Walker Blue. Joe would have to sleep in his car tonight rather than chance driving back to Dallas. Gates then brought over a humidor and Joe selected a Nicaraguan cigar. He clipped the end and lit it. The tobacco tasted sweet, as though touched by honey, the smoke earthy. Joe was getting too comfortable.

"I guess it's time we talk about Edgerton," Joe said.

Gates examined his cigar, rolling it slowly between his fingers. "Yes, I suppose so."

"Tell me about the day you went to Albuquerque. I read your report. It said you wouldn't speak to the investigators. That you lawyered up."

"Of course I did. I had just learned that I was being investigated for corruption. I knew enough to heed the advice of my attorney, Irvin Ritterhouse. He was an old friend, and a hell of a good tax attorney. Not much of a criminal one, though, but he did keep me out of jail. He and the two other law firms I hired. Irvin died last year. Lung cancer." He again held his cigar out for inspection. "His last few months, he spent here. I set up one of the bedrooms for him. He'd outlived his wife. His two kids were miserable bastards. His elder son didn't even show up at the funeral." He paused, seeming to reflect. "But I suppose you're not interested in all that."

Gates went on: "Back when I was in Albuquerque, your counterparts came to talk to me. Irv told me to keep my yapper shut. His words, not mine. And I did. But afterward, after the hearings and the fines, and all the rest, I did talk to one of your agents. I told him all I knew about Arlen."

Joe had not found any report in the file documenting a follow-up interview with Gates. "Do you remember who it was you spoke to?"

"I don't recall the name. A Native American gentleman. Tall. I recall we talked about the Long Walk. And that's what makes me think he was Navajo."

Joe knew who the lead agent was back then. "Does the name Malcolm Tsosie sound familiar?"

Gates was thoughtful. "All I remember was our discussion about the Long Walk. He claimed Kit Carson was responsible for a near genocide. I suggested that while Carson brought about the surrender of the Navajo at Canyon de Chelly and the scorched-earth policy, it was probably not his intent to decimate the tribe. He did not much care for my account. He compared Carson to Hitler. I reminded him that Carson had married a Cheyenne woman, and he nearly ended the interview." He laughed. "It was my own fault for discussing a topic of such cultural import. Other than that, he was friendly enough."

"What did you tell him about Edgerton?"

"I told him I never saw Arlen that day in Albuquerque or since. When I got there, Arlen never showed up. Later, they said he'd disappeared."

"Why did you go to Albuquerque that day?" This was the test. The fishing trip story had been a sham. Joe knew that just as surely as he knew Gates had been involved in the corruption back in '88. But he also knew this old gentleman in front of him was working hard to try to redeem himself for that past indiscretion. The former congressman would either live up to the seemingly honorable image of a man who had learned from his mistakes or he would fall to his own vanity and self-righteousness and remain that man of twenty years ago.

"A friend had told me the ethics committee was going to announce the investigation and Arlen and I were the targets. I wanted to meet with Arlen to exchange notes. Please don't ask me the name of the friend who told me. I can assure you she was in no way involved."

"So you knew Arlen was taking money?"

"No. I suspected he was taking money. We were often on the same side of the issues. And let me set the record straight. I did take the money. I took it not because I needed it but because I believed that was how politics worked. I'd been around it my whole life. A game of favors played by people who saw the deal as more important than the issue. Whoever wielded more backroom influence was the winner. I liked to win back then. And winning meant doing favors and then asking for favors. Foolish, yes. Naïve about what was really important, like self-respect and honor. Guilty as charged."

So Gates didn't know for sure if Edgerton was on the take? Then who else was in a position to influence the legislation?

"Tell me about Kendall Holmes."

"Have you heard the term *heterochromia*?"

Joe had not.

"People with two different-colored eyes. I don't know if that was the reason, but I never trusted him. It was that or the tinted sunglasses he always wore. Very self-conscious. And he looked like a mobster. They could have called him the 'Teflon Don,' too, because his association with Arlen and the corruption investigation never tarnished his political career. About four years after Arlen's disappearance, he won a state senate seat. And then a few years later, he was elected to the U.S. Senate. Very savvy in his political undertakings. Now I hear he might throw his hat in the next presidential primary. He's not a household name yet, but that doesn't matter. If the party likes you, you're in. And they like him."

"Mr. Holmes had told the agent investigating the case back then that he had gone to the airport to pick you up the day Edgerton went missing. Did you spend the rest of the day with him?"

"What I remember was sitting in the airport, furious, because he was about an hour late. I called Arlen's office, but no one answered. Ken finally showed and we did spend the rest of the evening together, waiting for Arlen. We had dinner and then started calling around when Arlen didn't show. We were at Arlen's office when the news broke about the ethics investigation."

"Did you tell Mr. Holmes about the investigation?"

"No, but I think he already knew. Arlen had friends, like I did. He probably got a tip. Ken was his chief of staff. Arlen would have told him to work up a spin. And Ken was a lawyer. Duke, I think. Maybe Georgetown. Never practiced, went straight into politics. A policy man."

They talked a little more, and Joe declined a second Johnnie Walker. When it was time to start the fifty-mile trek back to Dallas, Gates insisted Joe spend the night. The former congressman must have been a powerful persuader when he was in office, because Joe found himself not only accepting the offer but feeling indebted to his host.

No doubt Gates was still a master at the game of favors.

Both Dale and Andi were in the dark. This trip was off the books, so Joe could not call ahead to arrange the meeting before he flew to D.C., but at least Helena had been able to confirm the senator would be in town today. She'd picked Joe up at the airport and had driven him to the senator's office building. He told her if his meeting went well, he would have a story for her when he was finished. She said she'd wait for him.

Joe's plan was to hit up the senator cold. Not always smart when interviewing such a high-profile person, but it gave Joe the possibility of getting the story raw, which often proved more truthful (or sometimes more full of holes), and less likely to involve lawyers. If the senator refused to meet, Joe would at least try to get an interview with Malcolm.

The Capitol Hill police officer who worked the lobby of the Hart Building sized Joe up and offered a phlegmatic "May I help you, sir?" His stolid face and no-nonsense attitude made Joe suspect that important work was being done in the venerated congressional suites above. Work of a most high and noble nature. Work that would cause those upstairs to look upon Joe, a mere rube, as a distraction.

The officer picked up the desk phone and told someone on the other end that a BIA agent was here to see Senator Holmes. The call must have caused quite a stir in the senator's office, because Joe had to wait thirty minutes before the same officer got a callback. Joe secured his

Glock in a lockbox by the guard desk and passed through the metal detector.

When he got off the elevator, Joe found Malcolm waiting, holding out a hand. He looked like an olive tree offering a branch, tall, dark, rough, and a lot of seasons behind him. They shook and the former BIA agent apologized about their previous encounter at Grace Edgerton's office.

"It's customary for an agent to call ahead before asking to interview a senator," Malcolm said.

"I've never interviewed one before," Joe said. "I didn't know there was a protocol."

"It's okay. The senator was impressed with your work on the Edgerton case. I always believed he had run off. You proved me wrong. That art collector was never on our radar back then."

"He wouldn't have been because he didn't kill Edgerton."

"I thought the news said he did."

"I believe they're saying he's being investigated for his involvement with the case."

"Then who killed him?"

"That's why I'm here. I'm hoping the senator can help me."

They stopped outside a door.

"After I finish with the senator, I'd like to talk with you."

"Everything I know is in the file."

"Not everything. There wasn't much in the file on Holmes."

"There wasn't much to put in there."

"How long have you been with the senator?"

"Eighteen years."

"I'm sure you've gotten to know him pretty well. What do you think?"

"If you're asking if he's capable of murder, everyone is."

"You, too?"

Malcolm didn't answer.

"Why didn't you write up the interview with Ellery Gates?"

"He refused the interview."

"No. I mean the second interview."

Malcolm stared back at Joe, revealing nothing. The olive branch had been withdrawn. He was impassive. Still a good imitation of a tree.

"You traveled to Oklahoma and interviewed him."

"He refused that interview, too."

"How come there was no report in the file?"

"It may have been the year I left the BIA. Probably got lost in the shuffle." Malcolm smiled. It looked more menacing than friendly. "You're leaving, too, right? Retiring, I heard."

A man in a shiny blue suit and manicured hair hurried down the hall. Joe waited for him to pass, not answering Malcolm's question.

"How did you get this job?"

"During a follow-up on the case. I interviewed him. He offered me the job."

"Was that after you interviewed Ellery Gates?"

"I don't remember interviewing him."

"Holmes was a state senator then, right? How was he able to pay enough to hire you away from the BIA?"

"I wanted to leave and he was ambitious. He said he had his eyes set on a U.S. Senate seat. I took a chance. It paid off."

"I don't buy it. We do this job because we love it. You wouldn't have just walked away."

"I was tired of locking up my own people. Kendall wanted to help them. And the pay was good."

"So his job offer had nothing to do with what Ellery Gates told you?"

"I don't remember interviewing him." Malcolm opened the office door. "The senator is waiting."

Inside, a young woman sat behind a reception desk. She told Malcolm they could go right in.

They walked across the small, elegantly furnished waiting area, past the receptionist's desk, and into the senator's inner office.

Senator Kendall Holmes rose from behind his desk and came around to greet Joe.

"I'm glad you were able to bring Arlen's killer to justice. When his body was found, I was shocked. All these years, I always believed Arlen was relaxing on a beach somewhere." He motioned for Joe to join him on a museum-quality sofa, but Joe remained standing. "I met this Othmann fellow once or twice, at fund-raisers and art events over the years. I would never have suspected him of anything like that."

"He didn't kill Congressman Edgerton."

"Then how can I help you, Agent Evers?"

Joe looked at Malcolm. "I would prefer to speak to you alone."

"Of course."

"Give me a few minutes with the agent, Malcolm." He displayed a courteous smile, more mechanical than genuine.

"Yes, sir," Malcolm said. "And just to remind you, we have the Smithsonian event tonight."

"This won't take long," the senator said.

Joe looked around the room. On the walls hung tasteful black-and-white photographs of the senator posing with people, most of whom Joe didn't recognize.

"May I?" Joe said, pointing to the picture frames.

"Please."

Joe walked along the row. He recognized a few U.S. politicians and a few foreign dignitaries: Margaret Thatcher, Mandela, Gorbachev. Many of the photos were group shots of delegations. One photo caught his eye.

NAFTA ARCHITECTS
San Antonio, Texas
December 17, 1992

It was a photo of twenty or so individuals. A message was hand-written on the photograph: "We did it, mi amigo! Sylvestri Guillen."

"I don't see you in this photo," Joe said.

"I wasn't. Bush senior, when he was vice president, had asked Arlen to represent the border states during negotiations in '87. We worked closely with the Mexican delegation. When it was signed, a friend sent that to me. I'm very proud of my association with NAFTA."

Joe returned to the sofa. "Arlen was involved in several major initiatives. Indian Gaming. NAGPRA. NAFTA."

"He lived and breathed politics. I learned a lot from him. The country lost a great leader."

Joe studied the senator's eyes. Brown. When he blinked, blue appeared at the bottom edge. Then it disappeared. Contact lenses to cover up his heterochromia.

"There are rumors you might be running in the presidential primary."

The senator grinned. "I'm hearing the same rumors."

"After the Edgerton investigation, I'm surprised you were able to get back into politics."

"The voters in my district were amazing. It was four years after his disappearance and, of course, I was never implicated in the corruption probe. They saw through all that smoke and sent me to Santa Fe. Six years later, the state sent me to D.C. I'm very grateful for their trust, and I try to live up to it every day I'm here. I don't forget where I came from."

"Who do you think killed Edgerton?"

"I thought this Othmann fellow did. On the news, they talked about a theft from a dig site on the day Edgerton disappeared. Seems plausible."

"I'm sure back then you probably thought of someone, Senator. Who?"

He was thoughtful. "Is this off the record?"

"Yes," Joe said, lying.

"I never said anything back then, but I always wondered if Grace had gotten tired of Arlen's fooling around."

"With whom?"

"Faye, of course. I used to cover for him all the time."

"You know for a fact they were having an affair?"

"He would have me keep tabs on Grace, check her itinerary so he could block out hours. Jealousy can be a powerful force."

"That doesn't explain Nick, the driver."

"No witnesses. I guess Nick was in the wrong place at the wrong time."

"Is it possible that Nick or Faye was the target and it was Edgerton who was in the wrong place at the wrong time?"

"I suppose anything is possible. I didn't know Nick that well, but Faye went through boyfriends weekly. She even hit on me, but I knew she was trouble."

"Did you have a relationship with her?"

He shook his head. "I was very concerned about my political career. Working for Arlen was a stepping-stone. I planned to put in my time and then go out and run myself. I was always careful with sex, drugs, and money—the three vices of politics."

"How did you feel when you learned about the corruption investigation?"

"I was angry and scared. I couldn't believe he put me in that situation."

"So you believe he took the money."

"No. I didn't believe he took the money. When he disappeared, I was shocked. But later it made sense, especially after the ethics committee made their findings public."

"Did anyone try to bribe you?"

"Why would they approach me?"

"You were his policy man. He valued your counsel. People might see you as the person to influence."

"I don't care for your insinuation, Agent. The investigation showed that Arlen and Ellery both took the money. Not me."

"No, it proved that Ellery Gates took the money, but Arlen was never given the chance to defend himself and none of the money was traced directly to him."

"What about the bank account in Mexico City?" Holmes said. "That was linked to him."

"In name only. The bank officials never met Arlen, and the Mexico City attorney wouldn't talk to our agents back then. I'm pulling border-crossing records on everyone who worked in Edgerton's office. It'll tell me who went down to Mexico."

"I assume that's why you were so interested in the NAFTA photo. Well, your instincts are good. We regularly traveled to Mexico City. But what does that prove?"

"Do you think Cedro Bartolome will talk to me?"

"Who's that?"

"The attorney in Mexico City."

"Clever, throw out the name and see if I react," Holmes said. "Why are you so sure it was someone from Arlen's office?"

"Do you recall a Colt 1911 pistol that Arlen received from the Veterans of Foreign Wars?"

"I don't." The senator checked his watch.

Joe found it interesting he didn't ask the significance of the gun.

"I hate to cut this short," Holmes said, "but I do have to get to an event tonight. It's not polite to be late when you're the keynote speaker." He stood and held out his hand. "All this has been very interesting. Please let me know how you progress with the investigation."

Helena's Jeep darted across the outside lane and came to a stop at the curb in front of Joe. The cab she cut off blared its horn. Not to be out-classed, Helena fired off several expletives, a few of which made Joe blush. He quickly ducked into the car.

"Thanks for—"

"Cut the pleasantries. What's my story?"

"I'll give it to you on the way back to the airport. I need to get home and dig out my passport."

"An international man of mystery. Let's get married."

"If I told you Othmann is not a suspect in the murders, would you write about it?"

"If I can source it to someone close to the investigation."

Over the next half hour, while they crawled through rush-hour traffic, he told her about the threats made by Hawk Rushingwater, his organization, and his petition to the UN seeking to have the Navajo Nation secede from the United States.

When he finished, she grew sullen.

"I have a confession to make, Joe," she said after a while.

He was concerned by the change in her voice.

"I'm not the big political reporter you probably thought I was. I'm a gossip columnist. Beltway chitchat. This case is my big break. Thank you for trusting me with it."

He swallowed the lump in his throat. He'd led her astray with the story, but he was too committed to stop now. All he could do was push on. He tried to tell himself he would make it up to her when the case was over.

"You're welcome," he croaked like the frog he was.

❖

OCTOBER 27
WEDNESDAY, 5:50 P.M.
INDEPENDENCE AVENUE SW, WASHINGTON, D.C.

S enator Holmes had chosen to sit in the front seat tonight. Usually, he relaxed in the back, sprawled across the wide leather seat of the Lincoln, talking away on his phone. But not tonight. Tonight was different. It was business, but a different sort of business. Malcolm sensed it as soon as Joe walked out of the senator's office. Now he was waiting to hear what the senator had in mind.

"You've been with me a long time, Malcolm," he said. "A very long time."

Malcolm wished the senator would get to the point.

"Do you believe in my work?"

Malcolm groaned inwardly. Over the years, he'd come to hate D.C. double-talk. "Yes."

"I'm sure you want to see me continue my work on behalf of Native Americans."

Malcolm didn't bother answering.

They were coming up on the Smithsonian.

"We have a little problem that Agent Evers might unearth."

Malcolm suspected Joe had already unearthed the problem. Apparently, the same way Malcolm had unearthed it eighteen years earlier.

They'd never talked about the missing congressman after he was hired. When he had gone to Holmes's office back when Holmes was only a state senator, Malcolm questioned him about what time he had picked up Ellery Gates from the airport. Halfway through the interview, Holmes had said, "You know, I'm starting to realize that politics can be a dangerous business. I should consider hiring a bodyguard." The offer was made. At the time, Malcolm was coming up on a use-of-force review, which he wasn't sure would go in his favor, so he made his decision. And hadn't regretted it until today. But now he was in too deep. Joe might cause problems for Malcolm if the investigation gained momentum against Holmes.

"What do you need, sir?"

Holmes explained his problem and finished by saying, "So I need you to go down to Mexico City."

Malcolm nodded. Then he told the senator what he needed.

❖

October 29
Friday, 4:16 p.m.
Aeropuerto Internacional de la Ciudad de México,
Distrito Federal, Mexico

After his interview with Holmes, Joe had told Dale about what he'd learned. He went to his office to plead his case.

"I need to talk to the attorney in Mexico."

"Are you nuts? No way. You want to start an international incident. We go through State. Actually, Andi can go through State."

Since learning that it had been Stretch and not Joe that had been leaking information to Othmann, Dale's attitude toward him had improved. But suddenly they seemed at loggerheads again.

"And you're on leave anyway," Dale said, shaking his head. He made a shooing gesture with his hand. "Go home and rest. Take it easy. And find yourself a job. You're a hero now. The offers will be pouring in."

"Grace Edgerton and Senator Holmes both went to Mexico a short time before this Cedro Bartolome opened the account. He needs to be tracked down. He might talk."

"There's no reason for him to help you. You can't do anything to him. He knows that."

"Maybe," Joe said.

"Fine, take leave. Put it in. I want paperwork. And be careful."

Now Joe was in Mexico City, fighting his way through the airport to reach the exit. Outside, he found a taxi with a driver who spoke decent English. He flopped down in the backseat, pulled out a folded printout of a Google map showing Cedro Bartolome's law office address, and handed it to the driver.

"Andale, por favor," Joe said, reaching hard for his college Spanish.

The driver took off. Traffic here was worse than in D.C., all the drivers dark-haired Helena Newridges. If a single word could describe a city, the word for Mexico City was *crowded*. Cars on top of cars. People on top of people. And buildings sprouting up everywhere. He'd never experienced claustrophobia before, but he felt a pressure in his chest and an inability to expand his lungs to their fullest. He wondered if this was his first anxiety attack.

He turned on his phone. Two messages. The first was from Chris Staples. "Did you leak that story? Four days before the election. You couldn't wait four fucking days? We needed closure, not this. Not this, goddamn it!" Staples had banged the phone on something. "And I hope your arm hurts."

The second message was from Andi. Joe had called her from the phone on the plane and told her about his plan. She'd been pissed, but after she cooled off, she'd agreed to help him—unofficially. In the message, she gave him the name and number to the FBI Legat, the legal attaché in Mexico City, but she wanted absolute deniability. "Lose my number," she'd said. He wrote down the information and tucked it in his wallet. Then he stuffed his pen in his breast pocket. It was a fine pen, gold-plated, a gift from Christine many Christmases past, like his tailored dark blue suit. Everything on him right now said class and, he hoped, money. It was part of his plan. He closed his eyes. It shut out the rush of life outside the cab's window.

Last night, he'd made a 7:30 flight back to Albuquerque, getting home at two in the morning. The little sleep he'd gotten had been restless, mostly because his arm ached. He'd tossed and turned, trying to find a position that lessened the throb. And when he finally had drifted off, he'd dreamed of ravens—or maybe crows. He didn't know for sure, but he assumed they were not seen as a good omen in a dream.

Now, in the back of the cab, his left arm a little stiff from the plane ride, he laid the copy of the *Washington Post*, with Helena's latest article, on the seat next to him. He stretched out his arm.

At least this case would be over soon, he hoped. Then he could take some time off. Get some rest. Give his body time to heal—but only if he got what he needed from Señor Bartolome.

❖

OCTOBER 29
FRIDAY, 4:37 P.M.
CAMPOS ELISEOS, CIUDAD DE MÉXICO,
DISTRITO FEDERAL, MEXICO

Malcolm sat behind the wheel of the rental car. Next to him was Raul. In the back, Snap, a strange creature, even when compared to the critter in the front. Raul had told Malcolm, in somewhat understandable English, that when Snap was young he used to catch pigeons so his family wouldn't starve. An American had watched him crack the neck of a bird and called the young boy "Snap." The boy took a liking to the name. Over the years, he'd graduated from birds to people. In between, there'd been a few cats and dogs. The scar on Snap's left cheek had been from a "pussy." Raul's incomplete set of brown teeth made an appearance when he smiled, and Malcolm wasn't sure if he'd been referring to an actual feline or joking about murder.

"L'me see?" Raul said, holding out his hand. Malcolm gave him the photo of Cedro Bartolome, which he'd taken from the law firm's Web site. It showed an older man with thick black hair, a thick black mustache, and a thick body covered in a tailored suit that did little to hide his thickness.

The late-afternoon sun glinted off Raul's greased-up hair as he bobbed to the music on the radio, a station he'd insisted on choosing when he'd gotten in the car. Malcolm rolled down his window now, even though the air-conditioning still blasted. His companions smelled like sweat and refried beans.

Earlier that morning, he'd spent four hours in Tepito (one of many ghettos in this vast city) trolling for the right bottom-feeder, flashing a photo of fifteen hundred dollars to prospective parties. He dared not carry that much money there. He also had photos of two thousand, three thousand, and five thousand, just in case. The two locos stinking up his car went for the fifteen hundred. Back in D.C., Holmes had given him twenty thousand dollars in cash. Money to hire local talent, he'd said. Since there would be no receipts, Malcolm would keep the rest. That and the three hundred thousand he'd told the senator he would need to take care of this mess would be his little nest egg.

Snap said something in Spanish. Glancing in the rearview mirror, Malcolm could see him smiling, the scar forming a giant half-moon dimple.

Raul looked back. Then he said to Malcolm, "You take us for food after?"

These dimwits were about to get more money than they'd seen in a year, and they wanted to shake him down for tacos and *cerveza*. "Yeah, sure."

Raul translated. Snap seemed pleased.

Malcolm had parked on the street by an impressive glass-sheathed office building. While he eyed the front entrance, Raul and Snap watched the cars coming out of the garage.

"Shit," Malcolm said.

Raul looked at him.

Malcolm pointed. Joe Evers had just stepped from a cab in front of the entrance. "Keep an eye on the gringo, *comprende*?"

Raul's head bobbed. Either it was a nod or he was dancing to the music.

❖

October 29
Friday, 4:58 p.m.
Office of Cedro Bartolome, Campos Eliseos,
Ciudad de México, Distrito Federal, Mexico

Joe had called ahead and arranged for a meeting with Señor Bartolome, explaining a deal he was putting together for the purchase of a textile plant outside of Mexico City. He'd scoured the Internet for translated news articles from Mexico, searching out actual financial stories. He found one that included enough details for him to create a convincing cover story. He simply changed the business names and locations

Now Joe sat in Cedro Bartolome's office, wondering when it all went bad. Bartolome had already called for security and was berating Joe for sneaking in under false pretenses.

"Señor Bartolome, please, if I can explain. Once you hear what I have to say, I'm sure you'll agree to help." A minute earlier, he realized he'd left his copy of the *Post* in the cab. The office door swung open and two burly men rushed in. They grabbed Joe by the arms, hoisted him up.

"This is really unnecessary," Joe said.

"Mr. Evers, you need to understand that a third of our fees come from international clients." Cedro Bartolome's English was impeccable. "If I divulge a name of a client, even from twenty years ago, our current clients will go elsewhere. I will not discuss this any further." He spoke in Spanish to the two men, his words sharp.

They hauled Joe to the door.

He tried one last time. "Check the *Washington Post* Web site. There's an article—" The door slammed closed.

❖

October 29
Friday, 5:07 p.m.
Campos Eliseos, Ciudad de México,
Distrito Federal, Mexico

The glass doors to the office building burst open and Evers came out, not looking happy. Two men followed. They stopped just outside the entrance and folded their arms across their chests in the universal pose of the tough-guy security guard. So the meeting had not gone as planned. That was good. Very good.

Evers climbed into the same cab he'd arrived in. A second later, it took off. Malcolm hurried to put his vehicle in drive, but stopped when the cab pulled to the curb on the next block.

Malcolm waited.

Minutes passed.

Evers was setting up surveillance. He wasn't finished. He'd been thwarted at the law firm and this was . . . what? Plan B. Follow Bartolome home? Malcolm was guessing, but it was sound logic. If he were handling the case, he would do the same. Any decent investigator would. Wasn't that why he was down here visiting this shithole—with the two fajita-smelling assholes next to him—because Joe wasn't such a loser after all. The washed-up prick was proving to be a lot more competent than he looked.

At six o'clock, a black Mercedes pulled in front of the building. One of the men who had tossed Joe earlier walked out. Next to him was the target: Cedro Bartolome. They walked to the car. The man opened the back door and the lawyer got in. The car drove off. Joe's cab followed. Malcolm followed the cab. Things were getting interesting.

They drove for a while. The buildings thinned out. Eventually, they came to a community of estates, each plot a few acres, all backed up to a hill. The Mercedes turned into a fenced property with a guard booth. The gate opened and the Mercedes entered.

The cab drove past the property.

Malcolm was unsure what to do. He slowed. Bartolome was his target, but Joe was a problem. An idea had been percolating in his brain since seeing Joe at the office building. Things happened in Mexico. Maybe he could take care of Evers first, and then he wouldn't have to rush the lawyer. He pondered this dilemma as the cab pulled to the side of the road and parked. Malcolm turned into the driveway of another estate. This one did not have a guard booth, but it did have a gate and camera. He angled the vehicle so its license plate was hidden. From this vantage point, he had a view of both Joe's cab and Bartolome's estate.

Five minutes later, the gate to the driveway that Bartolome's vehicle had turned into opened. A scooter drove out. The driver wore a black suit. Malcolm assumed it was the chauffeur. Joe's cab turned around and drove up to the gate. A few minutes later, the gate opened again.

Joe had made the decision for him.

"Okay, Raul. Time to earn your money."

❖

C ome in, Mr. Evers," Cedro Bartolome said, his face impassive as he stepped aside for Joe to enter.

Joe hadn't expected to be received with chuckles and backslaps. For a lawyer, providing information on a client, even one from twenty years ago, was no small matter, for it violated the touchstone of the profession. Joe understood how difficult this was for Cedro and was grateful for the opportunity to be heard. At the security gate, waiting for the guard to call up to the house, Joe had felt like a young boy asking his grade-school sweetheart out for a first date. He hadn't known what he would do if Cedro had refused him. Like a child, he supposed he would have hung his head, mumbled something incoherent to the guard, and left, vowing never to be so foolish again. But the gate had opened, and the taxi had followed the gravel path to the house. And Joe, like the boy who was told yes by his sweetheart, got a lesson in the old adage "Fortune favors the bold." Now he just hoped he could collect.

Joe followed the lawyer into an elegantly furnished sitting room. A crystal chess set topped a round table in the corner. Wooden bookcases lined the walls of the room, some titles in Spanish, many in English.

A woman entered. She carried a tray with glasses and a bottle of wine. Cedro introduced her as Daniela, his wife. She wore a simple blue evening dress. It was an elegant complement to a beautiful woman.

"Will you be staying for dinner, Mr. Evers?" Daniela's English was more British than American, and Joe wondered if she'd studied abroad. She was much younger than her husband.

He stood to address her. "No, thank you. I do not want to intrude. And I am sorry if my timing was poor."

"I am sure it could not be helped." She turned to her husband and her expression conveyed she was unhappy their evening had been interrupted. "Cedro is an important man." She offered a less than sincere smile. "It was nice meeting you, Mr. Evers."

Joe gave a slight bow. "And you, Señora Bartolome."

When she left, Cedro said, "We have a little Friday tradition. We either go out to dinner with friends or she lets the cook go early and prepares supper herself for both of us." Cedro tasted his wine, seeming to savor the experience. "She is somewhat protective of these evenings and detests when I bring work home."

"Believe me, I understand." Joe recalled his family dinners with Christine and Melissa. "And if you ever prepare the meal yourself, I suggest you don't just throw something together. You'll regret it later."

Cedro appeared confused. "Yes, I'm sure I would."

They sat on a flower-patterned sofa, which would have been gaudy in any room but this one. In the hands of the rich, gaudy often became chic. Cedro placed his wineglass on the gold-leaf coffee table.

"I read the *Washington Post* article," Cedro said, "and I have considered your request, but I have not decided on an answer. I must speak to my partners. We have a meeting scheduled in the morning. One question they will ask is whether this group, this Navajo NOW mentioned in the article, is currently on your country's terrorist watch list."

Helena's article claimed the BIA was investigating the money wired to Mexico to see if it was linked to the group. Such a link would show the money may have been an attempt to divert funds to finance terrorism. The theory was flimsy and full of holes, but it was Joe's only move. Helena unknowingly had built up a nonexistent terrorism angle. And Cedro was concerned, which had been Joe's intent.

"I can tie them to the money. Even if the U.S. government doesn't classify your actions as aiding a terrorist group, my investigation should be enough to put your firm and all of its accounts and business transactions under scrutiny. I'm sure your clients would not appreciate the attention."

Cedro seemed to consider Joe's words. "What assurances do we have that if I assist you, our firm will not be targeted by your FBI?"

"I—"

From another part of the house came the sound of splintering wood.

Then a woman screamed. Daniela.

Cedro jumped to his feet. Joe followed, reaching for his Glock as they ran, but the gun was back in his apartment in Albuquerque. They raced to the doorway through which Daniela had gone, down a hall, and into a brightly lit room, a huge kitchen—the kind usually profiled in magazines featuring luxury homes.

But the two skinny young men standing by the eight-burner stainless-steel stove would not have been part of the article. Neither would the knife held to the neck of a pale Señora Bartolome.

Joe took in the kitchen, assessing the situation. Granite countertops and expensive cabinets framed the room. A long scalloped-shaped island occupied its center. At the far end, behind the two men, an exterior door stood open, broken pieces of its wood frame on the floor.

The kitchen could easily fit two cars side by side or end to end. Plenty of space to move around. He searched for something with which to defend himself. Several food-laden plates sat on the island, presumably Daniela's special dinner: salmon. A cast-iron pan sat on the stove. Joe smelled fried onions and a weapon. He raised his hands and advanced to the right side of the island, moving toward the man who held the knife to Daniela's throat. He stopped when he was shoulder to shoulder with Cedro, Joe on the right by the stove.

"Everyone, calm down," he said, though he was sure his words were not heard over the rapid Spanish spoken by Cedro. Daniela was directly in front of them, held still by the greasy-haired man's arm around her neck, her blue dress protected by a red-flowered apron, the shade too close to the color of blood. Joe could not understand Cedro, but knew he was begging Snap not to harm his wife.

The second man, a handsome specimen with a nasty scar fracturing his face, had moved to the other side of the island and crept forward, trying to get behind Joe and Cedro. Handsome also wielded a knife, but unlike Snap, he looked like he'd used it a few times—and had enjoyed each and every occasion.

Snap glanced toward the rear door. Was he planning to flee? What was going on? Had Joe happened upon a robbery? A kidnapping? Cedro was rich, and ransom was big business in Mexico.

Joe's shoulders felt tight.

Handsome came around the end of the counter behind them, grinning.

Snap held the knife in his right hand, extended out toward Cedro, his left arm wrapped around Daniela. Her eyes were wide, fear apparent, but she seemed calm, as calm as any person could be in that situation.

"Is this your doing?" Cedro said to Joe. "Some kind of threat if I don't cooperate?"

Snap looked past Cedro at Handsome. Fleeing wasn't part of the plan. They were timing their attack.

Joe took a deep breath.

Fortune favors the—

He grabbed the frying pan and swung it at Snap's knife hand. He felt the thud in the pan's handle as the flat bottom made contact. Oil flew through the air and splashed Snap, Daniela, and the cabinets. The knife skidded across the island and fell off the other side.

Joe turned and stepped behind Cedro to face Handsome, protecting the lawyer's back, and hoping it would be reciprocated.

He heard a scuffle behind him.

Handsome said something in Spanish and then made several quick slicing motions with his knife hand. Joe didn't understand the words, but he could translate the gesture: I'm going to cut you good.

Handsome lunged, the blade coming at Joe's face.

Joe leaned to his right and swung the pan. Each missed the other.

Handsome lunged again.

Joe stepped back and his leather-soled shoe found spilled oil. His foot slid out and he fell. Handsome's knife cut the air above Joe's head as he landed on his back.

Handsome came in fast and hard, his knife in front of him.

Joe raised his legs and kicked, knocking Handsome back. He glanced around. Cedro exchanged blows with Snap. Daniela was also in the fray, striking her husband's attacker on the head and back.

Handsome came at him again, but this time he, too, slipped on the oily tile. His feet flew up from under him. Joe scrambled to his knees and was on top of him in an instant. He raised the pan and brought it down on his face. Then a second time. Two sickening tolls of a funeral bell. The man lay still. If he lived, he would have a few more scars, possibly some dents. Joe took the knife from his limp hand.

It was a stiletto. A thought flashed in his mind. He would finally use the word *stiletto* in a report.

He got to his feet.

Cedro lay on the floor, Snap kicking him, Daniela beating at the young man's head. Snap turned and punched her in the face. She fell against the cabinets and slid to the floor.

Joe raised the pan and threw it, hitting Snap on the shoulder. He started forward, this time careful of the slippery floor. The young man squared himself, fists balled, mouth in a snarl. Then he must have seen either the knife in Joe's hand or his partner on the floor. Snap turned and made for the back door. But Joe was on him. He wrapped his left arm around the man's neck. Snap resisted, but Joe had thirty pounds on him and, from this position, had the advantage. He tightened his hold, ignoring the burn in his stitched tricep, and held the knife against the man's neck.

Cedro lay on the floor, bleeding, his wife next to him, helping him, though she, too, was bleeding. Joe wanted to ram the knife deep, but . . .

He placed his right forearm against the back of Snap's head and locked his left hand onto his right bicep and applied pressure, continuing to grip the stiletto. Snap stopped resisting as Joe compressed the blood flow to his brain. Thirty seconds later, Snap was unconscious. Joe dropped him to the floor.

He closed the knife and tossed it on the island counter, not wanting it in his pocket when the police arrived. He didn't know how they would view an American who had been involved in an assault and was concealing a knife in his pocket. It might complicate his account of what had happened. He removed his necktie and secured Snap's hands. Then he sat down next to him and checked the man's pulse. He was alive. He'd have to secure Handsome, too. If he hadn't killed him.

"Is Cedro okay?" Joe said to Daniela. She knelt next to her husband, pressing a dish towel against his bloody face.

She nodded. Tears ran down her face. Her left cheek and forehead were bruised. Blood seeped from the corner of her mouth.

"Call the police," Joe said. "I'll take care of him."

She hesitated, looked at Cedro, then stood and hurried off.

Joe started to get to his knees.

Something crashed into his back. Before he knew what was happening, an arm wrapped around his neck, then another pressed up to the side of his head, the same as he had done to Snap. A rear naked chokehold. His breathing became difficult. Pressure built in his head.

"Dale lied," a familiar voice said. "You're not a loser. You're a pain in the ass."

Malcolm.

What was he doing here? It didn't make sense. . . . Then again, it did. It made all the sense in the world. Holmes had sent him here to silence the lawyer.

Joe grabbed hold of the forearm around his throat and pulled. Malcolm wheeled back and tightened the hold. Joe's vision blurred. He willed himself not to go unconscious.

"It's nothing personal, Joe."

It wasn't going to end like this. Not like this. Not on a kitchen floor among strangers, so far away from Melissa. His vision faded to gray.

He raised his left hand to his chest, groped under his suit jacket, found what he was looking for. He pulled it out. He was weak, so weak. The voice in his ear was now echoing in his head. He raised his right arm and jabbed backward, hard.

Malcolm roared in pain and let go of him.

Joe fell forward on his knees and gasped for breath. The blood rushed to his head and white spots appeared in front of his eyes. In a moment, they cleared and he saw the frying pan he'd thrown earlier. He grabbed the handle and got shakily to his feet.

Malcolm screamed as he pulled Joe's gold-plated pen from his right cheek. Fury blazed in his eyes, all the fury of a man who'd just been stabbed in the face. He held up the bloody writing implement, and his intent became clear. It was crazy, almost perverse, but it prompted Joe into action. He was not about to let himself be killed by Christine's gift. He swung the pan with all his strength, all that he had left, and it struck the former BIA agent on the left side of his head. The bell tolled again, and Malcolm fell to the floor. He did not move.

Joe surveyed the savagery around him.

Unlike the movies, this was how violence played out in real life. Sloppy and ugly. Nothing choreographed. A vaudeville tragedy. No applause. No curtain calls. No roses. Only blood and pain and soon-to-visit nightmares.

He hobbled over to Cedro, who was sitting up but not looking well, and took a seat on the floor next to him.

"You doing okay?"

The lawyer gave a weak nod.

Daniela returned, holding a phone in one hand, several towels in the other. She saw Malcolm lying on the floor but said nothing.

"Mind if I ask you a question?" Joe said to Cedro.

Sirens sounded in the distance.

"Who did you open the account for?"

"You are a persistent gringo." Cedro's mouth and cheek were swollen, so his words were not so well formed. "He said his name was Arlen Edgerton, but later I saw a photograph of the missing congressman and knew it was not him. This many years later, I fear I cannot describe him to you. I'm sorry."

Joe hung his head. All this, for what? Pointless. No, not pointless.

He had Malcolm, and that would tie Holmes to the corruption and a motive if he could flip the former agent, but Cedro's testimony would have tightened the case, connected the three murders to Holmes as well as to the casino money. A witness from the past was powerful. And to Joe, it was somehow the key. He needed to hear it from the lawyer, to place Holmes here, to know the truth; even it were circumstantial to the murders, it would prove to Joe he had the right man.

"I was bluffing about the terrorism angle."

Cedro smiled.

They listened to the approaching sirens in silence. Soon emergency vehicles were outside, police officers and medics inside.

"There is one thing I remember about the man," Cedro said as he was lifted onto a stretcher. "He had two different-colored eyes. Like the dog."

NOVEMBER 1
MONDAY, 8:03 A.M.
BUREAU OF INDIAN AFFAIRS, OFFICE OF INVESTIGATIONS,
ALBUQUERQUE, NEW MEXICO

Dale froze in the doorway to his office, briefcase in one hand, a Starbucks in the other.

"When did you get back?" he asked.

Joe reclined behind Dale's desk, feet up, papers and folders pushed to the side, two model cars seemingly discarded on the floor. "I caught a red eye."

Dale knew about Malcolm in Mexico City. Joe could practically smell his fear. He wanted to drag this out, wring out every ounce of pleasure from this confrontation, menace Dale like a cat menaces a cornered mouse. And today, for a change, Dale would be the mouse and Joe would be the big fat tabby with a mean disposition.

"What are you doing behind my desk?"

"Seeing what it's like to be an asshole."

"Get out of my chair."

"It may not be your chair much longer."

"What are you talking about?"

"Not me. Malcolm. He's been talking. Apparently, he's got a phobia about Mexican jails. And I can't blame him. The prisons down there really suck. He wants to be extradited back to the States. So it's been pretty much a tell-all down in Mexico City. He'll talk to anyone— the *federales*, the FBI, State Department, me. Hell, when I left, he was chatting up the guy mopping the floor at the police station. I don't think he wanted to go back to his cell."

"What's that have to do with me?"

Joe came around the desk. "You set me up, you son of a bitch."

"I have no idea what you're talking about."

"I'm talking about putting me on the case, giving Malcolm updates about the investigation, and blocking me every time I tried to talk to him or the senator."

"You're crazy. I—"

"You protected a murderer and almost got me killed."

"The senator sits on the committee that oversees the BIA. He's entitled to know—"

"Bullshit. You traded information for the promise of a promotion. But what I don't understand is why? You had a pretty much spotless career, not stellar—none of us do. So why? Why now?"

Dale didn't respond at first, but when he finally did, there was a visible droop in his shoulders.

"It didn't seem so wrong at first."

"That's what Stretch probably thought. But he knew exactly what he was doing and why: money. So he could afford to be superdad with trips and cars and tuition. The problem with him was that by the time I came along, he was already in too deep to Othmann to refuse. But you were different. You didn't owe Malcolm or the senator. So why?"

"I watched you finish your career with nothing more than a pension and a kick out the door. I didn't want that. The senator was going to owe me a favor. But I wouldn't have done it if I had known he was involved in Edgerton's death. I thought it was just politics. You know me. I wouldn't have protected a murderer."

Joe said nothing.

"What are you going to do now?" Dale asked, defeated.

Joe walked over to the bookcase beside Dale's desk, grabbed hold of one side, and shoved. The wall unit and the rows of model cars crashed to the floor. Die-cast parts flew across the rug. He crushed several under his foot as he strode to the door.

"We're even."

❖

NOVEMBER 2 (ELECTION DAY)
TUESDAY, 10:52 P.M.
EDGERTON FOR GOVERNOR HEADQUARTERS, SANTA FE,
NEW MEXICO

Grace Edgerton stood onstage, looking out over a roomful of volunteers and supporters who had come tonight to be with her while the votes were tallied. Now they cheered at the announcement. And Grace was moved to tears of joy, but her tears were not just for winning the governorship. That morning, she'd been notified by the FBI only minutes before their press release. Kendall Holmes had been arrested for the murder of her husband. The news went viral. The election alone would have paled in comparison, but the combination of the two overwhelmed her.

She stepped to the podium to deliver her acceptance speech. The applause and whistles and hoots continued.

Chris Staples, who stood to her right with Paige Rousseau, both clapping and smiling, leaned toward her and shouted to be heard.

"They love you, Madam Governor!"

Yes, they did. And she loved them. And it was only then, after all these years, that she realized how much she still loved Arlen. And that this election, like all the others over the past twenty years, were her way of honoring him and his memory, a way to carry on his work.

She raised her arms in the universal gesture of victory and imagined Arlen standing next to her as she accepted the governorship of this great state.

❖

NOVEMBER 13

SATURDAY, 9:48 A.M.

FAIR HILLS CEMETERY, ALBUQUERQUE, NEW MEXICO

G rass had not grown over the grave. This was hard country, after all. Fine things struggled in New Mexico. Joe never thought of grass as a finery, but its delicate blades and small stature and its thirst for water that outpaced rainfall put grass at a disadvantage in this harsh region. So Christine's plot remained barren. But it didn't matter. She was not below that brown dirt. She resided in Joe's heart and was part of Melissa's existence. She lived on through them.

Her headstone was modest. Nothing fancy. Christine hadn't liked fancy. She'd preferred plain and unobtrusive. So Joe had selected a simple marble slab with the epitaph BELOVED WIFE AND MOTHER.

"Miss you, Mom," Melissa said. They had walked hand in hand to her grave.

Joe listened to his daughter's words in silence.

Then she let go of his hand and went back to the car, leaving him alone with his wife.

Minutes passed. He felt at peace. It was a new sensation, one that he hadn't known since her passing. He wasn't quite sure how to feel about it.

"You know I miss you," he whispered. "Every day. Every night. Every time I see Melissa." A crow cawed from somewhere behind him. "I'm seeing someone now, but I'm sure you know that. She's nice. Broken, like me. I think that's a good thing, good for both of us. We can help each other."

A breeze floated by and carried with it the soft scent of sage. "Dale's on review, so they asked me to stay and run the squad. But I'm not sure if I want to go back. And I have another offer. The new governor wants to appoint me as her border security adviser. Fancy title. I told her I don't know much about border security, but she says she trusts me to do the job."

He smiled. "It's been a long time since anyone's trusted me."

ACKNOWLEDGMENTS

T HIS NOVEL WAS INSPIRED by an actual event that occurred in Chi Chil Tah (Navajo Nation), New Mexico. Several years ago, I was investigating a missing-person case with Navajo criminal investigator Larry Etsitty. While canvassing a community for leads, we were given information about an abandoned vehicle in the nearby woods. After a somewhat long and dusty hike through a thinly populated forest of scraggly junipers and oaks, we came upon a long-forgotten and fully stripped sedan. Three large bullet holes marred the windshield, and another pierced the driver's door. While the vehicle was never linked to a crime (except being the victim of abandonment, vandalism, and target practice), the scene stayed in my mind and eventually grew into this novel.

Few stories are written in a vacuum. They are the result of many interactions and much research. This book is no exception. My interactions involved working with the individuals who investigate violent crimes on the Navajo reservation. I would be remiss not to thank them for accepting me into their circles and sharing their personal experiences and views with me, whether at a crime scene or over coffee afterward. Many of those revelations made it into this book, in one form or another, or simply influenced the tone of the narrative. I offer my thanks and gratitude to all the officers and criminal investigators on the Navajo reservation and specifically to the following individuals: senior criminal investigators Larry Etsitty and Malcolm M. Leslie; criminal investigators Denise Billy, Darryl Boye, Christopher Tsosie, Robert James, and Charles VanOsdell; and evidence-recovery technicians Donovan Becenti and Randall Bluehouse. To the FBI agents and staff who work in Gallup, New Mexico, and who must handle the worst of the worst and see the most tragic of tragedies on a daily basis, I offer recognition of their difficult tour of duty.

As for the research that went into this book, I want to thank Richard Malone and Amy Wyman, investigators with the New Mexico Office of the Medical Investigator; plastic and reconstructive surgeon Nathan S. Taylor, M.D.; Professor David A. Phillips, Jr., University of New Mexico, Department of Anthropology (Archaeology); Professor Michelle D. Hamilton, Forensic Anthropology Center, Texas State University; Cindy Josley, Jenelle Yazzie, and Carol A. York, who helped me with Navajo language and traditions; the fine docents at the New Mexico Museum of Natural History & Science who took me into their work space and shared stories of the museum; and the many law enforcement officers and agents who answered my questions and provided me insight. While I took some liberties with the material presented, the accuracy and realism are accredited to these individuals. Where the information is wrong, I am solely to blame.

And finally a warm thank-you to all the individuals who brought *Dark Reservations* into the light: Ann Hillerman and Jean Shaumberg of Wordharvest, who host a truly wonderful conference and make everyone feel a part of their family; executive editor Peter Joseph, associate editor Melanie Fried, and the professional staff at Thomas Dunne Books and Minotaur Books who worked so hard to make my novel shine (many thanks to you, Peter, for your editorial guidance and sage publishing advice); Elizabeth Trupin-Pulli, a most genuine person and a most marvelous agent; David Shifren, Randall Silvis, and Victoria Thompson, my Seton Hill University writing mentors who transformed me into a writer; freelance editor Michael Dell, whose editing and story advice made my novel so much stronger; my Seton Hill writing community and writing group buddies who make the job of writing fun and not so lonely; and my early readers, Carla E. Anderton, Frank A. Fisher, Jennifer Felts, Rebecca Glover, Matthew Hellman, Mark Hoff, Stephen Marshall, and Laurie Wood Sterbens, who kept me on my authorial toes and challenged me to do better.

If I have forgotten anyone, please know you are very much appreciated and the oversight is my memory and not a reflection of your contribution.

SOUTH COUNTRY LIBRARY

3 0614 00302 6194

OCT 2 3 2015